The Rule of The Six 'P's'

by

George Donald

Also by George Donald

Billy's Run
Charlie's Promise
A Question of Balance
Natural Justice
Logan
A Ripple of Murder
A Forgotten Murder
The Seed of Fear
The Knicker-knocker
The Cornishman
A Presumption of Murder
A Straight Forward Theft
The Medal
A Decent Wee Man
Charlie's Dilemma
The Second Agenda
Though the Brightest Fell
The ADAT
A Loan with Patsy
A Thread of Murder
Harry's Back
Charlie's Recall
The Broken Woman
Mavisbank Quay
Maggie Brogan
Malinky
The Privileged Daughter
A Conflicted Revenge
Charlie's Swansong
The Rookie Suspect
No Sad Loss
Maitland

PROLOGUE

They called themselves the team.
However, both the police and the media had many names for them, but primarily knew them as violent, armed criminals.
Yes, they terrorised the customers and staff of the financial establishments they robbed, but curiously, in their long history of robbery they had never injured anyone.
Throughout mainland Scotland, these men practiced their profession with almost military style precision, using the same *modus operandi* for each robbery.
Their leader, a consummate professional, constantly reminded his associates of his rule of the six 'P's'.
Planning and preparation prevents piss poor performance.
Through the long years they were active, they were frustratedly pursued by the police and though through their intelligence network and paid sources the constabularies throughout Scotland had come to identify the members of the team, the police were unable to arrest them for without the evidence to convict them, it would have been a pointless exercise.
It was also suspected that the financial institutions the four men robbed were not without their own culpability, for the true figure of the money stolen by the robbers was sometimes believed to be inflated to reflect the bank or building societies own inept accounting.
Nevertheless, it was assessed by the police that throughout the years the true cumulative sum stolen must number at least hundreds of thousands of pounds…if not more.
However, what confused the police was that though the robbers stole untold thousands, none of the men displayed the trappings of wealth for each man lived a relatively austere life in his rented council home, drove second-hand vehicles, took occasional budget holidays abroad and continued to be employed too, dutifully paying their income tax and National Insurance stamps.

Warrants to covertly examine their bank accounts revealed nothing more than the earnings from their employment.
So, the police had cause to wonder, where and what had the four men done with the stolen money?

CHAPTER ONE

The crew of G Division's Golf Mike 4, Constable Pat Hanlon driving with Trudy 'Trood' McNamara in the passenger seat, grumbled and cursed at the lack of heating in the old and rusting marked Transit van as Hanlon cautiously drove from Haggs Road into the entrance of the Pollok Park.
"Old bus or not," he muttered, "I'd rather be in this than trying to negotiate this rutted track in a panda, Trood."
Her hands freezing despite wearing her police issue leather gloves that in turn were shoved into her armpits in a vain attempt to keep them warm, she sighed, "I'd rather be at home tucked into my bed than in *anything* else."
"What was the name of the reporter, again," he risked a glance at her as the Transit skewed and slithered along the track.
"Mrs Paterson. Jane Paterson," she replied, her breath creating a small fog of steam that drifted to the roof of the van.
Staring from the passenger window, she idly watched the snow-laden trees pass by and wondered not for the first time what mad compulsion had caused her to join the polis.
Peering through the windscreen, Hanlon asked, "And remind me. The body is supposed to be lying where?"
"Somewhere beside the Burrell Collection building," she yawned.
He smiled when he asked, "Late night, hen?"
"You know how it is when you're single and fancy free," she grinned. "Wine, song and a life of debauchery."
"Actually, with a missus and three weans, no, I don't. At least not any longer," his brow furrowed, then catching sight of a woman standing in front of the Burrell building who was frantically waving her arms to attract their attention, he softly added, "Here we go."
Hanlon stopped the police vehicle yards from the woman who dressed in a snow crusted balaclava, heavily quilted red anorak,

black coloured nylon waterproof trousers with snow boots on her feet and straining to hold an excited and large, black furred Alsatian dog on a lead, rushed to the driver's door.

And what the *hell* is she doing out in this bloody weather, Hanlon inwardly sighed.

"It's over here…" she pointed her arm and cried out, but was interrupted when sliding down the window on the door, Hanlon waved a hand and told her, "Mrs Paterson? I'll get out in a minute if you can step back with your dog and keep it under control, okay?"

"Oh, aye, yes, of course," the woman, her cheeks flushed with the cold, pulled at the agitated dog then stepped back several yards.

Getting out of the vehicle, Hanlon casually let his hand slip to his wooden baton in his trousers pocket, then staring warily at the dog that was straining at its leash, inwardly thought - if she lets it go, it's getting introduced to Mr Hickory.

Coming around the front of the vehicle, her head down against the pinpricks of sleet that battered against her unprotected face and flapping her arms around her body in an effort to keep warm, McNamara said, "You reported finding a body, Mrs Paterson. Where is it?"

"Oh, over there," she half turned and waved an arm in the general direction of the building that was hardly visible through the driving, sleety snow that was turning to rain.

"Sorry," she blushed. "Behind the building, I mean. It was really Robby who found her."

"It's a woman?" McNamara's eyes narrowed, then asked, "Is Robby there with the body now?"

"Oh, no, Robby's my dog," she bent to pat the furry monster.

"Maybe you could take us to where you found the body, Mrs Paterson," interjected Hanlon though from her tracks in the snow it was quite obvious the direction from which she'd come.

It took them several minutes blundering through the virgin snow to reach the corner of the building where Mrs Paterson and her dog's footprints continued towards the rear of the building.

"Can you wait here for a couple of minutes, please," he raised a hand.

"Will you be long, do you think? I didn't intend to be out here as long as I have and I'm freezing," she replied.

He glanced back at the Transit then with a reassuring smile, said, "The back door of the van's open. Go back there and get inside. We'll try to be as quick as we can," he smiled in the sure knowledge that if indeed it is a dead body, being the witness who discovered it would mean Mrs Paterson would be taken to Pollok Police station to provide a lengthy statement.

Walking together, one hand on their caps to prevent them from being blown away by the icy wind, they made their way around the rear of the building and walked in the footsteps that already were being filled in by the drifting snow.

"Try not to wander away from where she's already trod," Hanlon told his probationary cop. "If it's suspicious, the CID will want to know where we've stepped."

Thirty yards further on, the footsteps in the snow abruptly stopped in a whirl of disturbed snow for lying face down, lay the body of a dark-haired woman, though her face and most of her head was by now covered by snow. Her light green coloured dress billowed about and exposed her bare thighs and naked backside, though they could not see her lower legs or feet for they too were also covered by snow.

"Oh, my," Hanlon softly muttered while unconsciously shaking his head, then with his free hand reached for his personal radio. His throat tightening as he stared down at the woman, he pressed the button and said, "G375 to control. Regarding the call to Pollok Park, Eddie. You'd better let the CID know it's a code four-five, suspicious," then slowly added, "and they might want to bring the circus with them."

****

Detective Constable Ailish MacDonald eagerly licked her lips as she ripped open the paper and released the tantalising smell of her fish supper.

"Tea?" asked her neighbour.

Half turning, she nodded to Willie McBride, who carried the two stained mugs held in his shovel like hand.

"Aye, please," she stuffed a handful of chips into her mouth and smiled. "God, I'm starving," she sighed with pleasure, then turned as the phone on the clerk's desk rang.

"I'll get it," he raised a hand indicating she remain where she was then lifting the phone, said, "Pollok CID, DS McBride."

Breaking off a piece of the fish, she watched as his brow creased then heard him say, "Behind the Burrell? A woman? Right then," he grimaced then asked, "Has the casualty surgeon been called out? Good. We'll meet him there."

She saw him appear to listen, then shake his head and rub his hand across his brow when he replied, "No, wait till I get back to you. No need to call out the boss in this weather if it's some drunken bird got herself lost in the snow and froze to death. Right, we'll be there in about," his face contorted when he said, "say by the time we get through the snow, twenty minutes or thereabouts, Eddie. Right then, cheers," he ended the call.

Replacing the handset, he turned to MacDonald to tell her, "Dead woman behind the Burrell. Pat Hanlon's there with his neighbour and a woman who discovered the body, so wrap your chips, hen, we'll need to head out."

"Never rains…"

"But it snows," he grinned at her then wiping her hands on a tissue, she grabbed at her quilted anorak, scarf, hat and gloves from the desk.

****

It seemed to McBride who was driving the CID Vauxhall Astra, that the storm seemed to be letting up slightly and the snow turning to light rain as they approached the Haggs Road entrance to Pollok Park, the tyre tracks of the police Transit van still clearly visible and a guide for the Ford Cortina as it too slithered along the snow-covered track.

The windscreen wipers clearing away the slushy snow were now battling with falling rain and the car heater going at full blast, it took several minutes before they happened upon the rear of a Volvo estate car that in turn was parked behind the police Transit van.

They could both see the Volvo that they recognised as belong to Doc Smythe, the on-call Casualty Surgeon, was empty.

"Here we go," grimaced McBride as he and MacDonald, their coat collars turned up and both wearing woollen hats, exited their car and were immediately battered by the rain.

Only in Scotland could it snow one minute then rain the next, McBride inwardly sighed.

"Wish I'd wore my wellies," grumbled MacDonald as she trailed after McBride, who head down against the driving rain, followed the tracks in the snow towards the building.

Minutes later, both gasping for breath, they came upon the two cops and the doctor who were stood in a huddle, staring down at the body from which most of the fresh snow had been swept aside to enable Smythe to examine the body.

"Where's the witness, Pat?" McBride greeted Hanlon.

"Did you not see her, Willie? She's in the back of the Transit or she should be. That's where I sent her to get out of the cold."

Turning to MacDonald, McBride said, "Ailish?"

"Right, on it," she sighed and headed back the way she'd come, but turned when Hanlon shouted out after her, "Watch out for the big dog she's got with her."

With a grunt, she muttered, "That's all I need," then continued on her way.

Glancing at McNamara, McBride told her, "No need for us all to be here, Trood. Get yourself back to the van as well."

"If you're sure, Sarge?" she asked, hoping he was not joking.

"Aye, on you go, hen."

Turning to the doctor, he asked, "Apart from confirming life extinct, Doc, are you able to tell me what I'm looking at here?"

Taking a breath, Smythe glanced down at the dead woman then replied, "I can't tell you much, Willie, simply because she's almost frozen solid which in this weather, doesn't really surprise me. She'll need to be on a slab and defrosted before…"

"Defrosted?" McBride was aghast. "You're kidding me, right?"

"No, unfortunately, I'm not," he shook his head. "It was well below freezing last night and God alone knows how long the poor soul has been lying here, so her skin is rigid and I can't use my thermometer with any accuracy to even give you an estimated time of death."

He glanced upwards and continued, "The rain's helping, though because it's bringing a rise in the temperature. Now, as for this poor girl, what I can tell you is," he paused, "and mind, Willie, this is purely from my observations and as you can see, she's not wearing undergarments. That all said, it seems to me that she's suffered some extreme vaginal injury that seems to indicate she has been pretty badly violated and there's a definite bruising around her neck that suggests she's been strangled. However, without a proper examination and I'm going out on a limb here, mind, I'm of the opinion this woman was murdered."

Slowly shaking his head, McBride turned to Hanlon and exhaling, said, "Contact the control room, Pat, and have Eddie call out the DI and the duty Fiscal. I'll want the Scene of Crime here too and I know its Sunday evening," he raised a hand as though to ward off the expected complaints, "but suggest that because of the weather conditions they call out the mobile incident bus. Also," his eyes narrowed, "ask Eddie to let the Govan CID know we're engaged and they've to cover for us. Have your Inspector attend as well. He'll need to organise some relief for you guys who will have to cordon off this area."

While Hanlon stepped a few paces away to use his radio, McBride said to Smythe, "Thanks, Doc. I don't see any need for you to remain here at the minute, but if you could..."

"I'll have my statement and the life extinct chit delivered to your Pollok Office first thing tomorrow, before I attend at my surgery," he nodded to McBride.

Watching the doctor make his way back to his vehicle, McBride asked, "No sign of any handbag or anything?"

Waving a hand around him, Hanlon replied, "It might be lying under the snow, Willie, but I didn't want to disturb anything until you guys got here."

"Aye, you're right," he nodded then with a wry grin, added, "Looks like you've drawn the short straw, Pat. Are you able to hang on here while I go and use the radio in the car? When your Inspector arrives, I'll see you get relieved right away."

"Do that, will you," Hanlon shivered. "Me and Trood have not had our piece break yet. That and I'm not wearing my long johns and my balls have shrivelled."

****

Across the city in the first floor flat in Quarrywood Road in the Barmulloch area of the city, George Knox glanced again the wall clock in the front room.

He grimaced when he saw the ornate clock read fifteen minutes to seven and angrily hissing, slammed down the phone before returning to the front room.

His wife Rosie, sitting in one of the two armchairs facing the gas fire, glanced first at her five-year-old grandson who sitting quietly on the couch, was watching a pirated Worzel Gummidge DVD. Turning, she stared at her husband before asking, "She still not answering?"
"Bloody ridiculous," he hissed in response. "She should have been up here hours ago to pick up the wee guy."
"Maybe the weather…" Rosie began, but he scowled and she said nothing more, for she knew that when George was angry it was better to just keep her mouth shut.
Walking to the window, Knox stared down at the street below, brighter than it should be because of the heavy fall of snow and seeing that not just his own car, but also all the vehicles were completely whited out. Curiously, he saw that instead of snow, it was now a sleet like rain that was coming down.
Inwardly annoyed with himself for snapping at Rosie, he breathed deeply to calm himself, continuing to stare out of the window and watching a bus crawl along at fifteen miles an hour through the compressed snow that was rapidly turning to blackened slush as the sudden downpour of rain made its appearance. On the opposite side of the road, an elderly man held onto a garden fence, moving slowly, hand over hand on the fence as slipping and sliding, he tried to negotiate his way along the pavement.
Knox made his decision.
Returning to the phone in the hallway he dialled the number and when it was answered, simply said, "It's me, son. Nip up to our Kelly-Ann's flat and tell her to get her arse up here to collect the wee guy. Tell her to jump a taxi and remind her that he's got school in the morning. And tell her too that if she doesn't get her arse in gear, I'll slap her jaw for her, okay?"
He could almost hear the smile on Alex Hardie's face, for George Knox had never before raised a hand to his daughter though on occasion and only because of her attitude and behaviour, he'd been more than tempted.
"No bother, boss," the big man replied, "If she's not there, I'll find a phone and call you from there to let you know."
"Speak later," Knox abruptly ended the call.
****
Putting down the phone, Hardie sighed.

It wasn't the first time that George had asked him to chase up Kelly-Ann, a right wee slapper if ever there was one and he smiled at the memory of the last time he'd to visit her at her flat and tell her to contact her Da. Just in from the dancing at the Barrowland and half drunk, she'd grabbed at him and tried to entice him into her bed. Not that she wasn't an attractive enough woman and truth be told, she was definitely fanciable, but shagging her would have been disrespectful to George and that just was not on.

Walking back into the kitchen, he decided to finish his coffee before braving the elements and slumped down into the kitchen chair.

Of course, he thought, he could have made some excuse, told the boss that he'd had a drink and couldn't drive or some such story, but that wasn't his style. No, George had been good to him in the past, *was* good to him and he wouldn't let him down.

Besides, he reasoned, his flat in Reidvale Street wasn't too far from where Kelly-Ann lived over in Tullis Street with her son, wee Clint. No more than a mile and a bit, so it wouldn't take him too long to get there and back.

He finished his coffee then stood and stretched to ease the ache in his back, thinking that if it was open tomorrow, he might hit the gym at Bridgeton Cross.

Making his way through the second floor flat to the lounge, he glanced out of the window, seeing that at last the storm was apparently abating but had been followed by the rain.

Peering down into the street he saw to his dismay his car was absolutely covered in snow. Across the road and down behind the bushes, a train passed by sending clouds of drifting snow into the air. Bugger it he thought I'll walk.

It took the twenty-nine-year old and muscular Hardie a few minutes to dress, pulling on a pair of heavy corduroy trousers, a thickly quilted red coloured anorak and a pair of old heavy boots, a hangover from his days in the shipyards that he kept at the back of the cupboard. Grabbing a woollen tammy and a pair of woollen gloves from the same cupboard, he shook his head then grinned at his reflection in the hallway mirror before he left the first floor flat.

****

One hour and ten minutes after the report to the police about the discovery of the body, DI Roddy Williams, clad in a heavy duty coat, a pair of old police trousers, thick socks and wellies and wearing a woollen Rangers tammy, arrived at the locus to find the white-suited Scene of Crime personnel were struggling to put up a tent around the body that was now lit by the halogen lamps that mounted on metal poles, swayed dangerously in the wind driven rain.

Greeting a shivering Willie McBride with a nod, he said, "Bloody weather, eh? I called out a couple of the lads and they're here with me for getting the body to the mortuary and as I was pulling up, the incident bus has just arrived, so once we've had a chat, away and get yourself a hot drink, Willie. Right," he pulled his tammy down to cover his ears, "what we got?"

McBride recounted the discovery of the unidentified female and that the witness, a Mrs Jean Paterson, was now at Pollok Police station with Ailish MacDonald and providing a statement.

Blowing into his gloved hands, McBride continued, "The shift Inspector has organised a cordon and Doc Smythe has declared life extinct, but tells us that we'll need to get the woman defrosted before cause of death can be established. That said," he pre-empted Williams question, "he's of the opinion she's been brutally violated and there's what appears to be finger-marks around her neck that suggests strangulation. That and as you can see," he nodded down to the dead woman, "she's not wearing any underwear."

"Defrosted," Williams slowly repeated once more then shook his head, his face expressing the horror of it all. Staring down at the body, he sighed, "My God, what a thing to have to happen to anyone."

He frowned when he added, "So, no doubt it's definitely murder then, eh?"

"Looks like it," McBride nodded.

"Nothing to identify her?"

Waving his hands about McBride replied, "We didn't want to disturb the locus when we arrived and it's too dark now for a proper search so I'm thinking once the SOCO guys have done their bit, we remove the body and organise a search for the morning. If this rain continues," he risked a glance upwards to the dark skies, "it might make the job a lot easier."

Williams grimly smiled when he said, "Means the uniform will need to stay out here all night."

"Aye," McBride nodded, "we'll not be popular, but what else can we do?"

"Agreed," Williams sighed, then continued, "You away and get yourself a hot cuppa and when you're ready, come back here and we'll examine the body before we turn her over to the mortuary boys."

"Boss," McBride acknowledged with a nod and barely feeling his chilled feet, began to make his way through the trampled snow towards the incident bus.

CHAPTER TWO

It took Alex Hardie almost twenty-five minutes to make his way to Tullis Street during which he was sure the rain was starting to fall off, but in that short time the rain had turned the snow on the pavements and roads into a dirty coloured slush, making his progress on foot highly treacherous.

Turning the corner from Greenhead Street into Tullis Street, he smiled when he heard country and western music accompanied by loud voices coming from the open door of the Bowlers Bar that was located on the corner and directly across the street from Kelly-Ann's first floor tenement flat.

Albeit it was a Sunday night and the weather conditions were horrific, he grinned, trust the Weegies to make it to the pub for a pint and a singsong.

The door at the entrance to the close was ajar and pushing it open, he stamped his feet to shake off the crusted ice from his boots before making his way upstairs.

Listening at the door, he could hear nothing from inside then aware the bell wasn't working, pounded on the door several times.

Several minutes and more pounding on the door failed to rouse her then bending down, he opened the letterbox and shouted through, "Kelly-Ann! It's me, Alex! Open the door!"

Still there was no response and eyes narrowing, he could neither see nor hear any sign of life in the flat.

He had reached the point he was considering putting in the door when the elderly man across the landing opened his and said in a hoarse voice, "She's not in, pal."

Turning, he saw the man squint at him before he said, "You've been here before, haven't you?"

Recalling that Kelly-Ann had previously joked the old man was a right nosey bugger and never missed her comings and goings, he replied, "Aye, I'm a friend of the family."

Then thinking he'd missed her, that she was on her way to her father's house, he politely asked, "Do you know when she went out?"

"Last night about seven I think it was. All dolled up she was too," the old man replied.

Taken aback, Hardie stared when he repeated, "Last night? Did you not hear her come home then?"

"No," the old man shook his head then eyes widening, stared at the tall, brawny man whose bulk appeared even larger because of the heavy clothing he was wearing, and stammered, "It's not as if I'm watching her or anything pal, honest. It's just that I've got right good hearing."

"Calm yourself, old yin, I'm not suggesting that," Hardie smiled reassuringly, then asked, "Are you certain she didn't come home at all last night?"

"Oh, aye, I'm sure of it. I'm a hell'uve a light sleeper, so I am."

He frowned then taking off his woollen tammy to reveal a head of neatly trimmed blonde hair, Hardie rubbed wearily at his brow before nodding and telling the old man, "Right, then, if you hear her come home, you've to tell her to phone her Da right away. Will you do that for me, pal?"

"Aye, son, no bother," the old man smiled with some relief.

Hardie squinted when he stared at him, then asked, "Do you have a phone in the house?"

"A phone? No, son, I can't afford a phone."

"Here," Hardie fetched his wallet from an inner coat pocket then withdrawing a five-pound note, said, "That's for your trouble."

The old man's eyes lit up and he was about to thank him when Hardie added, "Mind now, if she comes home…"

"I'll listen out for her, son, I promise you."

"Aye," he stared meaningfully at the old man, then smiling humourlessly said, "See that you do."

****

Pushing open the door into the lounge of the Bowlers Bar, Hardie was met by a fug of smoke and body odour as the mostly middle-aged to elderly crowd sang along with the equally elderly guitarist to a cheery Willie Nelson song.

Making his way through the throng to the bar, he exchanged a pound note for coins and was pointed by the barman to the public phone on the wall next to the toilet doors.

Dialling George Knox's number, he greeted him with, "Boss, it's me. She's not at home. Has she arrived at yours?"

"No," Knox snapped back. "I haven't heard from her yet."

"I spoke with a neighbour," Hardie plugged a finger into his left ear to hear better, "the wee man across the landing. He says she left the house at seven last night all dolled up and hasn't been back home since. I'm thinking the dancing because she likes her Saturday nights at the Barrowland. What do you think?"

"Sounds about right," Knox sighed through the phone. "Are you going to wait for her to come home?"

"No point. I've bunged the wee guy a fiver to let her know you're looking for her, but if you can think of anywhere else she might be?"

"Oh, I can think of a hundred places and all with some guy she's met at the dancing," Knox angrily spat back, then almost as quickly, added, "Sorry, big man."

There was a pause before Knox quietly asked, "Do you think I should start worrying, Alex?"

Hardie knew, as did half of the city, of Kelly-Ann's reputation and how promiscuous she could be with a drink in her and so took several seconds before he replied, "Let's not worry, boss, until we have something to worry about, okay?"

The phone beeped and he inserted another ten pence piece, hearing it clink as it fell into the machine, then said, "Let me call on some of my mates and put the word out that we're looking for her."

"No," Knox angrily snapped back, then more softly continued, "It's bad enough I've a daughter that's whoring herself about the city with every Tom, Dick and Harry without broadcasting it about, Alex. No, if you can think of anything, then go ahead, but for the meantime, we'll just assume that she's with somebody and that she'll get in touch when she's…you know. Back home."

"Aye, okay, George, you're the boss."

He paused then asked, "I take it you and Rosie have got the wee guy with you, then?"

"Aye, he's here," Knox sighed, "and we'll keep him for the night. Chances are that his school will be closed tomorrow anyway, if this weather keeps up."

"According to the forecast, there's a big thaw on for tonight and if this rain doesn't let up, the roads will likely be cleared for snow."

"This is Glasgow, son," Knox reminded him with a smirk. "The best forecast is sticking your head out of the window and having a look upwards."

"Aye, right enough," Hardie smiled, then added, "I'll head up the road, but if you hear anything…"

"I'll let you know," Knox finished for him and ended the call.

He'd just replaced the phone on the cradle when he was tapped on the shoulder, by a busty black-haired woman in her mid-forties, eight inches shorter than his six feet two and wearing a far too tight black lacy bodice and a short, red miniskirt over which hung her stomach. He saw her eyes were puffy with the alcohol she'd consumed as her hand reached for his buttock.

"Haven't seen you in here before, honey," she drunkenly drawled.

"No, probably not," he forced a smile then deftly taking her wrist and squeezing just hard enough to make her wince, removed it from his backside before he asked, "Don't I know you?"

"Me?" she stared wide-eyed at him.

"Aye, were you not at school with my Granny?"

Before she could respond he released his grip and was making his way to the exit, smiling as and ignoring the angry woman who drunkenly screamed after him, "You…you think you're a smart bastard, do you!"

****

Returned to Pollok Police station, the body of the unidentified woman now accompanied by two detective constables and en-route and to the City Mortuary in Glasgow's Saltmarket, DI Roddy Williams cupped his hands around the mug and sipping at the steaming hot coffee, could feel the tingling in his toes that indicated the blood was returning to his feet.

He glanced at the ruddy cheeks of McBride and jealously wished he'd more meat on his bones to fight off the cold, like the tubby DS.

On the opposite side of his desk, Willie McBride tapped out two cigarettes from the pack and offering one to Williams, flicked open his Zippo lighter and lit both.

"What did the boss say?" McBride asked and nodded to the telephone on Williams's desk.

"Says there's no point in him coming out tonight, that he's trusting we'll have done the necessary and he'll call in here first thing in the morning."

"Aye, I suppose he's right. I mean, what's there to see? A frozen corpse lying in the snow?"

"Wonder how long she's been lying there?" Williams idly wondered. "I mean, if Doctor Smythe is correct and she's needing thawed out, how long does it take to defrost a body? And it then begs the question, how long was she lying there for her to *get* frozen?"

"In this weather," McBride's lip curled, "I don't suppose it would take too long. You were out there, what, forty minutes? Maybe an hour at the most and I bet you still can't feel your feet."

"Funnily enough," Williams sighed, "I'm just getting the warmth back into them just now."

The door was knocked and then pushed open by Ailish MacDonald who entering the room, addressed Williams when she said, "That was Pitt Street Control Room on the phone, boss. I gave them the parameters of a dark haired woman aged between twenty and forty and approximately five feet two inches to five feet eight inches, but," she shook her head, "nobody reported missing within the last forty-eight hours in the Greater Glasgow area matching the description."

"Did you mention the green dress?"

"Aye, I asked for a speculative check with that detail too, but again, nothing. Oh, and I've got the statements of the woman who discovered the body and the two cops as well, Pat Hanlon and Trudy McNamara."

"Okay, Ailish. How you feeling, hen? I know it's your first murder. Any thoughts on how she ended up there?"

MacDonald, standing with her back against the wall, accepted a cigarette from McBride who lit it for her then brow creasing, she replied, "Well, there was no vehicle parked anywhere around the locus and no access for a vehicle where she was discovered, so I'm thinking she's obviously been brought there. The atrocious conditions tend to make me think she was dead before she got there, because why take her there to kill her? I think she was killed elsewhere and carried to where her killer dumped her. The thing that bothers me," she gave an involuntarily shiver, "is that Doctor Smythe thinks she's been violated, so does he mean raped or with something…"

William softly asked, "You're thinking not rape, but something forced into her?"

"Aye," she slowly nodded and gave a light shudder, then her eyes narrowing, continued, "I mean, the state the victim was in with the cold and that, the doc must've had some reason to use the word violated, rather than saying she had been raped."

McBride leaned forward to tap some ash into the tin Williams used as an ashtray before he said, "Well, the post mortem will tell us if that's true, Ailish, but if what you're thinking is correct, I hope the poor lassie *was* dead before…well, you know."

"Is the DCI coming out tonight, boss?" she asked Williams.

"No, he'll see us in the morning and to be honest, there's not a lot more we can do tonight anyway."

He glanced at the window before asking, "What's it like outside, Ailish? Still raining?"

"Lashing down," she smiled, "If it keeps up, we might see a right good thaw by the morning."

"Bloody West of Scotland weather," McBride grumbled. "One minute it's like the Artic and the next it's pissing down. Not like down in Ayrshire…"

"Where it's sunshine the whole year round," MacDonald finished for him, then grinned at McBride's pretend scowl.

"Right," Williams slapped a hand down onto the desk, "I think you two have done enough for the night and as you're both out early tomorrow morning and the Govan pair are covering any calls that come in, you should get yourselves home. So, before we leave, anything I've missed?"

"The cops on the ground at the locus, boss," McBride's face twisted. "Was the Inspector okay about having them out there in this weather?"

"He'd no real choice in the matter, but that reminds me," Williams reached down and opened the bottom drawer of his desk. Fetching out an unopened bottle of whisky, he said, "I've promised him that I'd leave a dram for his shift before they go home as a wee thank you to the guys on the cordon."

"Aye, better them than me," McBride inwardly smiled at Williams thoughtfulness.

****

By the time Alex Hardie arrived back at his flat, the rain was coming down heavily and making an impact on the snow on the ground. Taking off his coat, he hung it across the top of the door of the hall cupboard to dry then pulling off his boots and soaked trousers, laid them on top of and beneath the radiator.

Padding in his socks to the bedroom, he pulled on a pair of tracksuit bottoms, all the while wondering where Kelly-Ann had got to on Saturday night and asking himself, what has she got caught up in that meant she hasn't arrived home?

It was the wee boy that he really felt sorry for.

Clint, he unconsciously smiled at the name, recalling when Kelly-Ann had her son, she saddled him with the name because as a wee girl, she'd loved the big American actor, Clint Walker, who'd played the part of Cheyenne Brodie in the television series, *Cheyenne*.

Clint was a definite granddad's boy and adored George Knox who if he had his way, Hardie suspected, would gladly have raised the lad rather than leave him at the tender mercy of Kelly-Ann.

Though he would never voice his opinion, it was Hardie's private belief she saw the small boy more as a hindrance to her social life than her responsibility to raise and care for him.

Still, he sighed, it really wasn't his concern and he was always careful when around the boss to keep his personal opinions to himself.

He was in the kitchen making a coffee when the phone on the wall rang.

"That you son?"

"Aye, it's me, boss. I'm not long home," he replied, then asked, "Any word yet?"

"No, nothing. I'm thinking about calling round the local hospitals, see if maybe she'd had an accident or something," he said and it was clear to Hardie there was worried unease in his voice.

"What about the cops, do you not think it might be…"

"Those sods," Knox growled. "They'd just love it if George Knox called to tell them I'm anxious about my lassie being missing. No, we do this ourselves," he grunted.

Hardie took a slow breath before he asked, "What if she's in the pokey, boss. Maybe she's been lifted for something."

There was a pause before Knox replied, "You have somebody you can ask, haven't you? A pal of yours if I remember correctly."

"There is somebody, aye, but I've not spoken to him for a while now. However, if you think it's worth asking, I'll give him a call."

"Will he take a bung?"

"No," Hardie shook his head, "definitely not. Archie's as straight as a die, but I'll likely owe him a favour, though."

"Do it, big man."

Hardie heard a deep sigh before Knox admitted, "I'm getting a wee bit worried, Alex."

"I'll call you back when I've spoken to him, boss."

"Thanks, son," Knox ended the call.

Stirring at the coffee, he reflected on the call and the boss's reluctance to contact the police.

Quite naturally, George Knox saw the cops as the enemy, for it was no secret the gangland boss was one of Strathclyde Police's main criminal targets and as one of his team, so too was Alex Hardie.

Taking the coffee through to the lounge, he sat in the comfortable armchair by the tiled Victorian fireplace and switched on the gas fire.

Sitting with the mug held in both hands, he thought of his time as one of George Knox's men, recalling how as a young and headstrong youngster, Knox had recruited him seven years previously from a life as a welder in the Fairfields Shipyard in Govan into the team of armed blaggers, nurturing him and teaching him how to avoid the pitfalls of the profession; a profession where too many would-be robbers thought they were a whole lot smarter than the cops that pursued them and where most, if not all, were now serving at Her Majesty's Pleasure.

But not George Knox or any of his team, he smiled.

It had been a tough apprenticeship, working under the boss and joining an already successful team of three, for there had been a lot to learn from the savvy and streetwise Knox.

Knox's team had always comprised of four men, but Ernie, who Hardie had never met, had succumbed to lung cancer and as the boss had intimated on the day he invited Hardie to join the team, "We never operate with any less than the four of us. Not if we want to stay out of the jail, we don't."

Now, seven years on, he had graduated to become the boss's right-hand man, a fact that had been accepted by the other two; Johnny Dunlop, the weapons man and wee Kevin Stobbie. Kevin the driver who, though he had never been professionally trained, drove like Jackie Stewart and could lay his hands on the getaway vehicles with apparent ease.

Seven years with the team, seven years robbing banks, building societies and the occasional armoured car, and not once had the cops ever arrested them and mainly because they didn't kick the arse out of it and did no more than two jobs a year.

He smiled at the memories of those times, but such was the boss's planning and attention to detail, so far they had eluded the best the police had thrown at them; the local Serious Crime Squad and their pals, the Scottish Crime Squad, who he knew was made up of officers drawn from all eight of the police Forces and who travelled the length and breadth of Scotland in pursuit of the team when they were pulling jobs throughout the country.

He had no doubt that somewhere in police headquarters, his picture and that of the boss and the other two, was probably thumbtacked to a board as major players.

Yes, on several occasions they had been *invited* into a number of police stations in Glasgow and Edinburgh and on Knox's instruction, always obliged the cops by attending, though never without legal representation.

During those times a succession of detectives interviewed them and no matter what was put to them, they always responded with 'No Comment,' and refused to provide alibis or any physical evidence such as fingerprints in the knowledge that if the cops had anything on them, they wouldn't be invited for interview; they'd be dragged from their homes at five in the morning and charged.

As Knox persistently told them, "It's up to the polis to find the evidence to convict us. We do *not* provide them with the evidence, so just keep schtum when they're interviewing you."

As so they stayed out of jail, though there had been a couple of close calls when they'd narrowly avoided being arrested.

Yet, though he knew it should, it didn't really worry him because without such evidence there was no case and the one thing the team were good at, very good at, was never leaving any trace of themselves at any of the jobs they did.

And though the cops were aware of their identities and that they were a team of armed blaggers, he smiled for as the boss often said, knowing something and proving it were two completely different issues.

Yes, they used shooters and yes, they terrified people, but not once had they ever hurt anyone and that, the boss constantly reminded them, would always work in their favour if the worst were to happen.

And the rewards?

He smiled as he sipped at his coffee, thinking of the money that with the incredible interest it earned, amounted to almost four hundred thousand pounds that was now his; money that was looked after by the wee accountant the boss had them use and who had squirrelled away his share and that of the others in a Cayman Islands bank.

Of course, the others had been at the game for a few years before he joined them and had earned an impressive amount in that time.

But the boss was a fair man and though Hardie was a relatively newcomer to the team, Knox always split the proceeds four ways and he was more than satisfied with what he had so far earned.

He sometimes felt a bit guilty, for it was the boss who did most of the work though, finding and planning the jobs then cleaning the money through the wee fat guy, Harry Cavanagh, an accountant who Knox trusted. And trusting the boss as they did, he had no problem convincing the other three that wee Harry was a safe pair of hands to handle the money and also ensured that for the time being until their retirement from the profession, none of the four lived beyond their means.

As for their weekly income, as far as the Inland Revenue and the cops were concerned, Jimmy and Kevin ran a couple of burger vans and mainly worked at fetes, showgrounds or the football stadiums at the weekends while the boss owned a small newsagent's shop in Duke Street that he had managed by a widowed woman he trusted. Hardie himself maintained an employment cover as a personal trainer and part-time steward, working regularly at a couple of pubs and nightclubs in the city at the hours that suited him.

Not that he minded the stewarding work for with his height and physique, he seldom had any trouble with the punters, drunk or otherwise.

No, it was the women he had to worry about for Alex Hardie had been blessed with good looks and a patient nature, something that he often called upon to resist the drunken women and their grasping hands.

Not that he didn't like women, but so far hadn't met the right one, other than…

A sudden memory caused him to smile.

His thoughts turned to the Glasgow scene and though he wasn't impatient to be done with it, he looked forward to the day when the boss called a halt and they all headed out of the country to collect their money in whatever country they each chose to settle.

They'd agreed a date for later this year when, the boss had explained, they had one last job to do and while they were still young enough to enjoy living abroad on the proceeds of what they'd robbed.

Jimmy at fifty years of age was the oldest of the team with Kevin and the boss both forty-eight and as far as he was concerned, he'd be happy to retire with them, for the money he'd earned would set him up in a bar and restaurant business in one of the Spanish islands where he could live a modest but more importantly, quiet life in the sun.

It had been suggested by Knox that Hardie either consider retiring with the other three or going on alone and recruiting his own team, but he'd declined and told Knox that he'd no interest in forming a new team. To his surprise, the boss had agreed and told him that even careful blaggers like them had a sell-by date and it was wise of Hardie to get out while the going was good.

Besides, he'd told Knox one night when they'd shared a bottle of Whyte & McKay, apart from an older brother Carl, who lived somewhere in England and who he never saw, he'd no one living that he cared for and wouldn't be too sorry to leave Glasgow.

It was that same night and maybe it was the whisky talking, but he'd had something in the back of his head that he'd suspected for a while and challenged Knox. To his surprise, he'd discovered the boss secretly hoped that he'd take on Knox's only child, Kelly-Ann, and make a wife of her and father to her son, Clint, but he'd quickly dismissed that notion.

"No, boss," he'd apologised with his heart racing, "much as I like Kelly-Ann, I'm afraid she's definitely not for me."

To his credit, George Knox had accepted that Hardie wasn't interested in his daughter and the matter was never again discussed or even hinted at.

His coffee finished, he decided to make the call he'd promised the boss and rising from the armchair, fetched a small black notebook from a top drawer of the dresser.

Turning the pages, he found the number he was looking for, then fetching the phone on its long cable back to the armchair, sat back down and dialled.

In the few seconds it took for the call to connect, he found his mouth was suddenly dry and almost hung up, afraid that maybe it might be she…

"Hello?"

He took a breath as the woman, her voice now suspicious, again said, "Hello."

"Ah, Helen, it's me, Alex Hardie."

There was a definite pause before she replied, "My God, Alex? Heavens above, how long has it been? Are you okay?"

"Me? Aye, I mean, yes, I'm fine," he hastily added. "You? You okay?"

Christ, he nervously licked at his lips and inwardly wondered, why is this so hard?

"Yes, well as okay as any woman who's five months pregnant," she softly giggled over the phone, a giggle that he knew so well and missed more than he would ever dare admit.

Stunned, he replied, "Oh, I didn't know. Congratulations. How are you keeping?"

"Ah, fine, now that the morning sickness is past. Just a waiting game now and you should see me. I'm already feeling like a weather balloon, I'm that big," she laughed.

Before he could respond, she said, "Is it me you're wanting to talk to or is it Archie?"

"Is he there? I mean, not that I don't want to talk to you," he hurriedly added, his face reddening and hoping she wasn't reading into anything.

Apparently, she didn't for she said, "Hold on, Alex, I'll shout for him to come downstairs," then added, "It was nice speaking with you. Take care now, bye."

He heard the phone being laid down, then Archie asking who it was before the phone was lifted.

"As I live and breathe, Alex Hardie. Don't tell me you're phoning to confess to a number of armed robberies, Mr Hardie?" asked Archie, but with a definite hint of humour in his voice.

"If I was, Sergeant Philips, and I knew anything about armed robberies," he smiled, "you'd be my choice of copper to tell. How you doing, pal?"

"So, so, Alex. Weather's a bit of a bugger, but I'm off shift for a couple of days so hopefully with this rainfall, the worst of the snow will be gone before I'm back out there, chasing the likes of you and your team."

Grinning, Hardie replied, "Wasting your time, Archie, chasing innocent men like me."

"Right then, you're on for something I suppose. What's up, pal?"

"It's personal, Archie. Pal of mine can't locate his daughter. He's getting a bit worried about her and I was wondering if you were in any position to ask your mob if they've heard anything about her."

"You think she might have come to some harm?"

"We just don't know," he sighed. "I'm more interested to know if she's in the pokey and if she is, we at least know then she's safe."

"I take it you haven't reported her missing?"

Pausing, he took a second to decide before he responded with, "It's Kelly-Ann Knox, Archie. George Knox's daughter."

Though Archie didn't know Kelly-Ann, George Knox was a name known to most if not all of Strathclyde Police and likely, throughout Scotland's CID units as well.

"Oh, I see," he said at last. "Describe her for me, please."

"Eh," he tightly closed his eyes to picture her in his head. "Five feet seven, slim build, jet black hair down to her shoulders, bit of a looker. Oh, and she's, ah, twenty-eight, no," he unconsciously shook his head, "she's twenty-nine-years of age. Same as you and me. And she lives in a flat in Tullis Street, over in Bridgeton."

"When was she last seen?"

"About seven o'clock last night going out dolled up, presumably to the dancing in the Barrowland where she normally goes on a Saturday night out."

"Right," Archie wheezed, "give me your phone number and I'll get back to you."

"I thought your mob had my number?" he grinned.

"Likely we have," Archie replied with a short laugh, "but not in my home I don't."

Hardie rattled off the digits, then said, "Thanks, Archie, I owe you."

"Aye you will you bugger."

"Oh, one more thing. Congratulations on the baby."

"Thanks, Alex. We're looking forward to it, but," he lowered his voice to a whisper, "pregnancy might be a cute thing for most people, but it comes with the down sides too. The mood swings. God, you can't imagine," he exhaled with a long drawn out sigh. Then, his voice returning to its natural pitch, he asked, "You still playing football?"

"No, gave it up years ago, but I'm still keeping myself fit."

"Aye, I heard," Archie laughed again, then ended the call.

****

It had been some time since he'd given Helen Philips, or Helen McCrory, as she'd been when the three of them had first met all those years ago. Sitting there with his eyes locked onto the fire, the memories came flooding back.

They had been tight once, the three of them, back in their Whitehill Secondary schooldays when he and Archie had represented the Glasgow Schools at the fitba; him the centre-half and Archie the goalie, two big lads who attracted the attention of the scouts from the First Division clubs in Glasgow, though to their mutual disappointment, neither actually made the grade.

Through it all Helen was their number one stalwart supporter, egging them on from the touchline and ready with the oranges at half-time and a flask of tea when the game finished.

The friendship had started on their first day at the secondary school, him and Archie pals since their Whitehill Primary days. Together in the school heading to their class and seeing Billy McPherson shoving the wee, slightly built girl with the big brown eyes and shoulder length hair, causing her to fall against the wall and make her cry, then her school bag bursting open and spilling her books onto the linoleum floor of the corridor.

Them almost as one taking an arm each before slamming McPherson against a wall and him running away greeting and grassing them in to the teacher.

It had earned them six of the best each and he unconsciously smiled for he could almost feel the stinging in his hands, even after all these years.

To their surprise, she had waited at the school gate for them and followed them up the road, confusing them as she prattled on like a budgie all the way till they broke off to go to their own homes.

It was the same the next day and the day after that; Helen waiting for them after school until at last, without any conscious agreement, the two had somehow become an inseparable three.

Then, their schooling completed, they went on to their respective occupations. Archie as a City of Glasgow Police Cadet, Helen entered into the nursing and him into the shipyard as an apprentice welder.

Somehow, the closeness between them just faded until one Saturday night drinking in the city centre, he bumped into the two of them and discovered them to be engaged.

Of course, he congratulated them and though his heart was broken at losing her, forced a smile and cheerily bought them a drink.

They'd just bought a house together, they'd eagerly told him and Archie had pressed their phone number onto him, insisting he get in touch and that they'd go out one night for a meal.

But he didn't phone though he'd kept the number, just in case.

Later, when they'd left the pub and him full of the bevy and angry with himself that he'd never spoke up and told her how he'd felt, how he'd come to love her, he found himself down in a pub in the Gallowgate and without any provocation, started a fight.

It was just as well the polis were called for he had been taking a right bleaching from the pub's patrons. But still fighting and him being a big lad handy with his fists, it took four cops to bundle him into the back of the van where they'd set about him and given him another bleaching.

Charged with a Breach of the Peace and Police Assault, he'd been detained in custody for Monday's District Court and appeared before the JP with a sore face and broken nose.

He hadn't known at the time that one of the punters in the pub who had thoughtfully watched him battling the cops, had been George Knox.

Appearing at the District Court as a first offender, he'd been heavily punished and almost panicked, for he hadn't that sort of money to pay the fine, but to his surprise discovered the fine was paid in cash. Initially suspicious of the slim built man who'd waited for him at the front door of the court, he'd followed Knox to the café in the High Street where over an all-day breakfast, Knox had slowly broken down his reserve, learned of his background and though he hadn't realised it then, was recruiting him to replace Ernie Wiseman, the man he later learned the team had lost to cancer.

The following week in a Shettleston pub, he was introduced to Johnny Dunlop who that day drove him to a deserted quarry in the Fife area where Dunlop familiarised him with a sawn-off shotgun and a 9mm Fabrique Nationale, the semi-automatic handgun he came to know well and which he later used on the jobs the team pulled.

To date, though, he had simply brandished the handgun, but never used the weapon on any of the turns.

He was also to later learn that George Knox never planned a turn unless every minute detail had been checked and re-checked and that, Knox drummed it into him, was the key to their success.

The six 'P's' rule, Knox called it.

Planning and preparation prevents piss poor performance.

He was also to learn that though the police had long since identified Knox, Dunlop, Stobbie and their deceased associate, Ernie Wiseman, as the four-armed blaggers, they were never able to gather any evidence to link the team to the robberies.

Though he was never to learn of it, some months after the death of Wiseman and though he had been unaware, he had been spotted by an off-duty surveillance officer associating with Knox and thus come to be identified and later assessed by the police as the replacement fourth man for the team.

He involuntarily smiled when he recalled their first job as a team, a Clydesdale Bank in Johnstone's High Street. The boss, Johnny and Kevin, the getaway driver, like him all dressed in brand-new navy-blue boiler suits with Nitrile gloves on their hands and wearing women's stockings over their heads; the three older blaggers calm and composed and him shitting a brick.

Getting out of the Transit van, his mouth was so dry he thought he might choke, his hands sweating and the wearing of the stocking mask caused him to feel so claustrophobic he had to vigorously resist the temptation to rip it from his head.

Johnny with the sawn-off pointed threateningly at the bank staff and customers, the boss carrying the black bins bags and nimbly vaulting over the counter to raid the tills and him with the semi-automatic in his hand to guard the door.

What had taken a little over two minutes seemed like forever and he was sure he'd lost a couple of pounds in perspiration.

Then, the only word used in all of the jobs, Knox's shout of "Done!" and it was out the bank and into the rear of the van.

There followed a hair-raising race by Kevin to the fields beyond Linwood, down a lane, a shuddering stop, stripping off the boiler suits, the gloves and the stocking masks that went into the rear of the Transit that they doused with petrol before setting it alight.

What seemed like an eternity, but was literally minutes later, the four of them into the two small saloon cars parked there and at a sedate speed, back on the road and making their way to the M8 and returning to Glasgow.

He smiled at the audacity of their turns, their trademark being new boiler suits and the new stocking masks and gloves for each turn and the one word that was shouted by the boss,

"Done!"

"If ever we get caught," Knox had grinned one time, "it'll be because the country's run out of new boiler suits."

Thirty-eight grand they'd stolen that day. His first job and he'd earned nine and a half grand, though he didn't see the money then or since, for it went in the boot of the boss's car to later be delivered to their accountant, wee Harry Cavanagh.

What he did see was a regular tri-monthly statement, forwarded to him by Cavanagh.

The statement intimated both his savings and the interest it earned and originated from a Cayman Islands based bank that once read, he would destroy.

Only twice in the seven years he had been a member of the team did the police come anywhere near to catching them. Once when a beat copper turned a corner as they were leaving a building society in Perth and who quite rightly backed off when Johnny pointed the shotgun at him.

A second time when a patrol car had fastened onto the back of the Leyland van they were using on a turn in Dunfermline. Fortunately, the police driver wasn't as good as Kevin, who lost him on a country road when the police vehicle wasn't as sharp on a bend as was Kevin and it ended up in a ditch.

His thoughts idly returned to Helen and he smiled.

Him and Archie were never that clever at school, but Helen persisted in tutoring them both, either at her home where her mother kept the three of them going on jam or marmalade sandwiches and orange juice or at Archie's house where his parents seemed to have an abundance of chocolate biscuits and tea and permitted them to use their 'best' front room to study.

Never at his house, though, for after he and his older brother were orphaned and Carl took off for England, he was left in the care to his aunt Martha, a principled, church-going spinster with strong Calvinistic values and a sombre nature who disapproved of him having friends visiting her fastidiously neat and tidy Duke Street flat.

However, Helen, it turned out, proved an apt teacher for to his surprise, both Archie and he passed their 'O' level exams that permitted him to apply as an apprentice welder while his long-time pal opted for the Police Cadets.

And now she was married to Archie, a Sergeant at Stewart Street Police Office and she was pregnant with his child.

He sat forward in the armchair and rubbed wearily with the heel of his hand at his brow.

If he had to lose her to another man, polis or not, he'd rather it was Archie Philips than anyone for his old friend was a good man and would take care of her, of that he was certain.

No matter that they were now on opposite sides of the law, he thought of Archie like a brother and Helen like...he shook his head and smiled.

He could never think of her as a sister.

Not Helen.

****

The phone rang and he glanced at the clock on the wall, seeing that it was almost eleven o'clock and that nearly twenty-five minutes had passed since he'd spoken with Archie.

"Hello?"

"It's me," he heard Archie sigh. "The good news is that there's no Kelly-Ann Knox been lifted in any of the city divisions, Alex."

He couldn't explain why, but felt his stomach knot when he asked, "And the bad news?"

"Sorry, pal, but there's been a woman's body found over in the southside of the city. In the Pollok Park."

CHAPTER THREE

DCI Martin Benson arrived early that Monday morning at Pollok Police station, surprised to find that DI Roddy Williams and his team were already there.

Dumping his overcoat on a chair in Williams's office, he greeted him with, "Morning, Roddy. I didn't think you'd get in so early after the night you had. How you feeling?"

"Like I've been pulled backwards through a hedge then battered on the head with a rolling pin. Apart from that, I'm fine," he grinned. "Coffee?"

"Aye, please and while you're fetching it. You have any statements I can glance through?"

"Just the woman who discovered the body and the cop's statements who attended the call are there in the file too," he nodded to a folder on the desk. "Mine and the two late shift, Willie McBride and young Ailish MacDonald, we've still to include ours."

Settling himself behind Williams desk, he opened a pack of Kensitas cigarettes then lighting one, took a deep draw before reading the statements.

The door opened to admit DS Willie McBride who yawning, said, "Morning, boss," and handed Benson a brown manila envelope.

"Doc Smythe dropped this off to be added to the statement file."

"Thanks, Roddy," he stared keenly at him, "How did you get on last night in the snow?"

"Bloody freezing it was and a hell of a start to nineteen-eighty-four. We're lucky though up here," McBride pursed his lips. "It wasn't as bad as last week when they six people down south died in the storms."

"Aye, that's the thing about the Scottish weather. It's a bugger one day then the next," he turned to glance out the window where the rain battered against the glass. "At least the heavy downpour's getting rid of the slushy snow."

Taking a draw of his cigarette, he asked, "You were on with young Ailish. How did she cope attending her first murder?"

McBride grinned when he replied, "I think she was more concerned about the freezing cold than the body, boss."

The door behind him opened to admit Williams, who carried in two mugs of coffee.

"Willie," he nodded at him. "Did you manage to arrange a time for the PM?"

"If you can make it, boss, there's an opening at nine-thirty this morning."

Williams glanced at Benson, who nodding, replied for them when he said, "That'll do us fine, though it would be nice to know who our victim is. Nothing back from any of the Divisions about a missing woman yet?"

"Nothing, boss," McBride shook his head.

"Any suggestions she might be a prossie that's not been reported missing?"

His question wasn't a shot in the dark, for a year earlier there had been two reported cases of prostitutes being taken from the city centre by a middle aged man in a dark coloured vehicle and raped in the nearby Bellahouston Park.

"Could be," McBride shrugged, "but if she was out on a night like last night plying her trade up in the drag, she must have been off her head because I can't imagine there would be many punters out driving in that weather."

"Point taken, Willie. What about the locus now that the snows melting. Anything turn up yet?"

The cops at the locus have been warned to report anything they might find there, boss, but there's been no word yet; however, I'll get on to the control room again and remind them to let the cops know," and then he left the room.

"You got the murder incident room up and running, Roddy?"

"All set up, boss. Mhari McGregor as the office manager and I've appointed two of the DC's to come to the PM with us, Ailish MacDonald and Ian Burns and they'll act as the production team. It'll be good experience for Ailish and Ian's a steady hand."

"Good," Benson nodded before adding, "Well it just remains for us to get ourselves together and we'll brief the team on what little we know so far. But for now, let's have another fag and this coffee."

****

There was nothing to suggest the body was definitely that of Kelly-Ann, so he'd decided to hold off phoning the boss till the morning in the knowledge that such information at that time of night would only drive George and Rosie mad with worry.

After a sleepless night, he made a strong coffee then seeing on the wall clock in the kitchen it was a little after eight and knowing that the boss would be up to get the wee guy ready for school, he lifted the phone off the cradle on the wall. Carrying it to the window, he glanced out and saw that the overnight squall of rain that had brought with it an increase in the temperature and had wiped most of the snow from the road and pavements, though not on the rough ground beyond the fence opposite the building.

Then he made the call.

"Alex," Knox sounded like he too had a sleepless night. "When I heard nothing last night, I assumed you hadn't found anything out. But you're phoning at this time of the morning. So, what's up?"

He'd practised what he was going to say, yet still the words stuck in his throat.

"Alex?"

"Boss," he took a deep breath, "nobody with Kelly-Ann's details was lifted anywhere in Glasgow on Saturday night."

There was a pause before Knox asked, "I'm guessing there's a but, coming."

He felt his throat constrict when he said, "Yesterday evening, a woman's body was found in Pollok Park behind the museum, the Burrell place. The general description fits Kelly-Ann."

Knox received the information in silence, then slowly asked, "The polis, they take bodies to the mortuary at the Saltmarket, don't they?"

"Aye, I think so."

He heard a soft sigh then Knox dully said, "I'll drop the wee guy at school then I'll pick you up. We'll go together and find out if it's her."

He could hardly swallow now, but managed to reply, "I'll watch for you from the window."

****

Ailish MacDonald daren't admit it, but she was more than a little excited at being part of the murder investigation team and even more so because she had been neighboured with Ian Burns, a pleasant and friendly individual who nearing retirement, had just a few months left of his thirtieth year in the job.

Though she knew from her detective training course at the Police College the duties of a Productions Officer, this was her first time actually doing the job and also the first occasion she would be attending at a post mortem.

Burns, heavy set with a florid face, thinning ginger hair, a ready smile and whose old suit was impregnated and reeked of the strong pipe tobacco he used, said, "Don't forget to stick some hand cream in your handbag, hen, for your top lip. The smell in the mortuary when the pathologist opens the body is…well, awful," he'd cheerily grinned at her.

Now with Burns driving the CID car through the slushy roads towards the Saltmarket, they were here and she could almost feel the excitement coursing through her body.

"Have you had your breakfast this morning?" he risked a glance at her.

"Yes, well, cereal and a mug of tea. Why?"

"Oh, it's just that you'll need your stomach lined with something to throw up, I mean," he teased her with a wide grin.

"Aye, very funny you old git," she pretended to scowl at him, but Ian wasn't the sort of man that you could fall out with for long and within minutes, he had her laughing at anecdotal stories of his numerous visits to the mortuary.

"I'm hearing that the woman hasn't been identified yet," Burns said. "Shame that nobody seems to be missing her, isn't it?"

"Maybe her prints will turn something up," she frowned, but then remembered that was supposing the poor soul's body had finally thawed during her overnight stay in the mortuary.

"Aye, maybe," he agreed with a sigh.

Turning through the open gate into the rear yard, Burns parked behind the CID car that had been driven there by the DI, who they presumed was now inside the building with DCI Benson.

Leaving his neighbour to fetch the brown paper bags and production labels from the boot of the car, Burns strode towards the back door of the mortuary, only to discover it locked.

Calling out to Ailish, he strode with her round to the corner entrance of the building then pushing open the door, they almost collided with three men stood in the foyer area.

One man wearing a green dustcoat, who was clearly a mortuary attendant, was directing the other two men to a waiting room further down the corridor.

Glancing at both men, Ailish saw the younger man to be tall, handsome and blonde haired and who was wearing a white polo neck sweater, dark trousers, a black leather blazer and carrying a dark rain jacket over his arm while the other man was in his late forties, of medium height, slim build with greying dark hair and wore a beige overcoat over a grey coloured, three-piece suit.

Following Burns along the corridor behind the men, she startled when her neighbour turned to glance at her and she saw his face to be grimly set and flushed.

The younger of the two men stopped to permit her to pass him by and flashed her a polite smile.

Burns pushed open one of the double doors at the end of the corridor that was marked 'Private' and holding the door open to permit her to enter, whispered, "Quick, let's find the boss."

Taken aback and a little confused, Ailish watched as Burns rushed along the corridor then ducked into a room. Following behind, she saw that the DI and the DCI were also in the room, and then heard Burns breathlessly tell Benson, "Boss, you'll never guess who's outside in the relatives' room."

Staring curiously at him Benson shook his head as Burns continued, "George Knox. Him and some young guy that's with him."

"George Knox? What the devil is he doing here?"

"Don't know boss, but he was speaking with Charlie. Want me to go and fetch him?"

"Charlie? Aye, bring him here and we'll find out what Knox is doing here."

Stepping around Ailish, Burns hurried from the room while Benson said to Williams, "Is there anybody else from the CID here that you saw, Roddy?"

Shrugging, Williams shook his head when he replied, "As far as I know, we're the only criminal PM that's scheduled for the day, boss."

"Eh," Ailish felt a little foolish when she raised her hand to ask, "who's George Knox?"

Benson glanced at Williams before he quietly replied "Knox is one of the top ten targets for Strathclyde Police, Ailish. No, I correct myself," he sighed. "He's the target for every bloody police force in Scotland. He's the main man of a team of four armed robbers that for years have been acting without impunity right across the country, hitting banks, building societies and sometimes an armoured car or what they now call a cash in transit vehicle. The bugger's been on the rampage for what?" he glanced at Williams as though seeking agreement. "Over ten years now?"

Before Williams could respond, the door opened and she turned to see the mortuary attendant ushered in by Burns.

"Charlie," Benson turned to the bewildered man, "the two men through in the relatives waiting room. Did they say why they're here?"

"Aye, they said they're waiting to speak with you about the young woman who was brought in last night."

"Me?"

Surprised, Benson turned to Williams who shaking his head, muttered, "News to me, boss."

"Well, not you specifically, Mr Benson," Charlie shook his head. "The older of the two guys, he said he wanted to speak with the CID officer dealing with the woman."

Charlie's eyes narrowed when he asked, "Don't you know about them being here? Do you want me to throw them out?"

Benson hid a smile for he very much doubted the elderly Charlie could throw a hissy fit, let alone a hardened criminal like George Knox and his pal out of the mortuary.

Shaking his head, he replied, "I'll see them in a minute. Can you ask Mr Morgan to delay the PM for five minutes while I have word with these guys?"

"Aye, sir, no problem," nodded Charlie, who though he'd no idea what was going on, sensed there was something amiss and self-importantly shuffled from the room.

"Right, Roddy, let's me and you go and speak with our George and find out why he's here."

****

Benson led the way into the relative's room to find George Knox and the tall, blonde-haired man standing quietly chatting together.

"Mr Knox," he greeted him, "I'm DCI Martin Benson of G Division CID and this is DI Roddy Williams. I understand you've asked to speak with the man in charge of the investigation regarding the woman brought to the mortuary, last night. Can I ask what your interest in the woman is?"

Knox stared at him for several seconds then his eyes narrowing in recognition, said, "Benson. Don't I know you?"

"Aye," he nodded, "It must be about ten years ago, when I was a DS with the City of Glasgow Flying Squad. I interviewed you about a robbery you and your associates committed at a building society in the city centre."

"*Allegedly* committed, Mr Benson. As I recall, you had no evidence and were acting on suspicion alone."

Benson allowed himself a soft smile when nodding, he replied, "Quite right. I was winging it and you walked away without being charged. Now, again, what can I do for you, Mr Knox?"

Knox, his face pale, bowed his head and took a breath and it seemed to Benson, he was trying to work himself into an explanation, when to his surprise, the younger man said, "We learned last night, Mr Benson, that a woman was brought into the mortuary from somewhere over in Pollok. The thing is, Kelly-Ann, George's daughter, nobody's seen her since Saturday evening and it's not like her to not to contact her Da."

"Sorry, who are you?"

He flashed a wide smiled before he replied, "Alex Hardie, Mr Benson. I'm a friend of George. We've not met, but I'm sure my name's known to you guys somewhere."

Benson flashed a glanced at Williams before he addressed his response to Knox, "The woman who was brought in. We've not been able to identify her yet. Can you describe your daughter?"

Again, it was Hardie who hastily replied, "Kelly-Ann's twenty-nine years of age, about five-seven tall with shoulder length dark hair and she's slim build too. We don't know what she was wearing when she left her flat."

Benson's brow furrowed, then staring at Knox, he said, "Before I start taking any more details, Mr Knox, I think the quickest solution to determine if it is your daughter is if you or Mr Hardie want to view the deceased…"

"Aye, I'd appreciate that, Mr Benson," Knox faked a cough to hide his nervousness, then glancing at Hardie, was about to speak when the younger man placed a hand on his arm and said, "Let me go, boss. I'll have a look."

"Roddy?" Benson turned to the DI who opening the door then led Hardie from the room.

"Can I ask you, how you knew about the woman being found?" Benson stared at him. "It's not in the papers or on the radio yet."

Knox raised his eyebrows and slowly shaking his head, replied, "I have my sources, Mr Benson, just as you have yours."

"Can I ask why you didn't report her to the police as missing?"

Knox smiled when he quietly replied, "Let's just say that it's not just the polis who would have a good laugh at my daughter being missing, Mr Benson. I've got enemies you wouldn't know about that would like to see me fall."

"Care to discuss these enemies?"

"No, but thanks anyway," he wryly smiled.

****

Roddy Williams led Hardie through the door marked 'Private' into a small viewing room, split in half by a plasterboard wall with a large viewing window that was curtained off.

"We were just about to commence the post mortem, so I'll need to ask the mortuary attendant to bring the deceased back from the examination room. If you give me a couple of minutes to make then arrangement, then I'll have the attendant draw back the curtain," Williams said and left Hardie alone in the room.

Staring at the window, he had a fearful apprehension of what was to lie beyond the curtain and when the door unexpectedly opened just four minutes later, he was so startled he almost jumped.

Taking a breath to calm himself, he watched Williams rap on the window with his knuckles.

The curtain slid back and he heard Williams say, "Mr Hardie?"

Stepping forward, he found he could hardly swallow as he stared down at the woman lying in the coffin, a brilliantly white sheet pulled up to her chin so that the only part of her exposed was her face.

He saw her dark hair was brushed back and lay neatly on the pillow supporting her head, her eyes were closed with a faint bluish tinge to her eyelids and her face whiter than he'd ever seen on anyone before.

"Mr Hardie," Williams stared at his pale face when he softly asked, "is that Kelly-Ann Knox?"

****

They returned to the relative's room where Hardie, still shaken from what he had viewed, stared at Knox, then slowly said, "George, I'm so very sorry."

"So, it's her right enough," he reached behind him as if to sit on the chair against the wall, but tearfully staggered slightly and was caught by Benson and Hardie who helped him onto the chair before he fell to the floor.

Unseen, Williams quietly left the room to fetch some water.

Taken aback that the boss was so distraught, he turned to the DCI to ask, "Mr Benson, are you able to tell us what happened to her?"

Though he stared down at Knox, he addressed Hardie when he said, "All I can tell you at the minute is that the woman you have identified as Kelly-Ann Knox was discovered in circumstances that suggest she was the victim of a murder. The post mortem that we are about to conduct might tell us more. Right now, though, I'll need you and Mr Knox here to give us a statement so…"

"George isn't fit to give you a statement the now," Hardie snappily interrupted. "I need to get him home and let his wife know what's happened to their daughter."

Almost immediately, he calmed himself, then holding up a hand as though in apology, added, "I promise you though, once I've got George up the road I'll come back here or go wherever you need me to go and I'll tell you as much as we know. I'm sure there's no urgency to get George or Rosie's statement right now, is there?"

Benson took several seconds to make up his mind then nodding, said, "Okay. Given the circumstances, I'll agree to what you suggest. Take Mr Knox home and let his wife know about Kelly-Ann. Once you've done that, I expect you to attend at Pollok Police station to give me a statement. Do you know where that is?"

"I'll find it," he grimly replied, then helping Knox to his feet, took his arm to steady him as they passed through the door held by Williams.

When they'd gone and the door was closed again, Williams, a glass of water in his hand, returned to find them gone and said, "Jesus, boss, that was a turn-up for the books. George Knox's daughter?"

After Benson explained about Hardie's agreement to travel to Pollok Police station, he frowned when he asked, "You think the young guy will come to Pollok and give us a statement?"

"Funny enough, Roddy, aye, I do."

"I'll phone the office and tell them to expect him if he gets there first."

"Do that and while you're at it, have someone contact Criminal Intelligence at Pitt Street and send us what they know about our Mr Hardie to Pollok, *post haste*."

"How did they know about the body being here at the mortuary?"

"No idea," Benson sighed. "I did ask Knox, but he dizzied me, said he has his sources like we have ours."

"Cheeky bastard. He's obviously referring to a polis somewhere that's tipped him off."

"Aye, Roddy, but Knox is a man I wouldn't underestimate either. Right, we'd better get into the examination room or Mr Morgan will be wondering where we are."

Walking along the corridor to the examination room, Williams said, "You know what this means, don't you?"

"Oh aye," Benson exhaled, "I know *exactly* what it means. It'll not just be us looking for a killer. George Knox will turn this city upside down until one of us finds whoever murdered his daughter and for the killer's sake, it better be us who finds them first."

CHAPTER FOUR

Alex Hardie took George Knox's car keys from him and drove the racing green coloured, old-style, but well-maintained Jaguar back to Knox's home in Barmulloch.

Sitting quietly in the passenger seat, Knox pondered who might have killed his daughter, but uppermost in his mind was how he would break the news to Rosie and to his grandson that his mother would never be coming home.

Concentrating on his driving, Hardie was having the same thoughts. He liked Kelly-Ann…*had* liked her, he corrected himself, then realised that though their paths seldom crossed other than at the Knox's parties or when the boss occasionally sent him to find her to bring her home to her son and even then, when she had a drink in her, he couldn't help himself and inwardly smiled, had to avoid her groping him.

She was waywardly promiscuous and known for it too, even by the boss and her mother, though her father was constantly warning her to mind the company she kept.

His eyes narrowed for it occurred to him then that he knew few of her friends, other than some of the women she hung about with at the dancing and even then it was just faces, no names or addresses.

His thoughts turned to his agreement to attend at Pollok Police station and provide a statement. The CID would want to know everything about her life and that might bring problems for he would need to be careful that whatever he told them would not infringe on George and Rosie's life. No, he mentally shook his head, he'd watch what he said for the polis would look for any opportunity to bang the boss up and if he got the jail, it was more than likely they'd all be arrested.

Turning into Quarrywood Road, he slowed the Jaguar then startled, corrected the wheel when the old car slithered in the slushy remains of the snow when coming to a halt outside Knox's close.

Switching off the engine, he was about to speak when Knox said, "You'll need to be careful when you're talking to the CID, Alex. Answer their questions, aye, but don't volunteer anything, particularly about the team."

"I was just thinking that, boss. I'll watch what I say."

Seconds passed before Knox continued, "They'll want to know everything they can about Kelly-Ann and likely they'll want to turn over her flat as well. I've a spare set of keys in here," he opened the glove box and handed Hardie the keys. "Take them with you and make sure you're in the flat when they're searching it."

Hardie's eyes narrowed when he asked, "Are you expecting them to find anything there?"

Knox sighed when he replied "I knew she was partial to a wee bit of blow, now and then, even though I was always warning her about smoking the dope. If you find any dope there in the flat before the CID do, pocket it or dump it down the lavvy."

"You want me to go there the now and search the flat?"

"No," he shook his head and his eyes narrowed in thought. "That guy Benson, the DCI. I remember a wee bit more about him now. Sharp as a tack he was when we crossed paths the last time, so he'll be expecting you at Pollok. I want him to believe he's getting our full cooperation and I don't want him to think we're holding back on him."

"I can leave you the motor and I'll get a taxi, if you want?"

"Take the Jag, I'll not be needing it. Besides, I want you to come back here when you're done being interviewed to tell Rosie and me what the CID know about her murder."

He took a breath then turning, he tightly grasped Hardie's left arm, then staring him in the eye, said, "One more thing, Alex. I know we had the last job planned for next week, but as of now, it's on hold. What I want is for you to find out, who killed my lassie. I want you to concentrate solely on going round her pals, the dancing, anywhere she was in the last week and find out who did her in!"

His voice broke and choked off a cough.

"Do that for me, son, won't you? And Alex," he released his grip, "whatever it takes, do what you need to do to find the bastard."

"Aye, boss, of course," he nodded, "Stand on me. I'll do my level best," yet wondered what the reaction would be if the CID were to learn about him speaking to what was likely going to be Crown witnesses.

Well, he thought, I'll deal with that when it happens.

"Right, I'd better get upstairs," Knox said in a reluctant voice.

"Good luck, boss," Hardie patted him on the arm.

He didn't drive off till he saw Knox enter the close then with a sigh, started the engine.
****

Her upper lip shiny with plastered on hand cream and, as Ian Burns had suggested, breathing through her mouth, Ailish MacDonald looked on in horror as Mr Morgan, the silver-haired pathologist, calmly dictated his actions into the microphone suspended on the wire above the examination table while throughout the procedure, the female Scene of Crime officer continually snapped photographs.

Growing up on a diet of American cop dramas like 'Quincy, ME,' never in her wildest imagination did she expect a human body to be so utterly dissected, as was the body of Kelly-Ann Knox.

Her knuckles white from tightly gripping the paper bag that contained the only item of clothing the body had still been wearing when discovered, the light green dress, she watched the pathologist hand small glass sample bottles to her neighbour that contained blood, stomach contents, hair and a sample of the deceased's liver and kidneys.

"So, she was definitely strangled then, Mr Morgan," she heard DCI Benson break into her thoughts.

"Oh, without a doubt," the pathologist replied. "I can say that prior to her death, this was a healthy young woman. You might also wish to note the marks on her wrists that suggest to me she was bound or manacled, though by what I can only venture a guess that it was something narrow, like wire perhaps or a small gauge rope."

But then he shook his head and brow knitting, added, "No, not rope. I believe rope would have left a more distorted pattern on the skin."

"Am I expecting too much, Mr Morgan, when I ask if the wrists were bound together or she was bond to something, like a bed, perhaps?"

Morgan softly smiled before he replied, "I'm sorry to say, Mr Benson, that is something I do not know nor do I wish to hazard a guess."

"However," he continued, "The cause of her death was clearly the Hyoid bone in her throat being snapped and her Trachea being crushed. This injury has prevented the flow of air to the lungs and that in turn proved fatal. You can clearly see," he waved Benson over, "that what appears to be finger marks on the skin. I would suggest that the culprit was facing her or perhaps kneeling over her, if she were prone. Curiously," his eyes narrowed, "I would have expected that while being strangled she might have fought her killer to release his or her hands from around her throat and in doing so, I would have discovered scratches on her neck. The lack of such scratches tends to corroborate the fact her hands were, as I suspected, bound or in some way incapacitated."

"And the obvious bruising to her vagina? I might be a layman," Benson took a breath, "but having attended more post mortems than

I care to remember, it seems to me that it's more than just sexual activity that's caused such an injury, Mr Morgan."

"Yes, I rather fear you are correct, Mr Benson," Morgan peered at the injuries. "The absence of underwear garments seems to suggest that perhaps prior to her death, some sexual activity has occurred. I will of course swab the young woman, but I can only speculate that something, some large object, has been inserted into her vagina that if she were alive, must undoubtedly have caused her extreme and agonising pain. Whoever committed such an awful act…" he slowly shook his head, seeking the words that would not come to him.

Taking a deep breath as though to clear his head, he exhaled then lifted one of her hands and said, "As you can plainly see, none of the manicured fingernails on her hands are broken, suggesting to me that prior to being bound she might not have been capable of resisting her killer."

"Drunk or drugged, perhaps?"

"Possibly," he nodded, "though a forensic examination of the samples I have taken will undoubtedly shed further light on that theory."

Standing to one side, Ailish MacDonald stared numbly at the corpse, unable to imagine what horror the young woman had experienced in the sure knowledge she was being strangled to death and inwardly prayed that the injury caused to her vagina did occur after she had been strangled.

Using the blunt end of small wooden toothpicks, they watched as Morgan took sample scrapings from under the fingernails, each sample using a different toothpick that he placed into a glass sample bottle held by Ian Burns, who then tightly screwed down the lid of the bottle before placing the bottles into a brown paper bag.

"So, there's little likelihood that her killer might have suffered scratches?" a frustrated Benson asked.

"If I am correct, I'm afraid not, no," Morgan shook his head.

Turning to the other detectives and the Scene of Crime photographer, Benson meaningfully stared at them in turn when he said, "Knowledge about the vaginal injury suffered by our victim will remain in this room meantime. Under no circumstances will it be discussed even among the team."

There was no need to explain his reasoning. As the SIO in the investigation, he wanted a piece of specialist knowledge that only the murderer could know and any sick or waisted individual that for any reason who tried to claim credit for the murder, could be eliminated from the investigation if they had no knowledge of what the pathologist had discovered.

Ashen faced as she listened to the DCI, Ailish could not avert her eyes from the mutilated body that lay on the examination table, then visibly startled when Burns whispered, "You okay, hen?"

"Eh, oh, aye, I'm fine," she gulped.

But he recognised she was not fine and so handing her the brown paper bags, firmly told her, "Take these through to the room in the corridor and start filling in the production labels for each item, please."

She knew he was being kind and rather than argue, did as he instructed.

Ten minutes later, Burns joined her in the room and said, "Time we were heading back to the factory, Ailish, but before we go there, we need to hand these sample bottles into the Forensic Laboratory at Glasgow University."

"The Uni? Why there and not the Pitt Street Lab?"

"These are human tissue," he explained, "and the Uni is better suited to examining the contents. Once that's done, they also have the facility to safely dispose of the contents."

"Oh, right," she nodded and asked, "Then do we drop off the clothes and other productions at Pitt Street?"

"No, we take them back to Pollok, lodge them through our Production Book, and then deliver them to Pitt Street. It's all to do with continuity. We've seized them so we sign them into our book and then get a signature when we hand them over to the forensic guys at Pitt Street. That way the defence in any subsequent trial can't accuse us of letting the productions out of our possession where the defence can claim they could have been contaminated by anything or anyone other than the accused."

Once settled in the car with Burns again driving, he asked, "How you feeling?"

"Queasy," she admitted.

"Right then, when we've made the delivery to the Uni, I've just the thing to settle your stomach," he grinned at her.

Forty minutes later, their samples dropped off at the University, they were sat in a crowded café in Woodlands Road enjoying their rolls and bacon and tea.

"Think the productions are okay left in the car, Ian?"

"They're locked in the boot, hen. They're fine," he assured her, "now eat your roll."

"Do you not think the boss will be looking for us?" she asked, her brow knitting with worry.

"It takes time lodging the samples at the Uni," he adopted a serious expression, "so if anybody asks, that's where we were."

"Oh, right," she smiled, then her brow creasing once more, asked, "Why did you get so het up about them two men who were at the mortuary when we arrived? I asked the boss and he told me that the older guy, George Knox, he was a top target for the Serious and the Scottish. But you seemed right angry when you saw them."

"The younger guy, I don't know him, but the older of the two, George Knox? He's a real bad guy," his lip curled and he shook his head. "Him and his team have been robbing banks and building societies and doing C-I-T hold-ups for about ten or eleven years, nearly. He's what the Criminal Intelligence boys call a Z listed criminal target."

"C-I-T?"

"Cash in transit. Armoured cars."

"Oh, right. George Knox," she thoughtfully bit into her roll. "I'd heard of him of course, but I wouldn't have known him if he passed me in the street."

"Aye," he sighed, "he's knocked over a lot of places throughout Scotland, has Knox, but never been caught, not once."

"And our victim, that was his daughter?"

"Apparently, yes."

"Poor man."

"Poor man?" he stared at her as though she were mad. "The buggers a bad bastard, Ailish, and don't forget that."

"But he's still lost a child, Ian, regardless of who he is and besides, it wasn't his daughter who was robbing the banks, was it?"

He suddenly smiled then sighing, replied, "You're too soft-hearted, hen, but you're right. Regardless of who you are, nobody deserves to lose their wean and particularly the way that poor lassie was killed."

"Who was the other guy with Knox, do you know him?"

"No, I don't. His son, maybe?"

He stared at her, then slowly grinning, said, "Handsome big fella, wasn't he?"

She blushed and lied, "I never noticed."

"Aye right, you never noticed," he teased her, then asked, "I thought you were seeing somebody?"

"I was for about two months, but he dumped me."

He stared at her, seeing a young woman in her late twenties, tall at five feet nine inches with shoulder length auburn hair pulled back into a pony-tail, large brown eyes and thought her to be very pretty before he kindly replied, "His loss, the wanker."

"Thanks," she grinned, "and you're right. It's his loss and he is a wanker."

Finishing his tea, he nodded then said, "We'd better get a move on, hen, and get back to the factory."

****

Had there been anyone there to ask him, Alex Hardie would have admitted that yes, he was nervous when he stopped the car outside the police office in Brockburn Road, thinking apart from that time he'd been arrested for breach of the peace and police assault, he'd never been inside a police station without a brief to accompany him. Switching off the engine, he stepped out of the Jaguar and turning up the collar of his rain jacket against the chilling wind, made his way into the single storey building.

Pushing open the inner door, he was greeted by a young, uniformed constable standing behind the bar who smiled, then asked, "Can I help you, sir?"

"My name's Alex Hardie. DCI Benson asked me to attend here to give a statement."

"Oh, right," the constable's brow creased before he replied, "If you take a seat, I'll phone through to the CID and get someone to come and speak with you."

He had been sitting for no longer than a couple of minutes when a middle-aged man with thinning brown hair and as tall as himself, but running to fat, pushed open a door and said, "Mr Hardie, I'm DS Willie McBride, if you'd like to follow me, please."

McBride led him through a short corridor then into a wooden walkway that in turn, led to a portacabin at the rear of the building.

Pushing open a door into one half of the portacabin, McBride bid him to sit down in front of a desk before he explained, "As you can see, we're a bit pushed for space in the main building."
Sitting behind the desk, he continued, "The boss isn't back from the post mortem, yet, but I understand you were related to the victim?"
"Not blood related," he shook his head. "I've been friendly with her father for a number of years," as likely you already know, he thought, "but he's obviously upset at what's happened to Kelly-Ann, so I'm here to give you what I know about her and anything that might help you catch who killed her."
"Okay," McBride slowly drawled, then said, "It's no secret the lassie's Da is known to us, Mr Hardie," then squinting, asked, "Is it okay if I call you Alex?"
"Fine by me…Willie," he smiled.
McBride smiled in return, then sitting back in his chair, peered at him before he asked, "Have you or George any idea who might have murdered his lassie?"
He surprised McBride when he asked, "Have you got children, Willie?"
His eyes narrowing, McBride nodded when he said, "Aye, a son and a daughter, both grow-up now with their own families. Why do you ask?"
Shaking his head, Hardie slowly replied, "I'm not married and I've no family, but stand on me. If we did know who killed her, there would have been no need for me to come here today. It would have been sorted, Willie, without involving you guys. So, tell me this and God forbid," he raised a hand with his palm towards McBride, "had it been one of yours, would you have done things differently?"
McBride stared keenly at him for several seconds, then sighing heavily, said, "As you say, God forbid it should ever happen to one of mine or any of my grandweans. Truthfully, I just don't know how I'd react," he slowly shook his head.
They sat in silence for several seconds before McBride rose to his feet and with a soft smile, said, "Before we start, I'll fetch us a coffee, but don't even think of trying to look though any of my files while I'm away."
Hardie smiled then using his forefinger to cross his chest, replied, "I promise. Milk only, please."

****

Rosie Knox stared into the unlit fire, her mind and body numb while the tears dried on her cheeks.

Kelly-Ann dead?

She slowly turned to stare at her husband who sat in the opposite chair and who stared unseeingly at the fire, his thoughts with his grandson and how he was going to break the news to Clint.

But then he wondered, once the word went out that George Knox's lassie had been murdered, who would be the first to offer their sympathy?

Who among the criminals he knew in Glasgow would be the first to come to his door?

Who would look him in the face and say they were sorry to hear about it, want to shake his hand or pat him on the shoulder, but take pleasure that finally, after all those years, he had been knocked off his high horse. The untouchable George Knox, the man the polis could never catch or put away; he had at last been brought to his knees.

And he wondered some more; was Kelly-Ann's murder some sort of reprisal?

Had he unknowingly offended someone so badly that their revenge was to take his most prized possession, his only child?

He raised his head to stare at Rosie, her grief expressed in her face. Thirty-one years they had been wed. Married at seventeen without her parents' permission at Martha Street Registry Office in the city centre and though he wasn't the best of husband's, he still loved her. As far as he was concerned, she hadn't changed since the day they'd met.

She was as slim or so he thought, as the da he'd met her and her one true vanity, her shoulder length hair was also as blonde as the day they'd met, though nowadays with the assistance of a professional stylist.

Though now in her late forties, she was still a looker and he was proud that when he walked out with Rosie, she continued to attract stares from men of all age groups.

His eyes flickered for suddenly and without thinking about it, he recalled the day she'd delivered their daughter.

The midwife realising the delivery would not be straight forward had sent him down to the phone box on the corner to call for the doctor

to attend the small flat they had then, in Ruchazie. The bleeding that never seemed to stop and the midwife deciding not to wait for either the doctor or an ambulance. Him and the midwife, both bloodstained and between them carrying Rosie down to the wee van he'd owned and used for deliveries, him shoving the two of them into the back of the van then the mad dash to the Rottenrow Maternity Hospital.
The hours that passed, sitting in the corridor outside the delivery ward before the doctor took him into that small room, the walls painted green and white and smelling strongly of disinfectant and telling him how sorry he was, that there would be no more children, but that his wife and their daughter were both well.
Now, he wondered, why would I remember that and at a time like this?
He'd loved his daughter since the first time he'd laid eyes on her. He'd watched her grow up wild and stubborn, a free spirit his now dead mother used to call her.
Then when the teenage years set in, the arguments had begun in earnest.
First came the drinking and the partying, but it was to the men she'd become attracted to most of all.
Lots of men, his body gave a brief, involuntarily shudder at the memory.
His eyes narrowed and his brow knitted when he recalled their quarrels, the shouting and the cursing, the names he'd called Kelly-Ann and inwardly shivered with shame for he'd never be able to take any of it back and he'd have to live with those unkind and harsh words for the rest of his life.
The day she'd disclosed she was pregnant should have been a happy event for him and Rosie, but Kelly-Ann's utter refusal to name the father was like a slap in the mouth for them both.
As it happened, wee Clint was loved from the minute he was born. He found himself rising from his chair, then slowly moving towards his wife, his body shaking as he knelt beside her and taking her hand in his, he laid his head on her lap and when she gently stroked at his head, grief overcome him and he burst into tears.
****
While in the CID clerk's office waiting for the kettle to boil, Willie McBride took a minute to read the intelligence bulletin that had been

faxed to Pollok from the Criminal Intelligence Department at Pitt Street.

Scanning the two closely typed pages, he read that Alexander Meikle Hardie, aged twenty-nine, described as blonde haired, six feet two inches tall and of sturdy build, residing in a council owned rented flat in Reidvale Street in the Dennistoun area and who drove a red coloured, second-hand Ford Capri he'd purchased on the never-never. He was a Z target criminal and a member of the George Knox team of armed robbers. Hardie had one conviction almost eight years previously when he was fined for Breach of the Peace, Resisting Arrest and Police Assault (four charges).

"And nothing since," he shook his head for much as he hated to admit it, even to himself, he could not but admire the fact that George Knox and his team, criminals though they might be, during McBride's time as a CID officer had completely outwitted every attempt to capture or charge them with any of the numerous robberies they had committed.

"But time is on our side, Alex," he muttered to himself then poured the boiling water into the two mugs.

Returning to the portacabin, he placed a mug down in front of Alex Hardie, then fetched a packet of cigarettes from his drawer and asked, "Do you smoke?"

"No, I don't, but thanks anyway."

"Right, then," McBride lit a fag then fetching a pencil and a statement form from his desk, asked, "Kelly-Ann. Was she in a relationship, do you know? Did she have a boyfriend?"

"Not to my knowledge. Kelly-Ann," he grimaced as he wondered how he could explain her without sounding like he was demeaning her character.

"She was the type of lassie who liked, eh, how can I describe it…"

His pause wasn't lost on McBride who recognising that the younger man was having difficulty describing what he wanted to say, interrupted and softly asked, "Are you trying to say she liked the men, Alex?"

"Aye," his face contorted. "When she had a drink in her, she tended to be an easy pick-up for some of the guys at the dancing."

"Anywhere in particular she frequented when she went out?"

"I know that she occasionally went into the clubs in the city centre, but on a Saturday night, she usually went to the Barrowland.

Sometimes I did a favour for her Da and went there to fetch her and give her a lift home."

"Did she live alone or share a flat?"

"A first floor flat in Tullis Street. That's over in Bridgeton. She has a son, he's five, but when he was out dancing or clubbing, the wee guy would stay over at his grandparents; George and Rosie, I mean."

"You know we'll need to inspect her flat just in case it might be a crime scene."

"You think she was murdered there?"

"We won't know till we visit there," McBride shrugged. "Do you happen to have keys?"

"Aye," he nodded, "her Da gave me a set and I've brought them with me."

"Good. When we're done here, Alex, we'll go together if you're okay with that?"

"Of course, no bother," he nodded as he sipped at his coffee.

"What about employment. Was she working?"

"Did some part-time bar work when she could get it and on occasion, she helped out in her Da's shop in Duke Street, a newsagent's, but mainly George would sub her for the rent on the flat."

He didn't add that George did it mostly so his grandson could have a semi-stable home life.

"Now," McBride drummed the tip of the pencil on the desk, "her friends and particularly her male friends. Do you know any of them?"

They continued with McBride's questions for another fifteen minutes with Hardie answering them as best he could, but cautiously mindful that none of his replies in any way could provide the DS with information about George Knox or the other members of the team.

At last, McBride asked the question that Hardie knew must come and for which he had no answer.

"Where were you on Saturday night, Alex, through to the following evening?"

"I live alone and," he smiled, "I'm guessing your guys already have my address on file somewhere. Saturday night?" he shook his head. "The weather as it was, I stayed in watching the telly and no, I don't have anybody who can vouch for me being at home. The first I left the house was when George phoned me on Sunday evening about," his brow creased, "about seven, I think it was, asking if I'd go to Kelly-Ann's flat and tell her to phone him because she was overdue picking up wee Clint."

He smiled, then added, "That's the wee guy's name and don't ask."

Aware of the time of the discovery of the body, McBride muttered, "And you didn't get a reply."

"No, I didn't," he shook his head, "but I chapped the neighbour's door, a wee old man who's a right nosey bugger. He told me that she'd left about seven o'clock on the Saturday night, all dolled up and presumably going to the dancing. I bunged him a fiver for him to tell her when she got home that she'd to call her Da. The neighbour didn't have a phone, so I went across the road to the pub, the Bowlers Bar, and used their phone in the bar to ask George if she'd arrived at his place, but she hadn't. After that, I went home."

"How did you know to visit the mortuary this morning?"

"Heard it from someone that a lassie fitting her description had been found dead in Pollok Park."

"Care to tell me who told you?"

"No, sorry," he smiled.

The door opened and turning, Hardie saw it was Benson, the DCI from the mortuary.

"Ah, good, you made it," he nodded at him.

"Said I would and I'm here."

"Willie?" Benson raised his eyebrows at him and taking the hint, McBride excused himself and left the room.

In the corridor outside, in a low voice Benson asked, "Anything?"

"Nothing of note. I think he's being pretty straightforward with me and I'm of the opinion he's no idea who killed the lassie."

"Did he mention who tipped them off to attend at the mortuary?"

"He's not for telling us, boss."

"Ah, well, could have been anyone of seven thousand cops in the Force or maybe even one of our civilian colleagues. If nothing else, it saves us from some time-wasting inquiry, having to identify the lassie. What are you planning now?"

"He's agreed to come to the flat with me, if that's okay with you. He's got a set of keys from her father, so when I've wound up here, with your permission, I'll arrange a Scene of Crime visit there and I'll take somebody with me for corroboration."

"Right, do that and while you're away, I'll organise a briefing for the troops."

His eyes narrowed when he asked, "Where did she live, anyway?"

"According to Hardie, a flat in Tullis Street over in Bridgeton."

"D Division. Okay, I'll get touch with the CID at London Road and let them know we'll be working on their ground, doing door to door in the area. Right, who are you taking with you to search the flat?"

"I was thinking of Barry Connolly, boss. He was in the Serious Crime Squad, so he might have some information about Hardie that could be useful while we're in his company."

"Okay, do that and keep me apprised of anything you find. If the flat is our murder locus, Willie, I want us all over it from the minute you get there."

"Okay, boss," McBride nodded.

****

He agreed to meet the detectives outside the flat in Tullis Street and was escorted by McBride from the CID office to the foyer.

Nodding back at the DS, he was about to push open the door to the front of the building, but stood back when a woman carrying a brown paper bag entered, then stared at him in surprise.

"Oh, it's you," she involuntarily gasped and blushing, stared at the tall, blonde haired man.

"Aye, it's me," he smiled and holding the door open, asked, "Can I help you with that bag?"

"This," she clasped it to her chest as if fearing he was about to snatch it from her. "Eh, no, thanks," her face reddened even more.

"So, you must be a detective then," he continued to stare at her with a smile.

Ailish MacDonald stared back and nodding, found her voice to snap, "And you are?"

"Alex Hardie. I was a friend of Kelly-Ann. And you're Miss…?"

"DC MacDonald," she quickly replied to cover her embarrassment as she shuffled past him.

"Maybe I'll see you again, then DC MacDonald," he grinned at her as she walked off.

She neither replied nor turned to acknowledge him, aware her face was like a beetroot and inwardly cursing herself for behaving like a silly schoolgirl.

Making her way through to the CID clerk's room, she met Ian Burns who had parked the car in the rear yard and arrived via the back door.

Staring curiously at her, he asked, "You okay? You look as if you've dipped your face in a pot of boiling water."

"Thanks for those kind words," she scowled, then admitted, "I bumped into one of those guys that was at the mortuary. The younger one."

"Oh," he smirked, "the *handsome* one, you mean."

"Whatever," she scowled, yet much as it disturbed her, she inwardly agreed.

Alex Hardie was indeed a handsome man.

CHAPTER FIVE

He arrived outside the close in Tullis Street within minutes of the CID car and getting out of Knox's Jaguar, greeted the two detectives with a nod.

"This is DC Barry Connolly," McBride informed him.

With Hardie leading the way, the three men climbed the stairs to the first landing where he used the key to gain entrance to the flat.

Turning on the doorstep, he nodded across the landing and said, "That's where the old guy lives, him that says Kelly-Ann left the flat about seven on Saturday evening."

"Right thanks," replied McBride, who with his neighbour, pulled on a pair of nitrile gloves then added, "If you don't mind, Alex, hang fire here while we check the flat."

Raising his hands, he stepped back into the landing and replied, "No bother."

The detectives were no more than a few minutes when Connolly returned to the door and beckoning Hardie inside, said, "There doesn't seem to be any indication that she returned to the flat after she left on Saturday."

Leading the way through to the front room, he saw McBride stood there looking out of the window, but who then turned and asked, "You familiar with the flat, Alex?"

"If you're asking if I've been inside here, yes. If you're asking if I'm a regular visitor then the answer is no. Any time I've been here in the flat was to either pick up or drop off Kelly-Ann or the wee guy, her son."

He smiled when he added "There was no romance between us, if that's what you might be thinking."

McBride smiled then taking a breath, exhaled through pursed lips before waving a hand about the front room and said, "As you can see, there no apparent sign of any struggle here and as for the bedroom…" he led the way through the hallway into what was clearly Kelly-Ann's room. Pointing to the clothes that lay on the made bed or had fallen onto the floor, he continued, "As you can also see it looks like she's got herself dressed in here, maybe tried on a couple of outfits before she left the house."

His eyes narrowed when he asked, "I'm not trying to be smart or trick you, Alex, but have you any idea what kind of overcoat she'd have been wearing in this weather?"

Hardie stared at him then realisation setting it, he replied, "Wait. You're telling me she was found *without* a coat on? In this weather? Jesus," his face grimly set, he asked, "What *aren't* you telling me, Willie? What kind of state was she in?"

He didn't miss McBride's glance at Conolly before the DS replied, "For your information only, Alex, she was in a state of undress."

He didn't respond for several seconds, then quietly said, "I know that there's only so much you can tell me, Willie, and I won't press you further," he held up a hand, "but answer me one question. Please. You're telling me that Kelly-Ann was found in a state of undress. Are you inferring that somebody…some *bastard*…" he gulped, "that they raped her? Then they killed her and left her in the fucking *snow*?"

"You can't be telling her Da about this, Alex," McBride shook his head. "No father should hear that about his daughter."

Hardie reached behind him with one hand and feeling the edge of the bed, sat down and stared unseeingly at the floor, images of a laughing Kelly-Ann passing through his head.

Kelly-Ann swinging her giggling son about in her parents flat.

Kelly-Ann pouting at her Da, trying to weasel more money out of him.

Kelly-Ann full of the drink, trying to seduce him to stay the night in this very room.

He didn't see or hear Conolly leave the room, but then a minute later, the DC thrust a glass of water at him and said, "Here, drink this."

Nodding his thanks, he took the glass, guzzled some of the water then staring at McBride, said, "I'll need to tell her Da something, Willie, but this?"

"Whatever you tell him," McBride sighed, "he'll find out soon enough so on hindsight, maybe you'd better think about telling him the truth though how you'll phrase it, I have not a clue. Now her coat. Any idea?"

Hardie's eyes widened as he thought, then he said, "She's got a fancy green coloured hooded coat. She bummed that she got it in a Debenhams sale. I've seen her wearing that more than a few times."

McBride turned to the wardrobe behind him then rummaging through the hanging clothes, said, "No green coat here."

Turning to Connolly, he told him, "Go and chap next door, Barry, and get a statement from the old guy that lives there. See if he can remember exactly what time she left on Saturday night, if she got a taxi or a lift and in particular, what she was wearing."

"On it," Connolly nodded and left the room.

Turning to Hardie, he said, "By right's, it's the polis who should be attending at her parents' house to inform them of her death, but seen as how you and George were at the mortuary, Alex, that's unnecessary now. However, I'll need to ask you for the keys to the flat here."

His brow furrowed before he replied, "But you said you don't think she was killed here?"

"Aye, I know that, but the boss will want the Scene of Crime to go over the place anyway. There might be fingerprints that don't belong here or it might be that flat's been cleaned up since Saturday night. Either way, it'll need to be gone over. You understand?"

"What about me and George's prints? We've both been in the flat and her Ma too."

McBride wryly smiled when he replied, "I'm certain we'll have you and George's prints on file, but likely we'll need to get her Mother's prints, but if it's necessary, we can make an arrangement for that another day."

"I've a couple of questions I need to ask you, Alex, personal questions I'd rather put to you than have to ask her father."
"Go on," his eyes narrowed.
"Tell me what you know about Kelly-Ann's sex life."
He wryly smiled when he replied, "You want to know if she was fond of her Nat King Cole?"
"Aye, and if she had anyone in particular she was seeing regularly."
He hesitated before he replied with, "Kelly-Ann earned herself a reputation in the Bridgeton and Gallowgate area, a reputation she didn't really deserve. Of course, because she was George Knox's daughter, it was never openly discussed, but people round here, they knew," he nodded, "and for what it's worth Willie, it wounded her Ma and her Da what people whispered about her."
He grimaced, then thoughtfully added, "As for her having a regular fella? No," he shook his head. "I can't say that I ever heard her mention anybody regular."
"What about you, Alex and," he raised a hand as he softly smiled, "I have to ask."
"Me?" he took a breath, then replied, "Oh, aye, Kelly-Ann was a looker right enough and I'd be lying if I didn't admit she tried it on with me on more than a few occasions and particularly when I brought her home half-pissed. But I'm too close to her Da to take advantage, Willie, so no, I wasn't shagging her."
He got to his feet and said, "The wee guy. He'll need to stay with George and Rosie now. Can I take some clothes away for him?"
"Aye, of course, but I'll need to watch you take them," he replied with a grim smile. "Sorry, but I can't have you remove anything from the flat that I don't see."
"No problem," Hardie nodded.
"One other thing, Alex. You've already told us that Kelly-Ann lived here with her son, but what about the boy's father? Is he on the scene, do you know?"
He shook his head when he replied, "That was something Kelly-Ann kept to herself Willie. I don't know anything about him and as far as I'm aware, I'm certain that George and Rosie don't know either, because we think that Clint's father was a one-night stand; so no, to my knowledge and I think I can safely say, George and Rosie's knowledge too, Clint's father has never been on the scene."

Ten minutes later, a black bin liner filled with Clint's clothes clutched in his hand, Hardie left the flat, passing Connolly on the landing who gave him a nod.
****
In the flat, McBride asked, "How did you get on?"

"Got the statement," Connolly scowled then shuddering, added, "Creepy old bastard and the house stinks too," he grimaced. "He says she left about quarter past seven and he's pretty sure of the time because a film he was watching on BBC One, 'Return of The Gunfighter,' had started at half-six and had been on for about half an hour. Says he heard her front door banging shut and went to the window because he thought it was funny, her going out on such a shitty night, but there was a car down at the front of the close and he thinks it was a private hire because she got into the back, but he's not sure."

"Did he say what she was wearing?"

"Aye," Connolly nodded, "her green, hooded coat. Says he knows it was her because she was always wearing it."

"Any likelihood he's a suspect?"

"Highly unlikely because he's a weedy wee guy of sixty-eight who doesn't look like he could punch his way out of a wet paper bag. If what we're being told it true, that she was a fit young woman in her late twenties, he'd have been no match for her. Says as well that he doesn't drive and has no access to a vehicle. I've got his details anyway, Willie, so I'll do a PNC check when we get back to Pollok."

The front door was knocked and McBride said, "That'll be the Scene of Crime team, so while they're doing their stuff, why don't you nip down to that wee takeaway around the corner and see if you can rustle up a couple of rolls and two coffees?"
****
Returning to Quarrywood Road, Alex Hardie saw Johnny Dunlop's old style Landrover parked outside George Knox's close and guessed that likely Kevin Stobbie was upstairs too.

Grabbing the black bin liner from the rear seat, he made his way upstairs and it was a tearful Rosie Knox who opened the door. Seeing it was Hardie, the distraught woman flung herself sobbing into his arms.

Holding her close to him, her body shaking as she cried, he had never felt so helpless in his life.

Several minutes passed before he gently released her, then said, "Come away in, hen, and I'll get the kettle on," he whispered to her.
"No," she shook her head, took a deep breath then sniffed, "George's in the front room with the boys. You go and I'll fetch you a cuppa."
Handing her the bin bag, he made his way along the hallway and could hear wee Clint in the bedroom that had been decorated with cartoon figures on the wall and spaceships and planes that hung on thin threads from the ceiling.
Slowly pushing open the door, he saw the tousled haired five-year-old, blessed with his mother's fine features and dark looks, playing on the floor with his battery-operated train set, then glancing up, stared with tearstained eyes at Hardie.
He forced a smile and said "All right, wee man?"
Almost immediately he thought, what the hell am I thinking? All right, wee man? How the *fuck* can he be all right after being told his mother's not coming back to him.
Wordlessly, the child shrugged then bowing his head, continued to play with his train set.
Words failed Hardie so softly closing the door, he continued into the front room where he saw Knox sitting in his usual armchair facing the gas fire.
Johnny Dunlop sat in the opposite armchair while Kevin Stobbie sat on the couch.
"Lads," Hardie greeted them with a nod.
His face unusually pale, Stobbie replied for them both when he said, "Bad business, big man. How did you get on at the polis station?"
He removed his rain jacket then hanging it over the back of a wooden chair set against the wall, lifted the chair to set it down between Knox's armchair and the couch, before he quietly replied, "I spoke to a DS called McBride and gave him a statement."
Shaking his head, he continued, "Just told him that we didn't have a clue who might have did this to Kelly-Ann. He was asking about her pals, who she hung about with, but," he shrugged and glanced at Dunlop and Stobbie in turn, "you guys have known her longer than me. You probably know as much about who she hung out with than I do. In short," he exhaled, "there really wasn't much I could tell them. Then McBride asked me to go with him and another guy to her flat. George," he nodded at Knox, "had given me the spare keys.

They wanted to check if that was where she'd…" he paused, then swallowing said, "Where she'd been killed."
Turning to Knox, he raised a hand and hastily added, "But it wasn't. McBride said they'd still need to have their crime scene guys go over it for prints and bloodstains just in case it had been cleaned."
"Do they need mine and yours?" Knox turned to ask.
He wryly grinned when he replied, "McBride said not to bother because they've got ours anyway. Oh, and they've held onto the keys, but I brought some clothes for the wee man."
"Thanks, Rosie will be pleased you did," Knox replied, his voice dull with anguished pain.
He sat in silence for several minutes, broken when the door opened and Rosie, carrying a tray with mugs and a plate of sandwiches, entered and laid the tray on a small table between the armchairs.
Knox raised his head to ask her, "How you doing, hen?"
She tried to smile, but it turned to a grimace.
Embarrassed for her, the other three men turned their heads to stare elsewhere as Knox rose from his chair to take his wife in his arms. Unabashedly, he hugged her then released her to permit her to leave the room.
Resuming his seat, he stared at the three men in turn, then clearing his throat, his gaze turned to Hardie and asked, "What did you find out about her being killed, Alex."
"It's going to upset you, boss."
"I'm already fucking upset, son. Tell me."
He licked nervously at his lower lip before he softly replied, "She was raped, murdered and left in the snow in the Pollok Park. I'm guessing from what I was told last night, somewhere near to the Burrell museum."
He paused then continued, "I can't say for certain, but the way the guy McBride questioned me, I figured they don't have a clue at the minute who did it."
The watched as Knox's face turned pale and his knuckles turned white as he tightly gripped the arms of the chair.
Clearing his throat once more, his voice low and strained, he forced himself to remain calm when he asked, "What do we know about what happened to her? Anything you learned?"
Hardie replied, "Her green coat, you know the one with the hood that she always wore? It's missing from her wardrobe and from the way

McBride was interested in what coat she might have been wearing when she went out on Saturday night, I think it's fair to assume she must have been wearing it, but it wasn't found with her body. That and," he paused, "McBride said she was found in a state of undress."
"A state of undress," he slowly repeated then, his voice almost a whisper, he asked, "What the fuck does that mean, son?"
"I'm thinking, boss, that it's polis speak for her being stripped or maybe some of her clothing was missing. You know," he could feel his neck burning from embarrassment, "her underwear."
There was a silence before Knox asked, "So, whoever killed her, he raped her and dumped her without any clothes on?"
"Jesus, George," Dunlop leaned forward, his hand spread as though in plea, "you shouldn't torture yourself thinking about it.
"What else can I think about, Johnny!" he snapped back, then almost as quickly, raised a hand in apology and added, "Sorry. I'm not myself, the now."
It was Stobbie, who till now had said nothing other than to rise from the couch and handing them mugs of tea, though none had any appetite for the sandwiches, then asked, "So, what's the plan?"
Knox glanced at Hardie before he replied, "The job for next week is off and…"
"That's not what I meant…" Stobbie's face flushed.
Dunlop sharply interrupted with a shake of his head and said, "It's okay, Kevin, I think we know what you mean and there's no need to explain, George. Family comes first and besides," he smiled at them in turn, "we've done well with you running the team and we're ahead of the game, so why don't we just call it quits now, find the bastard that did this to Kelly-Ann and bring forward our retirement."
Knox wasn't expecting this and taking a breath glanced at them in turn, seeing first Kevin Stobbie, grim-faced but nodding, then Hardie also agreeing with a nod.
He could feel himself welling up and tightening his lips to avoid showing his emotion, nodded to make it unanimous.
Seeing how upset Knox was, Hardie quickly said, "The boss has given me the job of finding whoever did this, so if you two guys are okay with that?"
"Anything you need, big man," nodded Dunlop.
"Definitely okay by me," agreed Stobbie, his head bowed and his face still pale.

"Right," Hardie glanced at Knox as though seeking permission to begin, then said, "here's what I'm thinking."

****

When DCI Martin Benson entered the small, claustrophobic room at Pollok Police station that was to serve as the murder investigation incident room, his eyes immediately smarted as the fug of cigarette smoke enveloped him.

"Right, then," he waved the team down to whatever they could sit on, lean against or tried to poke their heads in through one of the two doors that accessed the room, "smoke if you must and here's what we know so far."

He stared round the room, trying to pre-judge how the information might be received.

"The victim is one, Kelly-Ann Knox, aged twenty-nine years, a single parent with a five years old son and who resided in a flat in Tullis Street, over in Bridgeton. Miss Knox was discovered last night in the snow behind the Burrell Collection building in Pollok Park, partially undressed which seems to indicate that she might have been sexually active prior to her murder. Whether the sex was consensual or she was the victim of a sexual assault is not at this time established, though the indication from the post mortem is that it was *not* consensual."

Once more he stared round the room, then catching his breath, continued.

"In the meantime, it is *my* opinion and mind, this does *not* leave the room, that injuries sustained to her wrists suggest either consensual *rough* sex or more likely, she was forcibly restrained then raped. When we catch the bastard that murdered her, we'll find out for certain," he added, but did not mention the awful damage to her vagina.

"Now, for those of you a little younger in service or do not as a matter of course read the intelligence bulletins distributed from Pitt Street," he again stared meaningfully around the room, "I have to inform you that our victim is the only child of one, George Knox."

He paused, seeing a few heads turn and a low murmur erupt that he quickly silenced when raising his hand, he continued with a nod, "Yes, Knox is likely well known to many of you as the most successful and prolific armed robber in the history of both the former City of Glasgow Police and now Strathclyde Police, as well as our neighbouring Forces throughout the central belt of Scotland. He is a dangerous individual and forget that shite about him being untouchable, he will be caught in time. However, it's not our job in the investigation to catch Knox, though," he softly smiled, "it would be a right good bonus. It *is* our job to catch his daughter's killer and, on that point, I have something to say."

"I do not want anyone in this room to consider George Knox's daughter to be anything but a murder victim. I do not want to hear the old adage of fly with the crows, shot with the crows' shite. That young lassie was a mother with a young child and she *was* brutally murdered. I do not care about her family background. This investigation *will* accord her the same intense commitment to catching her killer as we would a Catholic nun. Am I *absolutely* clear on that?"

There was a few nodded heads and mutterings, but Benson wasn't happy with the reaction to his warning and raising his voice a pitch, said again, "Am I *clear*, folks!"

"Yes, boss," and "Aye, boss," was the louder response.

"Thank you," he forced a smile. "Right then, to continue. George Knox and one of his team of blaggers, a younger guy called Alex Hardie, were aware that our victim had not returned home on Saturday evening after a night out and presumably had actively been searching for her. Someone," he raised a hand as though apologetically, "and I do not suggest it was anyone here, tipped off Knox about a body being discovered and to the DI and my own surprise, both he and Hardie attended this morning at the mortuary. At this point in time, I'm not so much interested in who tipped off Knox, but bear it in mind when conducting your inquiries should you come across anyone who you consider might be his source."

Benson did not make the allegation, but left his officers in no doubt he suspected the source to be a police officer or a civilian working for the police.

"Now, we have no suspect at this time; however, according to what I've learned from our colleagues at Criminal Intelligence in Pitt Street, it's more than possible that during his robbery career, Knox may have pissed off some of the criminal community in Glasgow or elsewhere who rather than having a go at him, have exacted some form of revenge on his family."

His face registered his sombreness when he said, "Kelly-Ann was his only child and frankly, when DI Williams and I spoke earlier this morning with Knox, he was distraught and rightly so. But that concerns me, folks, for if he *should* suspect that his daughter was murdered by someone seeking to get at him, we could be looking at open gang warfare in the city and let me remind you," he took a deep breath, "Knox and his team have access to firearms that they use to carry out their robberies."

He paused for several seconds to permit the team to mull over his words, then continued, "However, the other side of the coin is that our victim, who again according to Criminal Intelligence, is a lassie that enjoyed socialising and the company of men, might just have fell foul of a right bampot and we could be looking for an individual. If that *is* the case, then for the killer's sake, we'd better find him before Knox does. Questions."

A young fair-haired DC raised a hand to ask, "You're suggesting, boss, that Knox and his team will also be out hunting the killer?"

He smiled when he replied, "God forbid the victim was *your* daughter, Paul, but would you sit on your arse or wait for us to catch him?"

The DC, Paul Devine, blushed then shaking his head, replied, "Probably not, boss."

"Anybody else?" Benson cast a glance around the room and when no one raised a hand said, "Right, I'll turn you over to Willie McBride who went with Barry Connolly to the victims flat and let him tell you what he discovered."

"Boss," McBride acknowledged with a nod, then began, "One of Knox's team, the guy Hardie who was with him at the mortuary, met us at the victim's flat with keys. At first glance, it doesn't seem to have been the locus of the murder, but the SOCO are there the now turning the place over. What we did learn from a neighbour, an old guy who lived across the landing, was the victim left her flat sometime between seven and seven-thirty on Saturday night and at that time she was wearing a green, hooded coat. According to the neighbour, she was always wearing it when she went on her nights out. Anyway," he shrugged, "the coat was not found on the body so we must assume it's missing. We don't have a photograph or anything of the coat other tan it was purchased from Debenhams, so all I can say is if you come across a green hooded coat during your inquiries, bear it in mind."

He turned to Benson to explain, "I'll get an Action raised, boss, and contact the store to see if I can get a better description of the coat." Benson nodded in acknowledgement as McBride continued.

"According to the neighbour who's a nosey old bugger, the victim got into what he thinks is a private hire taxi. He thinks it was a taxi simply because she got into the back seat. If you recall, it was blowing a storm on Saturday night before the city was awash with rain, so there's every likelihood there wouldn't have been too many private hires on the road."

He turned to DS Mhari McGregor, the appointed office manager and said, "If the neighbour is correct, Mhari, it sounds like she's phoned for a taxi if it was waiting for her, so it might be worth a few Actions contacting the private hires in the Bridgeton area."

With a glance at Benson who nodded, McGregor replied in her soft, Inverness lilt, "I'll see it gets done, Willie."

"The only other thing of note is the young guy, Alex Hardie. He as good as admitted that our victim wasn't averse to sleeping around and as far as he knew, she'd no particular man in her life. He also admitted that she'd tried it on with him on a number of occasions, but says that he never took up her offer because of his close relationship with her father. For what it's worth, boss," he turned to glance at Benson and his face creasing, he said, "I tended to believe him about that."

Tight-lipped, Benson knew from his experience that being an armed criminal did not necessarily make a man a liar, and nodding, then asked, "Anything else, Willie?"

"No, other than Hardie also suggested that she was a regular at the dancing in the Barrowland."

A few of the team watching could not miss seeing Benson grimace.

"Oh, and Barry Connolly is at the flat with the SOCO supervisor," McBride added, "and he'll phone in if they've discovered anything of note."

"Right thanks, Willie," then turning to the team at large, asked, "Any more questions?"

A hand was raised at the back and expecting the inevitable question, acknowledged with a sigh, "Yes, Elaine."

DC Elaine Thompson, grey-haired and at five feet ten inches with the stature of a wrestler, was a CID officer for over twenty years.

Cocking her head to one side, her eyes narrowed when she asked, "Any thoughts that it might be Bible John come back to haunt us, boss?"

It was the question Benson had been dreading for almost without exception, every CID officer in Scotland knew of Bible John, the man who between nineteen-sixty-eight and nineteen-sixty-nine, was suspected of murdering three women. All three had been escorted from the dance at the Barrowland Ballroom by their killer and though having carried out a rigorous investigation, the police had failed to catch him. The name had been applied to the killer by a sister of one of the victims after overhearing the suspect quoting the Bible to his victim.

Years later, the name Bible John continued to haunt those officers who had worked on the murder investigations and their failure to arrest the killer had been a thorn in the side of the Glasgow police since that time.

Benson stared at Thompson, then replied, "We've no way of knowing that, Elaine, but rest assured, with the technology and experience we have these days, if that bastard has raised his head again, we'll catch him this time. Now," he turned to glance around the room, "any other questions?"

When nobody replied, he nodded and said, "DS McGregor has a number of Actions ready to go, folks, so finish your fags and coffees and I'll see you again at five here in the incident room before you knock off."

CHAPTER SIX

Though he wasn't certain, Alex Hardie supposed that the Barrowland would not open till late evening, but guessed that the administration and cleaning staff would likely be in early on Monday morning to clean and clear away the debris from the weekend. Located in the Gallowgate area of the city, the Barrowland Ballroom had opened in nineteen-thirty-four as a dance hall and concert venue for both local and international performers with a capacity to accommodate just over two thousand customers.

Justifiably proud of the building, the Glaswegians delighted in the famous names who visited or performed at the venue that weekly, drew enormous crowds from within and outwith not just the Glasgow area, but the world at large.

The building also shares its premises as a market place and is known colloquially by the Weegies and throughout as, 'The Famous Barra's."

Washed and shaved, Hardie glanced at the kitchen wall clock and finishing his second coffee of the morning, decided to walk to the Barrowland.

Glancing out of the window, he saw that there was a steady fall of light rain and from the hall cupboard, fetched a full-length hooded oilskin coat and golf umbrella.

Fifteen minutes later, striding eastwards along the Gallowgate, he was beginning to think not taking the car had been a bad idea, for the wind was now blowing horizontally into his face and he'd been forced to fold the brolly for fear of it blowing inside out.

His hood up, he trudged on then passing Bain Street, headed for the front door of the Barrowland building.

It was then he saw the grey, Morris Ital with the distinctive aerial on the roof, parked outside the building entrance and recognising it as a CID car, decided to pop into the small café on the opposite side of the road that gave him a clear sight of the entrance.

The café had few customers at that time of the morning and so he was able to sit at a table near the back of the café that permitted him an unobstructed view through the front window.

"What you having?" asked the middle-aged waitress with a world-weary expression.

"Ah, do you do espresso coffee?"

"We do white coffee and we do black coffee, we do coffee with sugar and coffee without sugar, but nothing fancy though," she sighed.

He refrained from smiling, then replied, "White coffee, please, and a roll and bacon."

"And do you want sauce on the roll?"

"Ah, no sauce."

She stared down at him then, her brow knitting and as if making a momentous decision, she said, "You don't look like a runner so you can pay before you leave."

Again, he supressed a smile and nodded in response.

Minutes later, the waitress returned with the coffee and the roll that to his surprise, were both delicious.

He glanced at his watch and seeing it was just after ten o'clock, wondered how long he'd have to wait.

Fifteen minutes later and conscious of the suspicious glances from both the waitress and the man behind the counter, he was just about to order a second coffee when he saw two women walk from the narrow road, almost a lane, that exited onto the Gallowgate.

His eyes widened for he recognised the shorter of the two and without realising it, quietly muttered, "Hello again, DC MacDonald."

He watched as MacDonald climbed into the driver's seat while the second woman, tall and grey-haired, got into the front passenger seat. A minute later, when the car had driven off, he went to the counter to pay his bill and received a wide and surprised smile for his generous tip.

Leaving the café, he was pleased to see that for the moment, the rain had ceased and if nothing else, it had driven off most of the snow from the pavements onto the gutters in the road, creating a brown, slimy slush that sprayed everywhere when driven over.

Crossing the road, he found the front entrance doors to the building locked, but a handwritten sign pointed visitors around the corner to the staff entrance in Gibson Street, the narrow street from where the two CID officers had exited.

Pressing the bell for the staff entrance door, Hardie was greeted by a familiar face.

"Bloody hell, as I live and breathe. Alex Hardie."

The heavy-set man who was wearing a pair of jeans that were too tight for his waistline and a crisply white shirt with the sleeves rolled back onto hairy forearms and a navy-blue tie, was as tall as Hardie, though prematurely bald and in his late forties.

Reaching out he cheerfully shook Hardie's hand.

"Long time no see, pal, how you doing?"

"Fine, Mark, just fine," he replied, then asked, "Okay to come in and have a quick chat?"

Mark Ritchie, the general manager of the building, grinned widely before he said, "No problem pal. Come up to the office and I'll stick the kettle on."

Hardie followed Ritchie through the building and into the staff corridor on the upper floor where the administration offices were located, nodding to a few people on the way that included several cleaners and two security staff who were known to him.

"Sit down, sit down," Ritchie grinned at him and calling out to his secretary, shouted, "Avril, stick the kettle on, hen. We've got a visitor."

Avril Collins, a tall, willowy blonde just turned thirty-three who, Hardie recalled, was rumoured to do more for Ritchie than secretarial work, popped her head into the room then in a husky voice, smiled at Hardie and said, "Hello, stranger."

Hardie nodded to her and saw that she wore her customary short pencil skirt that showed off her long legs and briefly recalled a time, almost a year previously when she spent the night at his flat.

That night had ended badly for unknown to him at the time, she had been keen to break off with Ritchie and was seeking a new relationship with him, while he had simply understood it to be a one-night stand.

Though neither had been in touch since that night, if Ritchie had suspected anything he'd never contacted Hardie or indicated that he knew.

"Two coffee's please hen," Ritchie broke into his thoughts.

With a meaningful glance at Hardie, she left the room.

Settling himself behind his desk, Ritchie asked, "So, what brings you back to the Barrowland, Alex? Looking for some stewarding work?"

Hardie knew that Ritchie, with dubious friends in Glasgow's underworld, kept a finger on the pulse about what was happening in the city and who was doing what to who and why. Therefore, there was no doubt in Hardie's mind that he must be aware his former chief steward was now a member of George Knox's team of armed robbers.

However, he knew that Ritchie must also be aware that to maintain the illusion of being employed, Hardie continued to perform stewarding work and so replied, "Not today, Mark. I'm here to ask for your help."

"Anything I can do to oblige an old friend," with a grin, Ritchie spread his hands wide.

"Ten minutes ago. The two CID women who were here told you about George Knox's daughter. Did you have anything to tell them?"

Ritchie's face clouded over then leaning forward, his hands clasped together on his desk, he shook his head and replied, "Bad business about Kelly-Ann, Alex. Tell your boss I'm really sorry."

"The CID?" he prompted.

Ritchie stared at Hardie for several seconds then with a sigh, said, "They asked the usual questions. Did I know her? Yes, I knew her," he nodded. "Can anyone say if she was here on Saturday night?" He pursed his lips when he answered his own question, "I can ask around, I told them, but you'll remember, Alex, what this place is like on a Saturday night, it's literally jumping, even with the shitty weather we've been having."

He rubbed wearily at his brow, then continued, "They asked me, what staff did you have on duty?"

"The problem as you well know, is that we don't have just the regulars on duty, but we bring in a couple of dozen part-time staff as well and it's usually cash in hand, so we don't keep records for them. Christ," he shook his head, "I've over a hundred or more people in here looking after anything up to a fifteen hundred customers, some who are only here for a couple of hours or so because they then move on to the clubs in the town or come here later after the pubs throw them out. I've the security team for both inside the place and doing the doors too, then there's the bar staff, the cleaners for the toilets, there's the technicians doing the lights, the musicians and *their* roadies as well as my own admin doing the cashing up."

"I remember," Hardie permitted himself a soft smile. "Bedlam, it is."

"Aye, bedlam hardly describes it," he said, then again grinning widely added, "but I love it."

"So, you were here on Saturday night then, Mark. Did you happen to see Kelly-Ann?"

"Truthfully?" his face clouded over. "I have to admit I'm a bit uncertain if she was here because I can't recall seeing her on Saturday," he shook his head. "Are you *definite* she was here?"

"This is her usual haunt on a Saturday, usually trying to find herself a click."

He stared thoughtfully at Ritchie, for it wasn't like the big man to be uncertain who was in his dance hall on Saturday night, recalling that Ritchie used to boast about his elephant memory for faces.

Kelly-Ann had been well known as a flirt and particularly with the stewards, for Ritchie, himself a former steward and weightlifter, employed tall and muscular individuals in the belief that their imposing presence was often enough to prevent trouble rather than have to sort it out.

Ritchie smiled then sighed, "She was a looker, right enough. Anytime I did see her in the place she usually had some guy hanging onto her."

"Here we go," Avril, using her shapely hip, pushed open the door carrying a mug of coffee in each hand that she laid down onto the desktop.

Staring down at Hardie, she asked, "You're here about Kelly-Ann?"

"You know?"

"Yes, the CID women, they were asking me about her, if I knew her."

She wryly smiled when she mocked, "I mean, who didn't know Kelly-Ann?"

Almost immediately, her expression turned to one of shock at her own disrespectful comment and her hands clasping at her face, she stuttered, "Oh, God. I'm so sorry. I can't believe I said that like the way it come out. The poor girl."

"I'm sure you didn't mean anything by it, hen," Ritchie soothingly replied with a glance at Hardie as watching, they saw Avril suddenly turn and rush from the room.

"You'll put the word out, Mark, that if she *was* in here on Saturday night, I need to speak to anyone who saw her or spoke to her."

"Aye, no problem, big man."

His eyes narrowed and he stared meaningfully at Hardie when he softly asked, "I take it you're acting on behalf of the family, trying to find out who did this?"

He didn't want to get into a conversation about George and Rosie, so stood up, his coffee untouched, then leaning across the desk, shook Ritchie's hand when he replied, "Anything you hear, I'll be grateful."

At the side door as he prepared to leave and though the rain was still off, it was then he recalled he'd left his umbrella lying in the café across the road.

"Bugger," he gritted his teeth at his forgetfulness and striding across the Gallowgate, pushed open the door to the café.

The waitress, smiling as she recalled the good-looking big tipper, fetched the umbrella from behind the counter then coyly handing it to him, said, "I thought you'd be back."
He grinned his appreciation and nodding his thanks, turned towards the door.
About to open it, he paused when through the glass he saw two men getting out of a silver coloured Range Rover that was parked at the entrance to the Barrowland.
The taller, heavier set of the two men was the driver and wore a Burberry coat while the other man, the one who piqued Hardie's interest, was a face he had not seen for some time. He had encountered the man only once before, but had never forgotten him. Finding the doors to be locked as did Hardie, he saw the men reading the sign that directed them to walk the few yards around the corner.
"Everything okay?" asked the waitress from behind him, confused why he was stood motionless at the door.
He turned to smile at her then nodding, replied, "Just catching my breath."
She hesitantly smiled as he stepped into the street, but walking away from the café, his thoughts were filled as to why, James 'Foxy' McGuire and another man who though they'd never met, he guessed *must* be Peter Donaldson, the drug dealer who was McGuire's boss, were visiting the Barrowland and so soon after the CID and himself.
****

With DC Ailish MacDonald driving, her neighbour Elaine Thompson fetched her cigarettes from her handbag and about to offer one to MacDonald, muttered, "Oh, I'm forgetting, hen, you don't smoke when you're driving."
Shaking her head, MacDonald replied, "Not since I burnt a good jacket when the fag fell into my lap, I don't. So, what did you make of that guy, Ritchie, the manager?"
Lighting her cigarette, Thompson's brow creased when she said, "Big fella right enough. I've got it in my head I've seen him before, but I don't recall all the men I've bedded."
MacDonald laughed as Thompson sniggered, then added, "I can't really decide anything about him. Half of me thinks he's a sleazy type and a bit out of character for running the Barrowland. I'm not saying he's a Ned or anything, but I got this vibe from him that I can't explain," her face creased. "I think what I'm trying to say is the

company that runs the place have always been known to operate a right, law-abiding dance hall and he just does not fit the type of manager I was expecting, you know?" she turned to glance curiously at MacDonald.

"Can't be easy though, running a place that size with the numbers that use it and trying to keep the neds and the drugs out. I mean," she risked a glance at Thompson, "I've been there a few times off-duty and I know the stewards check handbags and the like, but if the druggies want to get their stuff into the dancing to sell it, I'm sure they'll find a way and let's face it; if neds frequent the dancing, how do you tell them from the ordinary punter that just wants a good night out without any hassle? Anyway," she continued, "what's your take on what he said of our victim."

"That she was a slapper? Typical male bullshit," Thompson scoffed. "A lassie goes out for a good time, picks up a bloke and shags him and she's a slapper? Aye, right! What does that make our gender opposite's then, or is it only the women that are the slappers?"

MacDonald, recognising that Thompson was again on her high horse, bit at her lower lip to refrain from sniggering.

Several seconds passed before Thompson sighed, "What do you think about my question to the boss, that it might be Bible John again?"

"Those murders were way before my time, Elaine, but you," she risked another glance at her, "you're former City of Glasgow. Did you work on those investigations?"

Thompson, staring moodily through the windscreen, slowly shook her head then said, "I *was* in the CID then and working out of Baird Street at the time, but I was kept on the book dealing with the Divisional crime while some of the more experienced guys were seconded to the investigation. That doesn't mean I didn't hear what was going on, though. I know that those guys put their heart and soul into finding him and they worked long hours too, even after the serious crime budget had run dry and they weren't getting paid for their overtime. It didn't prevent the newspapers and particularly that rag the 'Glasgow News' giving them a right kicking, though, making all sorts of allegations about incompetence and shite like that. Believe me when I tell you this, Ailish," she shrugged, "it affected some of them too, them that had daughters. Do you know," she turned to stare at the younger woman, "the nightlife in Glasgow took years to get over what that bastard did to them three lassie's. Parents wouldn't let their daughters go for a night out without ensuring they were accompanied by their pals, for fear of Bible John getting them."

"And do you think it might be him again?"

"Honestly? No, I don't," she shook her head. "The MO is different, but that doesn't mean to say we discount him as a suspect."

"Do you think the boss *will* consider him to be a suspect though?"

"Martin Benson? He's a good guy and competent too, so I'm guessing he'll keep his options open."

"What about the manager at the dancing, Ritchie. Do you think he'll get back in touch with us if he hears anything?"

Thompson's eyes narrowed when she replied, "I don't know about him, but his secretary? I think she might. She struck me as the type that wouldn't mind a handsome young detective spending some time with her," she mischievously grinned.

MacDonald smiled when she said, "You're inferring that our Avril might be a slapper?"

"Aye, I suppose I am," she continued to grin.

****

The very question that MacDonald posed to Thompson was running through DCI Benson's head; could it be that Bible John *had* struck again?

Seated at his desk in the G Divisional headquarters in Govan's Orkney Street, Benson had also been asked that question by *his* boss, Detective Chief Superintendent Keith Meadows, who phoning from Pitt Street, had warned, "Once the media learns the lassie was probably at the dancing in the Barrowland, as they undoubtedly *will*, Martin, you can bet the buggers will be all over the story like a bad rash on a weans arse. I know I'm pressurising you," he grunted, "but do your best to try and tie down her movements prior to her murder and let's pray she was *not* at the Barrowland on Saturday night."

"I'll do my best, sir, and I'll let you know how my guys get on with their interviews at the Barrowland."

"Thanks, Martin and there's one other thing you should be aware of and," he paused, "I must stress, this is for your ears only. However, that said, if you believe it will progress your investigation by taking anyone else into your confidence, then I will leave it to your judgement."

His curiosity aroused, Benson asked, "And what is that, sir?"
"Now that the worst of the bad weather seems to have passed, I am informed by the Commander of the Scottish Crime Squad that his squad based at our Stewart Street Office intend resuming their surveillance of George Knox and his team. I have insisted, however, that while they have their task, our priority is finding the killer of a young woman. Yes, you will assist with any pertinent information that will not compromise your investigation and, while the Commander has agreed to a *quid pro quo* arrangement, I fear that it will in actuality be a one-sided bargain. You know as well as I do those squad buggers would sooner sell their weans than give up their Intel. However, I have also informed the Commander that should the need arise, your contact with the Stewart Street team will be DI Alice Meechan, who I understand is a Tayside Police Officer."
"Alice Meechan," Benson slowly repeated, then shaking his head, added, "I don't think our paths have crossed."
"She's not known to me either," sighed Meadows.
"Either way, sir, if I do have any cause to contact her and I do meet with some difficulty, I'll let you know."
"Good man, Martin, I'll be in touch," Meadows ended the call.
Staring down at his desk, Benson reflected on the conversation and thought, that's all I need. My guys trying to investigate George Knox's daughters' murder and I can't even tell them that the Scottish will be watching not just Knox, but their every move too.
****

Retracing his steps on his return to Reidvale Street, Alex Hardie was deep in thought and made the decision not to inform George Knox about seeing Donaldson and McGuire going into the Barrowland, trying to convince himself that their visit could be nothing to do with Kelly-Ann.

However, try as he might, he had this niggling thought that it was just too coincidental that on the Monday after her body is found, two of the most notorious gangsters in Glasgow show up at the very place where she frequented most, if not every Saturday night.

And on that point, his forehead creased; why did he have this increasing doubt that Mark Ritchie had lied, that the manager who prided himself in knowing everyone who visited his dance hall, yet was *uncertain* if Kelly-Ann had been there on Saturday night? After all, he unconsciously shook his head as he tried to make sense of it,

Kelly-Ann wasn't just another punter, she was George Knox's daughter and to those in the know, well known in more than one circle.

So then, why didn't Ritchie just say no, she had or hadn't appeared as usual?

It was that one word he had used, that he was *uncertain*, that made Hardie suspicious; a get-out word for Ritchie?

Neither yes nor no?

That *one* word that left a lingering doubt in his mind.

A lingering doubt that the more he thought of it, the more convinced he became that Ritchie was lying.

But why?

He paused to permit a bus to pass by then quickly strode across Bellgrove Street.

Once more, his thoughts returned to seeing Donaldson and McGuire, the druggie double-act.

Peter Donaldson was known to him by reputation only and only once had he crossed paths or rather, crossed swords with Foxy McGuire.

It had been about six years, maybe seven years previously, not too long after he'd just been taken on as the fourth man in the boss's team and was still regularly stewarding, maintaining his cover of working a regular job.

It had happened in the city centre at the door of a pub in West Regent Street, a Saturday night, he recalled as his eyes narrowed in thought.

McGuire, with a couple of teenage toe-rags in his wake and full of himself, had tried to push past him and his fellow steward, Andy Watson, to enter a pub that was already heaving with bodies.

Watson, a nice and respectable older man, had politely refused entry due to the overcrowding in the pub, whereupon McGuire had spat onto the pavement then come out with the old chestnut, "Do you know who the fuck I am!"

He recalled the incident as though it were yesterday, not knowing at that time who McGuire was, though Andy had obviously recognised the gangster.

While the five feet six inch and rake thin McGuire squared up to Watson, he had seen the young buck behind McGuire reach towards his back pocket and had acted instinctively by booting the guy squarely in the balls.

As the young man cried out in agony and dropped squirming to the ground, a flick-knife fell from his hand to bounce along the pavement.

Turning from Watson towards him, it was evident that McGuire was either tipsy or drugged and fists drawn back was ready to have a go; however, the sudden presence of a police panda car rolling down West Regent Street had alerted the second teenager who dragging the cursing McGuire away from the door, left their injured pal writhing on the ground as abandoning him, they staggered away.

Fortunately, the two cops, a man and his female partner, were acquainted with Watson and so it was the injured ned and his flick-knife that were taken away in the patrol car.

His brow furrowed when he thought of that night for he had not come across McGuire since that time, though heard stories about his treatment of drug debtors or those who by deed or word had offended his boss, Peter Donaldson.

Yes, he involuntarily nodded as he strode along.

He was now convinced that the visit by Donaldson and McGuire was not coincidental and must be somehow related to Kelly-Ann.

However, that now posed a difficult question.

How the hell was he going to find out what if any connection there was between George's dead daughter and those two gangsters?

A slow smile crossed his face as a possible solution presented itself.

CHAPTER SEVEN

DC's Thompson and MacDonald arrived back at Pollok Police station where they informed the DI, Roddy Williams, that according to the manager, Mark Ritchie, he had no knowledge of Kelly-Ann Knox being in the dance hall on Saturday night.

"And this guy, Ritchie, he can speak for all the staff?" Williams peered at Thompson.

"No, boss, but he's said that he'll put the word out among his people to ask if anyone who knows our victim can categorically state she was there on Saturday night. He's preparing a list of his staff who were on duty at the weekend and once we've got that, we can do the rounds and ask if any of them remember seeing our victim."

"And was he cooperative?"

"Well, clearly he isn't happy about the Barrowland being tainted once again by the suggestion that a woman might have been there, then later found murdered. Too many recent memories of you know who and the impact on his weekend takings would be catastrophic if the media find out our victim was at the dancing, then taken from there and killed,"

sighed Thompson, "and needless to say it would suit him if we can't prove she was at the dancing. As for him getting in touch," she shrugged uncertainly, "we only have his word that he will, but I'm thinking we maybe give it till tomorrow and we'll make a repeat call to find out if he has put the word out to his staff. We'll need to go back anyway to collect the staff list from him. We *were* thinking of popping back today sometime," her eyes narrowed as she stared at him.

"No," Williams shook his head. "We need the manager's cooperation, Elaine, so no need to piss him off. Leave it till tomorrow midday, then he can't complain he's not had enough time to get the list together."

"Boss," she acknowledged with a nod.

At a prompting glance from MacDonald, Thompson added, "Oh, and we spoke with Ritchie's secretary, a woman called Avril Collins. We didn't get a real opportunity to speak to her alone and she did say she couldn't tell if our victim was there on Saturday night, but we've the feeling that she might give us a phone on the QT without her boss knowing."

"Okay," Williams nodded, "as I said, Elaine, give it till tomorrow then pay this guy Ritchie another visit. For now, though, keep the Action and in the meantime, see what Mhari McGregor has lying in her basket for the rest of the day."

When they'd left Williams office and were heading for a coffee prior to speaking with the McGregor, MacDonald asked, "This is my first murder investigation, Elaine. I thought the DCI would be here to run things?"

"He'll be down at Govan running things from there, hen. Roddy is his deputy SIO and he's more than capable of making day-to-day decisions about how to progress the investigation. Anything that is of importance, Roddy will phone him. Right, you get the coffee's in while I go and pee."

****

When they left George Knox's flat, Kevin Stobbie drove Johnny Dunlop home to his end-terraced two bedroomed house in Skerray Quadrant in the Milton area of Glasgow, but declined the offer of lunch with Dunlop and his wife, Liz.

"Thanks, big man, but after hearing about Kelly-Ann," he grimaced, "I'm not in the mood for socialising."

"Aye, I know how you feel," Dunlop sighed. "When you think about it, Kev, the time we've been together with George and Rosie, we've seen that lassie grow up. It's a bad day for us all that some bastard has taken her from us."

He turned to Stobbie and placing a hand on his shoulder, said, "Now, you sure you won't come in for some scoff? I'm not happy about you going home alone to that flat of yours. I know what you're like, wee man. You'll only brood about this."

"I'll be fine," he forced a smile and when Dunlop got out of the Mercedes 190 saloon, gave him a wave before he drove off.

Turning onto Castlebay Street, he glanced in his rear-view mirror and saw the Ford Cortina with the two men following some distance behind.

Two streets further on, he saw the Cortina replaced as the eyeball vehicle by a light-coloured Ford Cortina and with a grin, shook his head.

Once more checking his rear-view mirror, he smiled at the tail and idly wondered if the cops were aware that he'd clocked them when he'd left George's flat in Quarrywood Road, but hadn't bothered mentioning it to Johnny whom he was certain, likely would have been unable to resist the urge to turn and give them the finger.

He'd long ago accepted that if you were a member of an armed robbery team, surveillance was an occupational hazard and he'd become used to it, so used to it he was certain that nine times out of ten, he could spot a tail car within minutes.

His face clouded over when it occurred to him; the cops would know that Kelly-Ann had been murdered, so why the hell were they tailing him today? Surely even they would realise that it was unlikely the team would be out blagging the day after her body had been discovered.

With a sigh, he decided to ignore the surveillance cars and headed home to his fifth storey flat in Summerton's Glenavon Road.

As he drove, he gave thought to Kelly-Ann's murder.

When Jimmy had phoned with the bad news, he had fought hard to keep his emotions in check and unable to find any reason not to visit George and Rosie, it was even more difficult keeping himself together at their flat.

He hated himself for deceiving George and Rosie, hated himself that for all these years he had betrayed them and hated himself even more for not being a man, for not standing up and telling them.

But now, it was too late for Kelly-Ann; however, a glimmer of hope beat in his breast, maybe not too late for the truth.

Arriving at the multi-storey building, he parked his Mercedes in the car park adjacent to the building in a spot where he could see it from his kitchen window to keep an eye on it.

Stobbie loved his car, albeit he'd bought it second-hand, but dreamed of the day when he'd be able to afford a brand-new motor and getting out of it, gently run a hand across the smooth, polished surface.

He never allowed any of the team to drive the Merc and was constantly the butt of good-natured jibes about it by the other three, who mercilessly teased him.

On one occasion, the mischievous Jimmy Dunlop had pinched the car keys for an hour, causing Stobbie some anxiety when he couldn't find them. But, he inwardly grinned, he'd solved that problem by confiding to Alex Hardie and swearing him not to tell Jimmy, that he'd affixed the spare key to the car where only he and Alex knew where to find it.

Locking the car, he walked towards the building, stifling a grin as he ignored the dark coloured Ford Escort that passed by on the access road, the two occupants, a female driver and her male passenger both fixedly staring straight ahead.

For once, the lifts were in working order, but mindful of his fitness, the wiry Stobbie had made it a habit to use the stairs and began to jog up to the fifth floor.

Pushing open the door into the landing, he heard his name being called.

"Hey, Kevin."

Turning, he saw a figure, a man he realised in that instant, dressed in dark clothing and wearing a balaclava.

"What the…" was all he managed before being viciously struck on the head.

His knees buckling beneath him, he fell to the floor, dazed and his vision fading, but with no time to protest. When he saw his assailant swinging what looked like a baseball bat, in vain he tried to reach out with raised his arm to ward off the next blow that suddenly came down and again struck him on the head.

Then his world went black.

Staring down at the unconscious Stobbie, the man raised the baseball bat then once more, brought it down onto Stobbie's head, hearing with satisfaction the crunching noise as the fallen man's skull split open.

With a satisfied sigh, the assailant removed his balaclava and turned to check he had not been seen.

Making his way along the corridor to the small room that housed the waste disposal chute, he pulled open the door then entering, opened the hatch and dropped the bat down the chute, listening for a few seconds as it clattered off the sides of the chute as it fell, before the man turned and scurried off from the room towards the stairs.

****

Martin Benson was at his desk, his jacket hung behind his chair and his sleeves rolled up as he worked his way through a pile of paperwork that demanded his attention.

When his door was knocked, he irritably called out, "Come in."

The door opened to admit a slim, attractive woman in her late twenties to early thirties he guessed, five feet eight inches tall, her shoulder length auburn hair professionally styled and wearing a white blouse and an olive-green skirted suit.

"DCI Benson," she greeted him with a smile, her accent clearly east coast.

"My name's Alice Meechan. I understand my Commander spoke with your Mr Meadows?"

He laid down his pen and returning her smile, replied, "DI Meechan. Yes, Mr Meadows did inform me that the Scottish Crime Squad has an interest in my investigation, that you were surveilling our Mr Knox and his team. Please," he waved a hand, "sit down."

When she'd settled herself in the chair opposite, he politely asked, "Can I get you a tea or coffee? Water perhaps?"

"No thank you, sir," she continued to smile, but Benson had been a copper for twenty-four years and wasn't taken in by her charming beam.

The pleasantries exchanged, he leaned forward to ask, "What can I do for you, DI Meechan?"

She stared at him for several seconds, seeing a balding man with greying hair and a pleasant face, before she said, "I came to see you to work out some ground rules between us regarding our joint interest in Knox."

Almost immediately, some inner sense warned Benson that he was about to be coerced, and so he asked, "And what exactly do you propose about these, eh, ground rules?"

"Well, sir," she slowly drawled, "as you will be aware, my team and I have been after Knox and his three accomplices for some time now…"

"Without much success, I gather," he smiled widely at her.

"Yes, that may be," she forced a smile in return.

"However, several weeks ago, my team followed George Knox when he and his associate, Kevin Stobbie, travelled to Clydebank where both men paid some attention to an armoured truck that was at the time delivering cash to the rear of the Clydesdale Bank in the shopping centre there, on Sylvania Way. It is our assessment that Knox and Stobbie were reconnoitring the delivery of the truck for a cash in transit robbery, a robbery that we also believe is imminent."

"That seems a logical conclusion," Benson pursed his lips then, his eyes narrowing, he asked, "How exactly do you think this pending robbery will affect my investigation into the murder of Knox's daughter?"

"Well, sir, we in the Scottish Crime Squad would take it as a great favour if you and your team could keep your contact with Knox and his associates and anyone acquainted with them to a minimum, so that they are not spooked and will go ahead with the robbery. This is a *tremendous* opportunity for us to catch them in the act," she coyly smiled and, to his surprise, he wondered; is she flirting with me?

He slowly nodded then, as if coming to a decision, calmly said, "DI Meechan, I am currently investigating the murder of a young woman, a single mother, who not only was brutally strangled, but horrifically sexually violated too."

As he stared at her, he saw her pale.

"Now, you're asking me to keep my officers contact with her parents and anyone she knew to a minimum so you can arrest the father and his associates?"

He paused and his face contorting, said, "Regardless of who my victim's father might be, DI Meechan, might I remind you that he has just lost his daughter, his *only* child and mother of his grandson. Well," he sat back and staring impassively at her, continued, "as far as I'm concerned, *my* priority is to find the sick bastard that killed this young lassie and if it means you and your squad have to try that wee bit harder to catch the man who's been running rings round you for a number of years, then no, I will not under *any* circumstances instruct my officers to refrain from doing their duty and *their* duty is to catch a killer!"

Forcing himself to remain calm, he continued, "Now, if you wish my officers to report anything that they believe is significant in helping you to arrest Knox, I will issue that instruction, but," he couldn't contain his anger any longer, "do *not* come in here to my office and try to charm me into sitting back so you and your squad can play at fucking cowboys and indians!"

Her face as white as a sheet and grimly set, Meechan rose to her feet and turning, wordlessly left the room.

When she'd gone, he slowly exhaled and rubbing at his face, reached for the telephone.

Dialling the internal number that took him through to the DI's room at Pollok, when his call was answered, he said, "Roddy, it's me. Listen, I've just had a DI Meechan from the Scottish Crime Squad in here. I'm going to have to speak to all of the team tonight, so keep them all there and I'll see you when I arrive for this evening's briefing."

****

In his kitchen making himself a late lunch, Alex Hardie's thoughts continued to trouble him for he had now convinced himself that there had to be a connection between Kelly-Ann and the two gangsters visit for if they were visiting the Barrowland, it was obvious they were meeting with Mark Ritchie.

Staring unseeingly at the fry-up that sizzled in the pan, he wondered again about contacting Avril Collins.

His thoughts turned to their night in his flat and if he were honest with himself, he had enjoyed her company.

It was the next morning when things had turned sour.
Avril's subtle suggestion she tell Ritchie she was breaking up with him to begin a new relationship without any discussion with Alex had more than annoyed him. The heated argument that ensued ended when in tears, she had cursed him then grabbing her coat, fled from the flat.
Yes, they had met several times since, but she had always been more than cool with him and though he hadn't heard to the contrary, guessed she was still with Ritchie.
So, he wondered again, how would she react if he were to phone her and ask about Kelly-Ann? Would she be receptive to a call or would she simply tell him to eff off?
The spurting fat from the frying pan alerted him to his lunch being overcooked and hastily, he ladled the food onto a plate and settled himself at the small, gateleg table.
Yes, he'd do that. When he finished eating he'd phone Avril and find out if she could confirm Kelly-Ann *was* at the dance hall on Saturday night and, his eyes narrowed, if Avril was keen to talk, maybe chance his arm and ask why Peter Donaldson and Foxy McGuire were visiting Mark Ritchie.

****

Returned to the top floor of Stewart Street Police Office where the Scottish Crime Squad had their suite of rooms, DI Alice Meechan, sat at her desk, bridled with rage that DCI Martin Benson had spoken to her in that manner.
Who the *fuck* does the old *bastard* think he is, she inwardly snarled. She lifted her head to stare at the wall opposite, the pin board covered with surveillance photographs of George Knox and his team, some of which went back years.
Since her appointment to the Squad three months previously and taking over one of the two the Glasgow teams, she was more than conscious of her predecessors' failures and had made it her mission to arrest Knox's gang, but to date without success.
Now this opportunity had presented itself to capture the gang when they hit the armoured car in Clydebank, but it was now jeopardised by Benson's detectives who likely would be swarming all over the gang in their search for the daughter's killer.

The open door to her office was knocked then entered by DS Barney Fellowes, a large, bearded man who was the popular, senior DS in the Unit and by virtue of his experience, her number two.
"A word, boss?"
Meechan indicated he come in and coldly nodded to the chair in front of her desk.
She was acutely aware that Fellowes, a Lothian & Borders Police Officer, disliked her and she had sought any opportunity to have him transferred from Glasgow to the Edinburgh headquarters or the satellite station at Stonehaven.
As for Fellowes, he not only disliked Meechan but also mistrusted her and on several occasions, had openly questioned her decisions regarding the deployment of the team that in turn led to her scathing comments on his recent annual appraisal.
However, Fellowes, with twenty-eight years' service compared to Meechan's ten years and a wealth of CID experience, had neither interest in Meechan's career advancement nor internal politics and continued to take delight in irritating her.
Right now though, he inwardly decided, was not the time for confrontation.
"We have a problem," he began.
Her brow furrowed as he continued, "Like you instructed, we took on Kevin Stobbie this morning and watched him pick up Jimmy Dunlop from his home. We followed them to George Knox's place and plotted up around the flat. When Stobbie and Dunlop left, he dropped off Dunlop and headed home to his flat.
She stared at Fellowes grim face, then coolly asked, "And what?"
"I decided to give it an hour before standing down because frankly," he pointedly stared at her as though to remind her of his objection to her decision, "I didn't think Stobbie would be up to any mischief the day after Knox's daughter was murdered. Anyway, twenty minutes after we plotted up around the flats, a marked police car with uniformed cops and then an ambulance arrived at the flats. We didn't think anything of it at the time. I mean, there's about one hundred and twenty flats in the bloody building and it could have been for any number of reasons the cops and medics were there."
She could a feel a cold chill run through her when she said, "But?"
"The ambulance left, but the panda didn't, then five or ten minutes

later, the Maryhill CID arrived at the flats. I recognised one of the detectives, a DS I've done a few jobs with."

"Did you speak with him?"

He stared at her before he stiffly replied, "No way. You know the rules. We don't show out and don't let anyone, not even the local polis know we're watching a place."

She smarted at the rebuke, but before she could respond, he continued.

"At the time there was nothing to indicate the ambulance had anything to do with Stobbie, but out of curiosity, when I got back here five minutes ago, I phoned my contact. It *was* Stobbie they took away. Someone attacked him in the corridor on his landing and he was found unconscious suffering from head wounds. He's been taken straight to the Neuro over in the Southern General Hospital in Govan and the words is, he might not make it."

"Does your source at Maryhill know you were watching the flats?"

He shook his head, then replied, "I told him I received a phone call that something was up in Glenavon Road."

She seemed to digest the information then slapping the desk with the palm of her hand, said,

"Shit. If Knox doesn't have a driver, that will put the robbery in Clydebank on hold."

Fellowes stared at her and slowly shaking his head, then sourly replied, "You don't get it, do you?"

"What? What do you mean, I don't *get* it, Detective *Sergeant*?"

"Don't you understand?" he stared curiously at her. "A target we had under surveillance was seriously assaulted while we were outside his fucking building! Fourteen police officers watching the building and our target is bludgeoned almost to death while we're sitting on our arses! Have you any idea where that leaves us? Christ, if the papers or the bosses find out, we're screwed!"

Her eyes fluttered as she realised the implication of what he said and worse, how it might affect her career.

Slowly and quietly, she asked, "Has the surveillance log been typed up yet?"

"No," he continued to stare at her, but now with suspicion written all over his face. "I haven't had the chance because like I said, we only got in just over five minutes ago."

"Did you make your team aware what you learned from your source at Maryhill?"

"I figured you should be the first to know," but he could read it in her eyes, what she was about to propose and recognised she was worried that the situation might do to her career prospects.

She licked nervously at her lips then with a glance at the open door behind him, said, "Then I suggest, DS Fellowes, that the *typed* surveillance log reflects the fact that after Stobbie dropped off Dunlop and then returned home, you immediately stood down the surveillance and returned to Stewart Street."

Stunned, he continued to stare at her when he asked, "You want me to doctor the times recorded in the log?"

"I'd rather you saw it as being sensible in that nothing reflects back on the Scottish Crime Squad that indicates we were present when a target was almost killed, that by the time the assault occurred we were off the plot and on the way back to base."

The royal 'we,' he thought, but it's me that's to falsify the log.

"I can't in good conscience agree with this, Ma'am…"

But he got no further when Meechan hissed, "Must I remind you, that *you* are a Detective Sergeant while *I* am a Detective Inspector and I am giving you a lawful command?"

But it wasn't lawful and he knew he must take some precaution to protect himself.

Seconds passed before he dryly asked "And the written log?"

"Please ensure that it comes directly to me."

Minutes later and after delivering Meechan the written log, Fellowes walked from her office and thought, how the hell does she think that she can keep this under wraps when me and thirteen other cops were there and know about this?

****

It was the investigation's office manager at Pollok, DS Mhari McGregor, who took the phone call from Criminal Intelligence at Pitt Street.

Hurrying through to DI Roddy Williams office, her soft Inverness lilt becoming even more noticeable as she gasped, "Boss, Kevin Stobbie, George Knox's wheelman. He's been discovered outside his flat badly injured, but no update as to his condition. However, Maryhill CID are treating it as an attempted murder."

"Bloody hell that puts the cat amongst the pigeons. Any details of what his injuries are?"

McGregor shook her head before she replied, "Nothing other than he's been blue lighted to the Neuro at the Southern, so I'm guessing head trauma."

"Right," Williams reached for the phone, "I'd better let the boss know."

****

Across the city, Alex Hardie dialled the number for the admin office at the Barrowland and to his relief, it was Avril Collins who answered.

"Avril, it's me, Alex Hardie. Can you speak?"

"Hello, Elsie," he heard her respond and guessed there was someone close by. "What can I do for you?"

"Are you able to meet with me? I need to speak to you."

There was definite pause before she replied, "I'm a bit busy at the minute, Elsie, but I can meet you after work, say five-thirty at the wine bar in the Tron Theatre?"

He knew the place well and that it was located only a brisk five-minute walk from the Barrowland.

"Right, I'll see you there," he smiled at the phone as she ended the call.

Glancing at his wristwatch, he saw he had two hours to kill and decided to phone George Knox.

The call was answered by Rosie still sniffing her tears, but pleased to hear from him.

"He's lying down the now, son, getting a bit of rest. He didn't sleep a wink last night."

"Don't disturb him, Rosie. How's the wee guy?"

"Clint? I'm worried about him. George tried to explain that his mammy isn't coming home again, that he's going to be living with us now, but it just seems to have passed right over his head. I mean I know he's just five," she sniffed again, "but he's always been a right smart wee guy. I think it's just that he doesn't want to accept what's happened, you know?"

"Anything I can do, Rosie? I mean, do you want me to take him for an overnighter or something, get some pizza delivered and spend some time with him?"

"That's awfully good of you, son, but right now I think he's better off here with us for the minute. Not that he doesn't think of you as anything but family," she hastily added, "but I think it's more for George's sake than the weans, you know?"

"Aye, you're probably right. Okay," he exhaled, "tell the boss I phoned and I'm still on it and if there's anything he needs to know, I'll be in touch."

CHAPTER EIGHT

He'd decided if he was having wine, he'd jump a taxi and arrived at the Tron Bar in the Merchant City's Chisholm Street ten minutes early, then ordering a glass of red wine and with a nod to the barmaid, secured a table from where he could see the entrance door. It was a little after five thirty when Avril Collins pushed open the door, a silk scarf hiding her long, blonde hair that was piled up on top of her head.

When he'd spoken with her earlier that morning, he recalled she had worn a short, denim skirt and a maroon coloured, long sleeved blouse. Now, as she walked towards him and removed her black raincoat, he saw she wore a bright yellow, cashmere top and a knee length dark green skirt and idly wondered, did she change for me?

She stared quizzically at him as he got to his feet and asked, "What?"

He smiled when he replied, "It never ceases to amaze me how attractive you are."

"Flatterer," she jokingly scoffed as he took her raincoat from her and handed it to the waitress who hovered nearby.

When he'd sat down, he ordered her a white wine, then said, "As we're here and if you've no plans for dinner, I thought we might order from the menu?"

"You ambushing me, Alex Hardie?" she softly smiled.

"Something like that," and politely asked the waitress to return when they'd perused the menu.

Several minutes later and after they'd placed their order, she began, "You needed to speak to me. I'm guessing this is about Kelly-Ann?"

He took a breath before he replied, "When I spoke with Mark this morning, Avril, I got the impression he wasn't telling me the whole truth. Do you know if Kelly-Ann was at the dance hall on Saturday night?"

Her brow furrowed as she hesitated before answering, then slowly nodding, said, "Yes, she was there, but you have to understand why Mark didn't admit that to you."

"He's worried that if the newspapers find out, the punters will stay away and the profits will drop," he drily replied.

She took a breath as she nodded, then said, "I'm sorry, Alex. I wanted to tell you, but…" she shrugged.

"He told you to keep your mouth shut?"

Her face reddened as she again nodded.

"Who else has he told not to say she was there? The security staff?"

"Them and the other staff," she agreed with a nod. "He told them not to mention it, that it would be bad business for the police to know because the papers would get a hold of it and if profits dropped," she shrugged, the inference clear.

He kept his anger in check when his voice almost a whisper, he leaned forward to continue for her, "And I'm guessing that their jobs are on the line if they talk about it or tell anyone and in particular, the police?"

Tight-lipped, once more she nodded.

He was prevented from carrying on with his questions when the waitress arrived and with a smile served their food.

He suddenly found he'd lost his appetite and picked at his food, seeing too that Avril wasn't enjoying hers.

Catching the waitresses eye, he ordered two further glasses of wine, then when she'd gone, said, "Look, I know the position you're in, that you're afraid if Mark finds out you've told me, you'll lose your job and you'll not want to risk your relationship either, so…"

"My what," she interrupted him with a fierce glare.

"You and Mark. I mean, you're together, right?"

Her shoulders sagged and she frowned when she replied, "Alex, Mark and I haven't been an item for over a year. That ended after, well, you know, that night," she blushed.

"You mean, the night we spent together?"

"Yes," she replied, though a little sharper than she intended.

Genuinely surprised, he said, "Oh, I'm sorry, I didn't know."

"Well," she brusquely said, "if you'd bothered to keep in touch, you would have."

They sat in silence, each staring at anything but each other, until at last, he said, "If you're not together any more why are you still there, Avril, working for him? I mean, you're a smart woman and I remember that you've a university degree in business so, why haven't you moved on?"

Her eyes widened when she replied, "He pays me well and because…" she paused, then continued, "Let's just say that I know some of his secrets."

He stared at her, trying to decide what those secrets might be, then his face lit up with a slow smile.

"He's skimming off the top of the profits and you know about it, don't you?"

She glanced at him, then sharply said, "I never told you that."

"You didn't need to," he smiled. "When I was stewarding there, I used to wonder why Mark always insisted on being present at the dancing on a Saturday night, the busiest night of the week, when as the manager with a couple of deputy managers he can call on, he could easily have taken at least one weekend a month off."

He nodded slowly as he continued, "It's because he needs to be there to do the books, isn't it? He needs to maintain a weekly presence because if he *wasn't* there and the company discovered that there was a discrepancy in the ledger for just one Saturday night, they might wonder at that and start to investigate why that was. So Mark needs to be there *every* Saturday night to maintain the same balance in the books."

He could see she was rattled and so raising a hand, said with a shake of his head, "Don't worry, I'm not interested in Mark's little scam, Avril, but I am interested in why Peter Donaldson and his thug pal, Foxy McGuire, visited Mark this morning just ten minutes after I had left him."

He watched her face pale and she took a quick sip of her wine before she replied, "Honestly, I really don't know, Alex. When they arrive," she gave a short shiver, "that rat faced McGuire, he's a slimy bastard, so he is. He makes my skin crawl each time he looks at me."

"I'm guessing then that today wasn't their first visit to Mark?"

Lowering her head to stare at the table, she shook her head and replied, "No, they've visited him on a couple on a couple of occasions, now. Three in fact, counting today," her eyes narrowed as she recalled. "Mark closes the door when they're in his office and," she lifted her head to stare at him, "you might remember, he never usually closes the door."

"Is Mark permitting Donaldson to sell his drugs in the dance hall?"

"I honestly don't know," she shook her head, "but if he is, then it's because they've threatened him. He might be a thief, yes, but he's never condoned nor permitted drugs to be brought into the place," she vigorously shook her head.

"So you have no idea why they were there?"

"No, I haven't, but I do know they're putting pressure of some sort on him, because after each visit, Mark is pretty wound up when they've gone."

He saw her turn to grab at her handbag and she was about to rise from the table when he gently grabbed at her hand and asked, "Are you leaving?"

She didn't withdraw her hand, but her face paled and when she stared him in the eyes, he saw the hurt and disappointment there when she replied, "You got your money's worth for the food and glasses of wine, Alex, so if you don't mind?"

Suddenly feeling like a right shit, he slowly nodded, then said, "Avril, I'm sorry. I really am. Look," he hastily added, "I know you're thinking the worst of me right now, but I did want to see you. Please, finish your wine. Let's forget about everything, but catching up. What do you say?"

The anger in her eyes died and slumping back down into the seat, she slowly nodded.

Staring at her, he wondered; why didn't I take up her offer for a relationship when I had the chance?

****

DS Mhari McGregor took the call from the Forensic Laboratory at Glasgow University and scribbling on her notepad, confirmed, "You'll have the written results typed up and ready for collection by Wednesday? Great, thank you."

Tearing the sheet from her notepad, she made her way along the narrow corridor to Roddy Williams room where she found him in conversation with Martin Benson, who she guessed must have just arrived for he was still wearing his overcoat.

"Ah, good, you're here too, boss," she greeted both men.

"I'm just off the phone with the Forensic people at the Uni," she brandished her handwritten note. "They've tested our victims' blood and the other samples and discovered high traces of cocaine in her system."

"Bloody hell," Benson glanced at Williams in surprise. "Her Da won't be happy when that little chestnut gets out."

"Unless he already knows she was doing drugs," Williams suggested.

"Mhari," Benson turned towards her, "the young guy, Hardie, Knox's man. Didn't he say in his statement that there was no likelihood of her doing drugs, that if her father had even suspected anything like that he'd have gone nuts?"

"That's correct, boss. Willie McBride took Hardie's statement and he added a bit at the end that he was of the opinion that Hardie was being truthful."

"Well, I think that's an important development, Roddy, so with the news about Kevin Stobbie," he glanced at his watch, "once the briefing is over and if you're not too anxious to get home for your dinner, I think it's about time we perhaps paid George Knox a visit at home."

****

Mark Ritchie closed and locked the drawers in the filing cabinet, then placed the keys in the top drawer of his desk.

His mind on the earlier visits, he thought what a shitty day I've had. The CID women, they were easy enough to handle. All he had to do to get rid of them was to promise them a staff list that he'd get Avril to attend to.

Turning, he slumped back down into his desk chair and his eyes narrowed when he thought about Alex Hardie. He had been a bit more difficult to deal with for knowing him of old, he knew the big man was nobody's fool. Had he convinced him that he couldn't recall seeing Kelly-Ann on Saturday night?

No, he wearily shook his head; he knew in his gut he had not.

Alex would be back, of that he was certain and how he'd handle that when the time came, he didn't know, for it wasn't just Alex he had to deal with. Kelly-Ann's Da, George Knox, was known throughout the city, Scotland even, for being one of the most successful bank robbers ever *and* he used guns when pulling his jobs, too.

Then there was Donaldson and his twisted pal, McGuire, and what he knew about them and Kelly-Ann.

There was no dealing with those pair.

"Keep your mouth shut," Donaldson had warned him with a slap in the mouth.

Yes, he could have picked up the bastard and broken him across his knee, but there was McGuire with the open razor in his hand and one to one, he knew he stood a good chance.

But not against two of them, so had been forced to take the crap Donaldson had dished out.

As much as it had infuriated and embarrassed him being treated like that, he also knew that if he'd fought back, there would have been repercussions.

So, hating himself for accepting their shit, he'd let himself be pushed around and threatened like he was a nobody.

But he'd took it and kept his mouth shut, the wisest choice if he wanted to continue walking and keep his balls.

Suddenly feeling parched he rose from the desk and strode over to the water cooler on the side table where he filled a paper cup.

Gulping down the water, he took a deep breath and wondered; was it time to take what he'd squirrelled away and head for the hills?

He thought about the Spanish bank account and the thousands he had skimmed from the Saturday takings.

Nobody else knew about it; nobody except Avril, but he knew she wouldn't talk. Not Avril and once more he regretted two-timing her, but whether his regret was because she'd found out about him shagging the barmaid or getting caught, he wasn't certain.

Of course, if he did bugger off, as soon as he was gone the company would discover the Saturday scam he'd been working and there would be a hue and cry out for him.

He glanced at the clock and made his decision, but before he left, there was one more thing he'd need to do.

He'd need to try and set things straight, if for nothing else than to ensure he'd sleep at night.

Sitting back down at his desk, he grabbed a sheet of paper and a pen and started writing.

****

The elderly Indian consultant neurosurgeon shone the torch into Kevin Stobbie's eyes and slowly shook his head.

Turning to the Ward Sister, he asked, "Has this poor man's family been informed about him being brought here?"

Glancing down at the chart she held in her hand, she slowly shook

her head before she replied, "There's no next of kin noted her, Mr Singh, but as it's an assault, I'm sure the police will have the details of any family. Do you wish me to phone, ah," she glanced down again, her eyes narrowing, when she read out loud, "Maryhill CID?"
He stood upright, but continued to stare down at Stobbie before he replied, "Tell them that I must undertake emergency surgery to relieve the pressure on his brain, that it might be advisable that the police inform his family to attend here as soon as possible."

****

Following his briefing to the investigating team and his instruction to them that anything they learned about the Knox team's activities regarding robberies be intimated to DI Williams, DCI Benson grabbed his coat and with Williams, made their way out to the rear yard at Pollok Police station.

Roddy Williams drove the car to Quarrywood Road and parked outside the close.

"How do you want to handle it?" he turned to ask Benson.

The DCI shrugged before he replied, "Okay, we know who George Knox is and what he's done and what he's wanted for, Roddy, but right now, as far as I'm concerned, he's the grieving father of a murdered daughter. Let's just go in with cap in hand and break the news about the cocaine. It might be that he can tell us something about it and that in turn might give us a clue about who killed her."

They left the car and reaching the door on the first landing of the building, it opened before they knocked.

Rosie Knox, her face drawn and pale, stared at them in turn then, said, "I saw you draw up. I'm Rosie Knox, Kelly-Ann's mother."

She stood to one side to permit them to enter, watching them as they passed her by then led the way down the narrow hallway to the front room where they saw George Knox sitting in an armchair, a young boy standing beside him.

Knox turned to the boy and said, "Away into your room, Clint, and play with your train set the now, son. Your Granny and me need to speak to these men."

The boy, his eyes hooded, stared at the two detectives then shuffled out of the room.

"A handsome wee lad," Williams smiled at Knox, who nodded when he replied, "Thank you. As you'd expect, he's having a right hard time of it right now. Please," he pointed to the couch, "sit yourselves down."

Behind them, Rosie said, "I'll stick the kettle on," but hesitated at the door when Benson raised his hand to stop her, then said, "Firstly, again," Benson said, "we're sorry for your loss. Any differences you might have with the police, Mr Knox," he turned to him and raised a hand again as he shook his head, "have nothing to do with how we intend conducting our investigation. I have to start with assuring you and you, Mrs Knox," he nodded towards her, "that me and my team will do everything we possibly can to find out who killed your daughter."

They both stared silently at him, then slowly nodding, Knox replied, "Thank you, Mr Benson. I appreciate that."

Rosie too nodded, then left the room to boil the kettle.

It occurred to Williams that they must have been expecting a visit if not from the police, then someone for within a couple of minutes, Rosie was back through to the front room with a tray on which rested a teapot with matching milk jug, sugar bowl and china cups and saucers and a plate of biscuits.

Knox rose from his chair and brought over a side table that he placed between the armchairs and the couch to permit Rosie to lay down the tray.

Once all four had been served, Benson began, "I know this is the most difficult of times for you both and for the wee lad, but there's some information I need to obtain from you and please," he again raised a hand as though expecting protest, "anything I ask of you is for the investigation only. Nothing you tell me will be divulged to any other source."

Knox glanced at his wife then said, "Go ahead, ask away."

"Unfortunately, right now we're no further forward than we were yesterday when Kelly-Ann was found. As you are both aware, a post mortem was conducted this morning and we received the result of some tests, late this afternoon."

He paused, knowing this would upset them, then said, "Kelly-Ann's blood indicated that she had been using cocaine. Were either of you…"

But he got no further for Rosie, her hands to her face, loudly cried out, "No! Not my Kelly-Ann!"

That'll be a no then, Williams inwardly thought.

However, it was Knox's face that interested Benson and Williams for though he was clearly shocked by Benson's disclosure, his expression quickly changed from pain to anger, and then he quietly asked, "Have you any idea who might have given her the drugs, Mr Benson?"
Shaking his head, he replied, "No, I was rather hoping that you or Mrs Knox might have some idea?"
Her head bowed and her face covered with her hands, Rosie shook her head as she quietly wept.
Trying with difficulty to maintain his composure, Knox then asked, "Are you working on the presumption that whoever gave Kelly-Ann the drugs might have killed her?"
"Truthfully? We just don't know enough yet."
Several seconds of silence followed, broken when Knox asked, "Were you able to confirm where she went on Saturday night?"
Distraught, her hands at her face, Rosie suddenly got up from her chair and hurried from the room.
He waited for a few seconds till the room door closed behind her, then said with a sigh, "Not yet. I had two of my officers make inquiry at the Barrowland where we understand she was a frequent Saturday night attender, but the manager there had no recollection of seeing her there. However, he's drawing up a list of the staff and tomorrow we'll start interviewing them to try and determine if any of them recall seeing her on Saturday night."
Benson glanced at Williams, then said, "I'm afraid that we have some more bad news for you, Mr Knox."
His eyes narrowed as Benson continued, "We heard that earlier this afternoon, your associate, Kevin Stobbie. He was discovered badly injured outside his flat in, eh…"
"Glenavon Road," Williams finished for him, then his brow knitting, he asked, "You hadn't heard?"
Knox's mouth fell open when he stuttered, "Kevin? But he was just here earlier this morning. Him and Jimmy Dunlop. After they'd heard about Kelly-Ann."
His head shook as though disbelievingly when he asked, "What happened?"
"Frankly, we don't know the details because it's the Maryhill CID that are investigating the incident. What we were told is that he had been assaulted and suffered severe head injuries and he's been

admitted to the Neurological Ward at the Southern General Hospital, over in Govan."

"Shit!" Knox suddenly rose to his feet, his fists clamped to the side of his head as he anxiously strolled about the room.

Staring at him, Benson slowly said, "Mr Knox…George. I need to ask this. Do you think or do you know if what happened to your daughter and Stobbie being attacked, are they related?"

Taking a deep breath, he slowly exhaled to calm himself, then staring down at Benson, said,

"To be honest and I know you've no reason to believe me, Mr Benson, because we both know that as far as the polis is concerned, I'm a criminal and your lot have been trying to lock me up for a long time now. But the truth is," he frowned as he slowly shook his head, "I have no idea, none whatsoever, but trust me, if I find out..."

He didn't finish the sentence.

Taking a deep breath that he slowly exhaled, he then asked, "Kelly-Ann. Her body. When will you release her to us?"

"I'm sorry, Mr Knox, that's up to the Fiscal. In a murder investigation, the deceased's body is usually kept…"

Knox raised a hand and interrupted with, "Oh, aye, I've heard about this before. It's if you arrest somebody and in case there's to be, what is it you call it again?"

"A defence autopsy," Benson replied.

Nodding as though in acceptance of the explanation, Knox continued, "Thank you for coming, Mr Benson and eh…"

"DI Williams."

"Yes. As you'll probably realise," he shrugged, "my wife Rosie and me, we're going to need time to take this all in at the minute and I'll be going over to the hospital to find out how Kevin is. The Neuro, you don't happen to know…?" his eyes narrowed.

"It'll be ward sixty-five," Williams helpfully replied, then got to his feet with Benson.

"Drive in through the main gate off the Govan Road and then drive straight on. It's in the big new building three hundred yards in on your left."

"Thanks, I'll find it," he nodded then led them to the front door.

Once the detectives were gone, Knox checked on Rosie in the toilet and found her sitting on the toilet pan, weeping.

He stood in the doorway and softly asked, "You okay, hen?"

"Drugs, George," her face wrinkled with the horror of it. "She had used drugs! I never knew," she sniffed and wiped her nose with a hand towel. "I thought I knew our daughter, but fucking *drugs*!"
"Granny?"
He turned to find Clint standing behind him, his young face creased with worry as he stared at Rosie.
"Come in here and see me, my wee lamb," she held out her arms.
He pushed past his grandfather and rushed into her arms.
Knox watched as she tightly crushed the boy to her, then softly told her, "Kevin Stobbie's been attacked, Rosie."
"Dear God," her lips trembled, then asked, "Do you think it's anything to do with…you know?"
"Oh aye, it's too coincidental not to be," he noisily exhaled through pursed lips, then added, "The polis didn't know all the details because it happened outside his flat. I'm going to phone Jimmy and find out if he knows anything, then I'll phone Alex and let him know. Once I know you're going to be okay, hen, I'll go to the hospital and visit him."
"Just go," she waved a hand, then added, "I'll be fine, George, honestly. Go."
He was turning away when her brow wrinkled as she stared at him, then called out, "Wait. If somebody's tried to," she glanced at the wee boy, fearful of using the word kill, then grimaced, "you know, Kevin. Does that mean that you and Jimmy and Alex, you might be at some kind of risk too?"
"Christ, I hadn't thought of that," he stared thoughtfully at her. "I'd better phone them right away to warn them, just in case."
She lifted Clint to sit him on her knee, forced a smile and said, "Do that and while you're phoning, I'll get you something to eat before you go to the hospital and the dinner on for this big boy."
Stroking Clint's hair, her eyes still bright with tears, asked, "Chips, fish fingers and beans, eh? What do you say?"
For the first time that day, the young boy hesitantly smiled.
****

In the CID car downstairs, Benson stared through the windscreen when he asked, "I'm pretty confident he didn't know about her using the drugs or Kevin Stobbie being attacked."
"I agree," Williams started the engine, then with a glance at the front room window upstairs, added, "You're thinking that both the lassie's

murder and the assault on Stobbie are linked?"

As Williams pulled away from the kerb, Benson nodded, then said, "There's nothing to indicate they are, but my gut's telling me otherwise, Roddy. First thing tomorrow morning, I'll do the briefing. I want you to take a turn over to Maryhill and see what you can find out about the assault."

"Okay. This thing with the Scottish, this DI Meechan. Didn't you say that they had resumed their surveillance on Knox's team?"

Benson's eyes narrowed in suspicion when he replied, "Aye, I did. You're thinking they might have been on Stobbie and Dunlop when they left Knox's flat?"

"Just a thought," mused Williams.

"Aye, but maybe not too far off the mark," he replied, his thoughts turning again to Meechan, who from the second he'd set eyes on her decided her to be a right sleekit woman.

****

DS Barney Fellowes glanced up when the door to the Sergeants room opened to admit Shona Burns, a Strathclyde Detective Sergeant slightly junior to him whom he trusted, not just as a fellow Scottish Crime Squad colleague, but also as a confidante and who, like him, had no time for Alice Meechan.

"Shut the door," he began, "I've something to tell you."

It was highly unusual for the Sergeants room door to be closed and her brow creasing with suspicion, she did as he said, then took her chair at her desk before asking, "What's going on, big man?"

Informing her of the assault upon Kevin Stobbie, he saw her jaw drop when he related Meechan's instruction to erase the fact that the surveillance had presumably been present outside Stobbie's high rise flats about the time the assault occurred.

"Is she daft or what? There was a full team there, Barney. How the hell does she think she can doctor an operational log? Is she naive enough to think we're all going to lie for her?"

He sighed before he replied, "I'm of the opinion that when the team hear about Stobbie being assaulted, she'll think that by changing the time we left the plot they'll just assume that it must've happened after we'd left the locus."

"Like fuck they will," exploded Burns, "because we all saw the ambulance and the uniform cops arrive and for I for one will not lie for that manipulative cow!"

"Remember, Shona," he raised a hand to calm her, "what she thinks and what we know are two completely different things."

However, Fellowes could not help but smile at Burns' outrage. Nodding, he continued, "And *that's* why I thought you should know. When the proverbial hits the fan, as undoubtedly at some point it will, she'll try and lay the blame at our door because she'll point out that she wasn't on the surveillance and therefore had no idea of the time changes in the log."

A slow smile crossed Burns face when nodding, she replied, "And because there's nobody to corroborate you when you explain that she instructed you to change the log, she'll deny she knows anything about it."

Her brow knitted when she asked, "What about the original written log?"

"She ordered me to hand it over; however," he grinned, "I took the liberty of photocopying it before I gave it to her and that's why I'm bringing you into it."

Burns nodded in understanding when she said, "So if I'm asked, I can truthfully say that you told me what she did and you were concerned enough to make a copy of the log."

"Exactly," he grinned.

"What a tangled web we weave, when first we practice to deceive," she smiled at him.

"And where did you drum up that wee chestnut from?"

"Drum it up? That's Sir Walter Scott, ya ignorant Edinburgher," she grinned widely.

****

As he expected, George Knox had to wait for several minutes before Johnny Dunlop calmed down, then told him, "Rosie suggested that we might be at risk, Johnny, so watch yourself when you're going out."

"At risk from who?"

"That's the problem," sighed Knox, then added, "The CID who were here earlier, the guy in charge of Kelly-Ann's investigation. He asked if I thought that her murder and Kevin's attack might be linked."

"What *do* you think, George?"

Knox slowly exhaled before he replied, "Honestly? I've no idea and while I'm on, have you heard from Alex?"

"No, should I have?"

"I tried to phone his flat, but there was no reply. If he phones you, give him the bad news and get him to call me."

"Are you going to see Kevin in the hospital?"

"Aye, once I've had something to eat. Rosie won't let me out the house without some dinner in me because I've not had anything all day."

"Right, then when you're leaving, bell me and then pick me up. You're not going out alone."

"Okay, old yin," he smiled warmly at Dunlop's concern, then before ending the call, added, "I'll see you soon."

CHAPTER NINE

They had decided to move on to a wine bar on the corner of Albion Street and Argyle Street where finding a dimly lit table in the farthest corner from the door, the second bottle of wine and the ambience turned the conversation to more light-hearted issues.

She surprised him when out of the blue, she confessed that she had never imagined herself working in the Barrowland and instead had envisioned a career in accountancy. Then, with an embarrassed smile, admitted when in her early twenties she had turned down the opportunity to live in London where a former boyfriend had promised to introduce her to a modelling agency owned by a friend of his.

"And why didn't you take up the chance to go? I mean," he gave her a wide smile, "even you must admit you're a real looker."

"Oh," she blushed, "I *did* travel down. However, the modelling agency," she used her forefingers to make italics in the air, "as it turned out, was a front for posing naked while dirty old men took photographs of me at about fifty quid an hour."

"You were going to earn fifty quid an hour?" his face expressed his surprise.

"No, not me," she frowned. "That's what the punters paid to take the pictures. I was getting about four quid an hour with the opportunity to do some *private* work with the punters where I was assured I could earn a lot more."

"Sounds like prostitution," he smiled a little uncertainly.

"Oh, believe me, Alex, it was," she scowled. "Half the girls I saw there were either so spaced out or too young to realise what was going on."

She shook her head in disgust then added, "Pathetic is the only word I can use to describe it. A dingy disused factory done up like some sort of sheiks harem. No way was I going to take my clothes off for those dirty bastards," her eyes flashed venomously.

"And the boyfriend?"

"Ah," she grimaced, then sighed as though at a painful memory.

"Well, my refusal to be involved didn't go down too well and," she drew a sharp breath, then her voice a soft whisper, said, "He put me in hospital for almost a week."

Hardie said nothing, his face expressionless, but hating the unnamed man who had beaten her.

She shrugged and then, her face reddening, quietly said, "It must be the wine that's loosened my tongue, because it's a very embarrassing story and even today," she took a deep breath and turning to stare at the ceiling, her eyes shiny with unshed tears, added, "I can't believe I was so *bloody* gullible."

"No, Avril," he leaned across the small round table to lay his hand gently upon hers, then said, "It's a very *sad* story. Taking a young woman's hopes and dreams then destroying them? You must have been devastated and though I don't know this guy, he sounds like the type of man I wouldn't get fed up punching."

She smiled then joked, "My knight in shining armour."

Now it was his turn to blush, before he quietly replied, "No, I'm not a knight, Avril, but there's some things a man shouldn't do and top of the list is to hit women or weans."

He wryly smiled when he added, "Saying that, it's not the first time when I've been stewarding I've had to wrestle some drunken, out her face lassie to the floor who's kicked off, but never to hurt them, you know?"

They sat in silence for almost a minute before nervously licking at his lips, he said, "Look, the elephant in the room. The last time we…"

"No," she held up her hand to interrupt. "I know what you're going to say, and *please*, no!"

She paused, her eyes boring into his, then continued, "That night, I came on too strong and I realise that now. Alex, I'm a thirty-three-year-old woman with no boyfriend and no family I can call my own and, well, to be honest, I was feeling lonely and though I was supposed to be Mark's girlfriend, I was feeling I don't know…" she shrugged, "neglected, maybe? Certainly, taken for granted. That and I was already suspecting he'd been seeing one of the barmaids and as it happened, I actually caught them at it."

"What, playing scrabble," he teased her with a mock expression.

"Oh, very funny," she smiled, then continuing to smile, said, "You're a good-looking man, Alex, and though I hear the rumours about you, I also suspect that you're a good man too. So, that night I was feeling a bit vulnerable," a tear escaped her and taking another deep breath, she said, "Look at me, crying like a baby."

He fetched a pale blue coloured handkerchief from his jacket pocket that he handed to her.

Dabbing at her eyes, she forced a smile and said, "I don't see any happy ending for me, but it's nice to know that you and I can be friends."

He wondered if they could be more than friends, but was astute enough to realise that if he dared broach the subject right now, she would assume that he might be taking advantage of her openness and so instead told her, "Look, probably the best thing you can do right now is go home and get a good night's sleep. And if you're okay with it, maybe you and I could meet again, but this time for a real dinner date and *not* because I need information from you."

Her eyes narrowed when she stared at him and asked, "You're serious."

"Yes, why wouldn't I be?"

"There's what, three or four years between us?"

"And if I were thirty-three and you, twenty-nine, that matters why?"

"Phew, I don't suppose it does matter," she happily shrugged.

"No, Avril, it doesn't matter and for what it's worth," he gallantly took her hand in his as they rose from the table, "I think I'm getting the best part of the deal."

She could feel a lump in her throat and unable to speak, simply nodded her thanks.

After settling the bill, he escorted her out into the soft rain and sheltered with her under her umbrella, his nose wrinkling at the faint and pleasant fragrance of her perfume.

They waited for almost five minutes until he was able to hail a taxi. Turning, he said, "I'm sorry, I have no idea where you live."

"I'm over in Cardonald," she replied. "It's a council semi where I used to live with my dad, but he passed a few years ago," she sadly smiled.

Closing the door behind her, she turned to see him using his thumb and pinkie finger as though using a phone to indicate he would call her.

He watched the taxi drive off then glancing up at the waterfilled clouds, waited patiently for another taxi to pass by.

It had, for some unknow reason he couldn't quite explain, pleased him that she was no longer in a relationship with Mark Ritchie.

Glancing up at the rain filled sky, he couldn't imagine what it had cost Avril to admit her past about the boyfriend who had put her in hospital, yet felt oddly privileged that she trusted him enough to disclose it.

But sympathy was no reason to start a relationship, he knew, no matter how attractive or intelligent she was.

Still, he smiled, it would be interesting getting to know her a little better and stepping from the shelter of the doorway, raised his hand attract the attention of a passing Hackney cab.

****

In his rented, second storey flat in the blonde sandstone tenement building in the city centres West Graham Street, Mark Ritchie quickly packed a suitcase, collected his documentation for the Banco de Santander, then panic seized him when he discovered that he could not find his passport.

"Shit, shit, shit," he repeated over and over as he anxiously pulled out drawers, then ransacked them, throwing clothing and other items about the bedroom. From there he moved to the second bedroom that he used as an overflow for his wardrobe, then onto the front room where the sideboard was also pillaged, but without success.

His heart racing and his breathing becoming more erratic, thoughts of what might happen to him if he didn't escape Glasgow this evening filled him with dread, for it was not just the ignominy of arrest and prison he feared; the truth being that the police and the court were the lesser of two evils.

No, what he feared was being dragged from the River Clyde minus his fingers, toes and his testicles.

Why, oh why did I write that *fucking* letter, he inwardly fumed.

He was about to give up his frantic search when a sudden thought struck him and almost racing through the flat, stumbled into the kitchen where dragging open a drawer, he found his passport jammed in at the back.

With a sigh of relief, he kissed the cover of the passport like it was some lost lover then shoved it into his inside jacket pocket before fetching his suitcase from the bedroom.

With a final look around the flat he headed for the door.

Making his way around the corner into Scott Street, he struggled up the steep hill and down the other side to emerge onto Sauchiehall Street where perspiration running down his spine, he hailed a black Hackney cab. Minutes later, he was dropped off at the Central Station and glancing at the iconic overhead clock, saw with relief he was almost forty minutes early for the London Euston train.

Time for a drink, he decided.

Thirty minutes later he was at the ticket desk.

"Return?" asked the ticket attendant.

"No, pal," he smiled, "I'm a definite one-way."

****

Arriving home, Alex Hardie didn't immediately see the red light winking on his answer machine, but when he did and replayed the message, his face turned pale and his blood froze.

Dialling George Knox's number, it was Rosie who answered.

"Thank God, Alex, that you're alright son," he heard her say, her voice choked with emotion.

"Is he in?"

"No," she replied, her voice low and casting her eyes towards the partially ajar bedroom door because her grandson slept in his Granny's bed, too fearful to sleep alone in case a bad man came to get him like they got his mother.

"He's away more than two hours now. He was picking Jimmy up first then going to the Southern to see Kevin."

"How bad is he, Rosie, do you know?"

"Only what the polis told us and I've not heard anything since."

"Right, I'll head over there the now."
"Alex?"
"Aye?"
"Be careful, son," she warned him, her voice breaking with emotion.
"I will, Rosie, I promise."
Replacing the phone into the cradle, his thoughts turned once more to seeing Peter Donaldson and Foxy McGuire at the Barrowland.
Kevin badly injured?
What the *hell's* going on, he wondered?
Striding into the kitchen to collect a bottle of water from the fridge, he returned to the hallway and lifting his overcoat, was about to grab for his car keys then remembered; he'd been drinking.
No sense, then, in giving the cops an opportunity to arrest him.
Lifting the phone, he dialled the number for a private hire taxi.
****

Getting out of the taxi cab in Redpath Drive at the end terraced two-bedroom house she'd taken over after her widowed father died, Avril Collins was still smiling, her thoughts full with the promise of a date with Alex Hardie.
She'd long held a torch for Alex and though she knew of the rumours about him being involved in robberies, chose to believe that he really was a good man, a man she could live with.
A man she could really call her own.
Or am I being too optimistic, she wondered with a frown.
Unlocking the front door at the side of the building and stepping into the small hallway, her thoughts filled with the evening and smiled while admitting to herself it had gone even better than she'd dared hope.
Yet there lingered a doubt; was she reading too much into his kind words?
In the neat and modern kitchen, she boiled the kettle and was opening the fridge door for the milk when she glanced at the photograph pinned there by a sticky post-it, a photograph of her taken by Mark Ritchie a number of years previously, she forcing a smile as though enjoying the photographer's attention.
It was then she knew she'd never really been happy with any man. The affair with Mark had always been one-sided, his needs coming before what she wanted from the relationship and once more regretted her two and something years with him.

Milking her tea, she inwardly admitted that yes, Mark had been good for her at a time when she had been at her lowest ebb; losing her father to a devasting illness, being dumped by her then boyfriend of three years and made redundant from her job at the bank and all within the space of six months.
Slumping down into the kitchen table, she remembered with vivid clarity that the job at the Barrowland had been a lifeline she had badly needed, personal assistant to Mark the manager.
Her brow creased when she recalled thinking at the time it had been strange that even with her accountancy background he had always insisted on managing the books himself.
It had taken her just a few weeks to discover why, that he was skimming money from the profits as well as regularly paying wages to ghosts; temporary staff that did not exist.
When he realised she had worked out his money-making scheme, he had increased her wages on the condition she told no one and to her shame, needing the job and with a substantial rise, she had agreed.
And so she had kept his secret for all that time, though how long he had been at it prior to her discovery of his theft, she never discovered.
They had become lovers shortly afterwards with Mark promising that when the time came, they would leave and set up home together.
She had known it was a lie, that he was merely keeping her sweet and biding his time to take off with his money as well as turning a blind eye to his numerous betrayals with other female staff.
Her one chance to break the cycle she had found herself in was the night with Alex, the night she remembered with shame when she had tried to coerce him into a relationship.
Sipping at her tea, she self-consciously smiled and again worried; did he really intend phoning her?
Is it possible he was just being kind?
With a sigh, she finished her tea and rinsing the cup, decided there was little point in sitting worrying about it then switching off the kitchen light, made her way upstairs to bed.
****
The taxi dropped Alex Hardie at the front entrance to the Neurological Wing of the Southern General Hospital where in the brightly lit foyer he found George Knox and Jimmy Dunlop standing beside a hot drinks machine.

No one else was in the foyer area.

"I only got in and heard the message on my answer machine," he gasped. "How is he?"

Knox, a plastic cup of coffee in his hand, shook his head before he replied, "We don't really know, son. The nurse upstairs told us he's in surgery, that the consultant, a Mr Singh is operating right now, but what his condition is?"

Again, he slowly shook his head.

"You wanting a coffee or something," asked Dunlop, jiggling a handful of change in his hand.

Hardie shook his head as Knox indicating with a nod that they all move towards the seating area, said, "The nurse knows we're down here and said she will give us a shout if she hears anything."

When they were seated, Hardie asked in a low voice, "Any idea who attacked him?"

Dunlop stared at Knox who taking a deep breath, replied, "We don't know and honestly, haven't a clue. It was that detective in charge of Kelly-Ann's murder, Benson, that told me when he visited me. All he could tell Rosie and me was it's the Maryhill CID who are dealing with it, then he asked if it had anything to do with Kelly-Ann getting killed."

He stared at Knox and Dunlop in turn, then made his decision.

"I might know something, boss, but I'm not sure if it's of any significance."

Knox stared at him for several seconds then said, "Go on."

"Like you said, I went to visit the Barrowland and spoke to Mark Ritchie, the manager. I've known him for a few years and before now he's always been straight with me."

"But?"

"Well, Ritchie has a memory like an elephant. He can always tell the regulars like Kelly-Ann; who's in the place or who's missing, you know? Anyway, he told me that he was uncertain if he saw Kelly-Ann last Saturday night and it was that one word, him being uncertain. It's just not like him," his brow knitted and he shook his head. "He's either a 'yes they're in' or a 'no they didn't come' man, do you know what I mean?"

"You think he's told you a porky?" asked Dunlop.

"At the time I couldn't say for certain he'd told me a lie, but I'd got this feeling he'd not told me the truth," he nodded.

"Anyway, earlier this evening I met with his personal assistant for a drink. She's a pal of mine from when I worked there," but decided not to go into any more detail. "She told me that Kelly-Ann *was* there on Saturday night and she didn't know either," he shrugged, "why Ritchie just wouldn't tell me that."

He glanced again at Knox and Dunlop in turn, but it was Knox who asked, "So why did this guy Ritchie lie? What's your best guess?"

"My best guess," he shrugged, "is that he's worried if it comes out in the newspapers that she was at the dancing then was taken from there and murdered, it will bring back all the problems the place had after the Bible John murders. The punters will stay away and the profits will plummet and if that happens…"

"Staff lose their jobs and maybe even the manager gets the sack, too," Dunlop interrupted with a nod.

"Exactly," Hardie agreed.

"I take it," Knox stared at Hardie, "that he's also told the CID that he doesn't remember her being at the dancing?"

"Aye, apparently."

"Stupid bastard," Dunlop spat out.

Knox took a deep breath then asked, "But how do you think that this guy Ritchie lying to you might be connected to Kevin getting battered over the head?"

"Like I said," Hardie raised a warning hand, "they might not be connected, but minutes after I left the Barrowland, I saw a guy who I thought was Peter Donaldson and Foxy McGuire, who I've met before, going inside the place. Avril, my pal, she confirmed it this evening it was them two."

"Donaldson and McGuire," Knox softly repeated, then almost spat out, "Those scummy druggie *bastards*!"

"Did your pal have any idea why they were there, Alex?" Dunlop asked.

"No," he shook his head. "All she could tell me was that when they were in his office, Ritchie shut his door, something he doesn't usually do and when they'd left, he was pretty wound up."

"There's something I need to tell you both," Knox stared at them. "When the CID came to the flat tonight, they told Rosie and me that after they did their Forensic checks they found cocaine in Kelly-Ann's blood."

It was Dunlop who broke the silence when he scoffed, "Kelly-Ann?

No way. It must be a mistake. Aye," he nodded, "I know she liked a wee bevy, but she wouldn't do drugs. Not that lassie. She was too devoted to her wee man."

"Thanks, Jimmy, I know you mean well, but it's no mistake," Knox wearily replied. "My lassie was doing drugs and that," he turned to stare at Hardie, "might be your connection with those two scumbags you saw at the Barrowland."

"But how does that relate to Kevin?" Dunlop insisted.

"The only thing I can think of," Knox shrugged, "is somehow Kevin found out and those two tried to stop him from telling me."

His face darkened, his hands clasped in his lap so tightly till the knuckles were almost white, when he continued, "They know if I found out they were dealing drugs to my lassie, I'd fucking murder them both."

They sat in silence for several minutes till Dunlop rose from the plastic chair with tubular metal legs, then moaned, "My arse is raw from sitting on this bloody seat."

Hardie smiled then asked, "Give me some change, Jimmy. I'll have a coffee after all. Boss?" he turned to Knox who declined with a shake of his head.

A bell chimed and all three turned to see a slightly built and wizened Indian man wearing green scrubs under a white coat, step out from the opening doors of the lift.

Glancing around, he caught sight of the three men then walked slowly towards them.

"Mr Knox?" he stared from one to the other.

"That's me. Eh, Mr Singh?" he stared at him with a furrowed brow.

"Yes, sir," he gave a slight bow, then his eyes expressing his sorrow, continued, "I am Singh. I am so sorry, but I come bearing the worst of news."

CHAPTER TEN

The Tuesday morning headline for the 'Glasgow News' was the murder of Kevin Stobbie, who the newspaper described as, *'A bachelor who resided alone in the multi-storey building in Glenavon, Road in the Maryhill district, Stobbie was a man long suspected by*

Strathclyde Police to be a key member of a four-man team of armed robbers who have for a number of years committed daring armed robberies throughout the length and breadth of Scotland.'
While the DCI in charge of the murder inquiry, Michael Thorburn, declined to comment on the ongoing investigation, the 'Glasgow News' surmised in its by-line that Stobbie's murder *'Is the result of an ongoing feud between the gang of robbers,'* who it wisely declined to name, presumably for fear of legal action against the newspaper, *'and a rival criminal gang in the Glasgow area.'*
"Pure conjecture," an irate Thorburn threw the newspaper onto his desk well aware that the by-line was simply an attempt to sensationalise the front page.
He glanced up when his door was knocked then opened by Roddy Williams, who asked, "This a bad time, Mike?"
Thorburn smiled and rising from behind his desk, extended his hand in greeting and said, "Long time no see pal. How's the wife?"
"What one? The second one that's making me happy or the first one that's screwing me for every penny I earn," he grinned at Thorburn, who indicated Williams sit down.
Raising a hand, Thorburn lifted the phone to call his CID clerk and requested two coffees be sent in, then asked Williams, "Still black with two sugar?"
"Yes, thanks," he nodded.
"Right then, Roddy, to what do I owe the pleasure?" he sat back with a grin, his hands clasped across his ample belly.
"Martin Benson sent me over, Mike. You know we've got George Knox's daughter's murder at Pollok?"
"So I heard. Anything doing there?"
"Nothing so far," Williams shook his head. "Benson's heard about wee Kevin Stobbie getting the message. Any suspects at your end?"
"Not a whisper. My guys have been chapping doors all yesterday and they're back there again this morning. It's the usual in these high-rise blocks as you'll remember. Three monkeys, Roddy; see no evil, hear no evil and definitely where the polis is concerned, speak no evil."
"Any Forensic?"
Thorburn cocked his head to one side to ask, "You're thinking that my murder is connected to your own investigation?"
"We can't dismiss it, but we've no evidence as yet to suggest they

are connected; however, it is something that we're going to have to consider."

"Well," Thorburn lifted the 'Glasgow News' from his desk and shaking his head, said, "this bloody rag isn't going to help any, fuelling the idea that the city is in the middle of a gang war."

He was interrupted by a uniformed officer entering the room with two china mugs of coffee.

"Thanks, Tom," he acknowledged the CID clerk, who closed the door behind him.

"So," he stared at Williams, "what can I do to help and vice versa?"

"Benson was thinking of a mutual exchange of information. At the minute all we have is that our victim had been using cocaine and that apparently surprised her Da and his wife. They'd no idea she was on drugs. What about Stobbie?"

"I have a report," he waved to a folder on his desk, "that the last time Stobbie was in Barlinnie, he was using heroin, but that was over thirteen years ago. When he was released eleven years ago, he was apparently clean then, but nothing since," he shook his head.

Then Thorburn asked, "What about your victim's movements prior to her murder? Have you managed to confirm where she might have been? I know from the Chief's daily synopsis she'd been found in Pollok Park."

"There was a suggestion that she'd been at the dancing in the Barrowland, but the manager there isn't certain, however, we've got people going back there this morning to obtain a list of the staff to try and determine if any of them recall her being there."

"God, I hope not," Thorburn stared with dismay at Williams, "because that'll bring out all the conspiracy nutters claiming Bible John's stuck again."

"Aye, exactly," Williams eyes widened as he blew onto his coffee to cool it.

"Okay," Thorburn sipped from his own mug, "we pool our information. So, now that's agreed, tell me, Roddy. What else is happening in your world?"

****

Arriving at the admin office in the Barrowland, Avril Collins greeted the cleaners with a smile then was a little taken aback to discover that Mark Ritchie, usually first in each morning, was neither at his desk in the inner office nor was it like him to be late.

"Elsie," she popped back out to the corridor to call to the cleaner, "have you seen Mr Ritchie this morning?"

The woman's face creased when shaking her head, she replied, "I've been here since the back of seven, Avril, and he's not been in since I was here."

"Right," she slowly drawled then re-entering the office, checked the wall calendar to ensure that she hadn't forgotten that he was attending a meeting elsewhere.

No, she unconsciously shook her head, there was nothing listed on the calendar.

Deciding to phone his flat, she called twice, each a lengthy call, but on both occasions there was no response nor did an answer machine kick in.

Where the hell is he, she idly wondered then settling herself behind her desk, was removing the grey plastic cover from her typewriter and startled in fright when a manila legal envelope fell from the keyboard onto her lap.

Her eyes narrowed as she lifted the sealed envelope, surprised to see that it was addressed to Alex Hardie and in Mark Ritchie's untidy handwriting.

She was about to reach for the telephone when she muttered, "Damn," for then remembered she didn't have Alex's home phone number.

Her eyes narrowed and rising from her chair, made her way to the large metal filing cabinet and pulled out the top drawer that contained the bulky file that contained the staff's personnel details.

Rifling through the file, she smiled when she saw with a relieved sigh that Alex Hardie's details had not been discarded when he'd quit his employment at the Barrowland.

Returning with the file to sit at her desk, she mentally crossed her fingers that he'd be at home and dialled his number.

"Hello?"

"Alex, it's me, Avril. Sorry to phone you so early, but…"

"Hi, Avril, what's up?"

She thought he sounded tired and was about to explain when the door was knocked.

Glancing up, she saw it to be the two women detectives from the previous day, recalling their names to be MacDonald and Thompson, and hastily said to Hardie, "Sorry, I have some visitors. I'll call you back."

Her first thought was, shit, they know about Mark skimming the money and that's why he's not here.

Forcing a smile, she said, "Good morning, ladies. What can I do for you?"

She was not to know that disregarding DI Williams instruction to call back at midday, Thompson had taken it upon herself to call early for the purpose of speaking with Avril.

"Just us again, Avril," the older woman smiled tightly at her. "We're here for the list your boss promised us. Is he in?"

"Eh, no, he's not. He's a little late this morning," she replied, conscious that her face was flushed and dreading that they knew she was lying.

"Oh, he is, is he," the detective coldly stared at her, then asked, "Do you have the staff list?"

"Ah, yes, I prepared it yesterday."

She could feel her body trembling and any second expected to be arrested for being complicit in Marks *fucking* scam.

Searching through her tray, she found the three stapled pages that she handed to the detective, who glancing thoughtfully at the closely typed pages, said, "That's more than I expected, but thanks. Had any more thoughts about whether or not Kelly-Ann Knox was here on Saturday night, Avril?"

Her mouth dry, she took a breath then heard herself reply, "I'm not sure. I usually work every second Saturday night to assist Mr Ritchie with the ledgers," she lied, "but I don't usually go down to the dance floor. Not my style," she joked, but saw that her witticism had fallen on deaf ears with the older woman though the younger detective, DC MacDonald gave her an agreeable smile.

Thompson stared at her for several seconds, then slowly nodding, said, "Okay. Now the staff that are on duty at the minute, will any of them have been working last Saturday night?"

"Eh," her brow creased when she replied, "not the cleaning staff, they're always early shift. There's the doorman on duty right now, the guy that let you in. He might have been stewarding, but I'm not certain. If you want to wait, I can check the duty roster and find out?"

"No, don't bother," Thompson glanced at the three pages, then added with a resigned sigh, "we'll have a word with him on the way out. The staff on here," she flicked a finger at the list, "if we can't contact them at their home phone numbers or their addresses, we'll probably be back to try and speak with them here, okay? You might want to inform your boss about that."

"Yes, of course," she again forced a smile, suddenly conscious she badly needed to pee.

She watched them leave and with a sigh of relief, left her desk to make her way to the loo in the corridor.

Five minutes later, her nerves shredded, she returned to her desk and phoned Alex Hardie.

****

George Knox stared dully at the cold fireplace.

Rosie had taken a taxi with the wee guy to his primary school over in Bridgeton to explain that his mother was dead and that he'd be living with his grandparents and asking that the school make provisions for him to attend a primary local to their home in Barmulloch.

He took a slow breath, deep in thought.

First Kelly-Ann, now Kevin.

What the hell is going on, he wondered not for the first time.

After they'd left the hospital, he'd first dropped off Jimmy Dunlop then firmly told Alex that no, he didn't need the younger man to come and sit at his house to protect him and Rosie and the wee guy.

"But boss," Alex had angrily argued, "what if Kevin's murder was a hit? Okay," he'd raised both hands as if expecting some protest, "we don't know why he was killed, but what if for some reason some *bastard* is out to get us all? Shouldn't you at least consider that you might be at risk? You, Rosie and the wean?"

Though it had never been spoken of, both he and Rosie were aware that Alex thought of them both as surrogate parents and that he'd do anything for them and wee Clint and that affection had included Kelly-Ann too, but right now he didn't believe that he and Rosie or the wean were at serious risk. Yes, it might come to that, but not for a day or two at the very soonest, for whoever killed Kelly-Ann and Kevin would realise the polis will be all over them all, watching and keeping tabs on the remaining three members of the team to try and nab the killer or killers.

Sitting back in the chair, his thoughts turned to what Alex had discovered.

Could it really be that Peter Donaldson and his rat-faced pal, Foxy McGuire, *are* behind the murders, he wondered?

If not the murders, then they certainly must have something to do with Kelly-Ann and her drug use and for that, his teeth gritted, his hands unconsciously clutching tightly at the armchair there *will* be a reckoning.

****

On the top floor of Stewart Street Police Office in the Scottish Crime Squad suite, DS Barney Fellowes glanced up when DS Shona Burns entered the DS's room and said, "Have you heard the news?"

"About Kevin Stobbie? Aye, it was on the radio, Clyde One, when I was coming in to work," he grimaced.

"Has she said anything about it?" Burns slumped down into a chair and stared at him.

"No, not yet. She's in her office with the door shut. I'm guessing she's on the phone sooking up to some boss, somewhere," he shook his head in disgust.

"What's the plan for today, big man? Are we still on Knox's team or are we pulling off because of what happened to Stobbie?"

"You're guess is as good as mine, wee pal. I can't see us surveilling Knox or his team after what happened and as far as I know, she…"

He was interrupted when the door was pushed open to admit DI Meechan who dressed in a black coloured skirted suit, said, "Ah, good, you're both here. I've spoken with the Commander who agrees with me that we should continue the surveillance on the Knox team."

"Are you kidding me?" an angry Fellowes stared unbelievingly at her. "They've just had their wheelman murdered, Knox's daughter was murdered three days ago and you think that him and the other two scroats are going to knock off a cash in transit delivery after what's happened?"

"I see no reason why they won't continue with their plan," she glared at him. "In fact, DS Fellowes, I've assessed that this is the ideal time for them to carry out their robbery, believing that we will pull off them *because* of what's happened."

"Un-*fucking*-real," he shook his head and turned away from her.

Openly provoked by his action, Meechan was about to rage at him, but was stymied by Burns who calmly said, "I assume, Ma'am, that you will be coming out with us on the surveillance for after all, *Ma'am*, you *are* the team leader."

It was no secret among the officers that she commanded that Meechan was as likely to become involved in a surveillance operation as she was to strip naked and dance the fandango, but coolly replied, "On this occasion, DS Burns, no. I will remain at Stewart Street and coordinate the operation from here."

Quickwittedly, Burns assumed an expression of innocence when she replied, "On *this* occasion, Ma'am? But you never come out on operations and frankly," she shrugged as she politely continued, "the team are beginning to question why that is. I mean, if you don't feel you're suitable to our type of work?"

Staring white-faced at the DS, Meechan was about to retort, but glancing hatefully at Fellowes, turned on her heel and left the room, slamming the door behind her.

"Cow," Burns muttered.

With a long, drawn out sigh, Fellowes turned to tell Burns, "Gather the guys in the main room, Shona. I have a cunning plan," he theatrically winked at her.

****

Restlessly, Alex Hardie paced the floor of the kitchen, his head a jumble of thoughts.

Kevin dead.

It was unthinkable.

Yes, the wee guy was one of the team and it was accepted by them all that they took their lives in their hands each time they were out on a job, but for all that and the police aside, he'd never known Kevin to have any enemies, anyone who would want him dead.

And the phone call from Avril, what the hell was that about?

He hadn't recalled giving her his phone number, but then realised it must still be in the staff files. Clearly, she had been in the office for when she'd ended the call she had said she'd visitors.

Who? Donaldson and McGuire again, his brow creased?

This is stupid, trying to guess what she's wanting he exhaled and shook his head at his own frustration.

He decided he'd little choice but to wait for her to call back.

Making his way to the bathroom, he'd just turned on the electric shower and stripped naked, stepped into the steaming hot water.

He'd no sooner soaped his body when the phone in the hallway rung.

"Bloody typical," he irately muttered then wrapping a towel around his waist and dripping water on the floor as he went, padded through to the hallway.

"Hello," he snapped.

Taken aback by his brusque response, Avril Collins tentatively asked, "Alex? You okay?"

"Oh, Avril, yes, I'm fine," he nodded at the phone, pulling his nose between his forefinger and thumb to remove the drips falling onto the phone. "What's up?"

"Mark Ritchie hasn't come to work today and I can't contact him. When I got to my desk I found he'd left an envelope for you with your name on it. It's sealed. Do you want me to open it and read it to you?"

Her heart beat a little faster and she waited with anticipation until he replied, "No, look. I'm in the shower at the minute. Give me half an hour or so and I'll drive over and meet you in the café opposite the main entrance, okay?"

"Okay," she replied then ending the call and though she couldn't explain why, smiled widely.

****

Shaved, showered and dressed, Hardie hurried downstairs to his parked Ford Capri then arriving at the car, hesitated.

George Knox, ever the meticulously careful man, had warned the team that it took but a few minutes to run their fingers around the external shell of their cars and particularly around the wheel arches and under the front and rear bumpers to check that the police surveilling them had not planted tracking devices.

Conscious it was approaching the thirty minutes he'd promised Avril and though he didn't think the cops would be out on the team after what had occurred with Kelly-Ann and Kevin Stobbie, he carried out the routine inspection.

Minutes later and having found nothing, he was behind the wheel and driving towards the café in the Gallowgate, all the while with one eye on the rear-view mirror, just in case.

Just over five minutes later he was fortunate to find an empty bay directly outside the café where he could keep an eye on his car.

Pushing open the door to the café, he saw Avril seated at a table near to the counter and with a lopsided smile, joined her.

The middle-aged waitress, recognising him as the generous tipper from the day before, raised an eyebrow and good-naturedly said to Avril, "Well, hen, now that I know he's yours, I'll not bother giving him a line of patter. So, what you lovebirds having?"

They both smiled at the banter, then ordering coffee and a roll and square slice for Hardie, waited till she'd walked off behind the counter before he asked, "Has he arrived at work yet or have you found out where he is?"

"Neither," she shook her head, then from her handbag, fetched out the envelope that she handed to him.

His brow knitted as he stared curiously at it, then tearing it open, began to read the single sheet of paper it contained.

"He's a right rotten writer," he shook his head and scowled, then handing the letter to her and aware he intended divulging the contents to her anyway, said, "You'll probably know his handwriting better than me, anyway. Please, read it to me."

Clearing her throat, she skimmed through the letter and he saw her frown as her eyes narrowed at the content.

Then in a low voice, she read aloud:

"Alex, I know you'll be aware I lied to you today. Kelly-Ann was in the dance hall on Saturday night and she was full of the Coke. I don't know for certain where she got it, but I can guess because those pair of ratbags Peter Donaldson and his pal, Foxy McGuire, are putting the pressure on me to let them deal in the ballroom. As for me, I had no option but to agree because if I refused, they threatened to," she paused and her face paling and swallowing tightly, glanced at him before she continued, *"cut off my balls and hurt Avril. I haven't been square with her and you probably don't know that some time ago, we'd broke up, but I can't be responsible for her getting hurt. As for Kelly-Ann, first of all, I know nothing about her murder, so please believe me, but if the cops are looking for suspects for killing her, I'd let them know about that pair of..."*

She grimaced apologetically and told him, "it's the C word, if you don't mind?"

He nodded with a smile that she should continue.

Secondly, I got one of the doormen to put her into a taxi and that's the last I saw of her. Anyway, I'm off for good. There's too much pressure between those scummies and my fear of being caught for my scam because you won't know this, but I've been screwing the company for years now. I've built up a wee nest egg that I'm taking abroad with me. I know I'm leaving a shit load of trouble behind me and I'm sorry I let you and Avril down. She knows about me screwing the company, but she's never been any part of it, so I hope she doesn't end up in the shit over what I did. Sorry, pal and please, can you let the police know what I've told you about Donaldson and McGuire and can you explain to Avril for me? Mark."

He took a breath and staring at her, could see the fear in her eyes; fear that Peter Donaldson and Foxy McGuire would take some sort of revenge on her. Reaching across the table, he removed the letter from her limp fingers then folding it, returned it to the envelope and placed it into the inside pocket of his jacket.

Inwardly he was absolutely incensed with rage at Ritchie's cowardly betrayal of Avril, leaving her to face Donaldson and McGuire alone.

"Here we go," the waitress cheerfully laid down two mugs and the plate with the roll, but the seeing Avril's face, asked, "You okay, hen? You want a glass of water or something?"

"No, I'm fine. Thanks, Donna," she forced a smile and waved the waitress away.

He knew he had to say something that would comfort and assure her, but was also aware that whatever he did say would commit him to her.

It was then he made up his mind and gently taking her hand, told her, "I won't let them or anyone hurt you, Avril. I promise."

She bit at her lower lip and he saw tears forming in her eyes when, her voice quivering, she asked, "How can you protect me, Alex? I mean you can't be with me twenty-four hours a day. If those two…" she closed her eyes tightly and paused, then re-opening her eyes, said again, "If those two decide that they're going to hurt me, then they will. I probably don't know as much about them as you do, but I know enough that they're really bad and that skinny one, McGuire, he hurts people. I've heard the rumours," she shuddered.

But not before I get to *them*, he inwardly thought as an idea began to form in his head; an idea that he decided not to share with her for fear that she might inadvertently disclose it to someone else.

However, his eyes narrowed, in the meantime there was another option regarding Ritchie's scam.

With no appetite for the roll, he suggested they return to her office then settling the bill, escorted her across the road where the duty doorman admitted them into the building at the staff entrance in Gibson Street.

Returned to her office, he sat her down at her typewriter then laid his idea before her.

Her eyes narrowing, she said, "So, you want me to type a letter supposedly from Mark that admits he stole money from the company?"

"Yes, and make sure there's quite a few spelling mistakes in the letter too, because I'm guessing he's not a typist?"

"No, he's not," she replied, her voice a mere whisper.

"Then, when you've typed the letter, we'll forge his signature. You can do that, can't you?"

"Well, yes," she agreed, but he could tell the doubt lingered there. Then she asked, "But why not use the letter he left you? I mean, that's in his handwriting isn't it and it's as good a confession as a typed letter."

"I know," he patiently explained, "but the letter also says Donaldson and his crony are dealing drugs in the place and without evidence, the police won't be able to arrest them. That means they'll still be out there and believe me, they'll find out the letter was handed to the cops and they won't be happy about it."

Then, his voice low, he added, "I'll deal with them in my own way, Avril, because I'm not letting them hurt you."

She had the good sense not to ask what his intentions were, but understanding his reasoning, began to type.

Thirty minutes later when her second attempt was finished, they again pored over it and finally agreed it contained enough details of Ritchie's confession. At his instruction, she also added a line that stated Ritchie did indeed see Kelly-Ann Knox at the dancing on Saturday night. He explained it would be better for her to inform the CID at Pollok before they discovered it themselves.

Her final act with the letter was forging Ritchie's distinctive scrawl.

"What you need to do now is phone the company representative and have them inform the company that Mark didn't show for work today and you've discovered the letter with his confession and his plan to go abroad, then contact the CID and tell them about Mark seeing Kelly-Ann here on Saturday. As for the letter," he smiled, "there shouldn't be any doubt about its authenticity because as Mark's secretary, you'll be able to identify the signature as being his. After you make your calls, I can only imagine the company accountants will be all over his office like a bad rash and of course, they'll want to check the ledgers."

"What if they call the police in to check the accounts? How will I explain he never let me examine the ledgers?" her face expressed her panic.

He grimaced then shaking his head, replied, "I think that's unlikely, at least in the beginning. If they had any chance of arresting Mark, then they'd probably call in the cops, but if he's on the run abroad and they've no hope of getting their money back, I think the company will probably try to keep it under wraps for as long as possible because they'll be worried it will attract bad publicity. I think we both know enough about Mark to guess that if he is away abroad and doesn't want to be found, he probably won't be."

He stared at her then encouragingly said, "You'll be under some scrutiny too, Avril, but don't worry about being nervous. They'll expect that. All you have to do is keep denying you knew anything about the ledgers, that it was Mark who insisted on doing the books, okay?"

"I'm not certain I can go through with this, Alex," her lips trembled.

He stared down at her then gently pulling her from the chair, hugged her close to him as her body trembled and her tears fell against his jacket.

"Yes, you can, Avril," he softly told her, "and I'll be here at five o'clock to take you safely home."

****

The unshaven man wearing the rumpled trousers and black leather jacket and who carried the battered suitcase, exchanged forty pounds sterling for Spanish pesetas, then wandered through Heathrow Terminal Three to the Iberia desk, where he loitered with a paper cup of weak coffee.

Almost with relief, he smiled when the tannoy announced that the flight to Madrid was soon to board.

Approaching the desk, he joined the short queue then minutes later, offered his passport to the smiling attendant who checking it, smiled and politely said, "Have a good flight, Mr Ritchie."

CHAPTER ELEVEN

With the surveillance team assembled in the largest room at Stewart Street, DS Shona Burns ensured that DI Alice Meechan was in her office then closed the door to the room before giving DS Barney Fellowes the nod that he could begin.

"Right, guys, as you all know, Tango Three of Knox's team, our very own Kevin Stobbie, met his maker yesterday and so we can assume that he won't ever again be coming out to play."

His comment drew some mirth, but then his expression changed when he continued, "The downside of Stobbie's departure of him shuffling off this mortal coil," with a smile he turned to Burns and said, "Shakespeare, Shona."

When the laughter died down, he continued, "As I said, the downside is that unfortunately we were outside his flat when the dirty deed was done. Now, this stays in the room," he cast a warning glance about the faces. "The DI in her wisdom," then ignored the rude groans and sarcastic grins, "has changed the log to indicate us leaving the plot prior to Stobbie's murder."

As he expected, there were several gasps and heads turning as the team glanced uncertainly about them.

It was a DC with a strong Fife accent who said, "I'm not speaking to that, big man. If she wants to corrupt the surveillance log, that's her lookout, but if I'm asked…"

He got no further for Fellowes held up a hand for silence, then said, "And that's why I've gathered you all together. If it *is* highlighted to the bosses that the log has been changed, I want you all to know that neither Shona nor I will condone what she's done and it's my opinion that you guys should be straight up, if the situation does arise. I do not want anyone here to risk their career because the DI has made what in my opinion is, a really stupid decision."

"Barney, maybe I'm being a bit naive here," began a young female detective, "but why is she even bothering changing the log?"

"Simply put, she's worried if it's discovered we were outside Stobbie's flat when he was murdered, it will reflect badly on her."

"So," the young woman's brow creased, "when and if the time comes, she expects us to lie to save her bloody career?"

A slow smile spread across Fellowes face when he nodded, then said, "The DI also wants us to continue our surveillance against

Knox's team this morning, in the belief that they will hit the cash in transit delivery down in the Clydebank."

"After everything that's happened? Bollocks," was one sharp response while others shook their heads in disbelief.

"Anyway," Fellowes, shrugged, "that's the instruction, so that's what we're going to do. However," he stared around the room with a mischievous glint in his eye, "I don't believe there's any hurry to get to the plot, so I suggest that we head for brekkies at the wee café on the Dumbarton Road, the one we used the other week. We'll meet there and have some scran before we get going. Once we're fed we can have another think about our plans for today. Everybody okay with that?"

There were plenty of knowing grins and nods before the meeting broke up.

****

Arriving at Pollok Police station, DCI Martin Benson joined DI Roddy Williams and the office manager, DS Mhari McGregor, in Williams' office to discuss the lack of progress in their hunt for the killer of Kelly-Ann Knox.

"The problem is, as I'm sure you're aware, boss," McGregor, a notepad on her knee, sat forward then said, "we've no confirmation she was at the Barrowland on Saturday night and without any information where she socialised that evening, we're on a hiding to nothing trying to trace her movements. That and there's nothing to tell us who she might have been socialising with."

"What about the suspicion she caught a private hire when she left her flat? Anything come of that?"

McGregor sighed before she replied, "I've had some of the team out on Actions contacting the local private hire companies, but some of them have admitted their records aren't as up to date as they could be. However, they'll put the word out to their drivers and it's the east end, sir," she reminded him and stared meaningfully at Benson, "so we're talking about several dozens of drivers, some of whom are renting the taxis and the callsigns from the owners and working for cash in hand, so they're not registered with the company. In short, I'm not holding my breath for a result, there."

He nodded slowly, then said, "Roddy, how did it go with Mike Thorburn over in Maryhill?"

"Like us, boss, he's keen to share what information he can and like us, has a niggling feeling that his murder and ours are linked somewhere. Though unlike us," he added with a sigh, "he's got a full twenty-storey building of flats for his guys to do a door to door, with a better likelihood that somebody might have seen something he can work with."

"Have you let Mhari know how we got on last night, at George Knox's house?"

"Aye, boss, I'm up to date with that," she interrupted with a nod.

"What about the list of staff from the Barrowland," Benson asked McGregor. "Did Elaine and young Ailish speak to the manager again?"

"We've got the list, boss, and I've a team working their way through it on the phones, but the staff we can't contact by phone, I'll need to raise Actions to have them visited."

"Okay," Benson rubbed at his forehead, then was about to speak when the door was knocked by Willie McBride who said, "Sorry to barge in, boss, but I've just taken a phone call from an Avril Collins who works in the Barrowland."

"And?"

"Well," McBride stepped further into the room, then glancing down at a scrap of paper he carried in his hand, said, "she told me she's the secretary to the manager, a guy called Mark Ritchie. It seems that Ritchie's done a bunk and left a letter confessing to stealing money from the company that runs the Barrowland. Also in the letter, he's apparently admitted he did see our victim at the dancing there on Saturday night."

Benson, his eyes suddenly bright, glanced at Williams then said, "That's the first piece of good news we've had. Now we have a starting point for our investigation."

"Aye, boss, but there's a downside too," cautioned Williams. "If the media get a hold of this information, we're going to be inundated with Bible John nutters."

"We'll deal with that if it happens, Roddy, but right now," he turned towards McBride and asked, "This woman Collins, did she say anything else?"

"Not about the victim, boss," he shook his head. "She did tell me she'd contacted the company head office and was waiting for some representative to attend at her office to deal with the situation. She sounded pretty nervous and it sounded to me like she might have been crying," he volunteered.

"Right then, Willie, as you've spoken with this woman, grab yourself a neighbour and get over to the Barrowland. I want you to find out what the score is with this guy who's disappeared and confirm this letter says our victim was there on Saturday night. If he's buggered off, we might be looking at a suspect for our murder."

****

In his flat in Barmulloch, George Knox was still trying to come to terms with losing both his daughter and his long-time friend in just two days.

While his grandson played in the spare room, he sat in the front room with Rosie, nursing a coffee and consistently going over in his head anything that wee Kevin had said, anything that might ring a bell and give some sort of clue as to who murdered him.

He glanced up when he heard the doorbell ring and watched as Rosie, rising from her chair, then said, "I'll get it."

A minute later he heard Alex Hardies voice telling her, "Aye, tea please, Rosie."

When the younger man entered the room, Knox nodded that he sit in the chair vacated by Rosie and asked, "Heard anything, son? Anything at all?"

In response and before he sat down, Hardie fetched the letter from his inner jacket pocket and handed it over to Knox.

Reading the letter, he saw Knox frown then ask, "This guy Mark. I take it he was the manager of the place?"

"Mark Ritchie, aye, but he's on his toes and I'm only guessing here mind, probably with a fair whack of the company's money. That and I'm also guessing he didn't want to be hanging around with Donaldson and McGuire on the scene."

Knox paled when he said, "So, it's likely they pair of bastards supplied the Coke to my lassie?"

Slowly nodding, Hardie replied, "It seems so, yes."

"Anything else that you can suggest?" he stared at Hardie.

His eyebrows narrowed before he replied, "You'll read in the letter, boss, that Ritchie knew that Kelly-Ann was full of the Coke on Saturday and that he told a doorman to put her into a taxi. It doesn't say who the doorman was, but I can find out from my friend Avril which stewards were on duty on Saturday night and when I speak to whoever this guy is, he might know which taxi company took her away from the dancing. You might not remember from your days at the dancing there," he worked at keeping his face straight, "but there's a taxi stance near the Barrowland and most of the drivers get their fares from the dancing."

"My days? Ya cheeky sod," Knox was forced to smile at the teasing jibe.

"Anyway," Hardie continued, "I'm hoping that I can track the driver down, see if he remembers picking her up and where he took her. Might give us something," he mused.

"Good one, son," Knox nodded. "That sounds like a starter for ten." Knox, a man who had left school aged fourteen with no qualifications and grown up initially serving as an apprentice in the Shettleston Ironworks, had what he jokingly called a degree in life. Calm by nature and never quick to judge, he had learned from an early age to consider all the facts and options before coming to a decision, an ability that had served him well. Clever and painstakingly meticulous and to the frustration of the police, his talent for organisation had kept him and his team out of prison, unlike many of his criminal peers.

Part of that talent had been recognising that the men who worked with him, other than himself and Jimmy Dunlop, who had wives and whose wives had no close ties to anyone, had no immediate family. Yes, Kevin Stobbie had a sister, but from whom he was totally estranged.

Alex Hardie had a brother who had abandoned him to an aunt that had died many years previously while the man Hardie replaced, the former associate, Ernie Wiseman, was a widower with no children. And so, the closeness and trust that developed between the men who had become the team, had formed them into their own family unit. Losing Wiseman to cancer, then Stobbie to murder had hurt George Knox as though the two deceased men had been brothers.

"Penny for them," Hardie softly said, bringing Knox back to reality.

"Eh? Oh, sorry, son. I was miles away," Knox exhaled.

"I can understand that, boss, given everything that you and Rosie have been through in the last couple of days."

"Right what was I going to say," Knox abruptly continued. "Aye, Kelly-Ann. It wasn't the Coke that killed her," he muttered, his fingers entwined on his lap.

Seeing the expression of surprise on Hardie's face, he continued, "I'm not for one minute excusing that pair, son, and they'll pay for giving her the drugs, but why I'm wondering, would they kill Kelly-Ann if she was a customer?"

"Just a thought, boss, and don't be jumping down my throat here," he held both hands up in a defensive posture, "but we both know she wasn't the most dependable woman when it came to looking for a job or keeping one and, you've said yourself in the past, she was always looking for handouts. So, is there any likelihood she might have been working for Donaldson? That maybe there was a falling out?"

Knox's brow creased and his lips tightened as he considered the question then slowly shaking his head, softly replied, "I just don't know, Alex. I'm *hoping* not, but then again, just how well did I know my own daughter?" he bitterly asked.

He paused as though deliberating, then said, "I know you're doing your best, son, but we need to find out more before we make a move against that pair. The last I heard, they've got some muscle working for them these days. You agree?"

He watched Hardie's face tighten and asked, "What?"

"I was thinking, boss, that the letter suggests they might have a go at Avril, so I was going to pay them a wee visit to warn them off."

"Remind me again, who is Avril?"

"Eh, she's the lassie in the letter there. A woman I know. She worked for Ritchie as his personal assistant."

Knox smiled then asked, "And how well do you know her?"

Hardie shrugged in return before he replied, "We're getting on okay, boss."

But then to his own surprise, he admitted, "I'd be gutted if anything happened to her. I've already told her that I'd look after her if Donaldson or that bastard McGuire tried anything."

There was a pause before Knox softly asked, "This lassie mean something special to you, Alex?"

He took a breath before slowly nodding, then said, "It's starting to look like it, boss."

Knox, a man brought up with old-fashioned Protestant family values, nodded then said, "If that's what you told her son, then that's what you do. You're nothing if you can't keep your word and particularly to a woman. How do you propose to go about it?"

"If you're okay with it, I was going to pay a visit to Donaldson and warn him off Avril. I was hoping to have Jimmy drive me to Donaldson's place and have him sit in the car outside with a shooter, just in case it goes wrong, you know?"

"Might be a bit dodgy if the cops are still watching us, son, but here's another option. Why don't you arrange a meeting with Donaldson, somewhere neutral where me and Jimmy can be there before you and back you if it goes apeshit."

"Boss," he waved a hand, "you've got enough going on with losing Kelly-Ann and Kevin. I appreciate it, but…"

"But nothing," Knox sharply interrupted. "We're a team, Alex, and I'm not going to risk anybody else."

Hiding his smile, Hardie nodded then agreed, "Okay."

"Here we go," Rosie pushed open the door, a mug of tea in one hand and a plate with two rolls in the other. "I know you said you're not hungry, Alex, but I've never known you to refuse a bacon roll."

"Thanks, Rosie," he smiled at her, then turning to Knox, said, "When I've had my grub, boss, I'll phone the pub Donaldson usually hangs out in and find out if he's there."

"Peter Donaldson?" Rosie sharply glanced at her husband before asking, "Why is Alex phoning him?"

"A wee bit of business, hen," Knox replied, his eyes meeting hers with the unspoken suggestion she doesn't ask and he'll not lie.

"Aye, well, you be careful round that man, Alex. I've heard he's bad news," she sniffed then left the room to check on her grandson.

"How is she holding up?" Hardie asked.

"I'm worried about her," Knox shook his head. "Right now she's got the wee man to care for and she's fussing over him. He's having a hard time of it, too, and keeps asking for his mammy, but what can we tell him," he sighed.

The sat in silence while Hardie finished his rolls, then getting to his feet said, "I'll make that call and let you know how I get on."

****

Instructed to wait in the staff canteen downstairs, Avril Collins nervously drummed her fingers on the table to, occasionally smiling at the curious cleaning staff when they caught her eye and who likely were also wondering where Mark Ritchie had got to and what the hell was going on upstairs in the administration offices.

Following her phone call to the company office two hours previously, John Bradley, the cheery representative she knew well from his visits to Mark, arrived with three other suited colleagues, one a frosty faced woman of indeterminate age, who after Bradley had read the typed note, curtly sent Avril off to the canteen.

Though she wasn't present, she had no doubt the offices would be getting torn apart as the four company reps searched for evidence of Ritchie's wrongdoing.

At last and two coffee's later, a worried Avril was summoned from the canteen by the same woman who neither spoke nor glanced in her direction as they made their way upstairs.

Ushered into Ritchie's office, she saw Bradley sat behind the desk with a younger male colleague sitting to one side of the room, a notepad in his hand.

"Ah, Avril, please," Bradley indicated with his hand, "take a seat." He didn't speak for almost a full minute, but stared down at the typed letter on the desk before him.

At last, holding the letter up between a forefinger and thumb, he asked, "Can you explain this?"

Her mouth dry and her stomach tensing, she shook her head then forcing herself to be calm, she replied, "What's there to explain, John. I arrived at the office to find that Mark, who's usually first in each morning, isn't here. I try to phone him at his flat to find out if I've missed some appointment he might have had elsewhere, but there's no reply. I wonder if he's had an accident or something, but decide to wait till lunchtime to phone around the casualty wards. I return to my desk out there," he nods at the closed the door, "take the cover off my typewriter and that letter falls onto my lap. At first," she shrugs, "I'm thinking it's a joke, but then realise if he's not here to explain the joke, well," she briefly pauses, then taking a breath, adds, "I phone you. I also phoned the police at Pollok about the bit that says Mark saw Kell-Ann Knox, the dead woman, here at the dancing, last Saturday night."

"And you've no idea where he might be?"

"Nope," she truthfully shook her head.

"Are you absolutely certain, Avril? I mean, you two being an item…"

"I'll stop you right there, John," she irately interrupted him, now into her role as the aggrieved personal assistant. "If you thought Mark and I were still having a relationship, then I have to inform you that ended a year ago when I found out he was shagging some other member of staff."

"Oh, I'm sorry," he was immediately flustered. "I didn't realise you'd, ah, broken up."

She seized the opportunity and went on the attack, irately telling him, "Yes, and if you think I'd any inkling that he was thieving money from the company, do you honestly believe I'd have kept my mouth shut? It's *my* bloody reputation too, you know."

She saw him nervously lick at his lips before he asked, "But the ledgers, Avril. Weren't you involved in…"

"Again I'll stop you there," she could feel her face redden and sensed the younger man sitting to one side, was shrinking into his chair and hoped it was from her anger.

"You might recall, John, that Mark insisted on being present at every Saturday night dance or show. No matter that even *you*," she forcibly pointed her forefinger at Bradley, "tried to persuade him to deputise on some Saturday's, he wouldn't and now we know why. And no," she shook her head. "Even with my accountancy qualification, he refused to permit me to assist him with the ledgers *and* if you recall, I actually once brought it to your attention."

"Eh, yes, of course," he nodded.

She could not believe her own audacity for she had lied about bringing it to his attention, but gambled that he wouldn't recall, that Bradley's pride would not permit him to refute her claim.

Her arms now folded, she stared at the flummoxed rep then softly said, "I can't believe he did this. The company have always been very fair with him and me, too. Are you able to assess how much he stole?"

Bradley blew through pursed lips, then shaking his head, replied, "No, not yet. We'll need to bring in a firm of Forensic Accountants and their investigation could take weeks, if not months," he sighed.

"What about the police? I phoned them," she began, "but that was after I contacted you first."

"And you did absolutely the correct thing," he hurriedly replied, then glancing uncertainly at the man sitting to his left, leaned forward onto his forearms and added, "If the police are made aware of a complaint of theft, that will be a decision for the Board."

Her mind racing, she thought, Alex was right, they don't want a public scandal.

Time for the distraught female, she decided and placing her face in her hands forced a sob, then said, "How the hell he managed to fool me all those years. God, I feel like a right idiot."

"Will you fetch Avril a glass of water," he turned to his colleague, who rushed from the room, preferring to leave Bradley with the apparent distraught woman than get involved.

Rising from his chair, he moved around the desk and uncertainly began to pat her on the back.

When the young man returned with the water, she wiped at her eyes and taking a drink, gasped, then asked Bradley, "Is there anything I can tell you that will help catch him, John?"

"Oh, no, my dear, I think you've done enough for today, but of course, if anything comes to mind?"

She favoured him with a wide though slightly teary smile then replied, "I'll be sure to phone you."

"Yes, well," he brightly said, "as I can clearly see you've had a bit of a shock, why don't you do yourself a favour and take the rest of the day off; go home and recharge your batteries, as it were."

With a subtle glance at the clock on the wall behind him, she could see it was gone five o'clock and as her shift finished at five-thirty anyway, it wasn't much of a favour.

However, with a nod and a grateful smile, she rose and left the office.

****

DS Willie McBride with his neighbour, Ailish MacDonald, arrived at Mark Ritchie's office to find the company's accountants sifting through the ledgers.

Introducing themselves to the man in charge, John Bradley, McBride asked to speak with Avril Collins and see the letter she had found.

His face screwed up as though in concentration, Bradley nervously asked, "Might I ask how the information you have about Mr Ritchie absconding with the company's money will be viewed by your superiors? I mean, will I be required to give you statement or something like that?"

McBride, not wanting to get caught up in what was a local Divisional CID matter and which should rightly be reported to them, deftly replied, "My concern, Mr Bradley is more to do with the murder investigation of Kelly-Ann Knox and the information that I believe is contained in the letter discovered by Ritchie's personal assistant, Miss Collins, that refers to our victim being here on Saturday night. So, if you please," he reached out a hand with the determined expression that the company rep should not even consider holding back on the letter.

"If you'll permit me to photocopy the letter first, for our records," explained Bradley.

"Of course," McBride graciously agreed.

The letter now in his hand, McBride then asked, "And where can I find Miss Collins?"

"I regret she was in a bit of a state so I suggested she go home. That was about twenty minutes ago," he grimaced, "but I can provide you with her home address and phone number, if you wish?"

"Please," McBride nodded, though slightly miffed that it seemed he was to a have yet another late finish.

****

As it happened, McBride and his neighbour were both unaware that they had just missed Avril Collins, when passing by in the corridor where the woman's staff toilet was located, were unaware that Avril had been inside repairing her make-up and was now standing just inside the door of the staff entrance in Gibson Street, waiting on the arrival of Alex Hardie.

Almost to the minute, she heard the door being knocked and opening it, was met by Hardie who grinned, then said, "Taxi for Collins?" Courteously holding open the passenger door of his Capri, he took advantage of her getting into the car to admire her long legs and wondered how she would react to his plan.

Driving out of Gibson Street, she was surprised when turning right instead of turning left, she curiously asked, "Is this an alternative route to Cardonald?"

"Ah, about that," he briefly glanced at her. "I had an idea and before you get mad at me, I thought a couple of days away from your place might just be wiser than letting you go home right now."

"Oh," she pretended to be surprised, "and just where do you consider it will be safe for me?"

"Look, don't think I'm trying it on, Avril, but I've a spare room and if you're in my flat for a few days I don't have to worry about you being alone in your place."

Thrilled though she really was, nevertheless she pretended to protest by asking, "And for these few days am I to wear the same clothes and underwear then?"

His face clouded for he hadn't thought about that, then pulling into the side of the road, sighed before turning to her and replying, "Here's what we'll do. We'll drive to your place, you can grab what you need then I'll drop you at my flat. I've a meeting tonight, a business thing, but you should be safe in my place as long as you don't open the door to anyone, okay?"

"Okay," she meekly agreed.

He started the engine again and driving off, asked, "Right, you can direct me to your house and while I'm thinking about it, how did it go when you reported to the company about Mark legging it abroad?"

With a grin she related the story of phoning the company rep, John Bradley, who later interviewed her and giggled when she told of her lie that she had previously warned Bradley of Ritchie's insistence he alone handled the ledgers on a Saturday night.

"Bloody hell, woman," he gave her an admiring glance. "I was worried sick you were going to be too nervous and give the game away, but it sounds like you completely charmed them."

Then he asked, "What about the cops? Did you phone them about Kelly-Ann being at the dancing on Saturday night?"

"I did and spoke to a detective who said he'd be over to get the letter, but he hadn't arrived by the time I was leaving."

"Good," he nodded.

Arriving outside her house in Redpath Drive, Hardie elected to remain in the car while Avril fetched her clothes.

Just over ten minutes later she returned to the Capri with a small suitcase and smiling, said, "That should do me for a few days anyway."

As the car drove off, they were not to know the phone in her house was ringing.

CHAPTER TWELVE

Returning to Pollok Police station, Willie McBride and Ailish MacDonald arrived just in time for the DCI's evening briefing. "Ah, good, you're here," he waved for them to enter the already overcrowded room.

"Anything to report?"

"I have the letter, boss," he brandished it like a trophy, "that confirms the manager's statement that says our victim was at the dancing on Saturday night. Unfortunately, it seems to be confirmed the manager, Mark Ritchie, has legged it and that he *was* ripping his company off. At the minute, the guy I spoke to, a company representative called John Bradley, says they haven't officially reported the theft to the police and I reminded him if they do intend reporting it," he smiled, "it's an E Division investigation, so it'll be London Road he contacts."

"Good man, Willie, we've enough on our plate with this murder. Go on."

"We missed Ritchie's personal assistant, Avril Collins, the woman who phoned in the information and there's no response to her phone, but we have her address so we'll catch up with her in due course and obtain a statement regarding her discovering the letter."

"Anything else?"

McBride shook his head, then asked, "What did we miss?"

"Not a lot," Benson sighed. "The team have contacted most of the staff by phone, but only a few knew our victim and none can remember seeing her on Saturday night, so those we haven't been able to contact will have their doors chapped tomorrow."

"Right," he turned to the room in general, "I've spoken with DCI Mike Thorburn over in Maryhill who's handling the Kevin Stobbie murder investigation, but they're no further forward to identifying his killer, though they still have a number of floors in the high-rise flats to check in their door to door inquiries. That and there's nothing coming in from any sources, so the games still a bogey. However, DCI Thorburn and myself remain of the opinion that both victim's murders are linked and we're going to continue collaborating our investigations, so if during the course of your witness interviews, you pick up anything that suggests a connection, bring it immediately to the attention of DI Williams, DS McGregor or myself. Understood?"

He saw a number of heads nodding and heard mutters of, "Yes, boss."

"Right then, any questions?"

There were none, so Benson dismissed the team till the morning, but beckoned that Williams, McGregor and Willie McBride follow him to the DI's room.

Once they were settled in the room with cigarettes lit, he asked McBride for the letter, then reading it, said, "Any hint from this guy Bradley how much was stolen by Ritchie?"

"He's no idea, boss," McBride shook his head, "other than to say they'll get a better idea when they bring in a Forensic Accountancy firm. However, the Barrowland dancing on a Saturday night, being the popular venue it is and particularly if there is a headlining group playing, he's guessing at thousands, possibly five figures or more."

"Bloody hell," Benson was impressed. "Five figures, eh?" Then to laughter, he grinned at the DI, "Sounds like what you made in overtime for the year."

To more laughter, Williams, replied, "The way my first wife's screwing me over for cash, boss, you might be right."

Turning back to McBride, Benson asked, "And you said they haven't yet reported the theft to the police?"

"No, he admitted the bad press could harm the company."

"This man Ritchie," Benson thoughtfully said, "he's either a suspect or he could be a vital witness for us if he has knowledge of who our victim might have been with at the dancing. Mhari," he turned to the DS, "create an Action for two of our guys to track down Ritchie. Find out where he is or where he's gone. I know the suggestion is he's abroad, but that could be a blinder to throw us off the track for the theft of the money. Needless to say, if we do find him then we can pass the information to E Division if they *do* receive a complaint about the theft of the money, but *our* priority is finding out what he knows about our victim's movements on Saturday night."

"Boss," she acknowledged and was making a note in her pad, only to glance up when McBride said, "If it's okay with you, boss, I'll take that inquiry on."

"Okay, Willie," Benson nodded in agreement.

"Right then, if there's nothing else?" he glanced at the other three, noting their shaking heads.

"Okay, we'll have an early finish this evening, so till tomorrow morning then."

As the other three rose from their chairs, Williams asked, "You coming straight here in the morning, boss, or do you want me to conduct the briefing?"

"You do it, please, Roddy. I'm to travel to Pitt Street to meet with Mr Meadows. He wants to see me and Mike Thorburn to discuss the murders and our thoughts on a possible link."

"Good luck, then," Williams nodded.

****

Across the city, the Scottish Crime Squad team had all returned to their Stewart Street base where DS Barney Fellowes knocked on Alice Meechan's door to inform her, "Ma'am, that's us back. Nothing to report regarding George Knox's team."

She barely glanced up before waving a hand in acknowledgement then dryly said, "Fine. Have the typed log sent through to me for my inspection."

"Of course, Ma'am," Fellowes nodded.

Returning to the DS's room, he grinned at DS Shona Burns then said, "She wants the typed log."

"And here it is, big man," she whipped a sheet of paper from the typewriter then flourishing it in the air, handed it to him.

He glanced at the sheet, seeing sequential times during that day typed down one side of the paper with the words, 'No movement' typed against each recorded time.

Grinning at Burns, he said, "She's not the only bugger than can falsify a log," then his forehead creasing, asked, "Did you get your washing done?"

"Aye, then I picked up the wean from school before I came back here. You?"

He took a breath before he replied, "Did a bit of shopping with Jimmy Butler. We popped into Ralph Slater's and I ordered myself a new suit for my daughter's wedding in July."

"Well," she grinned at him, "here's hoping you stay the same size and you won't if you keep stuffing yourself with kebabs."

Then, her expression changing to a worried frown, she asked, "What if her ladyship through there finds out we gave the team a day to themselves?"

He pretended to be surprised then holding up the sheet of paper, he replied, "I have no idea what you mean, Detective Sergeant Burns. Here's the log that shows we were all out on an operation and just like the one on Monday, when Kevin Stobbie got murdered, it must be true because madam there is about to sign it."

With a grin, he left the room to take the log through to Meechan.

****

Strolling through Alex Hardie's flat, Avril Collins was reminded of the one night she had spent in the flat that it was not only clean and tidy, but tastefully decorated too.

Watching her, he guessed her thoughts and remarked with a grin, "You think because I'm a man I must live like a pig?"

"No, not at all," she blushed, then with a grimace added, "Well, maybe. When I visited Mark's flat over in Garnethill, I spent half my time there picking up after him."

"Well, living with an aunt like I had, I'm domesticated," he smiled, "so you'll not need to pick up after me."

Glancing at his wristwatch, he continued, "Sorry, but I'm running a bit tight for that business meeting. There should be something in the fridge that you can grab for dinner."

"Oh, right. Do you know when you're coming home?" she asked, then, as if realising she was putting him under some pressure, hastily added, "I mean, I can hang on and rustle up something for us both, if you're not too late."

"Afraid not, Avril, I've no idea how long I'll be, but if I get the opportunity, I'll phone you here and let you know. In the meantime, I suggest you just go ahead and eat."

"Right," she nodded a little too eagerly, she thought and so forced a smile.

Their parting was a little awkward; he wondering if he should kiss her cheerio and she wondering if she should have walked him to the door with a peck on the cheek.

In the end she stood by the kitchen door and waved him off. Walking downstairs, Hardie's thoughts turned to the planned meeting with Peter Donaldson and Foxy McGuire. Though he didn't know Donaldson other than by reputation, his one-time confrontation with McGuire as well as his reputation caused him to suspect the vicious gangster was unlikely to arrive without some kind of weapon and possibly handers, too.

Getting into the Capri he continued to go over in his head the plan that he'd worked out with the boss.
Taking a breath, he started the engine and curiously, was surprised how tense he felt.
****

According to the dashboard clock, Hardie arrived three minutes before the meeting time at seven. Stopping the Capri on Monteith Row several feet from the rear of a new, silver coloured Range Rover that was parked adjacent to the gate that led down the steps to the front of the Peoples Palace. He recognised the Range Rover as probably the same one he'd seen them exit outside the Barrowland then glanced up and through the Capri's windscreen, seeing the dark clouds that once more threatened to unleash their full watery fury upon the streets below.

But for now, the rain was merely a drizzle.

He sat for a few minutes, slowly turning his head and peering into the darkness around the Capri. However, the slight fall of rain not only obscured his vision, but with the engine switched off, the windows quickly began to steam up.

He smiled self-consciously at the butterflies in his stomach and inwardly chided himself for feeling so foolish.

The plan was that the boss and Jimmy would be at the venue well before seven and though he had no hope of seeing them, trusted that they would be in a position to protect him if the meeting went sideways.

"Okay, Alex, here we go," he muttered to himself, then turning up the collar of his overcoat, got out of the car.

The Peoples Palace, constructed in the latter part of the nineteenth century as a museum and art gallery for the benefit of the common people of Glasgow and with a world-renowned glass enclosed winter gardens at the rear of the building, was designed to reflect the social history of Glasgow from the mid-eighteenth century onwards.

But at seven o'clock that evening, the beauty and majesty of the building was lost on Hardie, for his interest lay solely in the meeting with Donaldson and McGuire that had been arranged to take place at the ornate, terracotta Victorian fountain that lay directly in front of the building.

Halting in front of the open gate at the top of the steps leading down to the fountain, Hardie stared through the darkness and the falling rain and could see two figures, huddled beneath an overlarge umbrella and who were standing in front of the fountain. On either side of the fountain stood two more men, both tall and burly and dressed in dark clothing with both wearing the ubiquitous Glasgow headgear, the bunnet, and with their hands thrust into their coat pockets.

He smiled for he had been correct in his assessment; Donaldson and his sidekick had come with a couple of minders.

Once more trusting that as long as George Knox and Jimmy Dunlop were nearby he was safe, he began to walk down the stairs though he could not help but feel some trepidation.

As the seconds passed and as he descended the stairs, he fought the urge to glance at the area surrounding the fountain that was overgrown with thick shrubs and inwardly prayed to a God he no longer believed in that the boss and Jimmy were hidden somewhere in the foliage.

He stopped more than a few yards from the two men with the brolly and though it had been some years since he had seen him, immediately recognised McGuire and so assumed the other, a man his own height but with jowly cheeks and seemingly running to fat, must be Donaldson.

To his surprise, it seemed to Hardie that Donaldson was either born with a misshapen nose or at some time it had been injured for it turned up at the end so sharply it almost resembled a snout.

Turning to stare at McGuire, he noticed a white four-inch scar that run vertically down his left cheek and not recalling having seen it before, assumed it must have occurred since they first encountered each other.

He inwardly smiled, recalling that years before, George Knox had once taught him, "It's easier to begin being civil, son. Then if it's needed, you can work up to a rage. It's a lot harder than if you go in heavy-handed and have to climb back down to being civil."

And so, the lesson learned, he had decided that there was no reason to be anything but civil and greeted them with, "Mr Donaldson, Mr McGuire, my name's Alex Hardie. Thank you for meeting with me, particularly," he glanced up at the dark skies, "on such a rotten night."

Almost at once, McGuire mistook his polite civility for weakness and leaning forward from the umbrella with his bare head exposed to the rain, sneeringly replied, "Cut the crap, pal, what the fuck you wanting?"

It was then that Donaldson, his right hand holding the brolly, placed his free hand on McGuire's arm as though to restrain him, before asking in a high pitched, almost effeminate voice, "It must be important, Foxy, if Mr Hardie here thinks so by dragging us out on such an *awful* night. So, Mr Hardie, what can we do for you?"

Disregarding McGuire's hostility, he ignored the stick-thin man and concentrated on staring at Donaldson, before he replied, "I've no doubt you will know who I am, Mr Donaldson, and though we've never met, you'll also know that I run with George Knox and Jimmy Dunlop."

A slow smile spread across Donaldson's face when his voice almost a sneer, he said, "And I believe that also included Kevin Stobbie, but oh dear; I understand he's just been taken out of the game, or so I hear."

Hardie kept his face straight before he responded in a voice oozing menace, "That's correct and the man or woman who murdered Kevin; well, we *will* find them. Please be assured of that."

If he was expecting some sort of reaction to his comment, to his surprise it didn't show on either Donaldson or McGuire's face and in that heartbeat of a second, doubt crept into his mind; is it possible they had nothing to do with Kevin's murder?

"So, I reiterate, Mr Hardie, what can we do for you?"

"You'll be aware that Mark Ritchie is on his toes?"

He was pleased to see that simple statement *did* provoke a reaction, albeit slight, when Donaldson's pig like eyes widened and McGuire, his face contorting, turned to his boss then muttered, "What the fuck…?"

His eyes boring into Hardies, Donaldson coolly asked, "And why would that be of interest to us, Mr Hardie?"

"Well," he drawled, his eyes returning Donaldson's stare, "according to the letter that Ritchie left, he cited one of the reasons for him leaving town is that he was afraid of you and your pal there, Mr McGuire, because you had threatened him that if he didn't help you introduce your drugs into the Barrowland, you'd cut off his balls. The letter also indicated that you might hurt his personal secretary, Avril Collins, who I think is also known to you."

Even in the darkness, Hardie could see Donaldson's face pale at the thought such a letter might find its way into the hands of the police, then asked, "This letter, where is it?"

"In a safe place," Hardie smiled, knowing he had rattled Donaldson's chain, if not McGuire's, who continued to stare venomously at him.

"And your purpose in coming here tonight? Is it to gain some sort of advantage by letting us know you have the letter?"

"No," he calmly shook his head. "I'm here tonight to warn you both that Avril Collins is under my protection and that if any harm should come to her, I'll murder the two of you."

There was no immediate reaction from either of them for all of two seconds, but then he could see his threat had hit home.

It was then McGuire tried to lunge forward as though about to tackle him, but again was restrained by Donaldson who struggling to keep McGuire back, snarled at Hardie through gritted teeth, then softly replied, "I don't think you're really in any position to threaten us, Mr Hardie. In case you didn't notice, you're outnumbered four to one."

With a show of confidence that he scarcely felt, Hardie shrugged, then staring at Donaldson, thoughtfully replied with a cold smile, "Let me see. You, you fat fuck I can take with one hand. Your weasel of a pal there," without looking at him he nodded towards McGuire, "will go down next."

While they stared unbelievingly at him, he continued, "And as for those two gorillas you brought with you as your minders," he smiled as he nodded towards the one on his right who like the second minder, had realised something was amiss and both began to walk quickly towards the front of the fountain.

However, to Donaldson's surprise, almost lazily Hardie raised his left hand into the air and almost immediately, a shotgun blast echoed across the darkness.

Startled, Donaldson fearfully dropped the umbrella to the ground then both men stooped low and almost into a crouch as though fearing the shot was aimed at them.

The two minders also stopped dead, their heads swivelling on their shoulders as they scanned the darkness to their left, right and behind them.

"What the...?" began Donaldson and like the other three, continued to stare about him for the source of the shotgun blast.

His surprise was interrupted by Hardie, who evenly said, "You don't think I'd be stupid enough to come without my own minders, Mr Donaldson, do you? Now, we'll call it a night, but again, I'm warning you both. Continue with your own profession, if you want," he sneered, "dealing that shite that you peddle. But come anywhere near Avril Collins or *anyone* I hold dear and by Christ," both his face and his voice hardened, "I'll come for you and I swear to God, I'll make you suffer before I kill you."

He didn't wait for a response and though his heart was beating a tattoo in his chest and his legs were trembling, turned and thrusting his shaking hands into his coat pockets, began to retrace his steps to Monteith Row, forcing himself to walk slowly and casually away. Behind him, though he couldn't hear what was being said, he heard Donaldson trying to calm an enraged McGuire, but didn't turn for if either McGuire or the two minders had come after him, he knew he'd be alerted by another shotgun blast.

Reaching his car, his hands continued to shake as he fetched the keys from his overcoat pocket then getting in and starting the engine, took a long breath before he pulled smoothly away from the kerb.

As he drove, he regretted not asking Donaldson about Kelly-Ann, but Knox had been insistent that tonight was not the time.

"Besides," Knox had told him, "I've other plans for getting that information."

He hadn't pressed him what those plans were, but Hardie knew that when those plans *were* disclosed, someone was going to feel pain and lots of it.

****

Watching Alex Hardie walking off from the fountain, the larger of the two minders who'd stood to the left of the fountain, breathed a sigh of relief.

He hated working for the fat bastard Donaldson and as for McGuire, he was just an evil wee shite.

But he needed the money and the last person he expected to see that night was Alex, a man to whom he owed a great debt.

When he'd spotted who they'd come to meet, he'd pulled his bunnet tightly down and inwardly prayed Alex wouldn't recognise him.

He was relieved that it hadn't come to a physical confrontation, that after having their meeting, Alex had walked off though admittedly, he'd almost shit himself when the shotgun went off.

Now hurriedly making his way to the Range Rover to drive Donaldson, McGuire and the other minder back to The Talisman pub in Springburn, he inwardly grinned at the way Alex had dealt with the two sods.
Just a pity, he thought as pokerfaced, he held open the door for Donaldson, that the shotgun blast hadn't taken this prick's face off.

CHAPTER THIRTEEN

Wednesday morning began with what the Weegies call 'a right dreich day,' with rain pelting down onto the streets and soaking those unfortunate to be walking in them.
Lazily, Alex Hardie turned in his bed and though the blinds were tightly closed, he could hear the rain thundering against the single pane window.
Alarmed, his eyes narrowed and he startled for the briefest of seconds when he heard noises coming from the kitchen, but then relaxed when he remembered that Avril was staying with him.
Not in his room, he ruefully smiled, for returning home late last night, he had discovered her in pyjamas with his heavy cotton robe wrapped about her and to his surprise, she'd guessed he'd be hungry and had made him a chicken pasta.
While he ate, they had talked and though the conversation had become almost intimate, at no time did either he or she suggest sharing a bed.
When at last she had risen from the kitchen table, reminding him that whether Mark Ritchie was there or not, for now she still had her job to go to and with a gentle kiss to his forehead, left him to clear up.
He'd been tempted to take her in his arms, tear off her robe and pyjamas then carry her through to his bedroom, but with an inward jolt, remembered his promise to her that his flat was to be her place for safety, not an opportunity for him to come on to her.
Pity, he'd smiled at the thought and idly wondered; how would Avril have reacted if he *had* offered to take her to bed?
Swinging his legs out of bed, he idly scratched at himself then with a yawn, rose to his feet.

Recalling that Avril had use of his robe, he pulled opened a drawer in the large wooden chest of drawers and fetched out a loose-fitting navy-blue coloured tracksuit bottom and trousers, then pulled them on.

Rubbing wearily at his unruly hair, he made his way into the hallway and almost immediately, sniffed deeply at the tantalising smell of frying bacon.

Heading for the bathroom, he passed by the kitchen door and called out, "Morning."

Avril, her shoulder length blonde hair tied back into a tight ponytail and wearing a white blouse, black knee length pencil skirt and his black and white butchers' apron and shiny black low-heeled shoes, smiled then said, "Breakfast when you're ready, so you've got time for a shower before I serve it then I'm off in twenty minutes to work."

He stared at her for a few seconds, unconsciously smiling and before he replied, thought, this is a sight I could get used to then said, "I'll be quick, I promise."

As good as his word, within ten minutes he was shaved showered and dressed again in the tracksuit.

Rubbing vigorously at his damp hair, he returned to the kitchen where Avril placed a fry-up down on the table and said, "Sit."

"Yes, Ma'am," he grinned cheekily at her, then noticed when she sat opposite she had just toast and coffee.

"Too early for a fry-up?" he asked.

"No," she shook her head, then added, "I'm not keen for a big breakfast, but that doesn't mean I can't make you one," she smiled at him.

He saw her check her wristwatch and said, "You do know I'm taking you to work?"

"Oh, no," she waved a hand at him, "I'll get a bus or jump a taxi or something. You take your time and…"

But she got no further for he held up his own hand and interrupted with, "It's not open to debate, Avril. I'm not exposing you to any kind of risk."

Her face paled when she asked, "You seriously think that Donaldson and his pet dog might come after me?"

He couldn't help but smile at her apt description of Foxy McGuire, then told her, "Besides, I need you to check what security were on the door on Saturday night. Mark Ritchie's letter says that he left Kelly-Ann with one of the doormen to put her into a taxi. If I'm to find the taxi driver, first I'll need to speak to the doorman to get a description of the taxi."

"Oh, of course," she nodded, then smiling, said, "At least we'll get to spend a little more time together."

"And that's the other benefit," he agreed as he wolfed down his breakfast.

****

Within police headquarters in Pitt Street, Detective Chief Superintendent Keith Meadows was at his desk early that morning and requested that his secretary, Ellen, have the canteen send down a tray of coffee and bacon rolls for nine o'clock, the time his visitors were scheduled to arrive.

While he waited, he read the Chief Constable's synopsis of notable incidents that had occurred within the Strathclyde Police force area during the preceding twenty-four hours, making notes of any incident that he believed might require his attention.

Stubbing out his third cigarette of the morning, he emptied the ashtray into the tin bin beside his desk then raised his head when his door was knocked to see DCI Martin Benson standing in the doorway.

"Martin, come in, grab a seat," he smiled at him while almost on cue, Michael Thorburn, the DCI in charge of Maryhill CID, also appeared in the doorway.

When both men were seated in front of the desk, Meadows began, "Mike, any update on Stobbie's murder?"

With a frown, Thorburn shook his head before he replied, "Sorry, boss. I've had my guys turn the flats upside down, but the nearest I got to a suspect was an elderly woman on the third floor, that's two flights down from Stobbie's flat, saying that there was somebody, a man she thinks but she's not even certain of *that*, loitering in the stairwell the day before the murder."

"What about the murder weapon? I heard you'd recovered it."

"Aye, my guys found a baseball bat in one of the large rubbish bins that are located at the bottom of the chutes; you know, one of them big ones that have wheels at the corners? Anyway, there was blood and hair adhering to it, so it's at the Forensic Laboratory. I'm in no doubt it's the murder weapon, but whether or not they can get any prints from it," he shrugged, "I'll need to wait and see."

"Okay," Meadows slowly nodded, "keep me apprised because more than likely, the ACC will be asking."

Turning to Benson, he was about to speak when his secretary Ellen entered the room then, with a smile, laid down a tray upon which rested a pot of coffee, three cups and saucers, milk and sugar and three white paper bags, each containing a roll and bacon.

"Help yourselves, gentlemen," Meadows waved at the tray, then as Ellen let the room, asked Benson, "How's your murder investigation, Martin? Any further forward?"

"Ah, well, there's a story," began Benson, and recounted the circumstances of the discovery of the typed letter that contained Mark Ritchie's admission Kelly-Ann Knox was at the Barrowland Ballroom on Saturday night. He continued with the forensic pathology discovery that she was using cocaine and breaking the news to George Knox and his wife.

"How did Knox take *that* particular bit of bad news or did he already know?"

"No, I'm certain he didn't know, sir. Curiously though," Benson's eyes narrowed, "he never asked me if *I* knew or had any idea who was supplying her with the drug."

"I'm guessing you think *he* knows?"

"Well," Benson grimaced, "if he does know or thinks he knows, there will be hell to pay."

"That's all we need," Thorburn stared from one to the other. "If Knox goes after whoever he thinks gave his daughter the cocaine, we could be looking at a gang war here in the city."

Chewing thoughtfully on his roll, Meadows sipped at his coffee then asked Benson, "This man Richie who is on his toes. Is he a viable suspect for the murder?"

"At the minute, sir, they're all suspects," sighed Benson. "I've set Willie McBride the job of trying to track Ritchie down, but if he is abroad like the letter suggests…" he shrugged for there was no need to expand any further.

"Okay, then," Meadows slowly drawled, then added, "Let me know how McBride gets on."

"Sir."

"Now," Meadows glanced from one to the other, "this theory you both have that your murders are linked. Is there anything, anything at all and mind," he stared again at them both, "Andy Bartholomew *will* be asking me, to substantiate your theory."

With a subtle nod from Thorburn, Benson replied with, "No, sir, nothing at the minute other than we believe it's far too early to discount some sort of relationship. George Knox's only child and his long-time friend both being murdered within a couple of days of each other? Not that I or Mike here believe in coincidences, sir, but we have to face facts. The chances of both these victims who are connected to George Knox being murdered in such a short space of time; well," he shrugged, "we think the circumstances are far too high for them *not* to be linked."

"I can't disagree with you," Meadows sighed, "but in the meantime, without irrefutable proof they are linked, I want you to continue as separate investigations. However," he held up a warning forefinger, "continue with your exchange of information and if we do prove the murders are linked we'll form a combined task force at that time. Agreed?"

They both nodded.

"Any other business I should be aware of?"

It was Benson who replied, "Yes, sir. If you recall, you instructed me to provide the Scottish Crime Squad with any information that might be pertinent to their investigation of George Knox's team."

"Go on," Meadows eyes narrowed.

"I had a brief meeting with DI Meechan who frankly, didn't impress me," he huffed.

"However, I brought my DI, Roddy Williams into my confidence regarding your instruction and it was Roddy who posed the question; could the Squad have been following Kevin Stobbie on the day he was murdered?"

Meadows stared at Thorburn who holding up his hand, forestalled his question when he said, "Martin told me about the Squad's interest, boss, and Roddy's suggestion."

"Well, if they were following Stobbie on Monday, they certainly should have been in contact with you, Mike. But leave it with me. I'll give their Commander a phone and put it to him. Anything else?"

"Aye, boss," Thorburn boldly grinned. "If Martin's not eating his roll, can I have it?"

****

When he'd visited the Barrowland premises the day before, DS Willie McBride had sensibly taken the precaution of obtaining Mark Ritchie's address and though it was unlikely Ritchie would be there, decided that he and Ailish MacDonald would pay the flat an early morning call.

Hammering on the door provoked no response other than alerting an elderly lady across the landing to open her door, who leaning on a walking stick, demanded to know what the bloody racket was at that early time of the morning.

"CID, madam," McBride gave her a wide smile, ignoring the fact it had gone nine-thirty. "We're trying to raise Mr Ritchie. You wouldn't happen to know his whereabout now, would you?"

"No, I wouldn't," she frostily replied, but to their surprise, added, "If you really *need* to know, then speak with her downstairs, Elsie Balfour. She cleans and does his shopping for him, though I hear her own flat is like a midden," she loftily sniffed.

With that she irately slammed her door.

McBride looked at MacDonald and as one, slow smiles crossed their faces when McBride said, "Cleaning lady? Key to the door."

But, it didn't prove to be quite that easy for three minutes later when introducing themselves and requesting Ritchie's house key, Mrs Balfour, five feet nothing and eighteen stone of pure belligerence, scowled then asked, "You got a warrant, pal?"

However, if nothing else, Willie McBride was a resourceful man who after twenty odd years in the polis was used to thinking on his feet, and so replied, "No, but if I need to get one, hen, and I find anything in his flat that is even *slightly* illegal, then because you *also* go into his flat I'm jailing you as an accessory to whatever I can drum up. Savvy? That and I'll be asking the Social if you declare the money he pays you for doing his shopping and cleaning."

What occurred then, MacDonald later described with some glee and a wee bit of fiction, was a staring match that lasted almost a full minute before the plump woman snapped, "Fine!"

Reaching towards a plastic hook on the wall behind her, she handed McBride a tarnished Yale key, then slammed the door in his face. Grinning they could hear Belfour through the door, cursing and swearing as she moved along her hallway with most of her tirade directed at the 'fucking fat polis.'

"I've always had this winning way with women," he muttered.
In the bedroom of Ritchie's flat, it was obvious to the detectives that he'd cleared out in a hurry.
"And if he's been in a rush," McBride winked at her, "then guaranteed he's left something behind that we can use. The only thing we have to do now, is find it."
Over forty minutes had passed before MacDonald, conscientiously working her way through a pile of paperwork she'd discovered stuffed into a kitchen drawer, called out, "Willie, I think I've got something."
McBride stepped into the kitchen to find her bent over the kitchen table that was littered with paperwork and poring over a sheet of paper.
"What's all this?"
"Mostly bills, receipts, shite like that," she muttered, then handing him the sheet of paper, added, "But take a look at this."
His expression slowly changed to delight when he replied, "Young yin, I think you've just found the start of a paper trail."
****

After dropping Avril Collins at the door to the Barrowland with the reminder that she check out who of the security was on duty and if possible, working the door the previous Saturday night, Alex Hardie decide his next port of call would be George Knox.
It was when he'd got out of the Capri outside the close in Quarrywood Road that he saw the white coloured Transit van sitting fifty yards further down the street, adjacent to the post office cum grocery shop with its rear doors facing towards the close entrance that for some reason he couldn't explain, caused the hackles on the back of his neck to rise.
By now the rain had dwindled to a mere trickle and so, his overcoat collar up, he took a walk towards the van.
Approaching the van and furtively glancing at its rear windows, as he'd suspected the glass was covered inside with some sort of dark blue cling film and then he saw the front cab to be empty.
The side of the van bore the logo of a local building company.
Certain he'd seen the van some time before, though could not for the life of him recall where, he ignored it as he passed it by and headed into the shop where he saw the only customers were an elderly couple buying milk.

Standing behind them, he moved forward when they shuffled off and was greeted with a smile by the Indian shopkeeper.

Purchasing a packet of Trebor Soft Fruit Rolls for the Knox's grandson, Clint's favourite sweeties, he asked the helpful shopkeeper for a white, plastic bag to carry the sweets in.

Leaving the shop and again passing the van, he swung the bag nonchalantly as he walked, resisting the temptation to smack the side with his hand and call out to the surveillance officers he suspected were inside.

Though he was aware it wasn't unusual for the cops to surveil the team and he had accepted it as a part of the life he had chosen, Hardie thought it odd that they would be watching George Knox's flat, given that he and his wife were going through the ordeal of losing Kelly-Ann as well as the boss's long-time pal, wee Kevin. The more thought he gave it the more he believed it to be contemptible the cops could be so hard-hearted as well as thinking it was ridiculous they were surveilling the boss, for this certainly was not the time for the team to be pulling any jobs.

Unconsciously and also angrily shaking his head at their foolishness, he turned into the entrance of the Knox's close and made his way upstairs to their flat.

****

Inside the van, the two detectives watched Hardie walk off past the van, the younger of who held an SLR camera with a zoom lens attached.

"Do you think he knows we're in here?" he turned to ask his colleague.

The detective, sipping from a plastic cup filled with tea from his Thermos flask, shook his head.

"Nah," he confidently replied. "What you have to understand is that we give these guys too much credit. They're numpties, most of them and that's why they end up getting the jail, because we're a lot smarter than them."

Watching Hardie through the zoom lens till he disappeared into the close entrance, the younger detective was inclined to disagree and point out that George Knox and his team had never yet been caught and so never given the jail, causing him to idly wonder; who *really* were the numpties?

However, rather than get into an argument over it, he kept his thoughts to himself.
****

It was Rosie who opened the door to Hardie and with a humourless smile, said, "He's in the living room. I'll put the kettle on."

He found George Knox sitting in his favourite chair reading the 'Glasgow News' article describing the police attempts to trace the individual who had murdered Kelly-Ann Knox.

Though he hadn't discussed it with Rosie, it completely enraged him that the reporter had described her as the daughter of a leading figure in the Glasgow underworld, inferring that she too was somehow involved in crime.

He laid down the newspaper and turned to greet Hardie, who said, "The mob are outside, boss. They're in an old, white Transit van outside the shop down the road."

"Aye, I saw them this morning when I was going to collect the rolls and this rag," he disgustedly threw the paper from him. "At a time like this and with what we're going through, you'd think they'd better things to do with themselves, don't you?" he slowly shook his head.

Reaching for it, he folded the newspaper then laid it down on the carpet by the chair and nodding that Hardie sit down, asked, "How did last night go?"

"As we thought," Hardie sighed. "Donaldson seems like he might take the warning, but that wee rat faced pal of his," his brow knitted when he shook his head, "I just don't know."

"You any thoughts on them maybe having something to do with Kelly-Ann's death or giving her the Coke?" he stared at Hardie.

"No, boss, like you said, I didn't mention her at all. Donaldson did make a crack about Kevin, but I'm of the opinion that he said it just to needle me, not that he had anything to do with Kevin's murder."

"But you're not certain?"

"No," he admitted, "I'm definitely not certain."

"What about this guy Ritchie? Did they know he's done a runner?"

"They do now, because I *am* certain that wee nugget took them by surprise," he smiled. "I'm guessing they were relying on Ritchie to smooth the way for their dealers to operate in the Barrowland, but with him out of the frame, it kind of puts them on the back foot."

Knox slowly nodded in thought before he said, "This lassie you're friendly with, Avril. Is she staying on in the place and does she take over until they put a new manager in?"

"That I don't know. I dropped her at the Barrowland before I came here and told her to find out which doorman it was that Ritchie handed Kelly-Ann over to, on Saturday night. When I get the guy's name, I can ask him if he knows the taxi driver he called and if he knows where she was going to."

"I take it you know most of the stewards who work in the place?"

"Aye, I did boss, from the time I was working there, but there's probably some new faces working there now and Ritchie, he sometimes hired guys working cash in hand at the stewarding."

"Okay," Knox nodded, them smiling, asked, "What was the effect when Jimmy banged one off with the sawn-off?"

"Classic," Hardie grinned. "I thought they were going to shit themselves. You two played it perfectly. Where were you, anyway?"

"About thirty, maybe forty yards away in the bushes, dressed up like a pair of infantrymen and with black faces too," he smiled. "The night carried sound and we could not only see you, but hear most of what was going on too. In fact," he continued to smile, "Jimmy kept farting and I thought the minder that was closest to us *must* hear him, but he never turned our way."

"Well, it worked."

"Aye, son, it did."

The door opened to admit Rosie who carried in a tray with three mugs of tea and, whether he was hungry or not, two rolls and bacon for Hardie who didn't want to hurt her feelings and admit that just over an hour previously, he'd eaten a full fry-up.

It was a little later as he was about to leave Knox's flat that Hardie, with devilment in his eyes, said, "I was thinking I'd leave my motor parked outside the flats, then go out the back of the close, boss, and head across the field and come out at Olive Street. That will keep the buggers guessing, eh?"

But while he liked the idea of putting one over the police, Knox shook his head then said, "Do that, son, and they'll know we've sussed their van and they'll not use it anymore. Besides, they'll have their back-up vehicles parked in the streets round about here and anyway, it's handy knowing what vehicles they *are* using, so let's just play their game and pretend we don't know they're there."

"And *that's* why you're the boss," Hardie grinned at him.

****

In the van, the senior of the two detectives alerted DS Barney Fellowes that Tango Four was now exiting the close, was now into his vehicle and, "…it's an off, off, off east on Quarrywood Road, over."

Fellowes, bored witless and still unhappy with DI Meechan's decision to resume the surveillance, quickly decided there was little point in following Alex Hardie when the main man remained in his flat, so radioed that Tango Four be permitted to proceed unaccompanied.

CHAPTER FOURTEEN

When Avril Collins arrived at her office that morning, she was surprised to see a younger woman sat in her chair and about to ask who the woman was, heard her name called from through the open door that led into the manager's office.

Striding through, she saw John Bradley sat behind the desk, his suit jacket hanging on the chair behind him, his time loosened and his shirt sleeves rolled back onto his thick forearms.

"Avril, please, take a seat."

Her first thought was that he seemed ill at ease. Unaccountably irritated and confused, she remained standing and asked, "What's going on, John?"

His face reddened when he replied, "Ah, head office have put me in situ as the interim manager."

"And who's that at *my* desk?"

"Oh, that's young Sylvia from head office. She's only here temporarily too."

"So, I'm being let go?"

"Oh, no," he waved his hands in front of him as though trying to deflect her anger. "Head office have, how can I put this," he searched for the right words to calm her down, "asked that you take a few days off till we sort out what's went on here. With full pay, of course," he added with a forced smile.

"That suggests to me," she bunched her fists, "that I'm under some sort of suspicion."

"Oh, no, not at all, but with the ledgers now at the Forensic accountancy firm, head office have insisted we sort of start afresh, if you see what I mean."

"No, I *don't* bloody see what you mean!" she savagely replied, realising that she was now almost shouting.

A man not used to confrontation, he licked nervously at his lips then thinking he might appeal to her femininity, softly said, "Avril, I know that as a woman you likely trusted Mark completely and you were unaware of his theft of the money."

He could not know that it was entirely the wrong thing to say, but before she could protest at his overt sexism, he waved his hands in a downward motion and continued, "Please, just let things settle for this week at least. Believe me, I'm in your corner. When the dust settles and as soon as I can, I'll persuade the company that we need you back here as soon as possible because frankly, you have the best understanding of how things work around here and with the money that's already been stolen, the last thing the company wants is for the Barrowland to run at a further loss."

Whether she believed or could trust him to keep his word, she immediately realised was irrelevant for she had no choice other than to do as he said and leave.

Fighting back tears of indignation, she decided that though she were *merely* a woman, she was definitely having the last word, so taking a deep breath, coolly told him, "I am completely innocent of Mark Ritchie's wrongdoing, John, and if the company think they are going to use *me* as some kind of scapegoat, then you can tell them to prepare themselves for a court battle when I very publicly sue them for wrongful *fucking* dismissal!"

Turning on her heel, she quickly walked from his office and it was only when she entered the other office, she remembered.

However, glancing at the steel filing cabinet and with the young woman closely watching her, she knew she had no reason to check the staff duty list for Saturday night, so made her way out of the door.

Walking downstairs, she could feel tears of frustration dripping down her cheeks and on the ground floor, ducked into the ladies toilet to wash her face.

Staring at her reflection in the mirror above the hand basin, it occurred to her that right now, she had nowhere to go for she had no way to contact Alex, knowing he believed she would be working till he picked her up at five-thirty that evening.

Nor, she sighed, did she have a key to Alex's flat and her own house keys had been left on top of the dressing table in his spare bedroom. Her brow knitted as she pondered her predicament, then slowly, she smiled.

Her chequebook was in her handbag and so decided that she'd walk through the city to Union Street where she'd visit the Trees Restaurant for an early lunch, then treat herself to some retail therapy.

****

Hardie had been gone just fifteen minutes when the telephone rang. Rosie, who answered the call, shouted through from the hallway, "George, it's for you."

When he walked into the hallway with his eyebrows raised in question, she said in a low voice, "It's Harry Cavanagh."

Nodding, he took the phone from her and said, "Hello, Harry. What can I do for you?"

"George, first of all, sorry to hear about Kelly-Ann and wee Kevin. I can't imagine how you and Rosie are feeling. Anyway, I'll keep this short. Are you in a position to come in and visit me at the office?"

He knew not to ask why, but simply asked, "When?"

"Any time now or when it suits you."

"An hour?"

"That will be grand, George. I'll put the kettle on," Cavanagh replied, then ended the call.

"Rosie," he called her from the kitchen. "I'm away into the city to see Harry about a bit of business."

"What about them out there?" she cocked her head to one side.

"Oh, I'll take them on a wee jaunt with me," he smiled at her.

****

The younger of the two detectives in the van, grabbed at the microphone and in a low voice, said, "Stand by, stand by; Tango One standing in his close entrance. Looks like he's having a fag. Over."

Sitting with his driver in his surveillance vehicle in nearby Sheila Street, DS Barney Fellowes listened to the convoy acknowledging the information and wondered what Knox was up to. His Jaguar was parked in its usual position near to his close entrance, so why if he was about to depart, did he not simply go to his car?

"Looks like he's watching up and down the street, over," the detective in the van again broadcast.

Fellowes slowly nodded as he guessed Knox's plan, then lifting the microphone, informed the convoy, "Sound's like he's waiting on a lift. Stand by for a quick departure, over."

As it turned out, the detectives hadn't long to wait; however, it wasn't a car or a taxi that Knox watched for.

****

He saw the bus approaching from some distance and with a smile, flicked his cigarette stub into the road and waited till the bulky body of the bus passed the surveillance van then cut back into its own lane. For that brief few seconds, the bus hid him from the view of the van, then lifting the small, lightweight rucksack that lay at his feet, he sprinted to the bus stop that was located just yards from his close entrance, his hand extended for the driver to see.

As the bus slowed to halt, he knew that standing at the edge of the pavement so close to the stopped bus, the detectives inside the van would be blinded and unable to see him.

When the doors hissed open he was inside then paying the driver, opted for a seat downstairs
where he could watch the doors.

****

"What the…Fuck! Where did he go!" the young detective almost panicked when he realised that Knox had disappeared from the close entrance.

"The bus!" his colleague snapped at him.

"He's on the number fifty-seven bus!" the young detective screamed into the microphone.

"Calm down!" Fellowes voice thundered across the airwaves, then evenly instructed, "I want a footman to get ahead of the bus and find out if he's met anybody on the bus. Over."

****

Two bus stops further on, when the bus turned into Robroyston Road, Knox furtively watched as a young woman in her late twenties wearing her dark hair in a tight ponytail, light blue baseball cap, short navy-blue nylon rain jacket and blue denims with a handbag carried on her shoulder, hopped onto the platform. Though it was a bleak day, the woman had chosen to wear lightly tinted sunglasses.

He stared hard at her and with a dazzling smile, heard her apologising to the irate driver that no, she didn't have any change as she handed him a five-pound note and asked for a ticket to the bus's final destination, Buchanan Street bus garage.

He rightly guessed by handing over a five pound note she was delaying the bus from immediately driving off and by doing so she was buying precious minutes to allow her colleagues in the surveillance vehicles to speedily race from the nearby streets to get behind and in front of the bus in the event he got off, for its route was already known to them.

When at last he had collected her ticket and her change, he stared ahead and ignored her when she passed him by, then turning her head away to avoid any glance he might direct at her, took a seat somewhere behind him.

He inwardly smiled for he was almost certain it wasn't the first time he had seen the young woman though on the previous occasion some weeks previously, she had been driving a Ford Cortina, one of the vehicles that tailed him and Kevin Stobbie from Quarrywood Road through to Clydebank.

Good, he inwardly smiled with satisfaction.

Another face to add to the growing list.

And so it begins, he took a slow breath.

****

DCI Martin Benson drove directly from his meeting with Keith Meadows and Mike Thorburn to Pollok Police station where he found DI Roddy Williams at his desk.

"How did it go?" Williams asked laying down his pen and opening his cigarettes, then offering a Senior Service to Benson who took it and used an inscribed Zippo to light it.

"As expected," he took a deep draw of the cigarette then blew out a cloud of smoke. "The boss agrees with Mike and me that there's a strong likelihood both murders are related, but Mike's got nothing on his killer yet. The baseball bat used to murder Stobbie is at the Forensics, so he's waiting for feedback from them."

He picked a strand of tobacco from his tongue before he added "I told the boss and Mike of your suspicion that the surveillance might have been following Stobbie at the time of his murder. Meadows says he'll have a word with the Commander of the Scottish, but you know what the outcome of *that* conversation will be."

"Denial," Williams, wryly smiled at him.

"You know anyone in the Scottish you might be able to have a wee word with?"

"You think it's important?"

"Not so much that, Roddy, but that woman, DI Meechan," he almost spat the word out, "there's something about her that I don't trust. I wouldn't put it past her to complain about us failing to provide her with information we might collect during the course of our investigation and if push comes to shove, I'd like to have something that I can keep up our sleeve."

Williams' eyes narrowed when he replied, "There might be somebody. Leave it with me, boss."

"Okay. So, what's happening here?"

"Well, on the basis of the letter typed by the manager that Willie McBride brought back, I've sent a team to the Barrowland to interview any of the staff who might be there to ask if they know our victim and if so, to confirm if they did they see her on Saturday night with anyone. So far as I'm aware, they're still there so no update as yet."

"Is Willie with them?"

"No," Williams shook his head. "Him and Ailish MacDonald went to turn Ritchie's flat over in Garnethill, then phoned in to say they'd found something. That was over an hour ago," he glanced at his wristwatch.

"Didn't say what it was they'd found?"

"No, but they were phoning from the Fraud Squad office at Pitt Street and Willie said he'd update us when he arrived back here."

"Hmm," Benson's brow creased and he pursed his lower lip as he inwardly sighed, so much for me being the SIO with my finger on the pulse.

However, he had known McBride for a number of years and respected him both as a detective and a man who was more than capable of using his own initiative.

"Well then," he finally replied, "I suppose we'll just need to wait and see what he's got for us. So, how's about a coffee?"

****

Using a pair of high-powered binoculars, Johnny Dunlop stood in the front bedroom of his house in Skerray Quadrant, three feet back from the curtained window and as was his habit prior to checking out his firearms, routinely examined the area to the front of the house. All the parked cars there were known to him as belonging to his neighbours and there was nothing that piqued his interest or caused him to be alarmed.

Dunlop was more than careful, he was vigilant and acutely aware that if the cops came calling when he was at his stash, he was looking at a long-time care of Her Majesty's Ruchazie Hotel, also known as HMP Barlinnie.

Several minutes passed before he was satisfied that nothing was amiss, then returning his binoculars to the windowsill, made his way downstairs.

He could hear his wife in the kitchen making lunch with Clyde Radio blaring out at her usual ear-splitting decibels as offkey, she sang along to Bonnie Tyler's, 'Total Eclipse of the Heart.'

Much as Dunlop loved his wife, he would never describe her as a singer.

With a grin, he walked to the door of the kitchen and loudly called out above the racket, "Back in twenty minutes, sweetheart. Wee bit of cleaning to do."

"Right then, lunch when you get back in," she blew him a kiss.

Making his way to the back door, Dunlop opened it then peered out to ensure his elderly next-door neighbour was not in her garden. He liked Maggie and had known her since the day he and Liz had moved into their end terraced house, nigh on twenty years previously and they had both been more than supportive when the Big C took her husband. However, these days Maggie was becoming frail and a little forgetful and Dunlop believed the less she saw, the less inquisitive she would be.

Striding towards the fence at the bottom of his garden, he turned once more to confirm he was not being watched and pulling aside the hedge that covered the wooden fence, it revealed a gap through which his slim frame could easily pass.

The gap led into the rear, unkept garden of the semi-detached house in Egilsay Crescent that was occupied by Dunlop's mother's old school friend, Aggie Dawson, a widowed woman who had known him since he was a toddler.

At the bottom of Aggie's garden adjacent to the hedge was a large and sturdy built wooden shed with its door facing towards the dividing hedge. This door effectively meant Dunlop could enter the shed without being overlooked by any of the windows to the rear of the Egilsay Crescent houses that were adjacent to Aggie's.

Though the shed was located in her garden, the partially disabled woman had neither interest in the shed nor harboured any curiosity why Dunlop wanted it situated in her garden.

As far as Aggie, a lifelong member of the Socialist Workers Party, was concerned, as long as he continued to pay her a nominal monthly stipend for it to remain in her garden as well as the salary of a local woman who twice a week, cleaned the elderly woman's house, she was content not to ask any questions. That and nice woman though she was, it didn't escape him that when it came to money, Aggie was as tight as the skin on a black pudding that ironically, made his bargain with her that much easier.

In short, for the meagre cost of the rent of the ground and the cleaning woman's wage, Dunlop had a safe location to store his firearms that should the police come calling with a warrant, was not on his property; yet his weapons remained within easy reach if required.

Unlocking the Squire Watchman Armoured padlock, Dunlop opened the door then pulled the string that switched on the overhead battery-operated lights. He had no fear of light escaping from the shed for both windows, barred with steel rods were painted matt black.

Turning the dial on the safe bolted into the floor, he removed the sawn-off shotgun and cleaning materials then placing the shotgun onto a wooden trestle table, set to work.

Less than five minutes later, the weapon was cleaned and returned to sit in the safe alongside the 9mm SIG SAUER semi-automatic handgun and the 9mm Fabrique Nationale, the semi-automatic weapon usually carried on the jobs by Alex Hardie.

Satisfied that all was well, he glanced at his watch and softly whistling, locked the safe then switched off the lights in the shed. Securing the door, he carefully made his way back through the gap before finally turning to ensure there was no visible trace of his passage through the hedge.

Whistling as he returned to the house, he hoped lunch was tuna and mayo sandwiches, his favourite.

****

After he'd driven off from George Knox's flat, Alex Hardie took a circular route away from Quarrywood Road, all the time keeping a weather eye on his rear-view mirror; however, either he could not spot any surveillance vehicles that followed him or they had decided to let him run and their interest today lay with George.

Twice and without indicating his intention, he had abruptly stopped the car at the side of the road, once in Ryehill Road then a second time in Balornock Road and each time both watched the cars that sped past his Capri and his rear-view mirror for any sign of the surveillance.

On the second occasion, he was satisfied that he was not being followed and decided to go ahead with his plan.

He had discussed his intention with George.

Both were in no doubt that though it might not have been him personally, it was undoubtedly one of Peter Donaldson's lackeys who had supplied the cocaine to Kelly-Ann and thus he was ultimately to blame.

Acting as both judge and jury, Knox intimated he found Donaldson guilty and it was Hardie's job to provide the information that would lead to retribution.

That retribution would begin with Hardie checking out the Springburn pub, The Talisman, that was located in the Milton area of the city on Balgrayhill Road.

The pub was apparently favoured by Donaldson as an informal office and meeting venue for his drug dealers and was rumoured to be owned by him, though his name never appeared in any paperwork or above the door.

With his windscreen wipers brushing away the drizzling rain, Hardie turned on to Balgrayhill Road and followed the road that led him to the pub, then turned off the main road into Lenzie Place where he parked the Capri in the car park at the rear of a block of council flats. He knew it would be foolish to enter the premises without back up and decided instead to check out the cars parked in the waste ground beside the pub.

Getting out of the car, he opened the boot and pulled out an old, Stockman's full-length waxed coat. Pulling it on, he fetched a grey coloured bunnet from the pocket then opened a golf brolly. Closing the boot, he began to make his way to the pub's car park.

As he approached the pub, he saw a heavy-set man wearing a long dark overcoat and a bunnet who was standing on the veranda at the front of the pub and recognised him for what he was.

One of the minders from the previous evening and, Hardie surmised, likely keeping a weather eye out for any police activity that might turn its attention to the pub.

His head down beneath the umbrella, he slowed his step and a minute later, he smiled.

Prominent in the car park was the silver coloured Range Rover, the very vehicle he had parked behind when he'd met with Donaldson and McGuire at the People's Palace.

Pleased that he had confirmed Donaldson *did* in fact use the pub, he walked a little further on, then took a circular route to return to the Capri.

All he had to do now was figure out a plan to separate Donaldson from both his minders and his sidekick, Foxy McGuire.

CHAPTER FIFTEEN

Willie McBride knocked politely on the open door of Roddy Williams office then entering, beckoned that Ailish MacDonald follow him into the room.

Dragging in a chair, MacDonald sat on it while McBride occupied the vacant chair already there.

Nodding at Benson, he addressed Williams and said, "Sorry to sound a bit obtuse on the phone, boss, but I wanted to come back with as much information as I could."

Glancing at them both in turn, he continued, "We turned Ritchie's flat and it seems obvious he's taken off in a hurry."

Benson interrupted to ask, "Any suggestion our victim might have been in the flat?"

"None, sir," he grimly nodded, but added, "I've taken the liberty of requesting a Scene of Crime visit anyway and when they've a team available, they'll phone us here at Pollok and we'll meet them there, because we have a key."

He didn't bother explaining how he had come by the key and Benson didn't ask except to say, "So, what's this information?"

Half turning to towards her, McBride replied, "Ailish here discovered a bank statement in Ritchie's name for a Spanish bank." He fumbled in his inside jacket pocket and produced the sheet of paper, then reading the name, continued, "The Banco de Santander, Madrid branch. Armed with this knowledge, we visited the Fraud Squad at Pitt Street to inquire if they can help us identify any way we can trace Ritchie through his account. For example," he opened his hands wide, "any address in Spain he might have provided to open the account."

"And how did you get on?"

"Well," he took a sharp breath, "as we don't have a suspect *yet*," he grimaced, "I, ah took the liberty of informing the Fraud Squad's DI there that Mark Ritchie *is* a person of interest in the murder investigation."

Benson blanched before he said, "You didn't actually say that Ritchie is a suspect, did you?"

McBride, his face a picture of innocence that caused Williams to glance away to avoid being seen smiling, raised a hand as he shook his head to reply, "No, boss. I just let him know that it's imperative we trace Ritchie right away."

Slowly nodding and aware that across the desk, Roddy Williams was fighting a losing battle trying to stop himself from grinning, Benson asked, "Can he help?"

"Well," McBride drawled, "even where officially some countries do not have mutual treaties concerning the flight of wanted criminals, apparently there's an *unofficial* agreement within Interpol and that includes some of the member states like Spain and the UK, where the movement of large sums of money can be discussed without the necessity of involving political interference."

"So, even though we have no idea at this time how much money Ritchie has stolen, in a word, the DI will help?"

"He has to go through the Interpol's UK office in Manchester, but reckons if they contact their Spanish colleagues and the Spanish cops are willing, they might speak to the bank to try and obtain an address for us."

Benson stared hard at McBride before he asked, "And if they do get an address, I take it we'll need somebody to travel over there to interview this man Ritchie?"

Eyes wide, McBride nodded when he replied, "Probably, boss."

"And if we *get* the address, do you have anybody in mind for this Spanish trip, Detective Sergeant McBride?"

"Funny you should mention that, boss," his brow furrowed.

****

Alighting from the bus in Cathedral Street before it turned into North Hanover Street, George Knox slung the small rucksack onto one shoulder and deliberately maintained a steady pace as he strode eastwards towards the overhead railway bridge.

He resisted the urge to turn and stare at the young female detective who, he knew with certainty, would have alighted after him and was now following him.

Passing underneath the railway bridge, he continued at the same steady pace eastwards then as he turned left at the junction with Renfield Street, saw a familiar face across the road; a surveillance detective he'd seen several times before and who he guessed would be part of the foot team following him; usually a minimum of three, though sometimes as many as five, with surveillance cars in the adjoining streets.

Ignoring the detective, he continued to saunter down Renfield Street and crossed the road to the other side before unhurriedly and without warning, pushed open the door of the Maltman pub and stepped inside.

But then things changed.

As the door slowly closed behind him and aware that he had perhaps less than a minute before the surveillance would follow him inside, he hastily made his way to the wrought iron stairs at the back of the pub that led to the toilets in the basement, opening the rucksack as he went.

Within seconds, he had extracted the oversized workman's high visible fluorescent jacket, shrugged it on then added to his attire with a black coloured woollen tammy and a pair of dark coloured, heavy rimmed spectacles.

The backpack he crumpled up then shoved it beneath his arm under the jacket that he zipped up to his chin.

Seconds later, he pushed open the bar on the emergency exit door that led out to West Regent Lane, turned right and slowly made his way towards the junction of Hope Street where he skipped across the road through the traffic and into the continuation of West Regent Lane.

Not daring to look back for fear of attracting attention, he could only imagine the confusion that must have resulted from the officers who went into the Maltman, when they failed to find him there.

Exiting the lane on Wellington Street, Knox turned left and made his way southwards until he reached the building that housed the offices of Harry Cavanagh Accountancy.

It was at the door of the Victorian building he risked a glance about him, pleased that as far as he could tell, there was no trace of any surveillance officers or their vehicles.

****

DS Barney Fellowes was livid.

His driver decided not to say anything as Fellowes ranted and raved about the three footmen he'd dispatched to follow Knox.

"Jesus wept! It's a simple A B C follow. Sheila took him from the bus, the other two latch on then he goes into the Maltman! So how the *hell* can they have lost him in a pub!" he angrily shook his head.

The radio activated when his fellow DS, Shona Burns, said, "Sheila's discovered a rear emergency door's been opened in West Regent Lane, Barney. He's gone. Suggest we head back at the factory, over."

He sighed, realising that Knox had deliberately given them the slip, but then a horrible thought struck him.

Lifting the microphone, he quickly replied, "Roger, Shona. I don't think the turn's on, but we'd better head down and cover the bank in case he's decided after all to hit the cash in transit. All stations make your way to Clydebank and deploy in the plot-up positions as before. Out," he growled.

****

Harry Cavanagh heaved his tubby body from behind his desk and hurried round to greet George Knox, surprising the older man by giving him an embarrassingly tight hug.

Stepping behind Knox he closed the office door then nodding towards the outer office, explained, "The woman I've got working for me at the minute. She's pretty experienced and been at the job for over thirty years now. She's very competent and efficient, but I don't share too many details about my clients with her, if you get my drift," he raised an eyebrow.

Staring once more at Knox, he continued, "God, George, words fail me. Like I said on the phone, I can't imagine how you and Rosie are coping with such a terrible loss. Kelly-Ann and Kevin in such a short time. Here, pal, sit, sit," he led Knox by the arm to the chair in front of the desk that sat in the corner of the room by the bay window, then asked, "Can I get you anything? Tea, coffee, a wee nip?" Strangely touched by Cavanagh's genuine compassion, Knox declined then as the tubby wee man resumed his seat, said, "You seemed awfully anxious to speak with me, Harry. What's going on? Is there a problem with the accounts?"

"No, no, nothing like that," he quickly assured Knox. "No, the reason I needed to speak with you is, well; it's a kind of delicate situation, George."

"Delicate, how?"

"It's about Kevin's account. You know as well as I do that as a single man, Kevin's only family is a sister that, unless I'm way out of line, he didn't get on with. Do you know if that's still the case?"

"Paula? Aye," his lip curled when he thought of her. "At least, as far as I'm aware anyway. She buggered off to London years ago after ripping him off for a couple of grand, then married some toff down south. To my knowledge they've never spoken since. Why do you need to know this?"

"It's just that Kevin never left any instruction as to what I should do with his account if the circumstances ever occurred that…well, if he died, George."

"Oh, I see. You've got his money invested, but you don't know what to do with it?"

"Exactly," Cavanagh breathed a sigh of relief. "That's why I need some direction from you. Should I inform his sister or what do you suggest?"

"After she ripped him off," Knox scoffed, then shaking his head, added, "Kevin would turn in his grave, Harry. The woman's a bloody parasite as you well know."

"There is another option," Cavanagh slowly said. "Without disclosing any names or details, I had a similar situation a couple of years ago, just after I started my practice. Three clients entrusted me with their, ah, earnings and agreed that if any of them should die prior to closing their accounts, the deceased individual's investment would be divided between the surviving two."

Knox's face did not register the fact that knowing when Cavanagh had opened his accountancy practice, he had guessed who the team were; three older criminals from the Balornock area who concentrated solely on post office robberies during which one had accidently discharged his shotgun into his own leg and died of blood loss before his compatriots could get him to a hospital. The other two were caught soon after, but likely took comfort knowing when they were eventually released from prison, albeit at pensionable age, a nest egg would be waiting for them.

"Anyway," Cavanagh continued, "it's an option to consider."

He'd known Kevin Stobbie for a very long time and his eyes narrowed.

For several minutes, while Cavanagh occupied himself with paperwork that lay upon his desk, he gave the suggestion some thought.

According to Cavanagh, Stobbie's share of the takings from their jobs, when the investments were called in and converted to cash, amounted to something like five hundred and eighty thousand pounds. Split three ways, he reckoned that sum of money was the equivalent to eight, maybe nine profitable turns that had Kevin lived would have been split four ways.

However, acutely aware of the that the cops were increasingly becoming cleverer in their Forensic and surveillance procedures, further turns brought with them the fear of arrest and the possibility of losing everything that the team had worked for.

Besides, he inwardly shrugged Jimmy and Alex had already agreed to throw in the towel anyway.

He knew that he was making the decision for both Jimmy and Alex, but was confident they would back him.

"Do it, split Kevin's money three ways," Knox nodded, his face grimly set.

"Of course, George," Cavanagh politely replied, then a little hesitantly, added, "You do realise I will take a fee for the administration and my services? Say, one point five per cent?"

One point five per cent, Knox quickly worked out, was just over eight and a half grand.

"Seems a fair price," he nodded, for Harry Cavanagh was a businessman and to date had never put a foot wrong when looking after the teams individual portfolio's, as he described them.

Cavanagh continued, "The transfer should take no more than two days, George, and I'll update your accounts accordingly. Now, is there anything else I can assist you with?"

He felt his throat constrict for though he knew the day would eventually come, he still found it a little difficult to accept and particularly, with Kelly-Ann and Kevin's murders to settle.

Again, he knew that he was acting without Jimmy or Alex's approval, but would explain his reasoning to them later this evening. Clearing his throat, he slowly exhaled then said, "Some months ago, Harry, we spoke about a contact you have who can obtain genuine birth certificates and British passports."

Nodding and with a glance at the closed door, the astute Cavanagh pre-empted the request and softly replied, "I'll need photos of course and birth details as well as new names of your choosing. When you've decided on dates and destinations, I'll arrange flights and temporary accommodation details at wherever you, Jimmy and Alex decide to settle. Needless to say, the sooner I get the details for you, the quicker I can act and as for the payment, I'll simply subtract the fees from your individual accounts."

"Good," Knox added then his eyes narrowed when he saw Cavanagh's expression and asked, "What?"

"There *is* something else," the tubby man rose from his chair and turning walked to an old fashioned, tall, five drawer steel filing cabinet that sat in one corner of the room and was bolted both to the wall and the floor by heavy steel rods.

With his back to Knox, Cavanagh unlocked the cabinet then pulling open the second drawer, fetched out a cardboard file from which he withdrew a white business envelope that he placed on top of the cabinet.

That done, he returned the file to the drawer and relocked the cabinet while Knox idly wondered what secrets it must contain.

Returning to his chair, he leaned across the desk to hand the envelope to Knox and said, "Several months ago, Kevin contacted me for an appointment and gave me that envelope. He didn't say why or what it contains, but told me that if anything should happen to him, anything fatal, he said, then I was to make sure I give it to you."

His brow knitting, Knox stared with surprise at the envelope then accepted the letter opener that Cavanagh passed over the desk to him as the accountant discreetly pushed back his chair a few feet to permit Knox to read it in peace.

Slicing the envelope open, he extracted the single, handwritten A4 sheet of paper and began to read.

Glancing at him, Cavanagh was unable to discern from his expression what the letter contained and being the professional accountant he was, would never presume to ask.

After two or three minutes, he glanced at Knox, seeing his face impassive.

To his surprise, he then asked, "Do you have one of them thingy machines, Harry? One of them that tears the paper into bits?"

"Oh, you mean a shredder? Aye, there, the big black box on the table against the wall," he waved towards it at the side of the office.

When Knox was standing by the machine, he called over to him, "Just press the green button and slide the paper into the top of it."

When both the letter and the envelope were shredded, Knox pressed the red button on the noisy machine then turning to Cavanagh, said, "Thanks for everything you've done, Harry, and for what you are doing for me and the team. I'll be in touch with the details you need."

With a nod, he opened the office door and left.

****

Poring over a Vogue magazine while enjoying a delicious lunch at the Trees Restaurant in Union Street, then spending some time in the shops in Sauchiehall Street, Avril Collins had enjoyed her free day. Checking the time of her wristwatch, she saw it was close to three o'clock and though it was heavily overcast, decided to walk to Frasers in Buchanan Street to purchase some badly needed lingerie. While walking, she inwardly smiled, wondering if she should buy something sensible and practical or something racy, to taunt Alex. Alex.

The more she thought of him the more she wondered if there could ever be anything permanent with him.

Now thirty-three, she'd had her fair share of boyfriends, even a couple with whom she'd imagined spending the rest of her life with, but more for companionship than love.

However, none of the relationships had lasted more than two years and conscious that though she wasn't by any means approaching middle-age she harboured a secret she had never shared with anyone, not even the few female friends she had, for Avril yearned to be pregnant.

To have a child she could call her own, yet resisted the temptation to simply use a man to impregnate her.

No, if she were to have a child, she would do it properly. She'd find a man to love her and help her raise a child.

But, she wondered as she strolled through the city crowds, is Alex the man for that?

She'd heard the rumours about him, that he was a criminal, an armed robber who with his pals robbed banks and building societies.

Yet for a man who supposedly was earning a lot of money committing these robberies, she wondered; why then did he live in a council rented flat and drive a four-year-old, second-hand Capri? And why, then, was he still working as a steward at nights and weekends in the pubs and clubs in the city?

It just didn't make sense and not for the first time she wondered, are the rumours just that? Rumours?

Pushing open the heavy glass door, she entered Frasers store and still deep in thought, stepped onto the moving stairway.

The truth was she wanted to disbelieve the rumours, wanted to think of him as just a guy she could live with, someone she could trust who would never let her down.

But am I hoping for too much?

She stepped off the elevator into the store, still deep in thought.

Yes, she was conscious of the fact that at twenty-nine he was a little younger than she and felt her face unaccountably redden, but that didn't seem to matter to him.

She had no doubt too that with his good looks and build, he was a catch for any woman.

But do *I* appeal to him?

Slowly making her way through the store to the lingerie department, the doubts persisted, but mentally decided that whatever would be, would be, and for the time being, dismissed all thought of him from her mind.

****

Just as Avril Collins was entering the lingerie department at Frasers, Rosie Knox was standing on the pavement in Forge Street outside Barmulloch Primary School to collect her grandson Clint from his new primary one class.

When the mass of children came screaming through the gate towards the waiting parents, grandparents and carers, she grinned and waved at the excited little boy who ran straight into her arms.

Though it was less than a five-minute drive to Winifred Street; however, Rosie had promised the lad that on the way home, they'd stop at a shop near the roundabout in Broomfield Road and buy him his favourite sweeties, Trebor Soft Fruit Rolls.

Walking off from the school gate, her hand tightly gripping that of the excited small boy, Rosie was unaware of the black coloured Mark IV Cortina with the two men inside who paid more than a passing interest in her.

The driver, a large, stocky built man, turned as his passenger, who sported a livid four-inch scar on his left cheek, nudged him and said, "Right, nice and easy, big man. Let's find out if this is the regular route when she walks him home."

CHAPTER SIXTEEN

Though he took every precaution to check for police surveillance on his way home and confident in his ability to spot a cop, no matter how good they thought they were, George Knox was unable to confirm if he was being followed and not knowing if the police were following him always made him feel a little uncomfortable. Still, he felt relieved they had apparently pulled off him.

Alighting from the bus on Quarrywood Road on the opposite side of his flat, he glanced down the road towards the shop and saw the Transit van was gone.

What he did see was Alex Hardie's red coloured Capri parked beside his own Jaguar.

What he did *not* take any notice of was the dark coloured Mark IV Cortina a little further up the road that was parked facing away from him and in which sat two men.

What he could not know either was that the driver was watching him in the rear-view mirror and nudging his passenger, said, "That's him, Knox. He's just got off the bus."

Making his way upstairs, he pushed open the door to the flat and loudly called out, "Is that the kettle I hear boiling?"

Rosie poked his head out from the kitchen and with a pretend frown, said, "George Knox, I swear you're the only man I know who can hear teabags dropping into a pot from fifty yards away."

In the front room, listening to their patter, Alex Hardie smiled and once more thought, maybe someday I'll have a relationship like those two have got.

The ajar door was pushed open by Knox who said, "Glad to see you're here, son, I've just had a meeting with our accountant, wee Harry Cavanagh, and I have some news."

"Good or bad?"

"Good and a wee bit sad," Knox grimaced, then added, "Jimmy's due anytime, so if you don't mind waiting it'll save me having to repeat myself."

Glancing at his wristwatch, Hardie nodded before he replied, "I don't need to pick Avril up till five-thirty, so no problem, boss."

"We'll need to meet this lassie some time," he winked at Hardie. "She sounds as if she's a wee bit special, eh?"

He found himself blushing when he replied, "She's a looker right enough, but whether we're suited for a long-term relationship, I just don't know yet."

They both turned when young Clint walked into the room and shyly smiling at Hardie, run into his grandfather's open arms.

"How was the new school, wee man?" he affectionately ruffled the boy's hair.

"It's all right. I've made two new friends."

"Good for you," Knox enthusiastically grinned at him, then over his head, smiled with relief at Hardie.

Chasing Clint from the room to tell his grandmother to hurry with the tea, he said, "Rosie and me, we were really worried he might not settle in the new school, particularly after what happened to Kelly-Ann, so it's a damn relief to hear him tell us he's got some new pals."

"He's lucky to have the two of you," Hardie quietly replied.

"Aye," Knox nodded, then continued, "and that's half of why I made a decision today, son. A decision that will affect the three of us as a team."

He was saved from further explanation when Rosie, a mug held in each hand, entered the room.

"I forgot to get biscuits, but there's a piece and jam if you're hungry," she told them.

Grinning, Hardie took the mug and replied, "No, you're all right, thanks."

"Piece and jam," Knox shook his head and pretended to scowl.

She turned when the doorbell rang and frowning at her husband, said, "Just you sit there and relax, George, while I run and get the door. Me and my varicose veins."

Seconds later they could hear her high-pitched squeals of laughter and Jimmy Dunlop's voice as he threw his arms around Rosie and nuzzled her neck.

"Away you go, ya madman," they heard her cheerfully call out.

The door opened to admit Dunlop who turning back into the hallway, called out, "And don't forget, two sugar."

Glancing at Knox, Hardie inwardly sighed with some relief, for the sombre atmosphere in the flat had somewhat lightened and though he knew that both must still be grieving terribly, realised they were working hard at keeping their emotions in check for the sake of the wee boy. He also suspected that their real outpouring of grief still lay ahead of them.

"Right then, lads, what's the ten four?" Dunlop greeted them before slumping down into the unoccupied armchair.

Knox began by relating his visit to the city centre and his appointment with Harry Cavanagh, causing them to laugh when he described how he fooled the surveillance team that was following him.

Without interruption, he returned to his meeting with Cavanagh and told of the decision he had made on behalf all three of them that Kevin Stobbie's earnings from the robberies be equally divided between them.

"Aye," Dunlop agreed, "that cow of a sister of his, Paula. After what she did to the wee man, ripping him off like that, I wouldn't give her the time of day let alone his money."

Hardie had previously heard the story, so made no comment.

"And," Knox took a breath, "I also came to the decision that as a team, lads, we definitely call it a day."

Though they had already both agreed to finish the robbing, he was uncertain if they truly meant it.

He glanced from one to the other, but to his relief, they both nodded with Hardie commenting, "It's the right thing to do, boss. When it was just you and Rosie," he took a short breath, "it was worth taking a chance, but now you've got the wee man to consider."

He shook his head and glanced towards Dunlop, his eyebrows raised as though seeking approval.

"I agree with Alex," Dunlop nodded. "Besides, my Liz is nearly crippled with the arthritis in her hands and her feet and to be honest, she really needs a warmer climate. You know we've neither of us any family here, so if I was arrested I can't imagine how she'd cope without me and to be honest and though I haven't said anything before," he raised a hand as though in apology, "she's been at me to quit anyway. That and I've been looking forward to taking her to a warmer climate and with my daughter and her man and the kids living in Canada, there's nothing to keep us here anyway."

He shrugged then continued, "If I'm being truthful, George," his forehead creased as he stared at him, "I'm relieved. I'm fifty-two now and a man of my age shouldn't be running around like a daft thing, carrying a sawn-off and risking getting caught. Let's face it, if the cops jailed us, we're away for a minimum of anything between fifteen to twenty-five years and there's more than a likelihood at our age, George, we'd die in prison."

He took a deep breath, then added, "If anything, I'm thankful you made the decision rather than me having to come to you to tell you that I was thinking about packing it in."

Rosie entered the room, then sensing there was some deep conversation going on, wordlessly handed Dunlop his mug of sweetened team, then closed the door behind her.

"Thought I might have at least been offered a biscuit," he muttered, his eyes twinkling as Hardie laughed.

"What about you, son," Knox turned to Hardie. "You're still in your twenties. Are you sure you wouldn't want to stay here and try to set up your own team?"

He didn't immediately respond, but lowered his head for several seconds to thoughtfully stare at the carpet.

Lifting his head, he glanced at them in turn then settled his gaze on Knox before he replied, "You guys and Kevin, the three of you, you can't imagine how pleased I was to be accepted by you as a member of the team."

He licked at his lips then continued, "As for staying and setting up my own team? No, boss," he shook his head. "I'm more than happy with my share of the money that we earned so like you two, I'm heading for the sun."

"With this lassie, Avril?" Knox teased him.

"Who's Avril," Dunlop asked Knox, then stared at Hardie and said, "Don't tell me the big man has got himself a woman. Is she real or will he need a puncture kit in case she gets deflated?"

"Oh, she's *very* real," he cheerfully grinned at Dunlop.

"Right," smiling, Knox raised a hand and said, "I've asked Harry Cavanagh to get in touch with his pal that does the dodgy birth certificates, driving licences and British passports, so what I need from you two comics is the names you want to adopt for yourselves and your women," he smiled at Hardie and added, "that's *if* you're taking Avril with you. Passport photographs too and Harry suggests four at least and if we want, he can also arrange flight details for us too."

"What dates you thinking about for leaving, George?" asked Dunlop.

He didn't immediately reply, but then in a low voice, replied, "Any dates that suit you two, let me know and I'll tell Harry."

Dunlop sensed there was more to that response than Knox was letting on and staring keenly at him, asked, "What about you and Rosie and the wean? When do you think you're going to leave?"

He knew that they would protest and said, "I still have some unfinished business, Jimmy. I'll send Rosie and wee Clint, but I'm hanging on till I find out who killed Kelly-Ann and Kevin. Then, when it's dealt with, I'll join them."

A tense silence settled on the room, broken when Dunlop glanced at Hardie who gave him the subtlest of nods.

"Then, George, I suggest we send the women and the wee lad on ahead to get them out of the road and as for us two, we *all* stay until we're *all* ready to leave together. Right, Alex?"

"Right, Jimmy."

****

Foxy McGuire and his driver drove from Quarrywood Road directly to Peter Donaldson's luxury duplex flat in Park Terrace, overlooking Kelvingrove Park.

Leaving the driver sitting in the car, McGuire stood at the front door and after ringing the bell, he enviously glanced around him at the splendour of the terraced Georgian building.

This is what I want, he thought, and what I'll get for myself.

The door was opened by a slim built youth with almost cherubic features, no more than sixteen or seventeen, McGuire guessed, with shoulder length, wispy blonde hair who wearing a light blue coloured silk kaftan and a bright red lipstick, lisped, "He's in the shower."

The youth, who had he been female might have been described as beautiful, stood to one side to permit him to enter.

To McGuire's inward shame and revulsion, staring at the youth he felt himself become aroused and his voice quivering, stuttered, "Right then, let him know I'm here."

As though with a knowing smile, the youth returned his stare and nodded at him, then his bare feet making a soft, slapping sound on the tiled floor, with a deliberate teasing wiggle ascended the stairs and correctly guessed that McGuire was watching him.

Swallowing with difficulty, McGuire clenched his fists and reminded himself he hated poofs. They disgusted him and at any other opportunity, he'd have had no qualms and some fun punching the shit out of Donaldson's plaything.

However, now wasn't the time to fall out with the fat fucker and particularly with George Knox and his crew still to be dealt with.

Strolling with an arrogant swagger into the large and ornate front lounge, he padded around the brightly lit room where the light shone through the large bay window, touching and inwardly sneering at the pseudo art deco statues and wall tapestries that littered the room, mostly displays of young athletic male figures who were in the main, completely naked.

It was, as far as McGuire was concerned and regardless of its worth, it was all poofter shite and he'd not give it house room in a garden shed.

"Admiring my collection, Foxy?"

He turned to see Donaldson, his plump cheeks ruddy and his thinning hair still damp, wearing a black coloured, knee length silk wraparound that barely covered his portly figure.

"Not my style Peter," McGuire diplomatically replied, then as Donaldson waved a hand, settled himself down into one of the plush, pink coloured leather armchairs.

Slumping down into the matching armchair opposite, Donaldson said, "I'm having my young friend bring us some coffee. Now, tell me how you got on today?"

He shrugged before he replied, "The address was right enough. We got there just as Knox's missus was leaving the flat and we followed her to a primary school about a ten or maybe fifteen-minute walk away. She waited there and when she collected the kid, we took her back up the road."

"No trouble? She didn't see you?"

"No, of course not," McGuire sneered as if the question was stupid.

"Good. So, have you worked out what your time frame is for abducting the boy?"

"Abduct…eh, what?" he stared incomprehensively at Donaldson before he clicked. "Oh, you mean snatching him? Aye, probably tomorrow or maybe Friday."

"And where do you propose to hold him when you have him?"

"There's a flat over in the Ibrox area that a mate of mine rents out. It's empty the now so we'll take him there and when Knox comes to get him. Bang, he's a dead man," he grinned, his right forefinger extended and thumb cocked as he imitated holding a handgun.

"And the disposal of the corpses. How do you intend dealing with those?"

"Corpses?" his eyes narrowed.

"Well," Donaldson smiled humourlessly. "You won't be able to release the child, will you? He's a witness who even at his tender age, if asked will undoubtedly identify you from a line-up."

Inwardly angry with himself, McGuire hadn't considered the wee boy and though he was indifferent about killing the child, shrugged then replied, "There's the construction of a factory going on over in the Whiteinch area. I'll see they're put in with the foundations."

Donaldson stared at him and thought, he hasn't worked out the full details, but rather than provoke an argument with the volatile little bugger, said, "Good. Now, I assume you'll contact Knox by phone to let him know you have Kelly-Ann's boy?"

"No, I was thinking of sending him a message though his wife," he casually run a forefinger down the scar on the left side of his cheek.

"Not that I'm averse to sending such a dramatic message," Donaldson politely smiled, "however, there is the small detail of letting Knox know when and where he is to attend to collect the child. Will you have *those* details when you lift him from his grandmother?"

"Ah," thinking on his feet, McGuire replied, "I was considering leaving her with a note to tell Knox where he has to come to get the boy."

He turned when the young man quietly entered the room, his bare feet again making no sound on the thick pile of the carpet.

Laying down the tray onto the table in front of Donaldson, he softly lisped, "Anything else, Master?"

Master? McGuire's eyes widened and he almost choked as he fought back his laughter.

Pretending not to notice McGuire's red-faced amusement, Donaldson gently run his fingers along the youth's thigh towards his groin, then softly replied, "Not at the moment, dear boy. Now, off you trot."

His hand covering his mouth, the youth tittered then said, "I'll be waiting upstairs for you, when you're ready."

Seductively wiggling his arse as he left the room, Donaldson watched the young man with a smile then sighed at McGuire, "You really are the most frightfully narrow-minded man, Foxy."

He stared thoughtfully at McGuire, then continued, "As for leaving Knox's wife with a note as well as a fresh facial scar? Hmmm?"

His eyes narrowed as he gave it some thought, then shaking his head, said, "No, I don't think that's such a good idea at all."

"Why not?"

"Well, for one, it will give Knox the time and opportunity to make arrangements should he consider trying to rescue the child from your custody. Two, rather than come alone as you will instruct him, he will be all out for revenge and not only for you, ah, snatching his grandson, but also for slashing his good lady."

Hating himself for having to ask, he replied, "What do you suggest, then?"

"Perhaps you might consider my initial suggestion, Foxy, and phoning him with the instruction he has..." his eyes narrowed and he pursed his lips before he asked, "How long do you think it will take Knox to drive from his home to this flat in Ibrox?"

"Eh, no more than twenty minutes, maybe?"

"So, really, you're not certain?"

McGuire's face flushed as he retorted, "No, I'm *not* certain."

"Then," Donaldson coolly replied, "might I suggest that before you snatch the child, you drive between Knox's flat and Ibrox and you will know just how long he has before he arrives with you? That way you will also know if he does take longer than he should be, he *might* just be summoning assistance."

His throat was constricting and he wanted nothing more than to leap the short distance between them and pummel the fat bastards face, but instead nodded, then his voice gritty, said, "Good idea, Peter. I'll get it done."

But then as if seeking a problem, said, "I don't have Knox's phone number."

"You know Knox's name and where he lives, yes?"

"Aye, his address wasn't hard to find."

"Ever heard of Buzby?"

"Buzby?" McGuire's face reflected his confusion.

"The yellow cartoon bird that advertises the BT Directory Inquiries?" Donaldson sighed.

"Oh, aye, Buzby. Right enough," his face reddened at Donaldson's tolerant stare.

"Now, my dear fellow, anything else I should be aware of?"

"Mark Ritchie's bird, Avril. The tall blonde one that Hardie tried to scare us off. I was thinking of doing her, just to annoy the bastard."

"I assume you mean by doing her, you have in mind some sort of sexual assault?"

McGuire grinned when he replied, "That did cross my mind. That and giving her an extra wide smile to stitch."

Donaldson's brow thoughtfully knitted before he slowly shook his head, then replied, "Let's not unnecessarily shake a stick at our civil servants in blue, Foxy. While I appreciate your desire to copulate with the tall blonde lady, if we were to harm her in any way I have little doubt it will only attract the attention of the police and with our upcoming feud with George Knox, perhaps leaving her alone is the wisest choice. Besides," he sighed, "our issue is with Ritchie and if he has indeed buggered off without her, there is every likelihood she too was unaware of his decision to flee."

"So," McGuire's eyes narrowed, "you're telling me to leave her alone?"

"Yes, Foxy, that *is* what I'm telling you."

"Fine," McGuire snapped back at him, then petulantly folded his arms.

Slowly nodding, Donaldson cocked his head to one side as narrow-eyed, he stared at McGuire, then softly told him, "Just one more thing, Foxy. You are without a doubt a highly efficient asset to my organisation. I rely on you and your," he smiled, "very *capable* manner of dealing with those whose intentions might be to undermine my efforts to bring to my many customers the quality goods for which they pay so dearly. The fear and terror you strike in the hearts of my competition and those who would think they can rip me off are fast becoming legendary."

He paused for a few seconds, then continued, "This is why I trust you to be my lieutenant and why I pay you so handsomely. However," his voice hardened, "make no mistake, my dear man. While I appreciate that neither my decisions about running my organisation are to your liking nor is my personal lifestyle one you condone, my authority and my hedonistic sex life has absolutely *nothing* whatsoever to do with our business arrangement. You work for me!"

McGuire had not a clue what hedo-something meant, but rather than appear foolish and ask, kept his mouth tightly shut.

Taking a slow breath, Donaldson stared coldly at McGuire then continued, "That said I know that you covet my position as head of my organisation, but let me be crystal clear, Foxy. Fuck with me, or try to stab me in the back and no one will *ever* find your body. Are we clear?"

"Look, Peter, I don't know what you think…"

"Are – we – clear!" his face flushed, he angrily pounded a fist against the arm of the chair.

Swallowing with difficulty, McGuire nodded, then replied, "Yes, Peter, totally clear."

As quickly as he'd risen to temper, Donaldson calmed then smiling, rose to his feet and said, "I'll leave you to make the arrangements as we have discussed. Now, dear boy, if you don't mind seeing yourself out, I have to go upstairs and slap a perfectly round and nubile arse for an hour or two."

****

Returning to the car, he found the driver, big Lennie Campbell, snoring loudly, his head lolling against the headrest, his mouth open and a trickle of saliva running down his chin.

It was only when he sat in the passenger seat and deliberately slammed the door that the driver startled awake.

"Eh, where to Foxy?" he rubbed at his eyes.

"Back to Knox's street then I want to have a look at that flat over in Ibrox I was telling you about. I've had a thought," he narrowed his eyes as he lied to pretend Donaldson's idea was his own.

"I want to know how long it will take Knox to drive there after I've phoned him. I don't want to give him time to get his guys together and come up with some sort of an idea that they can fuck with us, know what I mean?"

"Righto," Lennie started the engine, then cautiously asked, "The boss okay with what you're planning? Taking the kid, I mean?"

He slowly turned to him, then winking, replied, "I think you and your pals forget who it is that *really* runs this mob. Between you and me, the boss is there to rake in the money, but it's *me*," he stabbed a forefinger into his chest, "that makes the day to day decisions."

Lennie said nothing but stared at the road ahead, concentrating on his driving and prepared himself to listen to another of McGuire's rants about Peter Donaldson.

He wasn't happy about the thought of kidnapping a wean. God knew, he'd done some stupid things in his life, but he'd never hurt a child.

As McGuire continued to run off at the mouth, Lennie's thoughts strayed to the meeting at the Peoples Palace, when him and big Deke had been told to stand by and mind Donaldson and Foxy.

He had been more than surprised and a little uncomfortable when Alex Hardie had appeared because neither Donaldson nor Foxy had given them any clue who they were meeting; just told then to stay handy in case there was bother.

He'd nearly peed himself when the shotgun went off.

Alex Hardie, eh?

It had been a wee while since he'd seen Alex, a young but competent guy that he liked and on occasion, when doing a couple of shifts as a bouncer at the Barrowland and for a while at a city centre club, worked with him for cash in hand when Alex was doing his gaffer.

Though he'd never admit it to McGuire or anyone for that matter, young Alex had pulled him out of a hole when he really needed the help.

It had been a couple or three years previously, when they'd been stewarding together, along with a couple of other guys at a fancy club in Royal Exchange Square.

He'd had a bad couple of days finding out his lassie was into the heroin and owed more money that he could afford to give her.

Course he'd thought about taking on the bastards who had let Charlene run up such a massive debt, but he was really out of his league and with no other option, actually considered doing a bank or a building society to get the cash.

Jesus, what an idiot he had been back then.

Finally, at his wits end and after Alex challenged him because he didn't have his mind on the job, in a moment of madness he'd admitted what was going on and to his shame, had actually shed tears of frustration at his helplessness.

The next thing he knew Alex was bundling him into the gent's toilet, telling the two young guys who were having a piss to get the fuck out and getting the full story from him.

Then to his astonishment, the very next morning did Alex not arrive at his house with the five hundred quid in cash and tell him, "Ask no questions and I'll not tell you any lies."

Even stranger than that, Alex didn't ask for a refund, just told him, "Pay the debt, Lennie, get your Charlene off the smack and we'll call it quits."

And he did just that.

Course, it wasn't easy getting her clean and truth be told, it nearly broke his heart seeing her begging and snottering and threatening and cursing and swearing like a fishwife; anything for a fix.

But between him, his missus and his auld Da, they did it. Aye, even though it meant locking her in the bedroom in his Da's cottage down in Ayrshire for nearly four, long and torturous weeks. The first two weeks was the worst, cleaning her vomit, her piss-soaked sheets and mattress and wiping her…well, it was like tending her again when she'd been a bairn

Nowadays, thank Christ, she was a different lassie. Healthy and in her own place with a cute wee wean and a man who was working regularly as a joiner and even knowing her background, was daft on her and their child.

Then to his shock, does Alex not appear that night at the fountain, a face he hadn't seen since that time.

He'd pulled down his bunnet, hoping Alex didn't recognise him and to his relief, apparently he hadn't.

He inwardly frowned, recalling that the last he'd heard about Alex was he was running with a crew doing banks, but didn't realise it was George Knox's mob; at least not till that night anyway.

"Eh, what?" he half turned realising McGuire was still running off at the mouth.

"I *said*, he might think that he's got his finger on the pulse about what's going on," McGuire snarled, interrupting Lennie's thoughts, "but he has no idea, no *fucking* idea, the things that I do for him. It's okay for him to sit up there on his high horse, playing at being the kingpin drug dealer in the city and shagging all them bum boys he brings home, but it's me who makes the arrangements for the stuff coming in and gets it distributed and me that deals with them that when they think they can rip us off. Me!" he pounded a fist into his chest, then paused for breath.

Lennie had no particular prejudice against homosexuals and though he was loathe to admit it, had recently learned his sister's teenage boy, a nephew he loved dearly and who as a wee lad Lennie used to take to the Celtic games, had disclosed to the family that he was gay. His brow wrinkled when he tried to recall the term they used.

Oh, aye, he'd come out of the cupboard or something like that.

Now, trapped in the car with McGuire, he had to listen to another of his homophobic rants and thinking of his nephew, silently wished he could just stop the Cortina, tear the bigoted wee shite out of his seat then kick him to death.

However, Donaldson was paying him a right decent wage and right now it was cash in hand that he badly needed for his lassie's forthcoming wedding, so like it or not, Lennie focused on his driving and mentally tuning out McGuire's rants, headed for Barmulloch.
****

DS Willie McBride was about to sign out of Pollok Police station when the uniformed CID clerk shouted, "Phone call for you, Willie. The DI at the Fraud Squad."

Ten minutes later, McBride was knocking on Roddy Williams door

and telling him, "Lo and behold, wonders will never case. That's a result through from the Fraud Squad, boss."
"Already? Bloody hell, that was quick."
"The power of the telephone," McBride grinned and sat himself down.
"The DI at the Fraud Squad," he began, "contacted the Interpol rep at Manchester who in turn was delivering a message from the," he paused to check his notes then to Williams amusement, badly pronounced, "Policía Municipal de Madrid…"
"You mean the Madrid polis," Williams fought back his laughter to smile at him.
"Aye, them. Anyway, they did us a massive favour, according to the DI, and they've spoken with the manager at the bank over there where Mark Ritchie held his account and managed to obtain an address for him at…"
Once more, he checked his notes, then laboriously recited, "Number twelve, Calle de Cuchilleros, or something like that anyway," he grinned. "The Spanish cops have discreetly checked the address and say it's a flat above a pharmacy."
"They haven't spoken to Ritchie, have they?" Williams asked, worried that they might have alerted him to the police interest.
"No, I asked that and they found out from the manager at the pharmacy who apparently owns the flat that he is living there and apparently on his own."
"Good," Williams nodded then reached for the phone. "I'll let the boss know you've tracked him down."
"So," McBride slyly grinned, "Do you want me to head home and pack a bag?"
Williams smiled before he replied, "The boss will make that decision, Willie, but you have to remember, I know it's in the pipeline for next year, but as I understand it, we currently don't have an extradition treaty with Spain so even if the bugger *were* to admit killing our victim or stealing the money, you can't arrest him."
"No, but I can speak to him and if he *is* guilty, when the treaty does come into force, we can arrest him there."
"Not if he's shot the crow, we can't," Williams retorted, then quickly turned to the phone and said, "Aye sir, it's Roddy here. Willie McBride's found out where the guy who buggered off is holed up in Spain."

To enable McBride to listen in, he turned the phone towards him. McBride could hear Benson sounded pleased, then the DCI quickly asked, "I suppose the bugger's wanting a wee jolly at Strathclyde Police expense?"

He grinned when he heard Williams reply, "He did wonder that, yes, sir."

"Tell him I'll speak with Mr Meadows in the morning, but till then he hangs fire on packing a bag. If the boss agrees, who did Willie suggest he to take with him?"

Meadows raised his eyebrows at McBride, who leaning forward towards the phone, loudly replied, "In fairness, boss, Ailish MacDonald was the one who discovered he'd legged it to Spain, so, if she's willing?"

There was a pause before Benson again said, "Let me speak with Mr Meadows, Willie, and I'll hopefully have a decision for you in the morning."

"Righto, boss."

After Williams ended the call, he nodded to McBride, "It's probably the best lead we've got for the minute, Willie, so if I were you, I'd give Ailish a phone at home and tell her to come in tomorrow with a packed bag and with her passport."

CHAPTER SEVENTEEN

After picking up Avril Collins from the side door at the Barrowland, Alex Hardie was shocked to learn that she'd spent the day wandering the town, though surmised that the half dozen shopping bags she'd placed on the rear seat seemed to indicate it hadn't been a completely wasted day.

"And this guy Bradley, he didn't say when you could return to work?"

"No," she shook her head, "but to be fair to him, Alex, I don't think he's pulling the strings. I've been thinking about it and my guess is that he might be on a sticky wicket too, because as the company rep for the Barrowland, he should have been on top on Mark and the fact that he's missed regular checks on the ledgers might suggest to the company bosses that he'd not been doing his job."

She shrugged when she added, "So, the chances are he might be for the sack, too."

"So, you do think they will sack you, then?" he risked a glance at her.

"Yes," she nodded, "I think they'll be looking for someone to take the blame and they'll want a fresh team in there with no lingering stink of theft. Let's face it," she added with a trace of bitterness in her voice, "I'm not exactly that high up on the food chain and I don't have any bosses that will support me if I am let go. That and can you bet that I won't get any kind of good reference, not when the word gets out about what Mark did. I'll be labelled the personal assistant who didn't have a bloody clue what her boss was up to."

He stopped the car outside his close and switching off the engine, turned to her and said, "If you are sacked, will you fight it?"

Her pent-up anger at the way she believed she had been mistreated by the company overcame her.

"Of course I'll bloody well fight it!" she snapped at him, then taking a breath, said, "Sorry, Alex. It's not fair to take it out on you, but apart from shop assistants, I haven't spoken to anyone all day. I suppose it's just," she paused and took another breath, then stroking back some loose hair from her forehead, continued, "I'm just so *bloody* angry at the unfairness of it all."

She welled up when she added, "That and I feel such a fool that Mark could have left me in the lurch like this."

He forced a smile then told her, "Let's get you upstairs and some food inside you. I make a mean sausage, fried eggs and chips and if you're *really* lucky, you might get beans with it too. Then when you've eaten," he nodded towards the rear seat, "I'll sit back and you can model the clothes that you've bought."

She smiled, her eyes shiny with unshed tears, then softly replied, "And will that include the lingerie?"

He stared at her for a few seconds then slowly exhaled.

"Oh, yes. Particularly the lingerie," he replied with a nod.

****

Sitting facing each other with their grandson asleep in the spare bedroom that was now his, George Knox stared at his wife and said, "You knew this day was coming, so it's time we were gone from here, Rosie."

She nodded in understanding before she asked, "When were you thinking we'd be leaving?"

He didn't immediately respond, but then asked, "Do you trust me?"

She stared irritably at him before she hissed, "George Knox! We've been together since I met you in third year at secondary!"

She stopped to take a breath, her eyes boring into his when she continued, "I've stood by you through thick and thin and never once have I *ever* questioned your lifestyle. Even though I knew you were making good money robbing the banks and whatever, I never asked you for any of that money though we both know it could have made our lives that much easier. No, you said it was our retirement fund that we couldn't be seen to be spending above our income and I accepted that *and*, I might add, without question! And now you ask me if I *trust* you? How fucking dare you!"

He couldn't avert his eyes from hers and staring at her, swallowed with difficulty before he softly replied, "Jesus, hen, I'm sorry and I unreservedly apologise. It was stupid thing to say. Please, Rosie, tell me you forgive me."

She slowly shook her head before she replied, "George, sometimes for the really bright man that I know you are you can be a right idiot. Okay, I forgive you, but just don't *ever* ask me that again. So," she folded her arms then took a deep breath, "what is it that you want to tell me?"

With some inner relief, he told her of his meeting with Harry Cavanagh and the arrangements agreed by Alex and Jimmy that they give up the robbing and leave the country.

"I know that was our plan," she stared at him, "but there's something else you want to tell me, isn't there?"

He took a breath then slowly releasing it gave him time to prepare himself for her objection.

"Me and the guys have already agreed that we won't be settling in the same islands. I was thinking we could go to Majorca, because we've been there before on holiday and you liked it in Palma, do you remember?"

"Aye, I remember I said I wouldn't mind if we had a wee place there. But, what about Clint? He'd need to go to school."

He smiled before he replied "I've already had Harry make some inquiry on our behalf. There's a school ten minutes from Palma that's for ex-pats, hen. It's fee paying, but the cost wouldn't bother us."

She stared suspiciously at him before she asked, "Just how much money do we have, George?"

"Well, for the years we've been robbing and after we've agreed to divvy up Kevin's share because he's nobody to leave it to, with a third of that and what I've salted away, we're looking at a little over six and a half hundred thousand pounds."

"Jesus Christ!" her eyes widened as her hand shot to her mouth. "George, that's a fortune! We're rich!"

"Aye, hen," he happily smiled, "and it makes up for all the things that you've had to do without during our marriage. There's enough there to buy ourselves a place outright, pay for the wee guys schooling and maybe look at a wee business like we've got the now. A Scots café, eh? I mean, there can't be many places in Palma where ex-pats can get a roll and square slice for their breakfast, eh?"

But then she remembered and her eyes narrowing, suspiciously asked, "What's the other thing you need to tell me?"

He hesitated before he told her, "I'm sending you and Clint on ahead of me. I want you both out of the country by Sunday."

"*This* Sunday coming?" her face expressed her shock.

"Aye, the sooner, the better."

Before she could argue, he held up a hand to explain, "Aside from the passports and a driving licence for you, Harry's getting you credit cards made up for the local bank where the money will be deposited and he's also arranging a rented accommodation till you decide to buy somewhere for us to live. If you remember when we were there we saw quite a lot of the estate agents were English speaking, so where in Palma we'll be living I'll leave to you to choose and sort that out," he pointedly stared at her. He then continued, "I want you to get Clint settled into the school and once you're both settled, by that time I should be coming out to join you. Maybe even sooner," he forced a smile.

She stared at him with dull eyes, then, her voice low and flat said, "You're staying here to find out who killed them, Kelly-Ann and Kevin, aren't you?"

He slowly nodded, then replied, "I need to finish it, hen. If I don't we'll never have closure. You know that, don't you?"

She could feel her chest tighten and her throat dry up before she asked, "What about Alex and Jimmy?"

He misunderstood her question and said, "Alex was saying he

fancies settling in Menorca and Jimmy is going to Paphos in Cyprus, then…"

"No, George," she vigorously shook her head. "I mean are they staying behind too? To help you?"

"Yes," he softly smiled, "they are."

"What about Kelly-Ann? We need a funeral, George. Will we come back for that?"

"When we leave, hen, there's no coming back," he raised a hand to quell her protest, then added, "Ever."

Taking a breath, he continued, "I've given it some thought, hen, and here's what I think is best. When we go, like I said, it'll need to be a clean break without the polis knowing where we've gone and that's why we'll be changing our names. I'm thinking I'll leave Harry Cavanagh to arrange a short funeral service at a crematorium and have him send the ashes to us. We can then have our own service for Kelly-Ann and have her interred where we can visit. I know," he held up a hand to protest, "that you'd probably want to say goodbye here, but God alone knows when the Fiscal will release her body and clearing out sooner than later might make the difference between me and the lads getting caught or getting away."

He could see that his plan for Kelly-Ann's remains was upsetting her and added, "Look, hen, I think it would be better for you if you were to remember her as she was, not as she is now. Besides," he forced a half-smile, "she wouldn't want her old Da to spend the rest of his days in the pokey, would she?"

She could feel the tears begin and as they trickled down her cheeks, she bit at her lower lip, then sobbed, "No, she wouldn't. Okay then, we'll do it your way. You make sure you find whoever did it, George, and you deal with them, but for Christ's sake, do *not* get caught."

****

In the kitchen of his house in Skerray Quadrant, chopping vegetables at the worktop while his wife Liz sat at the kitchen table with a Holland and Barrett hand cream, nursing her arthritic hands, Jimmy Dunlop was having a similar conversation.

"So, let me get this straight," she stared at his back. "I'm to bugger off to Cyprus while you stay here with George and Alex playing at …like them in all the films, what do you call them again? Oh, aye, sodding vigilantes!"

He sighed and turning to stare at her, quietly replied, "It's not like that and you know it, hen. You'll be going out there to pave the way for me coming out to join you. Wee Harry the accountant is arranging accommodation for you until you find us a gaff to live. You'll have access to our dough in a local bank and a driving licence so you can…"

"How the fuck am I supposed to drive with these!" she held up both hands and raged at him.

"Well, taxi's then, if you need to go anywhere," he calmly replied. "It's not as if Paphos is the other side of the world, Liz. There's more English speakers there than in bloody England!"

Her lips compressed tightly, she moodily lowered her head and stared at her clenched hands now resting on the table top.

"Look," he dried his hands on a dishcloth and moving towards her, bent down on one knee, "you know why I'm staying to help George. Me and Alex I mean. We're lucky, Liz, we've still got our lassie, even if she is married to that plonker. She's happy and she's got the grandkids. We'll have enough money to buy a place in Paphos," he tried to instil some excitement in her, "and maybe I'll start up my own wee plumbing business again and we'll still have plenty of dough to nip across the pond to see the grandweans now and again, eh?"

"What if you get caught? Have you thought about *that*!"

He knew that to argue would send her into one of her moods, knew also that her moods were more to do with the severe arthritis pain she was experiencing and so, placing both his hands-on top of hers, quietly said, "I won't get caught because the polis won't be involved. We're not doing any more jobs, Liz. This is purely personal for George, for me and for Alex. You knew wee Kevin and you liked him, too, didn't you?"

She couldn't help herself and tight-lipped, nodded.

"Well, this is for him and for George and Rosie's lassie. God forbid that anything should ever happen to our girl, but you'd want them to be there to help us, wouldn't you?"

She had little option but to agree with him and even though it went against her better judgement, again slowly nodded.

He smiled then said, "And the plus factor is, we've been to Paphos three times in the last six years, hen. Remember how your hands and feet felt when you were in the sun? Remember being able to walk

more than a hundred yards without being in pain, walking for nearly an hour by the time we left? Just think about that, too."
She stared down at her hands, then at her husband and inwardly wondered.
Was it worth it, risking the freedom of the man she loved just so she could feel free of pain?
However, it was, she suddenly realised, a decision that had been made for her.
****

Ailish MacDonald was beyond excited.
Her first major investigation and here she was, packing to fly off to Spain to interview what might be a possible suspect for the murder. She could hear her parent's downstairs, the usual argument over nothing and vowed one more time that when her salary was paid into her account she was off to the nearest estate agency to find herself a flat.
She'd worked hard at saving for a mortgage and admittedly, while her mother didn't take too much housekeeping from her, allowing her to bank even more money, the pressure of living at home was becoming increasingly unbearable and not for the first time wondered why her parents were still together.
The door to her room was pushed open by her seventeen-year-old sister, Greer, who surprised at seeing the packing and the suitcase, asked "What you up to? You going on holiday?"
"Something like that," she airily replied. "My neighbour and me are flying to Spain tomorrow to interview a suspect for a murder."
Impressed the sixth-year student flopped onto the single bed to ask, "Tell me about your neighbour. Is he good looking? A right catch?"
MacDonald smiled before she replied, "Willie's about forty-six or thereabouts. About three stone overweight, his hair's getting thin on top and he's happily married with two teenage sons, so no, I wouldn't describe him as a right catch," she smiled.
"Oh, a father figure," Greer grinned, then slyly asked, "How old are the teenage sons, then?"
The glance MacDonald returned put paid to that question, but of McBride, she said, "Aye, Willie's a real good guy," and continuing to smile, then added, "Funny, too."
The noise from downstairs had now graduated to shouting.

"You still thinking about moving out?" sighing, Greer rose from the bed.

"Definitely," MacDonald briskly nodded.

"Don't leave me here with them two," then one hand on the door, grimaced before she added, "Take me with you. *Please*,"

"I'll think about it," MacDonald promised.

****

Their meal finished, Alex Hardie rose from the table then rolling up his shirtsleeves said, "You can go in and relax in the front room while I clear up here. Put the telly on if you want."

She stood upright then reaching for him, pulled him close to her and said, "While you're doing that, why don't I model some of the things I bought today and you can tell me if you like them?"

Standing so close to her, he could feel himself become aroused and not trusting himself to speak, smiled as he nodded.

Minutes later, the crockery stacked on the draining board, he dried his hands then moved through the hallway to the front room only to find she was not there.

"Avril?" he loudly called to her.

"In here," he heard her reply then followed her voice to his bedroom. He could feel his heart beating wildly and his pulse racing as he pushed open the door to the bedroom.

Avril stood by the bed, her blonde hair bundled up on top of her head, hands demurely clasped in front of her, legs crossed at the ankles and wearing a black lace bra, minuscule black lace panties, black stockings buttoned onto a black coloured suspender belt and a wide, though slightly lopsided smile.

"Well, what do you think?" she softly asked him.

He stared at her then turning to close the door, told her in a husky voice, "I think it's time we had an early night."

CHAPTER EIGHTEEN

DCI Martin Benson arrived early that Thursday morning at Pollok Police station to discover that DI Roddy Williams was already at his desk as was DS Mhari McGregor, in the incident room.

"I'm beginning to think you live here," Benson sighed at Williams, then opening his pack of cigarettes, offered him one.

Williams grinned then rising from his desk, went to the door and shouted along the corridor, "Mhari, any likelihood you can rustle up another coffee for the boss?"

"Two minutes," was the answering cry.

Resuming his seat, Williams stared across his desk at Benson then asked, "Have you spoken yet to Mr Meadows about Willie and Ailish going over to Spain to see this guy Ritchie?"

"Called him at home last night," Benson confirmed with a nod.

"Good news and bad news, I'm afraid."

"And?"

"The bad news is that the boss wants a more experienced detective to accompany Willie, so regretfully, Ailish isn't going."

"Oh," Williams grimaced, "Willie phoned her last night to tell her she *was* going, so I'll have to break the news to her when she gets in."

"No, I'll do that," Benson shook his head. "Mr Meadows believes that if there is a likelihood that Ritchie *is* our killer, he wants you to go with McBride so you'll be off home packing your bag and grabbing your passport. It is up to date, I assume?"

"Aye, I had it renewed a couple of years ago. What about flights?"

"The boss told me he'll speak with the Administration Department at Pitt Street this morning to arrange your flight to Madrid. I'm told the Admin people will have your tickets waiting for you at Prestwick Airport and they'll also arrange for an Avis hire car to be made available to you when you arrive there, so don't forget to take your driving licence."

"Any idea when the flight is?"

"No," Benson shook his head, "but when Willie arrives, I'll have somebody drive you both to your place to collect your gear then take you straight to the airport. Better to be too early for the flight than too late."

He turned when Mhari McGregor entered the office with a mug of coffee in her hand that she handed to Benson, then said, "I've just taken a phone call from the incident room at Maryhill, boss. They've found a witness who swears she saw a man running down the stairs about the time that Kevin Stobbie was murdered."

"Any further details on this man?"

"The DS I spoke to," she hesitated, then shrugging, continued, "I don't think he wanted to say too much without his boss's approval, so he told me that DCI Thorburn isn't in the office yet, but he'll ask him to give you a bell when he arrives."

"Okay, Mhari, thanks and," toasting her with the mug, added, "thanks for the coffee, too."

****

Avril woke with her head resting on his chest her leg curled across his thigh and sensed that he too was awake.

She lifted her head from his chest then supporting it with her hand, softly whispered, "Thank you, Alex, for last night. I think I needed to…" she smiled, then said, "be relaxed."

"No more than me," he returned her smile with a grin then throwing back the quilt cover, swung his legs from the bed and naked, stood upright.

"Lie on for a while and I'll brew up some coffee. After all," he shrugged, "there's no need for you to rush to work this morning."

She turned on her back as he studied her then smiling, asked, "Is there any rush for *you* to get up?"

"No, probably not," he smiled, then continuing to stare down at her lithe body, added, "but if I stay in bed with you, there's a real likelihood I might not get out of it again."

"Then," she too swung her legs from the bed and arose. "I'll get the coffee going. You go and shower and while you're in there, run me a bath. After we're both dressed, why don't I treat you to breakfast somewhere?"

"Sounds like a plan," he smiled.

In the bathroom, while he shaved and showered, he thought of Avril and their lovemaking.

It had been energetic, almost frantic to begin with then gentler the second time and there was no denying they both enjoyed each other. Yet, still there was that lingering uncertainty in his mind.

That she was intelligent, beautiful and sexy, there was no doubt. But was he doing the right thing, inferring by his behaviour of protecting her and having her living here at his flat, albeit temporarily, that they could have a long-term relationship or was he merely leading her on with the suggestion of it?

He wiped the condensation from the mirror and stared at his refection.

A part of him worried that because of her previous failed relationships and most recently, with Mark Ritchie, she might become fixated on him and assume that when she learned of his plan to leave Scotland, she would be part of his life.

If he were truthful with himself, the last thing he wanted on his conscience was to be another failed relationship for her.

Yes, he continued to stare at himself, he could probably be persuaded to take her with him, but if it didn't work out, where then did that leave either of them?

His new identity would be at risk and the old proverb of a woman scorned would leave him vulnerable if she decided to call the cops on him.

Turning, he stooped and ran the hot water to fill the bath, then feeling guilt-ridden at his own indecisiveness left the decision for another time.

****

George Knox had a sleepless night and awoke irritable and grouchy, well, according to his wife, Rosie, anyway.

It was no secret to him that the cause of his restless night was the letter from Kevin Stobbie.

The details had not just surprised, but shocked him too and left him in no doubt who had not only murdered the wee man, but also the reason why he had been killed.

However, the information in the letter was so alarming that he could not share it with anyone, least of all Rosie.

At least, he swallowed the knot in his throat, not yet.

Sitting at the kitchen table, his breakfast hardly touched and his tea growing cold, he could hear the squeals of laughter as Rosie showered their grandson in the bathroom before taking him to school.

Because it was raining, he'd suggested that instead of Rosie and Clint catching the bus, he'd run them to school in the Jag, only for her to caustically retort, "Aye, well, if you're up for it or maybe you should try for another hour or two in bed. Kept me awake too, half the blinking night," she'd muttered.

"No, I'll be fine," he had finally persuaded her.

He took a breath and reflecting on his own feelings about the letter, his shoulders sagged and his head drooped for the only word that came to mind about how he felt was …betrayed.

Nevertheless, no matter what Kevin had done, he knew that there was only one course he could now take and that was to take revenge on the men who had murdered him and, his body involuntarily shuddered, likely Kelly-Ann, too.

Peter Donaldson and Foxy McGuire.

****

Informed by Mhari McGregor that she was to go to the DI's room, Ailish MacDonald was stunned when she saw the DCI, Martin Benson, behind the desk who nodded that she sit down, then broke the news that Roddy Williams would accompany Willie McBride to Spain.

"Oh," was her quiet response and though he could see she was bitterly disappointed, gently told her, "It has nothing whatsoever to do with your skill or competence, Ailish. Mr Meadows has decided that in light of the fact Ritchie might just turn out to be a murder suspect, he believes that a more senior officer should be present. You do understand that?"

"Yes, sir, of course," she numbly nodded, wishing nothing more than to get out and head for the ladies loo before she disgraced herself by crying.

"Have they already left, then?"

"They're on their way to DI Williams house to collect his luggage, then they'll be off to the airport."

He realised how disheartened she was and raising a hand, said, "However, I don't underestimate that you must be disappointed, but I do want you to know that it was you that led us to Ritchie and initiated this line of inquiry when you discovered that bank statement and I assure you," he sombrely nodded at her, "I won't forget that."

"Thank you, sir," her throat tightening, she found herself nodding in return.

He lowered his head and pretended he didn't notice how upset and close to tears she was and as she rose from her chair, he brusquely waved her away and said, "Right then, Ailish, I'll let you go, so away and find Mhari McGregor and ask her to give you something to do."

When she'd closed the door behind her, he breathed a sigh of relief.

Censuring a junior officer was something he could do and had done on several occasions, but disappointing a young and eager lassie like Ailish?

He exhaled as he thought, how crap am I at that?

****

He'd driven to a small café on Duke Street that coincidentally, was located directly across the road from George Knox's newsagent shop, but didn't bother pointing it out to Avril.

After a leisurely breakfast that she insisted on paying for, he told her, "I'll drop you back at the flat I'm going to chance my arm and see if I can find out who was on duty last Saturday night at the doors. If Mark Ritchie's telling the truth and I've no reason to think otherwise, I'll need to speak to whoever who put Kelly-Ann into a taxi, then trace the taxi driver to find out where he dropped her."

His brow creased when he continued, "And on that point, can you remember if I'm still on your staff list?"

"Yes, you are. That's why I had your phone number when I called you at home. You're still on the personnel file as a head steward. Why?"

"Oh, I'm thinking. You're currently suspended, but if I'm still on the staff list, I can pretend to be checking the availability of stewards for this coming weekend, so if I can persuade the lassie you mentioned who's at your desk to let me see it, I can find out who was on the doors last Saturday night."

"A shrewd plan, Mr Hardie," she smiled at him, then added, "John Bradley told me the girl's name is Sylvia, but I don't know her. I'd say she's in her early twenties and quite attractive too," she pouted.

"Then I can use my God given charm on her," he smiled.

"Not too much charm," she grinned, "otherwise I might become jealous."

He smiled, but thought, is that some sort of veiled warning?

"Look," she changed the subject and grimaced, "if I'm to stay at your flat for very much longer I'll probably need to return to my place to collect some more clothes."

"Let's think about that this evening," he smiled, then asked, "Other than my flat, is there anywhere else you might want to go and visit? I mean, a friend or family or somewhere?"

Her brow creased as she gave his offer some thought before she replied, "I might take a turn into Renfield Street and go to a matinee at the cinema, but that won't be till this afternoon, so no. Just drop me at your flat and I'll maybe get the place tidied."

"What," he grinned at her, "you think I'm living in an untidy flat?"

"No, it's not that," she blushed. "It's a woman thing. It's just that sometimes men can't see when something needs done or cleaned, like your oven, for example."

"Aye, right," he pretended to scowl, then finishing the last of his tea, nodded that they leave.

****

Harry Cavanagh had been busy, though mostly on the phone.

His contact Wattie, who owned the small, printing works in South Street, a man who Cavanagh had assisted with a low interest loan to set up the new business, had been briefed about the documents he was to provide and now awaited George Knox delivering the photos and the information to complete the passports, birth certificates and driving licences.

"How long do you think it will take you to assemble the doc's, Wattie?"

There was a pause while Wattie considered the question, then replied, "Once I've the information, give me two days, Harry, for delivery. But that's assuming your man provides the data I need by this evening, that is. Any chance you can gee him up about that?"

"I'll make a call," Cavanagh promised, then asked, "And your fee?"

"Let me think about that," Wattie replied before ending the call.

Cavanagh's next call was to a travel agency that he'd also help set up with a low interest loan and where the owner, Philip, had already committed himself to helping more than a few of Cavanagh's clients either flee or take a long sabbatical from the UK.

"And when I have the details, you can arrange flights with, say, a day's notice?"

"Don't see any problems there, sweet pea," Philip simpered on the phone. "However, can I suggest that if your clients wish to avoid too much attention, they avoid the major English airports and consider, say, Prestwick?"

"Prestwick?"

"I have it on good authority that the PCU down there…"

"The who?"

"Sorry, Harry, the Ports Coverage Unit," explained Philip. "The CID unit that keep an eye open for terrorists and travelling criminals;

those sort of people. Don't forget too it's still winter so travellers heading for the sun outwith the usual holiday season tend to stick out a bit. Anyway," he continued, "I have it on good authority that the PCU are in the middle of changing their police accommodation at Prestwick Airport because their offices are being refurbished and I'm hearing they are a bit disorganised at the minute. Prestwick being a busy airport for holiday destinations, the PCU *might* not be paying too much attention to just more Scottish holidaymakers, if you get my drift?"

Always one to take sound advice, Cavanagh replied, "I'll let my clients know and get back to you with flight dates and destinations as soon as I can. However, Philip, can I suggest a cautionary note about Prestwick? I'm of the opinion that my clients, who number three and two with their respective spouses, *might* just wish to depart from separate airports to avoid any casual interest in them?"

"Oh, I see," he heard Philip sigh, then after a lengthy pause, he said, "Well, in that case, might *I* suggest Prestwick along with the two other busiest Scottish airports, Glasgow and Edinburgh, where I'm sure they will be lost in the crowds of both Winter holidaymakers and business travellers?"

"That seems like a really good idea, Philip," Cavanagh added some enthusiasm into his voice for the travel agent's sake.

It was only when he'd ended the call that it occurred to Cavanagh. Resting his clasped hands on his portly belly, he reflected on his initial doubt about Philip.

Always keen to groom useful associates who would complement the contacts he was gradually building up to best assist the service he could provide for his clients, Cavanagh, now realised the travel agent's knowledge of what was going on at Prestwick Airport was beyond what he had expected and congratulated himself that Philip had indeed had been a real find.

****

After he'd dropped Rosie and Clint at the primary school, Rosie excused herself, telling him she'd shopping to do that included collecting the passport photos for the three of them and she'd see him later at home.

Waving her goodbye, Knox decided it was about time he took a turn over to Duke Street to visit his newsagent shop, a routine that he followed every few days and that he'd developed over the years.

It was as he arrived in Duke Street he realised that for the first time as far as he could remember, he had ignored his own golden rule of checking for surveillance and shaking his head in self-reproach, decided that the letter from Kevin Stobbie had affected him more than he thought and was still preying on his mind.

Parking outside the shop, he pushed open the door then held it as he politely nodded to the elderly woman who was leaving, her morning edition of the 'Glasgow News' and a pack of half a dozen rolls tightly clutched against her chest.

He almost grinned when he thought, only in Glasgow, for he saw her to be wearing her faded cotton dressing gown, slippers and with a brightly coloured scarf covering her grey hair that was tightly bound in curlers and guessed she was from one of the local tenements.

His visit to the shop was in reality a cursory visit because he trusted Emma, the middle-aged widow who managed the shop on his behalf.

"Morning, ladies," he called out to Emma and her teenage assistant, a cheerful young student who lived in a flat nearby and when she was not at Uni, worked during the day in the shop, at a local bar in the evening and also did an occasional Saturday night shift at a Duke Street chippy.

Where the hell does she get her energy, Knox had more than once wondered and though the girl was unaware, he admired her work ethos and privately instructed Emma to pay her a little above the average to help her with the cost of her studies.

"What brings you here today, George?" Emma cocked her head to one side to ask.

"Ach," he shrugged, "just at a loose end so thought I'd pop by and see how you're getting on."

"Away and put the kettle on, hen," Emma told her assistant.

When the girl had gone into the backroom, Emma quietly asked, "The polis, they any further forward about who killed Kelly-Ann?"

He leaned on the glass case that protected the cigarettes from being snatched off the counter and shook his head.

"Not that I'm aware, for they've not been back since they broke the news."

"How's your Rosie? She holding up?"

He thought about it before he replied, "The wee man's keeping her going, Emma. I think if she didn't have Clint to worry about, she'd be a whole lot worse off. As it is," he sighed, "I really don't think it's hit her yet that we've lost Kelly-Ann."

The door opened to admit a young woman in her mid to late twenties wearing jeans, a dark orange waterproof jacket and a baseball cap over her fair hair with the ponytail dangling through the plastic closure at the back.

Knox stepped back from the counter to lean against the back wall as smiling Emma stepped forward to serve the woman.

"Here we go," he turned as the young assistant came from the backroom with a mug of tea in each hand, one of which she handed to him.

"Thanks, hen," he smiled at her, but though his body language was relaxed, he could feel his body tense for the woman with the baseball cap, he suddenly realised, was nervous.

He heard her ask for a 'Glasgow News' and a packet of gum, then saw her hand over a five-pound note that she fetched from her jacket pocket.

That's when it hit him.

She didn't have either a purse or a shoulder bag with her and wondered, how many women carry their cash loose in a jacket pocket?

None or at least very few, he suddenly decided and his next thought was; she's a cop.

Sipping at his scalding tea, he knew the woman was taking pains to avoid glancing at him as Emma handed her the change from the five-pound note.

When the woman had left the shop, he asked, "She a regular or have you seen her before?"

"No," Emma curled her lip and thoughtfully shook her head. "She's new to me," then turned to glance at the assistant who also shook her head.

He was aware that Emma was staring at him, so explained, "Oh, I thought she looked like that lassie on the telly. You know, her on Take the High Road."

Emma's brow furrowed when she shook her head, then frowning, replied, "No, I don't watch it."

Five minutes later, his tea drunk, he left the shop and making his way to the driver's door, resisted the strong temptation to glance about him for watching police officers.

Getting into the driver's seat, he grinned at his own foolishness. Another face to remember, he inwardly smiled, then aware he still had to pass the message on about photographs and personal details, made the decision to visit Jimmy Dunlop and give the polis a wee day out.

****

Parking outside the Barrowland, Alex Hardie parked the Capri and locking it, had a cursory glance about him to ensure that neither the cops nor any of Donaldson's crew might be watching him.

Though not personally known to him, the steward on the staff door recognised Hardie and with a smile, politely informed him that Avril wasn't at work today.

Assuming from his comment the steward might have knowledge of Avril being suspended, he replied, "Actually, I'm going up to the office to see Mr Bradley."

"Oh, right," the steward nodded, "no bother big man."

Making his way to the manager's office, Hardie passed several staff members, mostly the predominantly middle-aged cleaners, who greeted him while some gave him good-natured jibes and grinned with offers of a quickie in any of the cupboards in the back rooms. With a wide grin and a red face, he declined the many carnal suggestions and arrived at the outer office that had been occupied by Avril, but was now the domain of the temporary secretary, Sylvia.

The young woman behind the desk who was banging away at a typewriter, glanced up when he rattled his knuckles on the doorframe and asked, "Can I help you?"

"Sylvia?"

"Who's asking?" she stared suspiciously at him.

"Hi, I'm Alex Hardie."

Her brow knitted and he repeated, "Alex Hardie?" and smiled at her as though surprised she didn't recognise his name.

"Sorry, you are?"

He could see through the open door that the manager's office was unoccupied and asked, "Is John not in today?"

She didn't immediately respond, but then with a frown, replied, "Mr Bradley is at the head office for a couple of hours. Can I help you?"

Bloody hell, he thought, this is going to be a hard sell.

Inwardly taking a breath, he delivered the lines he had practised in the car and replied, "Did he leave you any details about the

stewarding for this coming Saturday night?"
"Stewarding? I don't have a clue what you're on about," her eyes narrowed, then she added, "But if you want to come back in a couple of hours?"
"Look," he theatrically sighed, "I'm supposed to be organising the stewarding crew for Saturday's dancing. I need to get it done today, because a lot of the guys are cash in hand so they need to be informed a couple of days beforehand or they'll take up some other jobs in the pubs, okay?"
"Who did you say you are?"
"Alex Hardie," he waved at the filing cabinet.
Glancing to the cabinet where he'd waved at, still Sylvia didn't seem convinced.
"You'll see my name in the personnel file in there. It's in the top drawer," he pointed at the cabinet, inwardly thanking Avril for being so precise in her description where it could be found.
With one weather eye on him, she rose from her chair and made her way to the cabinet then retrieving the file, flicked through it.
Almost with a physical relief, she relaxed then nodding, said, "Alex Hardie. You're the chief steward?"
"That's me, Alex Hardie," he smiled as though confirming he was still in the post.
Striding towards him, she handed him the file, then said, "Here, you obviously know what you're looking for."
Taking the file from her hand, he nodded then stepping towards the cabinet, replied, "I'll need to check who's available for Saturday."
When she'd resumed her seat and continued typing, he reopened the top drawer and withdrew the file that was labelled, 'Stewards Shifts - 1984.'
Opening the file, he saw to his relief it was in date order and so the uppermost page was the previous Saturday night.
Running his finger down the page he saw that things hadn't changed much, the usual number of twenty-five stewards had been on duty with most of the names known to him.
"Should you not be taking notes or something?" asked Sylvia from behind him, her curiosity now again turning to suspicion.
"No," he shook his head, "most of these guys are known to me. I carry their phones number in my pocket book," he lied, slapping a

hand against the breast of his jacket where the inner pocket would be.

"Right," he added, "that's me. I've got what I need."

"Oh, okay, I'll let Mr Bradley know you were here," she forced a smile and stared carefully at him as though ready to judge his response.

"Aye, do that," he smiled then pretending ignorance, asked, "How come you're here? It's usually Avril that I find working here."

Continuing to stare at him, her voice lowered as though about to impart a secret when she said, "She's getting the bump. The bosses think she might have been into something with the last manager that was here. You'll probably know him if you've been working here. Mark Ritchie?"

"I heard something about him, aye," he shrugged, "but I thought it was just a rumour. Something about him getting fired?"

"He didn't get fired," she scoffed. "He fucked off with almost eighty grand that he'd stolen."

"Bloody hell," his expression was genuine for hearing the figure for the first time, he was genuinely surprised. "Are the polis after him, then?"

Now into her gossip, she again lowered her voice and with a glance at the open door behind Hardie, said, "That's why Bradley is at the head office. They're trying to decide if they're bringing in the cops. I heard him on the phone telling somebody the bosses know they won't get their money back, but they might lose a lot of credibility and the company's good name if it becomes public knowledge they've been ripped off, so right now they're having a meeting about it. Whether or not to inform the police," she added as though it needed explained.

"Wow," he shook his head. "Eighty grand, eh? What would you do with that kind of money?" he smiled at her.

"Put a fiver to it and pay off my loans," she moodily grunted, then turned away to resume her typing.

CHAPTER NINETEEN

The Ports Coverage Unit at Prestwick Airport had smoothed the way for DI Roddy Williams and DS Willie McBride through passport control and now seated together on the Iberia flight to Madrid, each enjoyed a San Miguel beer.

"So," McBride began, "we're booked into a hotel for the night then tomorrow first thing, we chap Ritchie's door and," he paused. "Do we interview him at his flat or haul him down to a local police station?"

"According to the note I was handed at Prestwick," Williams reached into his briefcase to fetch it, "when we get to our hotel, I've got a phone number here to contact a detective called Alejandro Perez of the Policía Municipal de Madrid, tell him which hotel we'll be staying at then ask that he meet us in the morning to take us to where Ritchie's flat is."

"So, it's up to us to persuade Perez let us use his police station for the interview?"

"Apparently," Williams sighed, a little anxious that the whole operation of travelling to Spain to interview Ritchie was, in his private opinion, a little harum-scarum.

Nodding, McBride didn't say, but had a private thought about how they would greet the Spanish Detective.

****

DCI Martin Benson was about to leave Pollok Police station when he was called back from his car by DS Mhari McGregor who told him, "Phone call boss. DCI Thorburn at Maryhill wants a word."

Returning to Roddy Williams office, Benson greeted Thorburn, who said, "You recall we discussed the possibility that the Scottish Crime Squad might have been on Stobbie when he was murdered?"

Benson took a breath before he softly replied, "I do."

"One of my DS's came to me in confidence. Seems he has a pal in the Squad who literally within an hour of Stobbie being attacked, was on the phone asking about the assault."

Benson thought for a few seconds then asked, "Why didn't the DS come forward at the time, Mike? The Scottish might have some information that could assist your murder investigation."

"Oh, don't worry about that," he could hear the scorn in Thorburn's voice. "I asked the same question and the stupid bugger claims that he didn't put two and two together until an hour ago."

"You think he's being straight up with you?"

"No, not at all," Thorburn was clearly angry. "He's sticking to his story but I believe he thinks he was doing a pal a favour by not mentioning it, though I'll never prove it, of course."

It was clear to Benson though from Thorburn's voice, the unknown DS had made a dire career error by not coming forward at the time.

"What's your next move?"

"I'll phone Keith Meadows and if he's not already spoken with the Squad's Commander in Edinburgh, it will give him some pull for me to interview whoever was on the surveillance at the time of the murder."

"You've not met their boss in Glasgow, DI Meechan?"

"No," Thorburn slowly drawled, "but you mentioned you didn't like her."

"Aye, I've no reason other than my inner sense, but it tells me she's not to be trusted, so if you do interview her, watch yourself."

"I'll bear that in mind. Did your guys get away to Spain okay?"

"They did. I sent Roddy Williams with Willie McBride instead of the young lassie, so I'll let you know how they get on."

"Speak soon," Thorburn ended the call.

He turned as the door was knocked to see Mhari McGregor grimacing at him.

"I know you're keen to get down to Govan, boss, but that was the DI from the Fraud Squad on the line asking if you'd give him a phone. It seems the owners of the Barrowland contacted E Division about Mark Ritchie and the DCI there passed them onto the Fraud Squad."

"So, there's an official complaint now?"

"There is," she nodded.

"Right, Mhari, I'll phone the Fraud Squad while you contact the hotel in Madrid the lads are away to and leave a message they've to phone you when they arrive."

His brow creased when he continued, "Might be an idea too, if you can get a hold of him, to phone the Spanish police officer who's their liaison and let him know as well you need to pass on the updated info. They'll need to be aware before they interview him that Ritchie isn't just a witness or suspect for the murder, but possibly a suspect for the theft of the money from his employers too. Also, with Roddy being away, I intend visiting the Knox's this evening, so I'd like you to come with me. Might mean you staying on a wee while longer tonight," he stared at her.

She gave him a soft smile before she replied, "Won't be the first time I've got home late boss, so long as you sign my overtime chit."
"With pleasure," he nodded at her.
****
As it happened, when George Knox visited Jimmy Dunlop he found that the Dunlop's had renewed their passports just eighteen months previously and had two spare photos each from the set they had sent off to the passport office.
Explaining the requirement for false names to match the counterfeit passports, driving licences and birth certificates caused great humour between the three of them as sitting in the front room with their coffees, they bandied names back and forth, some of which were quite ridiculous.
At one point, when Liz excused herself to use the loo, Knox said in a quiet voice, "I don't think I remember Liz being so cheery, if you don't mind me saying so, Jimmy."
Dunlop sighed as he nodded then replied, "Since I told her we'd agreed to chuck in the robbing, she's been a lot happier."
He stared keenly at Knox, then asked, "I suppose it's the same with your Rosie?"
"Aye, well, mostly. I've told her I want her to go ahead with the wee guy that I'm staying behind to finish it. Kill the bastards that murdered Kelly-Ann and Kevin."
"And she knows that the big guy and me are staying with you?"
"Aye," he nodded. "I told her that, but well," he shrugged, "it's like I gave her a shilling and asked for a tanner back."
As if something clicked in Dunlop's head, his eyes widened. "Wait, you said the bastards that killed Kelly-Ann and Kevin. You think…no, you *know* who did it? How the hell…"
But he was interrupted when the door was pushed open.
They both looked up when Liz poked her head into the room and said, "I'm away in to see old Maggie next door, Jimmy. I said this morning I'd pop in for a cuppa. Likely she's forgot to get milk again," she pulled a face.
"George," she turned her head towards him, "if you're away before I'm back, tell Rosie I'll give her a phone." Her eyes narrowed then she said, "Now I think about it, has there been any word from the polis about releasing Kelly-Ann for her funeral?"

"Eh, nothing yet, Liz," he shook his head and decided not to go into any detail.

"Ah, well, of course you'll let us know if you hear anything," she waved then closed the door behind her.

Dunlop's eyes narrowed as he stared at his old friend, then he quietly asked, "There's something you're not telling me, George. How the hell do you know who killed them?"

"Look," he pressed on and frowned at Knox, "we've been pals since primary when I used to kick your arse at the fitba' so don't give me that look."

"Aye, but don't forget you had a few years on me, ya bullying shite." Dunlop smiled then softly said, "What's going on, George? What are you not telling me?"

He took a breath and shaking his head, stared at the carpet for what seemed an interminably long time, while Dunlop patiently waited for him to open up.

"Harry Cavanagh had a letter for me. From Kevin."

"A letter? What kind of letter?"

"I haven't told Rosie. At least, not yet," he took a deep breath.

"Look, no pressure, pal. If you don't want to disclose to me…"

He raised a hand to stop Dunlop talking then slowly exhaling, made the decision if he was going to unburden himself, there was no man he trusted more.

"Kevin wrote a letter and gave it to Harry in the event he died or was killed."

"And?"

"He was Clint's father."

"Fuck off!" Dunlop suddenly rose to his feet, his hands at his head as he stared at Knox.

"You're joking, right? This is some sort of sick fucking joke, George!"

"No, I'm not joking. I only wish I was," he frowned.

"The letter. You got it on you?"

"I shredded it. I didn't want it being seen by Rosie, not till I'm in a position to tell her."

"But how…I mean, Jesus!" he slumped back down into the chair.

"Kevin said he bumped into Kelly-Ann about six years ago at the casino in Charing Cross. The one all them Chinese punters use."

Though neither Knox nor Dunlop were gamblers, they knew Stobbie liked an occasional night out at the tables and the casino was well known to them both for it once had been recce'd as a target for a job that they eventually passed on.

"He wrote that she was pissed and being her usual self," he grimaced knowing that with his old friend there was no need to explain further. "Said she was being hassled by a couple of Chinks, so he got her out of there. They jumped a taxi and he took her back to her flat. That was about when she'd just moved into it, do you remember?"

"Aye, of course I do," he nodded. "I was still doing a bit of the plumbing back then and fitted her bathroom suite."

"Aye, so you did," Knox smiled. "Anyway, Kevin wrote he didn't mean for it to happen and it was just the once, but a couple of months later she contacted him to tell him she was pregnant."

"And the wee bugger kept that secret all these years?"

"Apparently they'd both agreed that she wouldn't disclose to anyone about him being Clint's father."

"God, George, I don't know how I feel about this. I feel…I feel kind of let down, you know?"

"Oh, I know *exactly* how you feel, Jimmy, because I feel fucking betrayed," Knox angrily snorted.

They sat for a few seconds in silence, then Knox said, "There's more, though."

"Oh?"

"Kevin wrote that she told him Peter Donaldson and his pal, Foxy McGuire, started feeding her Coke for free, then tried to sign her on to smuggle it into the Barrowland for them as there was less likelihood of her being searched because she was so well known there."

His brow furrowed when he continued, "After she'd told Kevin about it he went to see them, threatened them that if they didn't back off, he'd see them sorted out. He didn't want to tell me because he wrote he owed me and knew I'd do them myself and get into bother."

Dunlop's face turned pale when his voice almost a whisper, he muttered, "The stupid wee sod. And they killed him for it, eh?"

"Oh, aye, no doubt about it in my mind. They've sorted him out first and I'm also in no doubt that they've killed my lassie too for grassing them into Kevin."

"Bastards!" Dunlop vehemently spat out.

He slowly shook his head, then asked Knox, "If you're right, George, then they've got to have guessed that Kevin told us about what they were wanting Kelly-Ann to do and if that's the case then we have to assume then that they'll be worried about us going after them."

He paused as he stared at Knox's pale face, then quietly continued, "I don't need to tell you that they will come after us unless we go for them first. And on that note," he knew his friend wouldn't be happy, but went ahead anyway, "I think you should take a shooter home with you; keep it handy in case you have any unexpected visitors."

Knox didn't like guns, a fact that Dunlop was aware of and with him being part of the team of armed robbers, more than once found himself the butt of good-natured jokes from the other three.

However, he inwardly argued, these were dangerous times and so with reluctance, he nodded.

Dunlop's eyes narrowed when he asked, "Does the big man know about any of this? About Kevin and Kelly-Anne, I mean?"

"No," Knox shook his head then said, "I'll tell him when I see him, but keep it to yourself for the minute. When Rosie knows, you can tell Liz."

"Stand on me, George," he nodded. "I'm schtum until you say the word. Now, how are we going to get those two bastards?"

****

After the call, Keith Meadows put the desk phone down and stared thoughtfully at his desk pad.

The Scottish Crime Squad's Commander, a Detective Chief Superintendent appointed by the Secretary of State for Scotland to the Squad from his parent Force, the Central Scotland Police, had been bluntly forthright.

DI Meechan, he had disclosed, had not been his choice for the position in the Glasgow office, but the politics of the position he held were such that he had little option other than to conform to pressure from the overseeing committee, who regulated how many officers he was entitled to recruit from each of the eight Forces that made up the complement of the Squad.

"DI Meechan," he had sighed, "is a very ambitious young woman who I have retrospectively learned, is prepared to climb over, backstab or bed her way to her advancement in the police. In short, she does every hardworking female officer a huge disservice because frankly, Keith, she is one devious bitch. Now, I realise what you're asking of me, so yes. If your murder investigation requires my officers to be interviewed, go ahead with my full consent. All I ask is that if your officers do find some wrongdoing among my team in Glasgow, I would appreciate the courtesy of a heads-up phone call prior to any official recommendation."

Having made the promise, Meadows lifted the phone and when his call was answered, he told DCI Thorburn, "Go ahead, Mike, and might I suggest that you and perhaps one of your DI's make the initial inquiry at Stewart Street. If you do find out anything of interest, please get back to me as soon as possible with a verbal brief before you put anything on paper."

****

Returned to his Capri, Alex Hardie gave some thought about visiting George Knox at home to let him know he had found out the name of the stewards the night Kelly-Ann was escorted down to the door by Mark Ritchie and that he intended visiting the first of them. However, he then realised it was more sensible to first visit the stewards and have a result for the boss and so, glancing at his wristwatch, started the engine and began his journey to where, at this time of the day, he was almost certain he'd find the first of them. Crossing the River Clyde on the Albert Bridge, he drove towards Springfield Quay and stopped outside one of the warehouses that lined the docks there.

No longer in use to store goods from the ships that regularly arrived from foreign lands, one of the large roofed warehouses had been rented by a smart entrepreneur who converted the interior to a gym where many of the stewards, who were employed in the evenings in Glasgow city centre, spent their days training or simply, hanging out with their pals at the small café bar within.

Pushing open the door, Hardie saw around two dozen men and a few women at the various training equipment that littered the warehouse and grinned at the many smiles and waves from some who recognised him.

His eyes searching the gym, he walked towards the man lying on a bench and lifting weights while another man stood above him, ready to take the strain of the dumbbells.

"How's it hanging, Sean?" he greeted him.

"There's a sight for sore eyes," the powerfully built, bald man, his naked torso and forearms gleaming with perspiration and tattoos, pushed the dumbbells upwards and when they were nestled on the rack, with a huge grin stood upright to grasp Hardie by the hand.

"Have you got a minute?"

"Aye, of course," the six feet seven-inch man towered over Hardie and correctly guessed that what Hardie wanted to ask him must be private.

With a hand on his shoulder and wiping at his torso with a towel, Sean guided him to a corner of the warehouse then asked, "Shoot."

When they were out of earshot of any other person, Hardie began, "You'll have heard George Knox's daughter Kelly Ann was murdered."

"Aye, I knew the lassie to see," Sean's eyes narrowed as he nodded.

"You'll probably also have heard Mark Ritchie's done a runner with money from the Barrowland?"

"I did hear a rumour," he slowly agreed again with a nod, though warily stared at Hardie.

"Ritchie left a note that have I saying he had nothing to do with her murder, but that last Saturday night at the Barrowland she was full of the Coke and he took her down to the door and had a steward put her into a taxi. What I'm needing to know is, Sean, you were on the door that night, so was it yourself that got her a taxi?"

The big man's eyes narrowed and he slowly shook his head before he said, "Not me, Alex. As I said, I knew the lassie, of course. We all did and to be honest," he took a sharp intake of breath, "I don't want to speak ill of the dead, but with a drink in her and…"

"It's okay, Sean," he held up his hand. "I think we all knew what she was like. But did you see her last Saturday night?"

"No," he slowly shook his head, "I can't say for certain I did, but you know what it's like at the Barrowland. It's usually the same crowd and the same faces and one night runs into another."

"Who were you working with on Saturday night? Can you remember?"

"Eric," he immediately replied. "Eric, the wee punchy guy. Sorry, but I don't know his second name."

Hardie smiled at the description, for he did know Eric's surname; McFee.

Eric McFee, handy with his fists, had lost more than a few stewarding jobs due to his quick temper and so earned himself the nickname 'Punchy.'

"I've not got his number."

"I might not know his second name," Sean grinned, "but I do have his phone number. I've got it in my jacket. Hang on," he said then walked towards the door where three coat rails were beside a number of old and dented metal lockers.

Returning a minute later, he handed Hardie a scrap of paper, then said, "I don't know much about Eric and to be honest, I was surprised that Ritchie took him back on, given his reputation I mean."

His lip curled when he added, "I never felt comfortable working with the wee guy. He'd start a fight in an empty house, that one and let's face it. We get enough agro from the punters, so we don't need that kind of hassle in the industry from one of our own."

"No, you're right," Hardie solemnly nodded, then with a quick grin, said, "Thanks, Sean. You still got my number in case anything about Saturday comes to mind?"

"You know me, Alex," he grinned back at him, then nodding at the scrap of paper in Hardie's hand, added, "I never throw away phone numbers in case I'm ever needing a favour."

Hardie slapped the big man on the arm, then said, "Be seeing you, Sean, and mind, if you hear anything?"

"I'll let you know," Sean finished for him, with a thumbs up.

Walking from the building, Hardie decided there was no need to hang about and getting in his car, began to look for a phone box.

****

Peter Donaldson turned to glance predatorily at the naked form of the sleeping youth lying on his left side in the wide bed, then very gently run a forefinger along the youth's spine, watching as the boy's body shivered with expectation before he turned to stare at Donaldson, who was also naked.

Watching Donaldson making twirling motion with his forefinger, the youth forced a smile then turned to lie face down onto the bed.

But then as Donaldson prepared to sit astride the teenager, the phone rung on the bedside cabinet and with an irritable sigh, he climbed off the youth.

Patting gently at the youth's backside, he whispered, "Stay exactly as you are. I'll be just a moment."

Snatching at the phone, he growled, "Hello."

"It's me," Foxy McGuire, sounding breathless, excitedly hissed through the phone. "Just to let you know I'm doing the snatch first thing tomorrow morning. When Knox's wife takes the kid to school. I'll ambush them on the Quarrywood Road at the junction of…"

He got no further for Donaldson, glancing quickly at the youth who stared back at him, said, "I don't need to know the details, Foxy. Suffice to say when you have completed your task, you can let me know."

But then as an afterthought, he asked, "When you say you are doing the snatch, Foxy, I assume you will have someone accompanying you?"

"Aye, Lennie, the big guy that does the driving for…"

"Enough!" unconsciously holding up a hand, Donaldson sharply interrupted him.

"Can I also assume that you spoke to our friend Buzby and have the phone number?"

"Yes," McGuire irritably replied.

"As I said, let me know when it's done, when our friend from Barmulloch is no longer a problem."

"Right," McGuire snapped back, annoyed that he was being so offhandedly dismissed.

Replacing the phone, Donaldson, his breathing becoming a little more rapid as he considered what he was about to do, with a smile leaned forward to whisper in the youth's ear, "Now, my sweet boy, where were we?"

****

In his top floor flat in Dalmarnock's Romford Street, Foxy McGuire stared down at the telephone, his face contorted and twisted with an intense hatred of Peter Donaldson.

He knew that the time for a showdown with the fat poofter was fast approaching and idly considered that once he'd settled the score with Knox, he'd do Donaldson soon after and bury the two of them in the same foundations.

But first things first, he thought and dialling the number for Lennie Campbell, told him that he was needed first thing tomorrow morning for the job they'd discussed.

"What time is first thing, Foxy?"

"Pick me up from my gaff at eight. That'll give us time to be in a position to grab the kid when he's getting walked to school."

It occurred to Lennie to ask, what if he's not walking, but getting a lift; however, he couldn't face an argument from the sod and so kept his mouth shut.

When the call had ended, McGuire took a breath to calm himself before striding into his bedroom.

From under the unmade, double bed, he fetched out a Cadbury's Roses chocolate tin. Opening the tin, he removed a bundle wrapped in a soft oily cloth.

Unwrapping the cloth it revealed a Luger semi-automatic pistol, a wartime World War II relic that he had obtained a year earlier from a junkie housebreaker, who had in turn had stolen the weapon from a house in Pollokshields.

Five nine-millimetre bullets also rolled out from the cloth, their brass tips dark and tarnished with age.

The housebreaker had confidently assured McGuire the weapon was unlikely to have been reported stolen for the householder, an elderly man, was known to dabble in knocked-off *objects d'art*, some of which the housebreaker had himself sold to the householder and which also accompanied the Luger out of a ground floor window.

And all it cost me, he grinned as he held the Luger up to the light was thirty quid and a bag of Coke.

Like most boys who grew up in Glasgow on a diet of cowboy and world war two films, McGuire had played in the back courts of the council tenements, practising with toy guns, pretend guns or sticks in a make-believe world where he had come to believe himself as heroic and, even though prior to the Luger he had never actually held a real firearm, was convinced there was little he didn't know about firearms.

In the privacy of his bedroom, the Luger in his hand, he pranced around the room, holding the pistol in both hands as he practised his stance, ducking behind the bed and pretending he was firing the weapon at an assailant standing in the open doorway, muttering, "Bang, bang," as though firing the weapon.

Satisfying himself that he was indeed a naturally gifted shot, he casually blew into the barrel just as did the heroes in countless cowboy films.

With a satisfied sigh, he imagined himself drawing a bead on a quivering and terrified George Knox then shooting him in the forehead.

His eyes narrowed as a thought came to him; wondering if he'd do the kid first to make Knox suffer even that bit more, seeing his grandson killed before his eyes.

Two bullets was all it would take and the other three?

Those, he smirked he'd save for Peter Donaldson and whatever wee poofter pal he was entertaining at the time.

CHAPTER TWENTY

After receiving the phone call from Detective Chief Superintendent Keith Meadows, DCI Mike Thorburn called in his DI to tell him, "Grab your coat, Calum, we're going to visit the Scottish at Stewart Street."

During the fifteen-minute journey from Maryhill to Stewart Street Police station, Thorburn explained why they were going there and that they had the express permission from the Squad's Commander in Edinburgh to conduct their investigation and ask any question of any member of the Squad.

"And," Thorburn grimly added, "if for one minute you suspect that I've missed something, Calum, or that any of the buggers are prevaricating, tell me and we'll treat them like any other suspect."

"Boss," Smith nodded.

Upon their arrival at Stewart Street they parked in the rear yard and ignoring the protocol of advising the resident DCI, Carol McQuade, of their visit, headed straight for the top floor.

Seated at her desk, DI Alice Meechan was startled when her door was knocked then pushed open by two men she did not recognise, but correctly assumed them to be police officers.

"Can I help you, gentlemen?"

Introducing them, Thorburn said, "I understand that you are the SIO in the surveillance operation that is currently being conducted against George Knox and his team, DI Meechan?"

"That is correct," she sniffed and politely offered them a chair.

Declining on both their behalf, Thorburn stared down at her then said, "You of course are aware that one of his team, Kevin Stobbie was murdered a few days ago in the block of flats where he lived?"
"Yes, of course," she forced a smile, yet could not avoid the cold hand that clutched at her stomach.
"My information is that your team were on Stobbie that day. Would that be correct?"
"Eh, yes, I believe so; however, the team were stood down prior to Stobbie being murdered. I have it recorded in their log."
"May I see the log?"
"Actually, sir, as the log is part of an ongoing operation, I must refuse."
"Why?"
"Sir?"
"Why *must* you refuse and particularly if the log corroborates what you've just told me?"
"Ah, well, if you insist, but I have to record the fact that you ordered me to hand over the log."
"Oh, I'm not ordering you to hand over the log, DI Meechan, but I am suspicious as to why you are reluctant to do so."
Her heart beating widely in her chest, she decided to say no more and rising from her desk, moved to a cabinet in the corner where she lifted out the operational logs. Forcing her hands to stop from shaking, she sifted through the sheets for the date of Stobbie's murder then extracted a sheet of paper that she handed to Thorburn. As he studied the sheet, he asked, "This time that's recorded for the stand-down. Is that correct?"
"Yes, of course. Why wouldn't it be?"
He stared pokerfaced at her before he replied, "Because my information, DI Meechan, is that it's a lie, that the time has been falsified."
She could feel her throat tighten and her face redden when she stuttered, "I have no knowledge of that, sir."
"Really? Is your DS Fellowes available for me to speak with?"
"They are currently out on the operation, sir, following George Knox."
"Then," he moved to one of the two chairs and sat down, "DI Smith and I will wait till they return."
****

George Knox locked the Jaguar then ignoring the Cortina that had stopped some fifty or sixty yards away, walked briskly towards the close entrance.

Had the cops known it, if they'd stopped him they would have discovered the bulge in the front waistband of his trousers was a nine-millimetre Beretta 92 semi-automatic pistol with a full load of nine bullets in the magazine.

One of several handguns that Jimmy Dunlop procured a number of years previously from different sources known only to him, Knox had previously fired the Beretta at the Fife quarry favoured by Dunlop for testing his weapons, where he discovered that he had absolutely no natural instinct for guns and indeed, firing the bloody things gave him the willies.

He glanced at his wristwatch and knew that Rosie would be collecting Clint from school, giving him some time to find a secure place where his wife or his grandson would not happen upon the gun.

In the end, after much thought, he realised that if trouble did come to his door the Beretta would need to be handy. High up in the hallway just behind the front door when it opened was the wall mounted electrical box for the flat, though even he at five feet seven inches needed to stand on a chair to reach it.

However, the height of the box off the carpeted floor meant that the likelihood of Rosie or particularly Clint chancing upon the handgun was nil.

Fetching a kitchen chair, he stood on it and opening the electrical box, saw there was sufficient room for the Beretta to fit snugly inside, though he realised he would likely have to explain to Rosie why the chair needed to be left in the hallway.

Making himself a coffee, he sat in the front room and considered the plan that he and Jimmy Dunlop had discussed.

Alex had recce'd the Springburn pub, The Talisman, that Donaldson hung out in; his unofficial office where he was known to do business, Alex had explained.

Knox, the architect for all their successful jobs, had always convinced the team that the more complicated a plan was, the easier it would unravel if things went pear-shaped.

Thus, his maxim was always, keep it simple.

And so the two men had agreed that accompanied by Alex Hardie, armed and parked nearby in the driving seat of a getaway car, they would first ensure Donaldson and McGuire were in the pub.
Then, when the two men left to enter Donaldson's silver coloured Range Rover, Knox and Dunlop would quickly approach the vehicle and shoot through the windows as many rounds at them as they could to ensure their deaths.
Jimmy had questioned, what if the Crime Squad were watching them that night?
However, Knox had reminded him that the cops seemed to favour dayshifts for their surveillance, for the team had never before hit a bank or armoured car in the evening or at night.
"And you think Alex will be okay with this, George?" he'd asked. "I mean, putting these two bastards down?"
"I think so, yes," he'd replied.
But then he recalled that just like him, Hardie had never actually fired the handgun he took on the turns and almost as an afterthought, added with a shake of his head, "If he's not up for it, I'll not hold it against him, Jimmy. Alex has been a good and trusted member of our team for years now, so if the big guy wants to renege on this, I'll understand."
He took a sip of his coffee and his thoughts turned to Rosie's shopping trip to collect among other things, the current photographs for both of them and wee Clint from the photographer's shop. Along with the information that he and she had agreed regarding their new names and with the Dunlop's photos and information that he would collect from Jimmy tomorrow morning, it meant he could visit Harry Cavanagh to organise the passports and other documents and get things moving.
If Harry was true to his word about the time frame for such arrangements, it might mean Rosie and Clint could be going abroad on Saturday night at the earliest, though he had already told her to be ready for Sunday.
Once the women and the wee lad were gone, they could then put their plan into action to murder Donaldson and McGuire and with luck, the three of them could be out of the country the following day. Yes, it sounded so simple.
He frowned, as he wondered; why then was he so worried?

****

The flight conveying DI Roddy Williams and DS Willie McBride touched down at Madrid-Barajas Adolfo Suárez Airport a little earlier than scheduled and, as they stepped off the stairs at the plane, both men were surprised to be greeted by two uniformed officers who determining their identities, touched forefingers to their caps and requested in broken English that the detectives accompany them. Carrying just hand luggage and a little confused, they followed the police officers across the tarmac.

Inside the cool shade of the building, they were further greeted by a tall, handsome, slim man in his mid-thirties and dressed in a light-coloured suit who in perfect English, shook hands and introduced himself as Detective Alejandro Perez. Then quietly explaining with a slow wink, informed them there would be no need to pass through customs or the passport control.

Being led by Perez through the concourse towards a suite of rooms that housed the airport police, Williams said, "I thought we were to contact you to let you know we'd arrived?"

"That was the plan, senor; however, I was contacted by your DS McGregor who explained there has been an update and a request you call her at your office."

Indicating a phone he could use, Perez beckoned McBride follow him into an outer office while Williams made the call, where he told him, "After I drop you at your hotel, do you wish to interview your suspect this evening or wait till the morning?"

"Probably an early morning call before he gets the chance to get his act together, Alejandro. Will we be able to use one of your stations for a formal interview?"

"I'll speak with my boss, but I do not foresee any problem," Perez nodded, then continued, "Unfortunately and though our governments continue to be in discussion, you are aware of course there remains no extradition treaty, so neither you nor I can arrest this man even if he admits his guilt?"

"Yes," McBride nodded, then pokerfaced added, "but if he does confess, me and Roddy will just beat him to death and maybe you can help us dispose of the body?"

Equally expressionless, Perez nodded before he replied, "It seems we have much in common, Willie. Perhaps we can discuss the details tonight over some beers?"

"Sounds like a plan," McBride grinned.

The door opened to admit Williams, who said, "I've spoken with Mhari," he told McBride then for Perez's benefit, explained, "Detective Sergeant McGregor. It seems that the owners of the Barrowland Ballroom have formally complained to Strathclyde Police, so Ritchie is now the prime suspect for the theft of about eighty thousand pounds."

"Phew," McBride's eye widened. "The Frauddies dealing with it or the local Division?"

"The Fraud Squad, but the boss wants us to concentrate on our investigation and if he bursts to the theft of the money, we'll not be able to arrest him yet," he sighed, "but we will take notes for compiling statements when we return to Scotland. If the extradition treaty agreement goes ahead next year, then the Fraud Squad will no doubt pursue him for the theft, but in the meantime because we have no jurisdiction…" he shrugged for there was no need for further explanation.

"Alejandro here," McBride inclined his head towards Perez, "will speak to his boss about letting us have a room at the local police station to interview Ritchie."

"You must understand," Perez explained, "if my boss agrees, it will be a courtesy only. We have no reason to detain or arrest this man Ritchie."

"Understood," Williams nodded then added, "In the meantime, Alejandro, if you can drop us at our hotel, perhaps you will permit us to buy you a beer?"

"For that," the Spaniard grinned, "there is no requirement for a treaty."

****

DS Barney Fellowes and the rest of the surveillance team parked their vehicles in the rear yard of Stewart Street Police station, then in two's and three's made their way upstairs to the suite of rooms. Pushing open the security door, Fellowes was met by a pale-faced DI Meechan who crooking a forefinger at him, abruptly said, "Come with me."

He glanced at DS Shona Burns, a glance that she read as, this doesn't sound good.

Following Meechan through the corridor to her room, he was surprised to see two men in suits seated in her office, who she introduced as DCI Thorburn and DI Smith.

"This is DS Fellowes," she turned to him then taking her chair, he noted right away he wasn't being given the offer to fetch himself a chair.

Meechan was about to speak when Thorburn raised a hand to stop her, then turning to Fellowes, asked, "I'm told that you were the operational team leader on the day that Kevin Stobbie was murdered, DS Fellowes. Is that correct?"

"Aye, that's correct, sir," he replied as calmly as he could, though he could feel his body tensing.

"I'm also told that your operational log for that day states you followed Kevin Stobbie from another targets house," he glanced down at the typed log. "Jimmy Dunlop, then when Stobbie returned home to the high-rise flats at Glenavon Road, you instructed your team to stand down. Is that correct, DS Fellowes?"

"After a short period of time, yes, that's correct, sir," and unexpectedly felt a calmness sweep through his body.

"And the time of the stand down that is recorded here, DS Fellowes, is *that* correct?"

Barney Fellowes had been a cop for twenty-seven years, nineteen of them as a detective with two stints in the Scottish Crime Squad; first as a DC and now as a DS.

So, he took an inward breath, it didn't take a genius to work out what the problem here was.

"No, sir that time is *not* correct."

"What the fuck…" a snarling Meechan almost sprung from her seat, but was immediately waved back down by Thorburn, who turning back towards Fellowes, asked, "Why is that not correct?"

"Might I be permitted to take a few minutes to fetch something?"

"Is it relevant to what you're going to tell me?"

"Oh, aye," he vigorously nodded, "it is."

He left the room and entering the DS's room just along the corridor, saw Shona Burns seated behind her desk, reviewing that day's log.

"What's going on?" she frowned at him.

"Can you come with me," he fetched paperwork from his desk drawer, "and whatever you're asked, tell the truth."

"Eh?" puzzled, she rose from behind her desk to hurry after him.

Returning to the DI's room, Fellowes turned and said, "This is DS Burns who was my deputy on the day that you're asking about, Mr Thorburn."

To Fellowes surprise, Thorburn smiled and said, "Hello, Shona, long time no see."

"Boss," she gravelly nodded towards him.

"I was Shona's DI at the Milngavie CID office," he explained, then turning to Fellowes, asked, "What is it you want me to see, DS Fellowes?"

"This, sir," he laid down the photocopy of the original, handwritten log for Monday, the twenty-third of January.

As Thorburn peered at the log, Fellowes said, "As you can see, the team were still operational at what I believe was the time Stobbie was murdered. In the team's defence," he hurried on, "we were all located within vehicles and at no time could we possibly have been aware of what was occurring within the high-rise flats, particularly on Stobbie's lading where I understand he was murdered. I regret that if you are here today to inquire if we might have saw anything that would be of use in your murder investigation, I'm sorry, but none of my team have any information that might help."

A tense silence had fallen on the room during which Thorburn glanced at Meechan, whose face was now as white as a sheet.

"So, DS Fellowes," the DCI slowly asked, "can you explain to me why the time on this copy handwritten log differs from the time on the official typed log?"

"Yes, sir," Fellowes coolly turned to glance at Meechan, "because I was ordered to change the time on the typed log to reflect that the team were stood down at the time of the murder."

Thorburn said nothing for several seconds, then asked, "And who ordered you to do this?"

"DI Meechan…"

But he got no further for she leapt from her chair and pointing a finger at him, loudly cried out, "He's lying! I do not know anything about this! He's saying this to get me into trouble!"

The other four in the room stared at her until at last, her eyes red with angry tears, she slumped back down into her chair, her eyes narrowing with hatred as she stared at Fellowes.

Thorburn tore his gaze away from Meechan to ask Fellowes, "And where is the original, handwritten log?"

"The last I saw it was when I handed it to DI Meechan, sir."

Thorburn slowly nodded as though in understanding, then asked him, "Did you question this alleged falsification of the log?"

"I tried to argue against what I was ordered to do, but I was reminded I was a Detective Sergeant being given an instruction by a *Detective Inspector*," his voice full of scorn as he pronounced her rank.

"A *lawful* instruction, she said," he turned to stare at her.

Thorburn was no fool and knew why DS Shona Burns had been brought into the room by Fellowes, but thought he'd better ask anyway, and so said, "DS Fellowes, you must realise this is a question of credibility. Your word only or do you have some proof of what you are alleging against DI Meechan?"

It was Burns who answered his question when taking a step forward, she replied, "Sir, Barney…DS Fellowes, I mean. He came to me immediately after having spoken with DI Meechan and told me exactly what he's just told you; that he was instructed to falsify the log and that's why we both agreed he would keep a photocopy of the original to protect himself against any allegation of his involvement."

Again Thorburn sat for several seconds before slowly nodding his head, he replied, "It's not my place to pass judgement on what I've been told today. However," he turned to Meechan, "I'll be going from here to Pitt Street to report to Detective Chief Superintendent Meadows what I've been told."

He held up the typed and photocopied logs before he added, "I'll be taking these with me. In the meantime," he turned to Fellowes and Burns "I suggest that you both prepare statements for your Commander who I'm certain will be in touch very soon."

Rising from his chair, he raised his eyebrows at his DI and said, "Calum?"

Taking the hint, Smith rose from his chair and both men left the room.

"You've fucked my career," Meechan snarled at them both, her face a mask of loathing.

"No," Fellowes sadly shook his head, "you fucked your own career."

****

Minutes later, returned to the DS's room, a shocked Burns quietly asked Fellowes, "What will happen now?"

He took a long breath before he replied, "I'm only guessing, but I think Meechan will be returned to her own Force with possibly the worst confidential report the Commander has ever delivered. Unfortunately," he grimaced, "shite always rises to the top of the water so I'm guessing she'll somehow survive, probably by fluttering her eyelashes and pleading that she was conned by an experienced DS and his pal, that being you," he softly smiled.

"As for us, you and I will be caught in the fallout, Shona. Me, because I falsified the report and though I should have gone above her head, I didn't report Meechan. I'll probably be going back to Edinburgh and likely bumped from the CID as well for bringing my Force into disrepute. As for you, I can only guess you'll be returned to Strathclyde, but whether you go back to uniform or stay in the CD," he shrugged, "depends on what kind of relationship you've previously had with that DCI Thorburn. If he liked you when you served together, he might speak up for you and see you're given the benefit of the doubt."

"What about the operation against Knox and his team?"

His eyes narrowed as his brow creased before he replied, "I'm only guessing, but the likelihood is that given what's happened today and the fact that Knox is probably grieving for his daughter *and* they're a man down since Stobbie got murdered, it might be put on hold for the time being."

He could not know that his opinion, pulling the surveillance of George Knox and his team, was exactly the opportunity that would assist them with their plan to murder Peter Donaldson and Foxy McGuire.

CHAPTER TWENTY-ONE

Unaware that George Knox had already decided that Kelly-Ann had been murdered by Donaldson and McGuire or that Knox and Dunlop had colluded how to deal with the pair, Alex Hardie continued to pursue his own inquiry to find her killer.

After leaving the gym in Springfield Quay, he had twice rung the phone number given to him by Sean the steward for their associate, Eric McFee, the punchy guy, but it was at his third attempt an hour and a half later, that the phone was answered.
Explaining who he was, McFee remembered him and told Hardie he was due to commence a stewarding job in an Irish themed pub in Queen Street in the city centre, but agreed to meet him in thirty minutes prior to McFee starting his shift.
Driving from his flat to the city centre, he gave some thought to McFee and what he remembered about the wee man.
Though Hardie didn't know McFee well and had never socialised with him, the one thing that struck him was a comment that someone had once used to describe McFee, saying that he suffered from the wee man syndrome, a popular term used by Weegies to describe individuals who mindful and resentful of their lack of height, were quick with their fists to challenge any perceived offence, no matter the size of their opponent.
"Hence his nickname, Punchy," he muttered to himself.
Finding a bay in Ingram Street where he parked the Capri, Hardie made his way to the pub, surprised to find that even though it was the late afternoon on a Thursday, it was heaving with punters. However, McFee had the good sense to stand just inside the door to await his arrival then shaking hands, invited Hardie to follow him through to the rear stock room where a couple of plastic tubular chairs and ashtrays indicated it was where the stewards took their break.
"So," McFee began, "what can I do for you, big man?"
Explaining that earlier that day he'd spoken with big Sean and his task to try and discover what happened to Kelly-Ann, McFee nodded then said, "Aye, she was at the dancing on Saturday night. I remember her. You must know what she was like, Alex," he grimaced as though worried about offending Hardie. "A couple of drinks or a bit of the white stuff up her nose and she was game for it with anybody or…"
"Wait" his eyes narrowed as he held up a hand. "You knew she was taking Coke?"
"Aye, I did," McFee sighed as though it were common knowledge. "I had to go into the ladies toilets about, oh," his eyes narrowed as he tried to recall, "Maybe eight or nine weeks ago, but to be honest I'm

really guessing about the date. There'd been a fight in the lavvy between two birds so me and another guy, a cash in hand like me, were sent to sort it out. Jesus," he shook his head, "getting between two guys is bad enough, but the women? I mean you must know what it's like, with them claws they call nails. That and you need to be really careful where you grab them or they're screaming sexual assault, you know?"

Hardie had to smile, having been embroiled in more than a few catfights himself.

"Anyway, there was about a dozen women in the toilets, mostly pissed and watching the scrap and egging them on. Kelly-Ann was one of them, but she was more interested in screaming that somebody had bumped into her because her line of Coke had fallen into a hand basin full of water and got diluted. That's how I knew she was doing the Coke."

"Oh, right. What about Saturday night, though? Ritchie saying he had brought her down to the door for a steward to put her into a taxi?"

"Not on my watch," McFee slowly shook his head. "I mean it was only last Saturday. I'd have definitely remembered that."

Hardie, now believing Ritchie had been lying, exhaled through pursed lips then standing up from the chair, said, "Thanks, Eric. That's been useful."

"Anytime, big man," they shook hands.

He left the noisy pub and blinking as he stepped into the bright sunshine outside, began to retrace his steps.

He had covered just thirty yards when he heard his name called and turning, saw McFee jogging after him.

Breathlessly, he asked, "Do you know what time Ritchie said he brought Kelly-Ann down to the door?"

"No," Hardie shook his head. "He didn't say a time. Why?"

"Me and big Sean, we took our break for a cuppa about nine-thirty, so we were off the doors for about twenty minutes."

"Oh, right," Hardie's eyes narrowed. "Who relieved you on the doors?"

"Just the one guy, eh, a new guy. His name is…" he tightly closed his eyes and clamped his teeth together as he tried to recall, then after a few seconds, with a triumphant grin, said, "Mickey, that's it. Mickey Rourke is his name. That's how I remember it. The same name as the actor," he smiled, pleased with himself, but then frowned as he added, "I think he came from the bar area to let us away, but I'm not sure."

"Mickey Rourke," Hardie slowly repeated, then asked, "You wouldn't have a phone number for him?"

"No," McFee frowned, then tapping the side of his nose with a forefinger, added, "but I do remember when I asked if he had just started full time, he said he was cash in hand, that he was already working a full time job with the security at Lewis's on Argyle Street."

Hardie clapped the smaller man on the shoulder and with a smile, said, "Thanks, Eric, I owe you one."

"No problem, big man," pleased, he turned and walked off.

Walking back to the Capri, Hardie decided to leave the car where it was, that he'd walk down to Argyle Street to try to find Mickey Rourke and rummaged in his pocket for more coins for the meter.

****

Rosie arrived home with her grandson and chasing the wee lad into his bedroom to get changed out of his school uniform, then asked Knox, "Why is there a kitchen chair in the hallway, behind the front door?"

"I'll explain later when Clint's in bed," he replied in a hushed voice as he helped her out of her jacket.

Bemused, she shook her head then told her husband, "I've a meeting tomorrow morning with the head teacher."

"Anything important?"

"No, I don't think so," she shook her head. "I think it's just to chat to find out how he's settled into the school since his mammy died."

Tears sprung to her eyes and Knox stepped forward to encircle his arms about her.

"God, I don't know why this is so hard," she sniffed as he hugged her to him.

"It's a lot to take in in such a short time, hen. Losing Kelly-Ann and with what happened to wee Kevin."

An overwhelming guilt overcame him as he remembered Stobbie's letter for never before had he kept anything from Rosie.

Throughout their married life, the ups and the downs and the trials that Kelly-Ann had put them through, they had always talked things out and on the occasions when like any married couple they'd argued, never went to bed without the issue between them being resolved.

"What's wrong?"

They turned to see Clint staring wide-eyed at them.

Knox stared down at him and pretending to frown, replied, "Am I not allowed to give my wife a cuddle, wee man? You want me to cuddle you too with my tickly fingers?"

His hands outstretched, he leapt at the small boy who ran off giggling.

"I'll get the kettle on," Rosie smiled through her tears and was turning towards the door when the doorbell rang.

His heart missed a beat and raising an arm to prevent Rosie from answering the door, hurried forward to peer through the spyhole in the door, then breathed a sigh of relief.

Opening the door, he saw DCI Martin Benson and a woman stood with him.

"I'm sorry to arrive without phoning first," Benson said, "but I thought it was about time I paid you another visit to let you know what's happening with the investigation."

Inviting them in, he stood to one side as Rosie took a breath to calm herself, then called out, "Will you have tea or coffee, Mr Benson."

"Tea will be fine, thanks, for us both," he made the decision then said, "This is DS Mhari McGregor, one of my team."

Leading them through to the front room, Knox chased Clint back to his bedroom with the promise if he was good, he could watch television later.

Once they were seated, Benson sighed then said, "I'm sorry to say we're not that much forward since the last time we spoke, Mr Knox. What we have learned is that Kelly-Ann was at the Barrowland ballroom on the night she was killed, though we've yet to determine if she left with anyone or where she went after the dancing."

Politely nodding, Knox thought, maybe where she went isn't relevant anymore since I now know who murdered my lassie; however, he said, "Can I ask how you found out she was at the dancing, Mr Benson?"

Certain that it would soon be in the newspapers anyway, he replied, "We have a letter from the manager who confirms he saw your daughter at the dancing that night."

Though already aware of the letter that Alex Hardie had discovered and of Mark Ritchie legging with the money, Knox realised he had to play the part of the grieving father and so, injecting some curiosity into his voice, he asked, "Why a letter, Mr Benson? Did he not tell you this himself?"

"A letter Mr Knox, because the manager has absconded abroad with a large sum of money that he stole from his employer. However, two of my detectives have tracked him down and they intend interviewing him tomorrow morning about anything he might know of your daughter at the dancing, anyone in particular she was with or if he knows where she went after the dancing."

"And this man, is he a suspect for her murder?" he asked.

"That I can't say, but as I have said, he is to be interviewed and that question will be put to him."

"Oh," Knox's brow furrowed, but he was saved from further remarks when Rosie entered the room with a tray of tea.

Once everyone was served, she sat in the available armchair and asked Benson, "Sorry if you have to repeat yourself, but is there any news?"

"Nothing other than what I've told your husband. We now know Kelly-Ann was at the dancing at the Barrowland and really, that's it."

He took a breath then said, "Mr Knox, I know you will have your own contacts in the city, people who perhaps aren't keen to come forward to speak with us. Have *you* heard anything?"

He shook his head before he replied, "Nothing."

"Is there any likelihood that Kelly-Ann was murdered because of, ah, your professional activities?"

Knox wryly smiled then replied "You think some bank or building society put a hit out on my family?"

Even Benson had to grin at that then shaking his head, said, "I take it that's a no, then."

"This thing, Mr Benson, that's in the 'Glasgow News,' the article that's saying it has a source that suggested it might be that headcase Bible John who's back, that it might have been him that killed Kelly-Ann? Are you investigating that?"

Benson grimaced before he replied, "Like any investigation that's ongoing, Mr Knox, we have to keep an open mind. Frankly, my opinion is that the 'Glasgow News,' a rag that I don't read, is more interested in selling newspapers than actually reporting facts. I can assure you and your wife that none of my officers nor anyone connected with Strathclyde Police has offered that opinion to the 'Glasgow News' and for what it's worth, I think the article is absolute rubbish."

Already having convinced himself who the real killers were, Knox's brow creased when he nodded in understanding.

"I have a question, Mr Benson," Rosie darted a glance at her husband. "If your investigation doesn't find out who killed my girl, when will the PF let us have her body?"

"That's a question for the PF, Mrs Knox, but I assure you that we're doing everything we can to find her killer. However," he shrugged, "the fact is I can't guarantee we will find who killed Kelly-Ann, but what I will say is that I will personally speak with the Fiscal to try and speed things up and have her released back to you."

"Thank you," she quietly replied.

"Well," Benson rose to his feet as did McGregor, "I'm sorry there's nothing more I can tell you at this time, but once my detectives speak with this man Ritchie who's abroad, if there is any further update, I'll be in touch."

Rosie glanced at her husband, but he subtly shook his head to indicate he would explain when the detectives had left.

Stood together in the hallway after seeing the detectives out and with the front door closed, Knox told her, "The manager of the Barrowland left a letter saying she'd been at the dancing last Saturday night, but Alex had already found that out anyway."

Nodding at the chair behind the door, she turned to stare suspiciously at her husband before she said, "Now explain this to me, George."

****

In the CID car in the street below, Mhari McGregor fastened her seat belt then remarked, "You were very polite to him, boss, calling him Mr Knox. But," she started the engine, "seeing as how the man is a Z tagged criminal, can I ask why that is?"

Benson took a few seconds before he answered, then his thick, bushy eyebrows thoughtfully knitting, he said, "I'm very well aware of George Knox's profession, Mhari, and the number of robberies he's committed or suspected of committing, but curiously, that has nothing to do with our investigation. As far as I'm concerned, George Knox and his wife are as much victims as is their lassie and *as* victims, they deserve the best of our abilities to find their daughter's killer and our support in their time of grief. Now that said," he turned to stare blankly at her, "how would you treat the Knox family?"

"Point taken, boss," she sighed.

****

Rosie Knox wasn't happy about having a gun in the house, an issue in which her husband agreed with her even though he laboured the point that it was for the protection of not just the two of them, but of young Clint too.

"So," arms folded she huffily replied, "am I to believe that me and the wee man are at risk every time we step out of the door?"

He swallowed tightly then shaking his head said, "It's more me that's likely to be the target of them two, hen, but if they come chapping at the door to get me, that's when it will put you and Clint in danger and *that's* why I've got the shooter here."

She stared dully at him then shaking her head was about to turn away when the doorbell rang.

He could see the fear in her eyes as he turned to peek through the spyhole, then with a smile, told her, "It's Alex."

"I'll stick something on for him," she sighed with relief. "You know what he's like, always hungry."

As she turned away, Knox smiled for she was like a motherly hen where the big guy was concerned, treating him like the son she'd always wanted.

He opened the door to Hardie who asked, "Was that a CID car pulling away?"

"Aye," Knox nodded as he closed the door behind him, "it was that guy Benson and one of his detectives, just to let us know they've confirmed Kelly-Ann was at the dancing on Saturday night."

"Anything else?" Hardie asked as he followed Knox along the hallway, pausing only to wink and wave at Rosie in the kitchen.

"Aye," Knox inclined his head that Hardie sit in the opposite armchair. "They've tracked down the manager, your man Ritchie, to somewhere abroad and two of Benson's people intend speaking with him tomorrow morning."

Hardie's face fell when he muttered, "Shit."

"What?"

Licking anxiously at his lips, he replied, "Ritchie's bound to tell them he left a handwritten note about Donaldson and McGuire trying to push their drugs in the dancing, not the note that I had Avril type and sign."

"And that's important, why?"

"Because it leaves her in the proverbial, boss. They'll probably guess that she's dummied up the typed note and wonder why? Then they'll drag her in and maybe charge her with something, I don't know what," he shook his head, "but being the cops, they'll not like what she did and go for their pound of flesh."

"What do you propose to do then?"

"I promised to protect her, but that was against Donaldson and McGuire," he shook his head again, "but there's no way I can protect her against the cops if they come for her. But now that they're in the equation, I suppose I'd better do something about it."

"Like what, take her out of the country with you?" Knox bit at his lower lip to stop himself from smiling.

Hardie grimaced before he admitted, "I had been thinking about it, so maybe this is just the motivation I needed."

"Well, on that point," Knox then explained about the requirement for passports photos and details in new names for the birth certificates and driving licenses too.

"I can do that," Hardie nodded, then added, "I'll get them delivered to Harry by tomorrow."

He saw Knox frown and sensed there was something else, so asked, "What?"

Glancing at the door as though expecting Rosie to step through, Knox shrugged before he replied, "I've something to tell you, but we'll wait till Rosie has fed you then take a turn out into the veranda for a fag.

As though on cue, Rosie stepped into the room with a plate of chips covered in salt, vinegar and brown sauce that with a fork, she handed to Hardie, telling him, "I'm guessing you'd no lunch?"

"How well you know me," he grinned at her.

Minutes later, when Rosie had delivered them both a mug of tea and left to prepare dinner for her husband, herself and grandson, Knox nodded that they move out to the veranda where he quietly told Hardie about the letter from Kevin Stobbie.

Visibly shocked, Hardie said, "I swear to you, boss, I had no idea."

"No," Knox shook his head, "neither did Jimmy or me, son, and I haven't told Rosie, either. There will be time enough for that when we're out of here and settled abroad, so keep it to yourself for the time being."

"Of course."

It was then he recounted the conversation with Jimmy Dunlop and their plan to murder Donaldson and McGuire.

When he'd finished, he stared at Hardie and could see the doubt in the younger man's eyes.

"You don't agree?"

"With the plan to knock them off?" Hardie shrugged. "It's not that, boss, it's just…"

"What then?"

"Well, that night I met with the pair of them at the Peoples Palace, I just got the feeling that, I can't explain it," he took a sharp breath, "but I just didn't figure them for killing Kelly-Ann."

Always conscious the simplest mistake in the profession he had chosen could land him in prison, Knox was never a man who dismissed an inner sense and after standing in silence for a moment, he asked, "This feeling you've got, son. Can you explain it?"

"All I can say," Hardie flicked the ash from his cigarette into the garden below, "is that Donaldson and McGuire didn't know you and Jimmy were watching out for me that night, so they weren't afraid of me, yeah?"

"Yes," Knox agreed with a slow nod.

"So, if they weren't at all bothered sneering about Kevin being killed and I know it sounds crazy, boss, if they'd had anything to do with Kelly-Ann's murder I think they'd have had a dig about it to me, maybe even to wind me up, but," he curled his lip and shook his head, "it wasn't even mentioned."

"If it wasn't them, Alex, who could it be?"

"Right now, I honestly don't know, but I'm going to ask a favour of you."

"And that is?" he stared curiously at him.

"Let me continue to ask my questions."

He leaned on the metal railing of the veranda and stared thoughtfully at the well-tended garden below as he continued, "Right now I'm trying to trace a taxi driver that might have driven her away from the Barrowland. There's a security guy, a fella called Mickey Rourke, who was working for cash in hand last Saturday night at the dancing and who works in Lewis's in the city. I tried to speak to him today, but he wasn't on duty. I'll get a hold of him tomorrow and hear what he has to say. Come on, boss," he urged Knox, "it can't do any harm."

"It won't affect my decision about Donaldson and McGuire, Alex," Knox harshly said. "Those bastards turned my daughter onto the drugs and they're getting done for that," he unexpectedly snapped at the younger man.

"And rightly so," Hardie softly agreed, "but let me follow up what I can, eh?"

"Okay," Knox sighed, but with a definite reluctance in his voice, then rubbing a hand wearily across his face, added, "but I need to ask. Are you in on the hit on Donaldson and McGuire?"

"I'm in," Hardie nodded.

****

Driving home from George Knox's flat, Alex Hardie gave thought to what he had agreed to; the murder of two men.

Yes, a right pair of scummy bastards that probably deserve it, but at the end of the day, he thought, murder is murder no matter who the victim is.

He'd never been involved in killing anyone, never even considered that one day he'd be in the position where he'd be asked to assist murdering someone, let alone the two drug dealers.

Yes, there had been times he'd been involved in physically hurting somebody and always men, never women though he had skelpt a few on the back of the head when he was stewarding and they were uncontrollably out of their faces and wild with the drink.

But being part of a hit team?

Not that he'd any sympathy for that pair of bastards. The misery they sowed among the folk in Glasgow turned his stomach and through the years, he'd known more than a few men and women that included a good pal, who'd overdosed themselves.

His brow creased as he thought, but do they deserve to be killed for turning Kelly-Ann on to the Coke?

He wasn't certain of the answer to that question, but then again, he argued with himself, she wasn't my daughter.

So, would it have been different for me if she *had* been my daughter?

Probably, he unconsciously nodded at the answer to his own question.
And did they kill her to keep her from telling her Da and to prevent the boss taking revenge on them?
Again, he wasn't certain though the likelihood was that they did or in the long run, would have.
So why am I still having this weird feeling, he wondered?
I'm not a cop, he inwardly argued, I've no training and I know nothing about looking for whoever killed her.
Am I being self-indulgent, trying to prove something to myself that I can find her murderer, do what the cops can't?
His thoughts turned to the boss telling him about the letter from wee Kevin; now that had been a shocker, he unconsciously shook his head.
Wee Kevin, Clint's father?
The wee scunner had kept that a real secret and for what, nigh on six years?
He would never had said to the boss, but there was no doubt in his mind that when Kevin took her home that night, and never in a million years was Kevin a ladies man, so more than likely Kelly-Ann was pissed and he'd no doubt it was she who persuaded Kevin into bed with her.
And good looker that she was, the wee man must've thought he'd won a watch that night, Hardie involuntarily grinned.
Christ, she tried often enough with me he continued to grin at the memory.
He turned slowly into Reidvale Street and slowed as he approached his close.
Sitting staring through the windscreen, he made his decision.
He'd speak with this guy, Mickey Rourke, find out what taxi he put Kelly-Ann into and once he'd found the taxi driver, ask if the driver remembered her and where he'd dropped her off. If he couldn't recall or if the driver did recall and the address was a dead end, then he'd chuck it in and finish his investigation.
His investigation, he almost laughed out loud.
Listen to me, like I'm a Weegie version of Columbo, he shook his head and sniggered.
Or, his brow creased as a thought came to him, maybe even send the information anonymously to the cops and let them deal with it.

He turned his head to stare up at his flat and saw the lights were on. It was then his thoughts turned to Avril and the detectives interview tomorrow in Spain with Mark Ritchie.
Once the cops knew she'd lied about the letter, they'd want to know why and she'd be forced to tell them about me persuading her to falsify the letter and that I have the original. That and she'd likely tell them too about Donaldson and McGuire and their relationship with Kelly-Ann.
Jesus, talk about a cat among the pigeons?
That and it could put a spoke in the boss's plan for the hit on the two of them, for it wouldn't take a genius to work out that when they were killed, it was me who knew about them using Kelly-Ann as a mule for getting the Coke into the dancing.
Then two and two would give them the boss and Jimmy.
He glanced again at the flat and exhaling, thought, it would be no bad thing to take her with me.
All I have to do before we skip the country is keep her out of the hands of the cops.

CHAPTER TWENTY-TWO

Friday 3 February 1984:
Detective Alejandro Perez, wearing dark sunglasses and as immaculately dressed in a light grey coloured linen suit as he had been the day before, was at the reception desk waiting when DI Roddy Williams and Willie McBride arrived downstairs, with the DS looking slightly the worse for wear after their session in the hotel bar, the previous evening.
Perez's eyes widened and he started to grin when McBride held up a hand then said, "Must've been something I ate."
"Aye, nothing to do with those eight bottles of San Miguel or the extra-large portion of paella," Williams shook his head.
"Ready, gentlemen?" Perez led them from the hotel towards the unmarked Seat police car, parked in the roadway a mere fifteen yards away.

Blinking in the bright sunlight both Scots wished they'd invested in sunglasses and almost immediately could feel the perspiration trickle down their spines.

****

Sitting at the kitchen table finishing his tea and toast, Lennie Campbell smiled at his wife, who in a voice filled with suspicion, asked him, "Why are you going out so early?"

"I'm picking up the boss. He's got something on this morning," he continued to tightly smile.

"But it's only gone quarter past seven," she protested, then her eyes narrowing, asked, "Is it the fat one or the wee creepy guy? Him you call Foxy?"

"Foxy," he confirmed with a nod, then with a sigh, he added, "Don't start, hen. I don't like working for that pair any more than you want me to, but it's an earner and we've the lassie's wedding to pay for."

"I know," she slumped down into the chair opposite then continued, "You know that Charlene wouldn't bother if it was just us and her man's folks, Lennie. Especially after all that we…that you've done for her."

"Aye, I know that, hen, but she's our only girl and I want her to have a day to remember. A day that celebrates everything she's been through and beaten," he nodded with fatherly pride.

She stared at him, a gnawing suspicion eating at her before she asked, "What is it that he needs done at this time of the morning, Lennie?"

He didn't answer, so she said again, "Lennie? What are you not telling me, you big bugger?"

He supped the last of his tea, then rising from his chair, leaned down to kiss the top of his pint-sized wife's head and said, "Don't be worrying about me, hen."

When he'd left the kitchen and after she heard the front door close, she slowly shook her head and thought, when have I ever stopped worrying about you, you silly man.

****

Alex Hardie had a sleepless night and rose from his bed feeling more restless than tired.

Turning to glance at Avril, he could see that she seemed to be asleep, but could not know that lying on her side facing away from him, her eyes were open and she too had had a restless night, though for a different reason.

Her thoughts had not permitted her to sleep for she had worried herself almost sick when he'd broken the news that the police might want to question her about the fake letter she had given them and in the darkness of night, when all her problems seemed to gather, she'd imagined herself being arrested and thrown into prison.

Hearing the door softly close, she decided to lie on for another few minutes.

A few minutes later in the kitchen and though he'd tried to be quiet, he turned to see Avril standing at the door, his dressing gown wrapped around her, her hair dishevelled, but in his mind looking sexier than ever.

"Morning, gorgeous," he smiled at her.

She blushed and running her fingers through her hair, replied, "Either you're short-sighted or you're starting to really fancy me, Alex Hardie."

There was no correct response to that he decided and so instead, asked, "What can I get you for breakfast?"

She exhaled as she sidled over to the kitchen table then slumping tiredly down into a chair, replied, "Just coffee for the minute, thank you."

He'd already prepared her a mug and placing it down in front of her, sat opposite, then staring soberly at her, said, "I know what I told you last night and it's a lot to take in, Avril, but if you do decide to come with me I'll need to get passport photos of you and a new identity to give to the guy that's organising it and sometime today, the earlier the better."

She licked nervously at her lips before she asked, "You really think I'm in danger of being arrested by the police?"

"I do," he nodded, then admitted, "and I'm to blame. If I hadn't persuaded you to type that letter…"

"You couldn't know at the time," she reached her hand across the table to rest upon his.

"I could have said no, but I didn't. Besides, who would have guessed that the police would have tracked Mark down? I mean, you said yourself that it was unlikely he would let himself be found."

"But they did find him, though God knows how," he bitterly replied.

She withdrew her hand from his then cupping both her hands around the mug, sipped at the coffee before she said, "You also think the company will fire me, even though I'd nothing to do with the theft?"

"That's what the lassie that was in your office told me, yes," he nodded.

"So, if I'm to accept your offer to go with you, what am I leaving behind?" her perfectly trimmed eyebrows knitted as she stared hard at him.

He realised it was a rhetorical question and waited till she continued.

"I'm thirty-three years of age, no husband or children, I've no job to return to, my home is a rented council property so I *need* to work to pay the rent, I've no family to speak of and the few close friends I have are all married and involved with their families. Socially," she sighed, "they've not a lot of time for me."

She paused and took a breath, then slowly exhaling, continued to stare at him before she said, "You're offering to take me abroad with you to God knows where because you've not yet said…"

"I hadn't quite made my mind up, but I'm thinking Menorca, maybe settling in the old city of Mahón," he interrupted with a soft smile. "I was there years ago in a place called Cala Pedrera. Lovely, it was and the houses were, well," his eyes shone with the memory, "spectacular is the only way to describe the place. There's a lot of ex-pat's there too, so English is pretty well spoken everywhere. And," he smiled, "there's a population of over ninety-thousand on the island so it would be easy for us to be anonymous there, particularly with our new names."

"Menorca," she slowly repeated, her eyes widening. "I've never been abroad," she blushed, then continued, "But, Alex, are you taking me because you feel responsible for me or because you think you might have feelings for me? Please, truthfully."

"Truthfully," he stopped smiling, his brow knitting, "I'm not one hundred per cent sure, Avril. You're beautiful and you're smart, so that's a definite bonus and the sex with you is," he shrugged, "wonderful. Yes, I feel responsible in that I've complicated your life, but I won't deny I have feelings for you. I've never," he made italics in the air with his forefingers, "been in love, but what I feel for you is real and right now, right at this minute, I want to be with you."

She didn't immediately respond, but then slowly shaking her head, said, "If I agree to come with you, I'll be bringing nothing more than a suitcase of clothes, Alex. I don't have any savings and I can't pay my way."

He leaned forward to tell her, "Let me assure you and I can explain later if you do decide to come with me, but money won't be a problem. I'm too young to retire," he smiled, "so I intend buying a small business and I've always fancied setting up a small a bar, somewhere to provide drink and maybe local food. If it makes you feel better about coming with me," he began to smile, "I'd be looking for a manager to run it. Somebody I can trust," he stared meaningfully at her, then added, "and we both know that you already have a background in finance, so that would be a definite bonus."

"And if this…" her brow creased as she paused, seeking the right words, "this *thing* we have at the minute; what if when we get to Menorca or wherever you decide, that this thing between us doesn't work out. What if you get tired of me or…"

He held up a hand to stop her and said, "If it doesn't work out, Avril, then it won't be because we didn't try to make it work. Yes," he nodded, "I know I'm asking you to take a chance on me, just as I'm taking a chance on you, but isn't it worth taking a risk?" he stared at her. "What's the alternative? You remain here in Glasgow, as you said, with no job, few friends and no future and the threat of being arrested hanging over you? Come with me," he urged her as he rose from his chair and walked to stoop beside her, his hands now holding hers.

"What's the Abba song again," he smiled. "Oh, aye…Take a chance on me?" he sang off-key to her.

"Now you're being ridiculous," she laughed while tears gently rolled down her cheeks.

"Yes, okay, I'll come with you," she finally nodded.

"Right, well," he stood upright, "let's get you fed then dressed and we'll head out to get some photos done. When we've got the pictures, we need to pick a new name for us both so that I can get the details to our guy for this afternoon, at the latest."

He left her in the kitchen to make herself some breakfast while he showered.

Stripping off in the bathroom, he felt a little guilty that he hadn't told her that he planned to send her on ahead, that he had to remain behind with the boss and Jimmy to settle a score.

But, he convinced himself, that was a conversation for another time.

****

Lying in bed in the comfortably furnished two-bedroom apartment above the pharmacy in Madrid's Calle de Cuchilleros, Mark Ritchie listened to the noise of the passing traffic in the narrow street below and with a slight groan, rubbed wearily at his forehead.

Too much time on his hands during the day had led to far too much red wine in the evening and this morning, he knew he was paying for it.

Idly scratching at his groin, he swung his legs from the bed and shakily got to his feet.

His first port of call was to make his toilet then decided there was an urgent need to hydrate himself and collected a bottle of ice-cold water from the fridge.

Wearing just the shorts, he padded along the tiled floor to the kitchen and was about to pull open the fridge door when the doorbell rang.

His eyes narrowed and he experienced a sense of panic for the in the short time since Ritchie had arrived in Madrid and been accommodated in the apartment, he had made neither friends nor knew anyone other than having a passing flirt with the middle-aged barmaid across the road, so had not an inkling who would be calling on him.

Slowly, he made his way to the front door and startled when the doorbell again rang.

Licking nervously at his caked lips, he pulled the door open to be greeted by a tall, swarthy man wearing a light grey linen suit who produced a small wallet, then said, "Senor Ritchie? Detective Perez, Policía Municipal de Madrid. May we come in?"

Without waiting for a response, Alejandro Perez stepped forward causing the surprised Ritchie to back away into the narrow hallway and that's when he saw the two men behind Perez and his heart sank.

The three detectives sat in the small lounge while Ritchie donned a sweat stained light blue, shirt he'd grabbed from the floor of the bedroom, then pulled on a pair of clean khaki shorts and leather sandals.

Returning to the lounge he ignored the two men and asked Perez, "What's this all about?"

Perez didn't respond, but turning to Williams, subtly nodded.

"I'm Detective Inspector Roddy Williams and this is Detective Sergeant Willie McBride, Mr Ritchie. We're from Strathclyde

Police. We're here…"
But he got no further for Ritchie held up his hand to snarl, "You've no right to be here. I know there's no extradition, so you can't touch me and," he turned angrily to Perez, "I've broken no Spanish laws."
There was several seconds of silence before Williams, his voice low, but clear, calmly replied, "Murder knows no borders, Mr Ritchie."
Shocked, he stared at Williams then, his voice faltering, said, "Murder? What the fuck are you on about? I haven't murdered…"
He stopped midsentence, his expression changing to one of understanding as he almost whispered, "Kelly-Ann. Jesus wept! You think I had something to do with that?"
Groping behind him for the arms of the rattan seat, he slumped down and continuing to stare at Williams, gulped then said, "I thought you were here for…well, something else."
"You mean the money you ripped off from your company?"
His shoulders sagged and his head bowed, then suddenly rising from his chair so quickly McBride did likewise in the belief that Ritchie was making a run for it, he waved a hand and said, "I need some water."
They watched him make his way into the kitchen then exchanging glances, Williams whispered to McBride and Perez, "We'll commence the interview here while he's no time to get his thoughts together."
They waited then in silence till he returned to the room and resumed his seat.
"Kelly-Ann," he shook his head. "I swear I know nothing about her getting murdered. Didn't you get my letter?" he glanced from Williams to McBride.
"We did," Williams confirmed with a nod.
"Then you're not here about the, ah, the money?"
Williams took a breath then explained, "As you quite rightly pointed out, Mr Ritchie, we have no legal jurisdiction in Spain at the minute. However, I can inform you that you are a person of interest in the theft of a considerable sum of money from your company and I'm in no doubt you will be pursued by Strathclyde Police regarding that issue."
Chancing his arm, Williams shrewdly asked, "I take it you're admitting the theft?"
Almost with relief in his voice, Ritchie slyly replied, "I'm admitting

to nothing, Mr Williams. Now, why *are* you really here? I mean," his eyes narrowed, "you did say you got my letter?"

Williams leaned forward to stare at him before he replied, "Aye, like I said, we did, but you have to realise that fleeing the country during a murder investigation after leaving a signed letter stating the victim had been in your premises and you had seen her on the night she was murdered. That leaves you as our number one suspect."

Bemused, Ritchie stared back at him before he replied, "Eh? A signed statement? What the fuck… But hang on, pal," he waved a hand. "Haven't you questioned Donaldson and McGuire? I mean, I thought it was them that done her in."

Now it was Williams and McBride who were confused, but it was McBride who asked, "Peter Donaldson, the drug dealer and his sidekick, Foxy McGuire? Why do you think it was them two?"

"I thought you'd read the letter?" eyes narrowing, he glanced suspiciously from McBride to Williams.

"Aye," Williams nodded, "but there was no mention of Donaldson or McGuire."

"Listen," frightened now, he began to get angry and insisted, "I wrote it all down, I told Alex how they were trying to get Kelly-Ann to bring Coke into the dancing and threatened to cut off my balls if I didn't let them and they'd hurt my secretary too!"

"Alex?"

"Alex Hardie. You said you got the letter. I mean, he must have given it to you if you have it."

"Wait," McBride raised a hand to stop him, his eyes peering closely at Ritchie. "You said you *wrote* a letter to Alex Hardie? You mean you *wrote* it by hand?"

"Aye, for fucks sake, what else would you think?"

McBride glanced at Williams who replied for them both when he slowly said, "The letter we were given came from your secretary, Avril Collins, and it was typed, Mr Ritchie. There was no mention of Alex Hardie receiving it and nothing in it that indicated Donaldson and McGuire were trying to recruit Kelly-Ann Knox to take cocaine into the Barrowland Ballroom."

Stunned, his face pale, he stared at Williams and shook his head before he stuttered, "That's not right. I *wrote* the letter and put it into an envelope that I addressed to Alex and said he'd to tell you guys about that pair. Besides," he vigorously shook his head, "I can't fucking type! That's why I had a secretary!"

McBride turned to Williams to dully say, "We've been sold a dummy, Roddy."

"Aye, so it seems, Willie," he thoughtfully sighed.

He took a breath then addressing Ritchie, said, "Right, it seems we didn't get the whole story then. So, Mr Ritchie, as you are already aware we can't arrest you for the crime of which you're suspected, but I am going to caution you and I want you tell to me exactly what you said in your letter and Mr Ritchie. If you want to absolve yourself from Kelly-Ann Knox's murder, do not even think about leaving anything out."

****

Lennie Campbell stopped the car on Broomfield Road adjacent to Broomfield Crescent.

Seated in the rear passenger seat, the Luger handgun in the rear waistband of his trousers uncomfortably pressing into spine, Foxy McGuire said, "Let's go over it again, big man. When they come alongside the motor, I jump out, push her out of the way, grab the kid into the motor and we're off."

"Aye, so you said," Lennie, sighed.

"You don't sound too enthusiastic about this," McGuire leaned across between the two front seats to snarl at him.

"It's fine, Foxy. No worries," Lennie raised a hand to calm McGuire and stared through the front windscreen.

But it wasn't fine. Grabbing a wean off the street worried the life out of him and he considered all the pitfalls.

The cops could be passing in one of their vans or somebody could see them and take a note of the motor's reggie plate.

Any number of things could wrong.

McGuire sat back down then said, "Once we have the kid we drive to the flat in Ibrox and I'll phone Knox and when he arrives," he grinned and made the sign of a gun with his forefinger and clenched fist, "he gets the message."

"Right," Lennie nodded, but he still had a bad feeling about this and though he tried not to think about it, his unpaid debt to Alex Hardie, Knox's pal, continued to trouble him.

****

George Knox had just got dressed and leaving the bathroom, saw

Rosie in the hallway wearing a light blue coloured blouse, knee length navy blue pencil skirt with dark tights and her blonde hair falling loosely onto her shoulders.

"My God, woman," he smiled with genuine pleasure, "you're a sight for sore eyes, so you are."

She blushed, then as if explaining her choice of clothes, said, "Remember I told you, I've a meeting this morning with Clint's headmistress."

"Eh? Oh, aye, of course."

"Nothing to worry about," she waved away his concern. "It's just a wee report to let me know how he's doing at the school," but then her eyes narrowed. "If we're leaving soon, do you think I should just cancel the meeting?"

"No," he quickly replied with a shake of his head. "Keep things normal. I don't want people getting suspicious about us taking off."

"So, we're really doing this, George?"

"Aye, hen," he replied with a nod, but sensing there was something amiss he placed a hand gently on her arm, then asked, "What's worrying you?"

She teared up when she replied, "It's going away abroad when we've not even buried Kelly-Ann. Leaving her like that without us being there for her service."

"I know it's going to be hard hen, but," he reminded her once again, "you know that she wouldn't want us to stay and risk me getting the jail, would she?"

"No," she nodded then taking a deep breath to compose herself, added, "You're right. Of course, you're right," and reaching across to hug him and peck him on the cheek, rubbed away with her fingers the trace of lipstick she left there.

They turned when Clint stepped out of his bedroom, his tie lopsided, as was his bright smile.

Staring at him, Knox tried hard to see any resemblance to Kevin Stobbie, but the wee boy was so like his mother he just couldn't see anything of Stobbie in him and inwardly thought; it doesn't matter who his father is, he's my grandson and I love him.

Curiously, he thought, making that decision seemed to calm him.

"I'm ready, Granny," Clint, his face flushed and his hair brushed and neatly parted, smiled up at her.

"Right," she brightly replied, "let me get my coat."
"You're not walking him to the school, are you?"
"Aye, for once it's a nice day," she replied.
"Listen, I've a better idea. Let me drive the pair of you, you go in and have your meeting and then we can visit Jimmy and Liz, pick up their photos and details and I'll drop you in town and you can deliver the photos and the script with the details to Harry Cavanagh."
Her face registered her confusion when she asked, "It's no bother, but wouldn't it be better if you did that?"
He glanced meaningfully at Clint before he replied, "I'm thinking if the you-know-who are on me today, they'll stick with me, but they'll not be interested in you doing a bit of shopping, if you get my drift."
Slowly nodding, she replied, "Aye, well, that means we don't need to hurry now, so, wee man," she turned to the child, "away back into your room and have another ten minutes playing with your trainset while your Granddad and me have another cuppa, eh?"
****

Alex Hardie drove the Capri to Bridgeton Cross then parking the car in Olympia Street, walked with Avril to a small photographic shop around the corner in London Road.
Fifteen minutes later, the photographer was satisfied with the snaps and for an two quid, promised to have the passport photos ready within an hour.
"That gives us time for some coffee," Hardie smiled as he led her to a nearby café.
While in the café, Hardie re-read the details of the names they were to adopt and was pleased that they had both decided that their destination would indeed be Menorca.
It was then he made his decision.
"There's something you need to now," he quietly began. "I'm sending you away first and I'll join you out there."
Her face placed when she hissed, "What do you mean? Sending me out there? Aren't you coming with me?"
"Yes, of course," he slowly waved his hand up and down to indicate she lower her voice. "I need to stay behind for a few days to tie up some loose ends, that's all. George and Jimmy, the guys I work with, their wives are going out ahead of them as well. The man who's organising the passports and the documents, he's arranging hotel

accommodation for Rosie and Liz, George and Jimmy's wives, and he'll do the same for you till I join you out there."

"Are they going to Menorca too?"

"No," he frowned, "we're splitting up, the three of us."

As a precaution, he made the decision not to disclose their final destinations and so told her, "I'm not certain where they're heading too, but we will be staying in touch through our contact, Harry."

She slowly nodded in understanding then, her voice faltering, asked, "And what if the reason you're staying behind for lands you in prison, Alex? What am I supposed to do then?"

He smiled when he replied, "You need to trust me because I promise you, Avril, you'll be taken care of. Harry, the guy who's arranging things for us, he'll see that you're all right. No matter what happens, I'll arrange for him to open a bank account in your name over in Menorca. There will be enough money in the account to tide you over for at least a year," he smiled then added, "unless you're a mad gambler. If you're careful, it will do you until you find yourself a job."

He took a deep breath, then confidently added, "But let's not think about that. I won't be any longer than two or three days behind you, then after we find a place and a business, you can decide if you want to stay with me or not."

"Oh, so whether or not we are a couple is up to me?" she coolly asked him.

He shrugged, then with a smile, replied, "We both know that women like to pretend it's the men that make the decisions, Avril, but the truth is we men only *think* we're in charge."

"And don't you forget it, Alex Hardie," she returned his smile, but fought back the anxious tears that threatened to spill over.

****

Lennie Campbell glanced at his wristwatch then turning his attention to the rear-view mirror, said, "That's nearly half past nine, Foxy. I don't think they're coming."

Slumped petulantly in the rear seat, McGuire snorted, "Right! Fuck this! What time do primary kids get out of school?"

"Eh, I'm a wee bit out of touch with the comings and goings of schoolkids, Foxy, but I'm guessing about three?"

There was a huffy sigh from McGuire, who then replied, "Okay, then. We'll be back here at ten to three and snatch the kid then. In the meantime, drop me at Peter's and I'll let him know what's happened."

"You're the boss," Lennie nodded and started the engine.

CHAPTER TWENTY-THREE

George Knox had gone through his usual routine when he'd gone downstairs that morning to start the Jaguar, but seeing and finding nothing, expected if the mob were there, the surveillance would pick him up when he started driving Rosie and the wee guy to the school. Driving on Broomfield Road, he'd paid no attention to the dark coloured Ford Cortina parked opposite the Broomfield Crescent junction.

Arriving at the school, he stopped the car thirty yards from the school gate and waited almost twenty minutes until Rosie, her face flushed, reappeared and got into the passenger seat.

"How did it go?" he asked as he smoothly pulled away from the pavement.

"As expected," she sighed. "The class teacher was there too and said that he's a bit quiet at the minute, but he's made a wee friend, a lassie who's being teasing him, but he seems to enjoy it and the teacher said they've been chasing each other round the playground at their breaks."

"A ladies man, eh," he smiled, but then almost immediately thought of Kevin Stobbie and the grin turned to a frown that thankfully, Rosie didn't notice.

When they reached Skerray Quadrant in the Milton area, Rosie cautiously asked, "Are we stopping for a cup of tea or anything?" Though he had been friends with Jimmy Dunlop for a very long time, Knox was aware that Rosie and Jimmy's wife, Liz, weren't always on the same page and through the years, social evenings with the four of them were rare.

"No," he shook his head. "I'll grab the photos and the paperwork and get you into the town for you to give wee Harry the stuff."

Almost automatically, he glanced in his rear-view mirror when he added, "I've not seen any sign of the mob this morning, but that doesn't mean they're not there. Once I've dropped you, I'll just head back home unless you want me to hang about for you?"

"No, you're all right," she shook her head. "I'm going to M and S for some new knickers. If we're going away forever, I want to take some extra with me. That and I'll get some things for Clint, too."

He gave her a lecherous grin then lewdly winking, suggested, "If you going for undies, get something nice and sexy."

She stared deadpan at him before she replied, "George, I'm nearly forty-eight. These days it's comfort rather than erotic."

"But you'll always look sexy to me, though," he tactfully said, earning himself a wide smile.

It took but minutes for him to collect the envelope from Jimmy Dunlop, then returning to the car, told her, "He was wanting us to come in for a cuppa, but I just said to Jimmy that we were in a hurry to get the stuff to wee Harry."

"Thank you," she gently touched his arm.

****

When they'd collected their photographs, Avril Collins too had decided if she was going abroad, she'd better get herself some lightweight clothes and personal items and so asked if Hardie would drop her into town.

"Actually, I've a bit of business to do in the city anyway, so I'll drop you in there and we can meet for a late lunch, if you're up for it."

Letting her out of the Capri in Clyde Street, Hardie continued to Wellington Street where after parking the car and ensuring as best he could he hadn't developed a tail, he climbed the stairs of the Victorian building to Harry Cavanagh's office.

The outer door was as usual, locked and after ringing the bell, it was opened by the grey-haired woman who scowling asked if he had an appointment with Mr Cavanagh.

Knowing full well he didn't, he replied, "Yes. My name's Alex Hardie and I have some information for him."

"Wait here," she rudely told him then closed the door on him.

Resisting the urge to grin, he knew from what George Knox had told him that wee Harry employed the woman for her accountancy skills rather than her courtesy and she was never to be trusted with any information regarding their business dealings.

Within a minute, the door was pulled open and with a deadpan expression, the woman curtly told him, "Go straight through, Mr Hardie."

Entering the inner office, he was greeted warmly by Cavanagh who ushering him into a seat, said, "Long time no see, my good friend. So, you're off for good, you and the lads?"

"So it seems," he smiled then removing the photographer's envelope with the photos from his inner jacket pocket, handed it with the sheet of handwritten paper to Cavanagh.

Glancing at the sheet, Cavanagh's head shot up when he said, "A woman's travelling with you?"

"Girlfriend. Avril Collins as she is at the minute," Hardie smiled, then added as he pointed at the envelope, then asked, "Is it a problem?"

"No, shouldn't be," Cavanagh glanced at the photograph then added, "You've picked yourself a bit of a stunner, there, Alex."

"I like to think so," he smiled, "and as you can see, her personal details are on the sheet."

"And I see you've chosen Mahon in Menorca?"

"Yes. I holidayed there once and liked the area."

"Oh, I see," Cavanagh's brow creased.

Worried that though Cavanagh said it shouldn't be a problem, Hardie pressed on, "Look, Harry, I know it's a bit of an inconvenience, but I'm prepared to pay that little extra if you can add Avril to the list."

"Well, in that case," he nodded, "we'll call it fifteen hundred for my fee and those of the printer and the travel agent, so yes, I'll get it done, Alex. Now," he stared keenly at Hardie, "can I suggest a change of name, that if you are considering settling over there, you do so with her as your wife? I mean you needn't be legally married."

Hardie's eyes narrowed when he asked why?

"Let me explain. I take it you're recorded by our friends in blue as a single man?"

"Yes, I suppose I am."

Cavanagh pursed his lips when he continued, "You are of course wanting to remain as anonymous as possible, Alex, and Menorca I presume being a Spanish island is populated by a predominantly Catholic society. Might I suggest that being a married couple is less likely to attract attention from nosey neighbours than a single man living with his girlfriend and thus less likelihood you might come to the attention of the local police?"

Hardie's eyebrows knitted as he considered the suggestion, then nodding, replied, "I take your point, Harry. Aye, go ahead and make us a couple. On that point, how long will it take for you to organise the passports and documentation as well as a hotel in Menorca for her to live until I get there and we find our own place? I'm keen that Avril leaves Glasgow as soon as possible?"

"Hmm, today is Friday. My man Wattie has the passports ready to be pasted and printed with your photos and your new names and I suppose I can urge him to create another for your girlfriend. With luck, perhaps get the documents to you for tomorrow evening?"

His brow knitted when he gave it thought before he added, "Hopefully, if the documents are ready and her birth certificate will be in her bogus maiden name, not the married name, so with luck I can arrange a flight for the young lady for say," he grimaced, "early Sunday morning, maybe Sunday afternoon some time?"

Nodding with relief, Hardie said, "That's grand, Harry. I've a feeling the cops might be…" but then held up a hand and smiling, continued, "Sorry, Harry, I forgot. You're never too keen hear all the details."

Appreciating that Hardie remembered to observe Cavanagh's one rule, he smiled then rising from his chair, made his way to the secure cabinet in the corner. From a locked drawer, he lifted out a bulky brown envelope that he handed to Hardie, then said, "Now that I know your destination, Alex, I'll contact the local branch of the Banco Bilbao Vizcaya Argentaria in Mahon. It's a well-established, popular bank and that's where all your money has been wired from the Cayman Islands. The bank's name is on the letterhead in the envelope. In the envelope is a grands worth of high denomination pesetas and that should be enough to see you through till the bank prints you a chequebook and cheque cards in your new names. There is," he added, "a letter of recommendation in the envelope too that simply identifies you as the holder of the account with the Cayman Islands bank, with a slip of paper that has a unique identification code to also identify you to the bank, so until you present the letter and the code there's no need for them to know your new name. Once they have the letter and the unique code, they'll activate your account and register you and your girlfriend as clients. The whole process should take no more than an hour and within a day or two thereafter you'll receive your cheque books and cards at your hotel."

"So, I don't need to produce anything other than the letter with the slip of paper and the unique code?"

"That's correct," Cavanagh nodded once.

"One question. How did you know to open an account for me with a Spanish bank, Harry?"

He smiled before he replied, "When George called in the other day, he said you were doing his head in talking about the Balearic Islands, so I put two and two together and voila," he waved his hands in the air.

"Bloody hell, Harry," impressed, Hardie smiled at him, "How the hell do you manage to cope making all these arrangements?"

"Easy," Cavanagh replied, "I'm brilliant at what I do. Oh, and modest with it," he smiled widely.

****

After leaving Cavanagh's office, Hardie started walking to Argyle Street and made his way along to Lewis's department store where he hoped to speak with the steward, Mickey Rourke.

As he ambled along, he gave thought to Cavanagh's suggestion that he and Avril pose as a married couple and wondered what her reaction to that would be.

She'll be pleased, I suppose, he thought.

His thoughts turned to the man he was looking for, Mickey Rourke, and inwardly hoped that he'd recall last Saturday night and putting Kelly-Ann into a taxi.

Once more it worried him that the boss had already made up his mind about Donaldson and McGuire. Yes, the two of them were a nasty pair of bastards, but again he wondered; why they would murder Kelly-Ann when apparently, they already had her recruited as their source into the Barrowland dancing?

Like the rest of the public, he'd read the 'Glasgow News' opinion that the killer known as Bible John had struck again, but didn't for one minute believe it.

No, she had been killed by someone who'd probably taken advantage of her drunken or Coked condition to abuse her. Too often he and his fellow stewards had prevented some chancers from taking drunken lassies out of the dancing or the clubs, recognising what the men were intent on taking sexual advantage of the women. Of course, not all the stewards were as diligent for more than a few of them were of the attitude if the women got themselves into such a state, then hell mend them.

However, was that the style of Donaldson and McGuire? Raping a drunk and drugged lassie?

The rumours he had heard about Donaldson, though he had no direct knowledge of the man, inferred that his sexual tastes lay elsewhere. But what about McGuire?

Did he somehow come across Kelly-Ann that night, rape her then kill her to keep her mouth shut?

He couldn't explain it in words, had no way of trying to tell George how he felt, but somehow Kelly-Ann's murder just didn't fit those either McGuire and certainly if the rumours were even half true, not Donaldson either.

With a sigh, he passed under the Hielanman's Umbrella then dodging and weaving through the midday crowd, crossed Argyle Street at the busy junction with Union Street before continuing on his way.

Minutes later he pushed open the heavy glass doors at Lewis's and making his way upstairs, asked a young female assistant where he'd find Mickey Rourke, the security man.

"Mickey?" she snorted. "Probably in the perfume department chancing his arm with the lassie's there."

Directing him to the perfume department and even though the store was busy, Hardie soon saw a dark-haired man of his own height, his hair tied in a tight ponytail and hanging over his white coloured shirt collar, wearing a company tie, black creased trousers and scuffed Doc Marten shoes.

The man, whose sleeves were buttoned at the wrists, was leaning forward with his forearms on a tall glass counter speaking with a pretty young assistant of no more than nineteen or twenty years of age.

As he walked towards them, Hardie could see the girl seemed to be embarrassed and inwardly smiled, for he guessed that the man, in Glasgow parlance, was giving the assistant a line of patter.

"Mickey Rourke?" he approached him from the rear.

Turning, the man who Hardie saw had shaved badly and who was smelling of a strong and pungent deodorant and who he guessed to be in his mid to late thirties, stared hard at him before replying, "Who's asking?"

"My name's Alex Hardie," he smiled easily at Rourke. "I was hoping to have a quiet word with you."

Rourke's eye crinkled as he studied Hardie before he softly said, "Alex Hardie. I know that name. You're in the stewarding game, that right?"

"That's correct, yes. A word?" he prompted Rourke.

Rourke pushed himself up from the counter then turning to the young girl, said, "Later, doll."

Turning back, he nodded that Hardie follow, telling him, "I'm due a break anyway."

Walking behind him, Hardie choked back a smile for he saw that Rourke didn't so much walk as swagger his way through the aisles till they reached a door marked, 'Staff Only.'

Pushing his way through, Rourke turned and crooking a forefinger at Hardie, wordlessly beckoned him to follow, then led him through a long corridor to a smoke-filled room where several store staff were seated at tables crowded with paper cups, juice cans and sandwich wrappers.

Settling himself at a table, Rourke pushed back the chair till it was balanced on the rear two legs and began to roll back his shirt sleeves to reveal that both arms were heavily tattooed in what Hardie believed was some sort of performance to impress him.

That done, he then said, "What can I do for you, pal?"

Sitting down opposite, Hardie replied, "I understand on occasion you work for cash in hand at the Barrowland and you were there on Saturday night?"

"That's right. There a problem?" Rourke's eyes narrowed.

"No," Hardie held up his hands and disarmingly smiled, "I'm just looking for some information that you might be able to help me with."

"What kind of information?" Rourke warily asked.

"Mark Ritchie, the manager. He left me word that a friend of mine got herself pissed out of her head that night and he had one of the stewards put her into a taxi to send her home. I'm trying to trace the taxi driver for a word."

Rourke leaned forward so that all four legs of the chair were now on the floor and clasping his hands on the table top stared thoughtfully at Hardie.

His brow furrowed and his lips puckered as though in thought before he asked, "And you think it might have been me? Who was this bird, anyway?"

"Her name was Kelly-Ann. Kelly-Ann Knox."

Rourke's face expressed surprise when he repeated, "Kelly-Ann Knox? The lassie in the papers that got herself murdered?"

As if she was looking for it, Hardie inwardly sighed, but then quietly replied, "You've read about it, then."

Shaking his head, Rourke frowned before he said, "Don't know that I can help you pal. I was working at the bar last Saturday night. You know the score, keeping the punters from snatching the drinks and keeping them in line from queue jumping."

"I heard that," Hardie coolly replied, "but I've spoken with the guys who were on the door that night, big Sean and wee Eric McFee. Eric said you let them away for their break for about twenty minutes?"

Rubbing at his chin, Rourke slowly nodded, then sighed, "Aye, he's right. I was sent down to the door for a wee while, but like you said I'm strictly cash in hand, so not a regular at the Barrowland and I don't know the steward's names or any of the punters there. This bird, this Kelly-Ann. Can you describe her?"

"Did you not see her photo in the newspaper?"

"Oh come on," he drawled and extending his hands as though in explanation, smirked. "You must know yourself, pal, that when the birds arrive at the dancing they're looking tasty, but after a few drinks or a couple of lines of Coke, most of them end up looking like they've been dragged backwards through a hedge."

"Rourke!"

They both turned to see a balding, heavyset, ruddy-faced man similarly dressed with a white shirt and company tie staring at them. "You're ten minutes too early for your break! Get your arse back on the floor right now!"

The man didn't wait for a response, but turned away and the door closed behind him.

Hardie saw more than a few of the staff on their break glance over at Rourke with smiles or grins at his embarrassment.

His face red with anger, Rourke hissed "Bastard!" through gritted teeth.

As he rose from his chair, Hardie quickly asked, "Do you remember Mark Ritchie telling you to put a lassie into a taxi?"

"Mark Ritchie?" his brow creased. "He's the manager, right? Eh, oh, aye, now you mention it," Rourke irritably replied, now anxious to get away. "There was a bird with a green coat on, but she was out of her face on the booze or the drugs."

"That'll be her, she wore a green coat," Hardie confirmed with a quick nod. "The taxi. What can you remember about it?" he persisted.

"Eh," Rourke hesitated tightly closing his eyes as if trying to remember yet seemingly keen to get back out onto the floor before his boss returned.

"It was a Hackney, aye, a black Hackney," he involuntarily nodded as he walked away. Then as he hurried off, calling out over his shoulder, "From the rank up the road. A Paki driver. Aye, that's right. The driver was a Paki."

Hardie watched an embarrassed Rourke hurry from the room, his swagger now gone and presumably because of his supervisor's humiliating telling-off.

A black Hackney car with a Pakistani driver?

Well, that shouldn't be too hard to find, Hardie thought, then rising to his feet, ignored the curious glances from a table of five women as he made his way from the room.

****

Laying his pen down onto the pad, DCI Martin Benson stared at what he'd written.

He was due to present a farewell speech that evening in the ex-serviceman's club in Whitefield Road to a retiring Detective Constable and speeches were just not his thing.

His thoughts turned to the earlier phone call from Roddy Williams with information that had certainly set the cat among the pigeons.

Lifting the phone, he dialled through to the incident room and said, "Mhari, it's me. How many of the team are in the office right now?"

"Eh, six, no, maybe seven, boss."

"Right, collect them together and I'll be through in a minute."

Replacing the phone, he tapped his fingers on the desk as he stared angrily at his pad then grabbed it and made his way through to the incident room.

Mhari McGregor sat at her desk while six other detectives stared at him as they came through the door.

"Sorry, boss, I'm one down. She's got an afternoon District Court appearance," she added.

"Right, listen in," he began. "I've just spoken with Roddy Williams over in Spain who interviewed Mark Ritchie, the manager from the Barrowland who buggered off with almost eighty grand of his company's money."

"Lucky sod," one of the detectives muttered, prompting Benson to respond, "Aye, maybe for now, but not when the extradition treaty goes through and we bring him back to Glasgow. Anyway, according to DI Williams, it seems that the typed letter Ritchie left that was handed to us by his secretary, Avril Collins, was a forgery. Ritchie's alleging that he hand-wrote a letter that contained much more information than was contained in the typed letter we were given by Collins. He further alleges he left the letter for the attention of Alex Hardie, one of George Knox's team, and in the letter asked that Hardie inform us our victim was indeed at the dancing last Saturday night. That and he also alleges Peter Donaldson and his pal, Foxy McGuire, might have something to do with the murder."

He stared at the detectives to allow it to sink in, before he continued, "For those of you who don't know them, Donaldson and McGuire are high profile drug dealers who are targets of the Scottish Crime Squad, our own Drug Squad and our Serious Crime Squad."

Pausing for breath, he continued, "Right, ladies and gentlemen, I want Hardie and Collins brought in to answer why they forged a letter for us and where the original is. If they refuse to come in voluntarily, arrest them on whatever trumped up charge comes to mind and lady and gentlemen," he stared at the DC's in turn, "I am *not* joking."

"Mhari," he turned to her. "Split the six into two teams of three and hit both addresses. When the rest of the team start arriving back, keep them here until we have Hardie and Collins in the office because if we can't find them at their home addresses, I'll want every known address for them turned over. Those two quite possibly have information we need and by heavens if they don't come across with what we need to know, then they'll find themselves at the Sheriff Court on charges of Perverting the Course of Justice!"

****

In the kitchen of his luxurious mid-terraced house in Park Terrace,

Peter Donaldson stood at the marble topped island, preparing the raw chicken and vegetables for that evening's meal.

Listening patiently as he worked, Foxy McGuire explained the details of the prospective delivery of heroin that if Donaldson agreed, would occur within the next six days.

"And our friends from Birmingham, they've agreed to our price?" he asked, his eyes concentrating on the precision cuts with the razor-sharp boning knife.

"Took a wee bit of persuasion," McGuire boasted, "but I beat him down to four big ones a kilo."

What he didn't admit was that the man from Birmingham had firmly stated that was the price and there was to be no negotiation.

"And you believe this to be a fair price for us, my dear boy?" Donaldson continued to concentrate on slicing and dicing his vegetables.

McGuire loathed being called 'my dear boy' and inwardly knew that the fat poofter would rue the day, but right now he needed him to agree to the deal and so enthusiastically nodding, then said, "Oh, aye. By the time we've added the adulterant, we can put it out at anything between fifty to seventy-five per cent profit, Peter."

Donaldson halted his cutting; wordlessly staring at nothing for several seconds, finally he agreed with a nod, then said, "Go ahead. Make the deal."

"Now," he turned to stare at McGuire, the large bladed knife held loosely in his hand.

"This issue with George Knox. Though you missed the boy this morning, you are confident you will be able to grab him this afternoon? I do not want Knox running around for any length of time unfettered and it would be unfortunate if he got it into his head to seek some sort of revenge before he was dealt with. In short, Foxy, he's a loose cannon and he must be put down. Is that clearly understood?"

McGuire didn't know what unfettered meant, but guessed it wasn't a good thing and so nodded when he replied, "Stand on me, Peter. The boy's getting snatched this afternoon and when I get Knox over to the flat in Ibrox, he's getting the message," he reached behind him for the Luger handgun and pulling it from his waistband, theatrically waved it in the air.

"What the fuck!" Donaldson's composure escaped him as he took a step backwards, the knife dropping from his limp grasp to land with a clang on the tiled floor.

"What are you doing with that thing in my house?" he screamed at McGuire.

"Don't worry, the safety's on," McGuire cackled then demonstrating his confidence in the weapon, pulled the trigger.

The loud bang that escaped the Luger startled both men as the bullet exploded from the barrel then struck the metal frame of the Aga range cooker, scoring it for several inches before it ricocheted to fly off at an angle that saw it rebound off the beautiful marble top then come to rest embedded in the plastered wall behind McGuire.

The ominous silence was broken when McGuire, shrinking into himself with his free hand held up protectively to his head, squealed, "Fuck!"

His eyes swivelling, he softly said, "Peter?"

The thinning crown of hair on Donaldson's head appeared above the worktop then his fingers clutched the rim of the marble worktop before his face that was purple with rage, popped into view.

Then he hysterically screamed, "You fucking idiot! You could have killed me!"

"Sorry," McGuire softly muttered.

"Sorry? Sorry!"

For once in his life, Donaldson's was speechless until he found his voice and through gritted teeth, hissed, "Get out, you fucking clown!"

His face paling and the Luger tightly clutched in his hand, McGuire turned on his heel and marched from the kitchen, all the while thinking, nobody calls me a clown and now more determined than before that when Knox was dealt with, he'd put a bullet into Donaldson.

CHAPTER TWENTY-FOUR

The two shopping bags in her hands, Rosie Knox decided that she'd go straight from the city centre to collect her grandson at school. Getting off the bus outside Barmulloch Primary, Rosie joined the throng of parents, grandparents and carers waiting for their children.

Though a few gave her some curious glances simply because she was a new face, she didn't acknowledge any of the nods, preferring to keep herself to herself.

At three o'clock, the bell rang and the adults at the gates, almost as one took an unconscious step forward as though failing to take that one step might inhibit them from identifying their children from the noisy horde that spilled out of the main door.

Glancing back and forth and even though she knew she had not missed him, Rosie sighed with relief when she saw Clint walking slowly from the door, then almost gasped in surprise for the small boy was hand in hand with a girl his own age.

As if suddenly aware they were being watched, the children released their hold and the little girl run towards the gate to be met by a woman in her mid-twenties who shyly smiled at Rosie, before taking the girl's hand and walking off.

"Hi, Granny," Clint wrapped his arms about her thighs to greet her with a hug.

A range of emotions swept through her for she knew that he would not be returning to the school on Monday, that on Sunday a new life awaited them in Palma and it was unlikely he would ever again see his new friend.

Taking his hand, she began the walk home, leaning down and whispering, "Got you something."

"What?" he eagerly asked.

She stopped walking then from her handbag, gave him a pack of Trebor Soft Fruit Rolls, his favourite.

Tearing off the wrapper he grinned with pleasure and they resumed walking.

As they made their way home, she questioned him about his day, who he'd played with, what lessons the teacher gave him, what he had for lunch, but being a typical five-year-old, the school day had now passed and was forgotten and he just could not remember.

They were just ten minutes into their walk when it happened.

Though the rain was off, it was very overcast and already the daylight was fading away.

Approaching the road junction with Broomfield Crescent, Rosie paid no attention to the dark coloured Ford Cortina parked at the side of the road and when she and Clint drew abreast with the vehicle, she

startled when the rear door opened and a wiry man dressed in dark clothes and wearing a stocking mask, jumped from the car.
Turning away from the man, Rosie instinctively raised an arm to shield the small boy, but was grabbed by the hair and her head painfully yanked back.
So sudden was the attack she had no time to call out or scream. The very act of being pulled backwards by the hair caused her hands to automatically flail wildly as she prepared herself to fall to the ground and thus she lost her grip on Clint.
Time seemed to stand still and, in the seconds that it took for her heart to beat twice, she stared down at her grandson and saw the shock and surprise on his pale face, but was then struck viciously by a fist to the face while continuing to be physically hauled backwards.
Falling heavily onto her back, Rosie had the presence of mind to turn onto her front as she collided heavily with the concrete pavement slabs, her tights ripping at the knees that skinned and almost immediately bled and her hands scraping painfully on the ground. But none of this mattered for she was too intent on seeing where her grandson was.
However, horrified, she raised her head to see the masked man grab Clint by his jacket and bodily hauling him towards the car, then heard the man loudly shout, "Go! Go! Go!"
Seeing the man bundle the small boy into the rear of the car, at last she found her voice and panickily screamed, "Clint!"
The car took off, its tyres squealing as the driver pressed down too quickly on the accelerator and threw the car into gear.
Still on her hands and knees, Rosie could only watch helplessly as the car sped off towards the Ryehill Road roundabout.
Stunned, she was unaware that the whole incident had occurred within just a few seconds.
"Jesus Christ!" she loudly wailed. "Somebody help me! Please!"
But there was no one around, no pedestrians near and none of the cars passing on the road stopped, though more than one driver stared curiously at the blonde-haired woman kneeling on the pavement.
Still shocked by the suddenness of the assault, Rosie scrambled to her feet, the palms of her hands bleeding, her knees achingly bloodied and a thin trickle of blood now dribbling from her mouth where she had been punched.
But then with a sudden burst of clarity, one thought came to mind.

"George," she heard herself muttering. "I need to get to George!" Ignoring the pain from her swollen face, Clint's dropped schoolbag and the shopping bags lying on the ground, Rosie almost fell as she pulled off her high heel shoes that she threw to one side and in her bare feet, began to run home.

****

The two male and the female detective assigned by DS Mhari McGregor to visit Avril Collins home in Cardonald, decided that as there was no reply to their knocking, they'd chap the doors of the neighbours houses for information.

While the two male detectives took the houses to either side, the female DC strode across the road where to her indifferent fortune, she happened to knock upon the door of the local busybody, a widowed woman in her mid-seventies whose pastime was regularly watching the comings and goings of her neighbours.

"Norman Collins lassie, the blonde one? Aye, I know her," the wizened faced woman, an unfiltered cigarette stuck between her thin lips, stared at the DC. "Not to speak to, of course. A bit too stuck-up for my liking," she huffed. "What do you want to know about her?"

"Does she live there with her father, then?"

"No, hen, he went to shake hands with auld Nick a while back, just like that crabbit bastard I was married to."

"She lives alone then?"

"As far as I know, aye. There was a guy visited regularly a year or two ago, but I've not seen him for a while."

"Do you know when the last time was that you saw her?"

"Phew," the crone shook her head, "not for a few days anyway. Why? What's this all about?"

"Oh, it's just she's a witness and we're keen to speak with her," the DC smilingly lied in the knowledge that divulging the real reason to the hag might tip off Collins she was being sought after.

"Does she have a car, do you know?"

"I know she drives, she used to drive her Da's old motor car, but I think she got rid of that a while ago."

"But nothing recent? She doesn't have a car now?"

"No, I don't think so."

"Does she have any other regular visitors?"

"Hmm, there was a big, good-looking young guy here a couple of days ago. He drove a fancy motor, red it was. I think he took her away in the motor."

"Can you recall what time that was and what day?"

"Fuck me, hen, what is this? Twenty questions? You're not asking much are you?" she took a deep draw of her fag. "It was about dinner time and this is Thursday, isn't it?"

"No, it's Friday."

"Are you sure?" her brow wrinkled.

"Yes, it's definitely Friday," the DC patiently nodded.

"See me, I'm always losing track of the days," she sighed. "It's an age thing."

"And the day?"

"What day?"

"The day the red motor driven by the big, good looking guy arrived and took Miss Collins away."

"What day was that?"

"That's what I'm asking you," the DC was beginning to lose patience. "Can you remember what day the red motor arrived?"

"Eh, it was Monday or maybe Tuesday."

"So, you don't remember?"

"No," she shook her head. "Every day is the same when you're my age."

"Do you know what the make and model of this motor was?"

"What motor?"

"The *red* motor."

"Do I look like I know anything about motors hen?" she scowled.

The DC bit back her sarcasm and forcing a smile, asked, "So you saw a good-looking young guy, in a red motor pick up Miss Collins from her house one day this week, but you haven't seen her since?"

"No, but I'll chap her door and let her know you're looking for her. Who are you, again?"

The DC irritably shook her head then said, "Just tell her the polis want a word and to contact us when she can."

"You're the polis? My, you're awfully young to be a polis, hen."

"Tell that to my teenage twins," the DC muttered as she left to join her colleagues.

****

"Slow down, Lennie! For fuck's sake, slow down! You'll have the mob stopping us for speeding!"

Lennie Campbell, his hands moist, his mouth dry and perspiration seeping through the back of his shirt to his jacket, licked nervously at his caked lips and wondered; what the *fuck* am I doing getting involved in this bloody thing?

In the rear seat, Lennie could hear the wee lad sobbing as McGuire forced his head down into the seat, then snarled, "Shut the fuck up or I'll give you something to greet about!"

"Come on, Foxy," Lennie pleaded, "There's no need for that. The wee boy's already terrified."

"Just drive, Lennie. Let me deal with this," McGuire sneered, then continued, "Did you see me smack her one? Right in the coupon I got her, the stupid cow."

It occurred to Lennie there had been no need to punch Knox's missus. Dragging her down to the ground should have been enough, but then again, he inwardly sighed, McGuire was a vicious wee shite and probably relished the idea of smacking a woman around.

"Bit of a looker his missus, wasn't she?" McGuire giggled from the back seat and it was then that Lennie realised; the wee bugger was on something. Coke, maybe?

"I never had time to notice," he dully replied.

"Oh, aye, what I'd do to your Granny, son," he giggled at the terrified boy.

"Christ sake, Foxy," Lennie had had enough. "You've got the lad, there's no need to taunt him. He's just a kid. You're supposed to be a bloody adult, so act your age!"

Taken aback, McGuire swallowed tightly at the rebuke, then mumbled, "I was only teasing him, Lennie. No need to get all het up about it."

"Aye, well enough with the teasing, okay? Now. The flat in Ibrox, does it have a phone?"

"A phone?"

"Aye, you told me you're going to phone Knox from there. Has it got a bloody phone, Foxy?"

There was a pause before McGuire admitted, "I'm not sure."

"You're not sure," Lennie twisted in his seat to stare at McGuire. "How the hell where you going to phone Knox then?"

"If the flat's not got a phone," he hissed in response, "I'll find a phone. There must be a phone box somewhere in Ibrox."

Lennie didn't respond, but shaking his head he thought, this is getting worse by the minute.

****

After leaving Lewis's store, Alex Hardie gave it some thought then decided the easiest way to ask the name of the Pakistani Hackney driver was to ask a Hackney driver.

Seeing a black cab approach with it's top light illuminated, he flagged it down then when in the back, said, "I'm not really going anywhere, pal, but I'll give you a tenner if you can tell me who the Pakistani driver is who drives a Hackney cab."

The young driver turned to stare at Hardie with suspicious eyes before he asked, "Why do you want to know, pal?"

Hardie already had his story concocted and replied, "He was at the rank in the Gallowgate last Saturday night and picked up a female pal of mine from the dancing. I only want to know where he took her because after he dropped her off, some rat mugged her and stole her handbag. That's who I want to find."

It seemed fair enough to the driver and a tenner for giving a name seemed a fair price, so he said, "He's not a Pakistani, pal. He's an Indian, a Sikh I think because he's got a thick beard and wears one of them bandage things on his napper," and whirled his fingers round his head.

"A turban?" suggested Hardie with a smile.

"That's it, a turban. Anyway, he's called Jan Singh. Well, it's not Jan, it's something else, but everybody calls him Jan."

Handing over the ten-pound note, Hardie said, "For another fiver, any idea where I can contact him?"

"Hang on."

He listened as the driver contacted his control room to ask if Jan Singh was on duty today, then heard the controller respond that Singh was due to commence work at the George Square rank at five that evening.

"Here, and thanks," Hardie handed the driver the five-pound note then got out of the cab.

He glanced at his watch and saw he had an hour and a half before Singh started work, so returning to where he'd parked the Capri, decided to return to the flat to ensure Avril was okay.

****

The three male detectives who attended at Alex Hardie's flat in

Reidvale Street had no luck either and after knocking on a few doors, were unable to ascertain if Hardie actually lived there. Returning downstairs to stand in the close entrance, the three men debated whether to hang on in the likelihood that Hardie might return to the flat or return to Pollok Police station for further instruction. Mindful of that evening's retiral function at the ex-servicemen's club and after some discussion, the men finally decided that it would be wiser to attend at the nearby London Road Police Office from where they could phone Pollok.
Had the men paid attention, they might have taken note of the tall, well-dressed woman wearing the headscarf who suspicious of them, walked by the close entrance.
Had the men looked closer, they might have noticed the woman was carrying paper shopping bags, some of which displayed the names of city centre department stores.
Had the men watched the woman as she passed them by, they might also have seen her stop at a close entrance further along the street where she entered the close, though they could not know that from there, she covertly watched them enter their vehicle and drive off.
****
When the front door was loudly banged, George Knox almost run from the front room with the intention of jumping onto the chair in the hallway to retrieve the handgun secreted there in the electrical box, but then he heard his wife Rosie cry out.
Dragging the door open, Rosie fell crying into his arms.
His eyes widened in shock when he saw her flushed face was stained with dried blood, her tights torn and her knees bloodied too.
"My God, hen, what happened?" he began then staring behind her, a cold hand grabbed at his heart when he asked, "Where's Clint? Where's the boy!"
Breathlessly, the perspiration pouring from every pore of her body, she sobbed, "They took him, George. Two men in a motor, they took him," she collapsed into his arms, her body shaking and exhausted at having run barefooted from Broomfield Road.
Half carrying, half supporting her, Knox stumbled with Rosie to the kitchen where she crumpled down onto a chair.
Grabbing a mug from the draining board, he filled it with cold water and urged her to drink, then said, "Slowly, hen. Tell me what

happened?"

The abduction of Clint Knox took just under half a minute. However, the retelling of the incident with his grandfather interrupting Rosie to ask probing questions, took over ten minutes as slowly, George Knox built up a picture of what had occurred.

At last Rosie, now calmed, her blouse soaked with perspiration and dried blood from her mouth as well as water spillage from the mug, Knox reached up to a cupboard from where he fetched a first aid box.

Gently dabbing at the cuts on Rosie's hands, knees and on her feet, he applied an antibiotic ointment, all the while reassuring her that yes, he would get Clint back and whoever had him?

They'd pay.

By Christ, they *would* pay!

"But why him, George?" she asked, distraught, her face tear stained and unable to comprehend what use a five-year-old boy was to anyone?

It was then the phone in the hallway rang.

****

It was approaching four o'clock when Alex Hardie turned into Reidvale Street, then shocked, slammed on the brakes to avoid colliding with a woman; Avril he suddenly realised, who stepped out in front of the car waving her arms.

When she'd dragged open the passenger door, he barked, "Bloody hell, woman! I almost run you over! What the hell you playing at?"

Breathlessly, she got into the car with her shopping bags then pulling the door closed, snapped, "Drive!"

Immediately realising that something was wrong, he put his foot down and drove from Reidvale Street, then turning the corner he stopped in Bellfield Street to ask again, "What's going on?"

"Three men," she gasped. "I think they might have been police; detectives I think. They were coming out of the close when I got back. They're away now, but I'm not sure if there might be someone still there in the close."

Slowly nodding in understanding, Hardie knew then that the CID must have learned from Mark Ritchie that the letter Avril had typed was a dummy, that the real letter had been addressed to him and now they were out to either arrest or at the very least, detain them both.

"Right," he exhaled, "here's what we're going to do. You can drive, you told me?"

"Yes," she nodded.

"I'll nip back to the flat on foot through the back courts and check to see if the cops are there. You give it five minutes then bring the motor back round to the close. If it's all clear, I'll wave from the window then you can come up and we'll grab a bag of clothes each. If you don't see me at the window, take off and book into a city centre hotel. If I'm arrested I'll tell the polis that I made you type the letter and, well," he shrugged, "if they believe me you're off the hook."

"And if they don't?"

He grinned when he took the sealed envelope from his inner pocket then said, "Hold onto this, then visit a guy called Harry Cavanagh who has an office in the building at number sixty, Wellington Street. You got that? Harry Cavanagh, sixty Wellington Street," he slowly repeated, as he stared at her. "You can trust him, Avril. He knows who you are and he'll explain everything and he'll help you to get to Menorca."

She felt the lump in her throat as she clutched at his arm and asked, "What about you, though? I'm not leaving without you, Alex."

Surprised at her reaction and more than he believed he would be, he gently removed her hand from his arm and smiled when he said, "The worst they can do is charge me for withholding evidence, so don't be worrying, okay? It might be a wee while, but I will find you. I promise."

Opening the driver's door, he got out then leaned in to also remind her, "Five minutes."

She glanced at her wristwatch, but when she looked up, he was already striding away.

****

Mhari McGregor glanced at the phone before she warily asked, "I take it you left the other two at the flat in case Hardie returned?"

"Eh, no. They're here with me at London Road. We weren't certain if you wanted us to come back to Pollok, Mhari."

There it was, the unspoken appeal.

McGregor tightly closed her eyes at their stupidity, but knew full well why they'd made that decision.

They were worried about missing the five-thirty kick-off that evening with the free swally and buffet in the ex-serviceman's club in Govan for the DC who'd finally completed his thirty years. Well, she inwardly seethed, they were going to be disappointed, so in a voice dripping with sarcasm, replied, "Hold on. I'll just pop into the DI's room and tell Mr Benson that none of the three of you thought that it might be important for you to hang back at Hardie's flat, just in the off-chance he *might* return to where he *lives*!"

In a heartbeat, the detective hurriedly replied, "No, don't be bothering him, Mhari. You're all right. We'll head back there the now, okay?"

"Fine!" she slammed the phone down.

****

Once she'd packed one of his sports bags with as much as it would hold, she'd swapped places with Hardie at the front window to watch if the police returned while he packed a leather holdall with some necessary clothing.

It was as Hardie was zipping up the bag he heard her urgently call out, "They're back!"

Grabbing both bags, he hissed, "Come to the door, quick!"

They almost collided in the hallway as they rushed to the door, then Hardie running ahead with the bags as Avril pulled the door closed behind her, both run down the stairs where at the ground floor landing, Hardie nodded towards the rear of the close, "This way! Through to the back!"

It was fortunate that the three detectives were unaware that the red coloured Capri parked a little further along the road outside the next close belonged to Hardie, for almost leisurely and more than a little disgruntled at missing out on the pay-off for their colleague, they took their time getting out of the CID car before entering the close. By then Hardie and Avril were quietly making their way in the fading light of the rear court to the adjoining close where first ensuring the CID car was unoccupied, they slipped into the Capri and drove off.

CHAPTER TWENTY-FIVE

She watched her husband retrieve the handgun from the electrical box and pleaded with him, "Just phone the police, George. Tell them what's happened. Let them handle it."
He shook his head as he examined the Beretta. He didn't know that much about guns and certainty not as much as Jimmy Dunlop, but he knew how to check the bloody thing was loaded.
Finally, he replied, "No, hen. Involving the polis would complicate things and this needs to be settled now so that it won't come back to haunt us."
"Then I'm coming with you," she stuck out her jaw, determined that he wasn't going alone.
He turned and placed his hands on both her arms then staring at her, said, "The guy on the phone told me that if I'm not there in twenty-five minutes, he'll hurt Clint. That was two or three minutes ago, so there's no time to contact Jimmy or Alex either and time's wasting, Rosie. No, you're not coming. What if it's a come-on and the wee guy is actually on his way here?" he stared at her. "I need you to be here if he arrives, okay?"
Grabbing his jacket, he was slipping it on when she hugged him to her and tears blinding her, whispered, "Don't get yourself killed."
"I won't," he forced a smile, "but if the worse does happen, mind and go and see Harry, okay?"
Her face screwed up as she fought back more tears and unable to speak, could only nod when he left, softly closing the door behind him.

****

Lennie Campbell stepped into the hallway when he heard the ground flat door open then inwardly sighed with relief when he saw it to be McGuire.
"You find a phone?"
"Aye, there was one around the corner that was working," his face creased with disgust when he added, "Bloody phone box has been used a toilet."
"So, he's coming then?"
"Aye. Where's the kid?"
"I got him quietened down. He's in there," Lennie cast a thumb over his shoulder, "watching the telly. I found a couple of videos of cartoons for the player," he added.

"Right," McGuire squared his shoulder, "let's see if we can find some bin bags."

"Bin bags?"

"Aye, for Knox and the kid when I plug them."

A cold shiver run down Lennie's spine when he asked, "You're going to shoot the kid?"

"Not unless you want to just strangle him or something?" McGuire smirked.

Then his face fell when staring at Lennie, he asked, "Did you think we'd be letting the kid go?"

"Eh, I thought," he hesitated, then said, "Aye, I thought when Knox got here, you were letting the kid go."

"What," he sneered, recalling Donaldson's warning, "so that he can finger the two of us if we get caught and the polis put us into an ID parade and we end up getting life? Not a chance," he shook his head.

"Right," McGuire continued as he stepped into the kitchen, "let's see if there's any bin bags here."

Hearing him rummage through the cupboards, Lennie turned and stepped back into the lounge.

The small boy sat on the edge of the couch staring at the television, but then aware the big man who'd been nice to him was at the door, he turned and tearfully smiled.

His face expressionless, Lennie stared back at Clint for a few seconds then slowly stepped back into the hallway and closed the door.

****

Alex Hardie drove them to the Sherbrooke Castle Hotel in Glasgow's south side, a hotel that was well known to him through his job as a steward.

He went on to explain that on several occasions, when the hotel hosted weddings or parties that the management suspected might become too boisterous, Hardie had been hired to provide stewards to oversee the events and that he was known to most of the staff.

"We'll be safe there till we're off," he told an increasingly anxious Avril, then with a grin, added, "There's no reason why the police would search for us there. And, eh, you don't mind us booking in as man and wife, do you?"

Surprised, she smiled when she replied, "Eh, no, not at all."

"So, if anyone asks, we're only recent married. Got that, Mrs Hardie?"

She blushed then replied, "Got it, Mr Hardie."

"Good," he nodded, "it means we share the room and it'll be one less worry for me; you being in your own room, I mean."

"Oh, of course," she replied, but a little disappointed that seemed to be the only reason he wanted to share and wondered, was he cooling off from her already?

Unaware that he'd inadvertently wounded her, he told her of Harry Cavanagh's suggestion that when they arrived in Menorca, they pose as a married couple.

She half listened and politely nodded, her thoughts straying as she continued to wonder just how long they'd last together on the Spanish island.

Arriving at the former baronial mansion that is set in its own magnificent gardens, Avril stared at the red bricked building with its rounded tower and he smiled when she told him, "I've known of this place, but never actually visited. It's stunning."

"Aye," he smiled, "and wait till you taste the food."

It was fortunate that the receptionist recognised Hardie and so the process of booking in was eased.

When they were settled in their room, he said, "I need to let George know where I am. I don't want to use the phone in the room just in case anything's overheard by the switchboard so I'll pop downstairs and use the public phone in the lounge. Do you need anything?"

"No, I'm fine thanks."

He stared at her, sensing that some sort of tenseness had arisen between them, but wrongly assumed she had been spooked by the near miss of being arrested by the CID.

"I'll be as quick as I can," he said then was gone.

Downstairs in the reception area, he used the payphone to call George Knox's number.

The phone rung once before being snatched up by Rosie, who said, "George?"

Stunned, he recognised the panic in her voice and said, "Rosie? It's me, Alex. What's wrong?"

Through her sobs, she quickly recounted the afternoon, Clint being snatched from her grasp, the phone call from the kidnapper and

George, now armed with a handgun, going to meet him to try and rescue the wee boy.

"Do you know where he's away to?"

"No, he wouldn't tell me. He told me to stay here in case Clint comes back, but I know the real reason. He was worried I'd try to follow him."

"Shit!" he loudly snapped, attracting some curious glances from a couple of women seated nearby who wore business suits.

His voice lowered, he told her, "I'll be right over."

Replacing the handset, he rushed back upstairs then entering the room, saw that Avril was in the bath.

Grabbing his car keys, he poked his head into the bathroom and breathlessly said, "Sorry, I need to go. Somebody's kidnapped Kelly-Ann's wee boy, Clint. I need to go and…"

Realising that to ask questions would only delay him, she interrupted and waving a wet hand to shoo him away, shouted, "Go, go, go,"

When he turned away, she called out after him "Be careful!" then heard the room door bang shut.

Tightly closing her eyes, she sunk down into the bubbles till only her face was above the water and found herself doing something she hadn't done for a very long time.

She prayed to God to keep Alex safe; Alex and the wee boy.

****

DCI Martin Benson instructed that a car be sent to collect Roddy Williams and Willie McBride, then glancing at his watch, sighed heavily.

Neither address for Alex Hardie nor the woman, Avril Collins, had turned up any information where they might be. Though Benson now knew the real contents of the letter that Mark Ritchie had left, he wanted his pound of flesh from those two miscreants who had led him and his team a merry chase by not passing the information the letter contained.

"Penny for them, sir."

He stared down at Mhari McGregor and slowly smiled, then replied, "Sorry, Mhari, I was miles away wondering where that pair of rogues are."

"Is it worth keeping the guys at their addresses this evening?"

He knew what was going through her head and shaking his, said, "No, get onto the control room and let the team know to return to the office. However," he stared meaningfully at her, "let them know too that when they get back here and if they do go down to the pay-off in the ex-serviceman's club, I want them bright-eyed and bushy-tailed to turn the houses tomorrow to bring Hardie and the woman here for interview. Got that?"

"Got it," she smiled and lifted the phone, but stopped and asked, "What about you, sir? What you up to?"

"Me," he sighed, "I need to go to the pay-off. I'm doing the speech and the presentation."

****

Driving with the Glasgow A to Z map open on his knees, George Knox stopped at a red light on Paisley Road West and glanced down at the map.

He wasn't familiar with the Ibrox area and tracing a finger along the main arterial road, saw that Copland Road was just along on his right and the address the man had given him, Rhynie Drive, was first left off Copland Road.

He startled when the lorry driver behind banged on his car horn and releasing the clutch, started forward.

Bloody hell, he thought and using his wing mirrors, tried to establish if the mob were on him.

Leaving Quarrywood Road, he hadn't given them a thought and his shoulders sagging, realised that if it came to using the handgun, there was every likelihood the mob would arrest not only the people holding Clint, but him too.

Sod it, he furiously gritted his teeth.

The wean is more important than me.

He slowed the Jaguar as the right hand turn for Copland Road loomed ahead and forced to halt to permit an approaching bus to pass by, turned quickly into the tenemented street, then almost immediately stopped outside a close.

Getting out of the car, he pulled down his plaid bunnet tightly on to his head and narrowing his eyes as the daylight faded, could see the turning into Rhynie Drive was a further 100 yards down the street.

Two small boys, no more than ten years of age who were sitting on a low wall outside the close with wooden sticks in their hands, stared curiously at him then at the gleaming car.

"Watch your motor for two bob, mister?" one of them strode towards him.

Stressed though he was, he had to smile in admiration at the brazen blackmailing wee shite in the knowledge that if he refused the two-shilling payment, he would likely find a scratch or two on the motor when he returned to it.

Rummaging in his pocket, he flipped a shilling towards the wee lad then sternly said, "You'll get another two shillings if you're still here when I get back and the car's not damaged."

"Right you are, mister," the boy, his eyes shiny at the thought of more money, grinned toothlessly at Knox.

Striding down towards Rhynie Drive, a half dozen scenarios raced through his head, none of which ended well.

His heart racing and his chest tightening with every step he took, he reached into his jacket pocket for the reassuring feel of the Beretta semi-automatic pistol.

The close at number four Rhynie Drive was across the road on his right.

Slowing his step as he walked towards it, could see that a large untended hedgerow hid the ground floor windows of the flat on the right while the curtains on the windows of the ground floor flat on the left were pulled together and obscured any view within.

Glancing upwards he could see lights were on in some of the flats while the remainder were in darkness.

The caller had said the name on the door was 'Jackson," but not on which floor the flat was located.

Entering the close, Knox could feel the adrenalin coursing through his body and hesitantly stepped towards the ground floor doors.

Removing the Beretta from his jacket pocket, he held it in his right hand behind his back and with his free fist pounded, saw the name 'Jackson' on the door to his left.

The door was snatched open by a large bullish looking man who stared curiously at Knox, then nodded with his head that he follow the large man into the flat.

The man then turned and in a deep bass voice, said, "Shut the door behind you pal."

Knox realised there must be at least two of them, because this was not the voice on the phone and turning, closed the door.

A second voice called out, "In here, George."

His throat tight and his knees shaking, Knox was wise enough not to walk by the large man who he knew would see Knox held the Beretta behind his back, and so said, "After you…pal."

Lennie Campbell smiled and nodding in acknowledgement of the sarcasm, walked ahead of Knox into the front room where the bright, overhead light was switched on.

He saw the furniture in the room had been pushed back against the wall and it did not escape his notice that a pile of thick, black coloured plastic bin bags had been spread out like a carpet on the floor.

In the middle of the room, a slighter, dark haired man was standing with his left arm wrapped around the small boy's throat.

His stomach clenched for he could see his grandson was pale faced, his lips quivering with fright and his body shaking.

In the man's right hand was a hand gun pressed against Clint's temple and though Knox had no knowledge of type or models, like most men of his generation had watched enough World War Two movies to recognise a German Luger pistol.

"Don't worry, wee man," he forced a smile. "Granddad will take you home soon."

"George Knox," the man slowly smiled at him then boastfully asked, "Do you know who I am?"

Knox, fearing the large man would finally see he was carrying a gun, backed against the wall and then slowly worked his way into a corner of the room, as he replied "No idea pal."

In the doorway, Lennie Campbell was growing increasingly nervous. He hadn't been happy about signing on to help McGuire with a murder, but persuaded himself that needing the money as he did, needs must.

But killing the wean?

"McGuire's my name. Some people call me Foxy because I'm a right sly bastard."

McGuire's eyes unsuspectingly followed Knox as he shuffled around the room with his back to the wall, arrogantly confident that Knox dare not try anything with the Luger pressed against the boy's head.

"What is it that you want from me, McGuire?"

"*Mr* McGuire, if you please," he smirked.

"Okay then," he sighed. "What do you want, *Mr* McGuire," Knox repeated.

"The satisfaction of seeing a big player like you squirming in front of me."

Knox didn't immediately respond, trying to judge if he could get a shot at McGuire before he pulled the trigger and blew out Clint's brains, but knew that neither was he a dead shot nor if he were, he'd never make it before McGuire killed his grandson.

Both men, their eyes locked together and intent on watching each other, took no notice that Lennie Campbell had left the room.

"There must be something you want to let the lad go, Mr McGuire," Knox nervously licked at his lips. "Money? I can pay you whatever you want."

"I don't need your money, *George*," he jeered. "I've got enough cash from my own business, a business your own lassie was helping me and big Peter with," he scoffed.

"So," Knox growled, "why did you need to kill her if she was helping you?"

McGuire stared curiously at him before he replied, "Is that what you think? That we killed her?"

Hearing this discussion about his mother, the little boy tried to twist his head to turn and stare at McGuire, but squealed when his head was viciously wrenched by McGuire's forearm.

"Now, your skinny pal," McGuire sneered. "I did do him right enough. Fucked him good with a bat, I did. Right on the noggin," he manically giggled. "His head, it bounced about like one of them wee plastic dogs you see with the nodding heads on the back shelf of motors, you know?" he sniggered.

"You killed Kevin?" Knox's eyes narrowed.

"Aye," he smirked, then his lip curling, he added with a long drawl, "Me."

Terrified, the small boy again tried to break free from McGuire's grasp, but was roughly choked as McGuire hissed, "Keep still, ya wee shite!"

Knox reached out with his free hand to calm Clint, only for McGuire with a shaking hand to extend his arm and point the gun at him while he screamed, "Don't fucking move!"

****

The Capri shuddered to a halt as Alex Hardie drew up outside the close in Quarrywood Road.

Jumping out from the car he raced upstairs where the door had been opened by Rosie who sobbing, rushed into his arms.

"God, son, I'm at my wits end, so I am," she cried into his broad shoulder.

Helping her into the flat, she was still wearing the stained blouse and skirt, her hair in disarray and he could not fail to notice the fresh abrasions on her hands and her knees as he sat her down in a kitchen chair.

Once again, she described the details of the abduction of her grandson.

Tensely pacing the floor of the kitchen and hating himself for it, he knew there was no other option than to wait for George to return with Clint.

If they ever would.

****

Their eyes remained locked as they stared at each other.

Knox, his back now against the wall directly opposite the fireplace with McGuire just six feet from him, saw in his peripheral vision the large man re-enter the room and slowly make his way towards McGuire.

Now there were two targets he had to contend with and in his helplessness, all hope within him died for he now realised that neither he nor Clint were going to leave the house alive.

His mouth as dry as a witch's tit, he pleaded, "Just let the boy go, Mr McGuire. There's no need for him to be harmed. You've got me, isn't that enough?"

As a show of good faith, he slowly withdrew his arms from behind him and his arm hanging down at full length let the wide-eyed McGuire now see the Beretta that he held in his hand.

"I'm just going to lay this down on the floor," he said and his eyes still staring into McGuire's, began to bend at the knees to lay down the handgun on the carpet.

His eyes trained on Knox as he slowly bent down. McGuire's full attention was on him and his lip again curling, he held the small boy tighter and was about to speak when…

Behind him, Lennie Campbell had made his decision.

Raising the heavy cast iron frying pan he'd brought from the kitchen in both hands, he brought the full weight of his eighteen stone viciously down to strike McGuire squarely on the head, feeling the shock of the contact reverberate through his hands and his arms, inwardly flinching at the cracking noise of broken bone as the frying pan landed.

McGuire, his skull shattered in several pieces that pierced his brain, crumpled like a marionette face down onto the floor, releasing his grip on both Clint and the handgun which bounced onto the carpet.

For a few seconds, nobody said anything, but the panorama was broken when Clint stepped over the fallen man to rush into his grandfather's arms.

Tearing his gaze away from McGuire, Knox stared open-mouthed at the large man who shrugged, then said, "He was going to, you know," he made a gun with his forefinger and fisted hand, grimaced then nodded meaningfully at the small boy.

"Even I'm not that much of a bastard to let that happen, Mr Knox."

Close to tears, Knox heard himself whisper, "Thank you."

Hearing a slight moan, they both turned and stared down at McGuire.

"Christ, he's still alive," Lennie muttered.

"Here," Knox thrust Clint towards the large man, "take the boy into the kitchen, eh…"

"Lennie."

"Lennie," he nodded. "I'll deal with this."

Taking Clint by the hand, Lennie led him to the door and almost had to drag the tearful small boy through the door before closing it behind them.

Fetching a handkerchief from his trouser pocket, Knox used it to first cover then pick up the fallen Luger that he put it into his jacket pocket and lifted the Beretta into the other pocket.

Turning over McGuire, saw that the skin on his scalp had burst wide open where he'd been struck and oozed dark, arterial blood.

Staring at him, he saw he was also bleeding from both eyes while an opaque liquid stained with blood leaked from his nose.

He watched Knox with glazed eyes and tried to speak, but could not form the words and even though he had no medical training, Knox correctly guessed McGuire had at the most, just minutes if not seconds to live.

"You were going to kill me and my grandson," Knox hissed at him. "Why? Is it because you killed my lassie? That you knew I'd find you?"

Tears formed in McGuire's eyes, eyes that begged Knox to help him, but he was wasting his time for George Knox had no intention of aiding the man whose intention was to murder his grandson.
Picking up the fallen frying pan, he rose to his feet and stared at McGuire one more time, then with an expression of extreme hatred, leaned down and once more brought it mercilessly crashing down onto his head.

CHAPTER TWENTY-SIX

When the doorbell rang, it was Hardie who beat Rosie to the front door by a hairs breadth then pulling it open, was delighted to see Clint stood there clutching the hand of a man he hadn't seen for some time.
Stunned, he stuttered, "Lennie? Lennie Campbell?"
Pushed unceremoniously to one side by Rosie, he grinned when she scooped the small boy into her arms, and to the lad's embarrassment, began hugging and kissing him through her tears of joy.
Dancing along the hallway, she suddenly stopped and turning, her face expressing her panic, she stared at Lennie and hissed, "Where's George? Where's my man?"
"He's okay, hen, he's fine," the big man lifted a palm to reassure her.
"He sent me here with the wee lad and to tell you, Alex," he stared meaningfully at Hardie, "he's away to finish it."
Frowning, Hardie indicated with a nod that Lennie come into the flat, then said, "You'd better tell us the whole story, big man."
While an overjoyed Rosie cared for Clint in the kitchen, settling him down at the table and began making his favourite meal of fish fingers, chips and beans, Lennie followed Hardie through to the front room.
Indicating Lennie sit, Hardie sat opposite and leaning forward in the chair, said, "Shoot."
Holding nothing back, Lennie related being hired by McGuire as a minder for both him and Peter Donaldson, "But when I saw you that night at the People's Palace, Alex," he shook his head in an

expression of self-loathing, "I began to question what the fuck I was doing working for that pair of evil shit's."

"It was the money, Alex," he took a breath and slowly exhaled, then raised his head to stare apologetically at him. "I needed the dough to pay for my lassie's wedding, the lassie you helped get off the smack. And this," his embarrassment was evident, "I began thinking to myself, is how I fucking repay you?"

He paused for a moment to reflect on his betrayal of his debt to Hardie then continued with McGuire's plan to kill George Knox and the boy.

"I'd convinced myself I needed the money, pal, but shit. Kill the wean? No way," he vigorously shook his head and waved his hands in front of him, "I couldn't be party to that. Never. So," he took a long sigh, "when Foxy was about to shoot your man, I pancaked him with a frying pan."

"You killed him?"

His eyes narrowed and he idly scratched at his head when he said, "I'm not sure. He was muttering when I took the wee boy out of the room into the kitchen, but he was dead when me and your pal put him into the plastic bags. Maybe it was me that killed him or maybe George Knox finished him off. Whatever, it *was* down to me," grim faced, he exhaled, his head down and his hands tightly clenched together.

"And I'm guessing that George is away to see Peter Donaldson?"

"Aye," confirmed, "he's gone after Donaldson. Told me to bring wee Clint back to his missus and tell you that he's away to get the fat bastard."

Hardie's face paled when he asked, "He's going to kill Donaldson?"

"Aye, Alex, I don't think there's any doubt about that. He's got Foxy's gun and he'd brought a gun of his own, so he's away, he says, to settle it once and for all."

"Shit! How long ago?"

"There's nothing you can do to stop him now, Alex," he shook his head. "He'll have arrived there before I got here."

"Where does Donaldson live, Lennie?"

"He's got one of them fancy mid terraced houses in Park Terrace over by Kelvingrove Park."

Hardie realised Lennie was correct, he'd be too late to stop Knox and his mind racing, asked, "McGuire's body. Where is it? Is it still in that flat?"

"No, Alex, and I'm wondering if I can ask for yet another favour."

"A favour?"

"Aye," he slowly nodded. "McGuire's in the boot of my motor and I'm needing a wee hand to get rid of him."

****

He spent almost fifteen minutes wiping down the flat's door handles and other surfaces in the rooms with a cloth soaked in bleach to ensure that there was nothing that could identify either Knox or the man Lennie as having visited the flat.

That done, he made his way back to his vehicle to find the two small boys, their sticks on their shoulders and diligently parading like Guardsmen up and down the length of the Jaguar.

Fetching a pound note from his pocket, he held it up and beckoning the taller of the two towards him, quietly asked, "When did the man or the woman come to look at my car?"

The boy's face creased as he stared first at the note, then at Knox, before he replied, "What man or woman? I didn't see any man or woman, did you?" he turned to stare at his pal.

The smaller boy shook his head then squeaked, "There wasn't anybody here, mister. We guarded your motor like you told us, didn't we?" and in turn sought confirmation from his taller pal.

As satisfied as he could be that the surveillance probably hadn't followed him after all, Knox tightly smiled then handing the smaller boy the note, said, "You guys did a great job, now see that you split that between you."

Having made two friends for life, he got into the Jaguar, started the engine and his heart still beating like a drum in his chest took a breath to calm himself before smoothly driving off.

****

Downstairs in the darkness of Lennie Campbell's Ford Cortina, he revealed to Hardie, "McGuire, he told me where he intended dumping your man's body and the wean. Even had me drive him there yesterday morning to check it out."

A little over twenty-five minutes later, they arrived at the darkened site in Clydeholm Road where switching off the car lights, Lennie cruised along the unlit road then stopped at a construction site.

"There's a gap in the hoarding there," he pointed it out to Hardie.

"McGuire's plan was to take the bodies through the gap then stick them into a pit where they're laying the concrete foundations tomorrow."

With an inward shudder, Hardie nodded then asked, "And there's no way he'll be found?"

"Not with a couple of ton of cement being poured over him, no," a grim-faced Lennie shook his head.

Even more nervous than at any time he had been with the team pulling jobs, Hardie helped Lennie remove the plastic binbag wrapped body from the boot, then lifting McGuire onto his shoulders, Lennie said, "Don't forget that other binbag, Alex."

"Eh? Aye, okay. What's in it?" he reached into the boot to grab it.

"The frying pan," Lennie smirked.

Awkward though it was, the two men managed to prise open the plywood hoarding and squeeze the body through, then together, carried McGuire to the deep trench that was to be filled with concrete.

"His plan was to put the bodies down there," Lennie nodded into the four feet deep trench, "then cover them with soil so they wouldn't be noticed when the concrete's poured."

"Did you bring a shovel?"

"Oh, aye, I did," his eyes narrowed when he remembered. "I'll fetch it."

Minutes later, when he'd returned with the shovel, Lennie volunteered to deepen the trench another few feet to bury the body, then used the soil to cover it.

Tamping the earth down with the shovel, he gasped, "That should do it."

It was then Hardie realised the frying pan was still lying on the ground.

"Ach, don't be worrying about that," Lennie shook his head. "That'll just go in the Clyde. I don't see me making a fry-up in that bloody thing now."

Returned to the car, Lennie said, "I'll drop you back at your pal's house, Alex. Can you tell him from me again, I'm sorry that I got involved with all this?"

"You saved him and wee Clint, Lennie. I'm sure the boss will be grateful."

"No need for his thanks, Alex. You pulled me out of a hole and I'm only sorry that I didn't remember it sooner. That and if I'd did as McGuire said, I'd never have forgiven myself."

"Anyway," he was a little embarrassed and paused before he added in a quiet voice,

"I'll not forget what you did helping to save my lassie."

****

Not wishing to draw attention from nosey neighbours, Knox parked the Jaguar in Lynedoch Place and in the darkness, walked to Park Terrace.

As the man Campbell had said, Peter Donaldson seldom if ever used taxis or used any other vehicles and so Knox experienced mixed feelings when he saw the silver coloured Range Rover outside the mid-terraced house, for knowing why he had come, he was both eager to get the job done yet nervous at what he intended doing.

Recalling also that Lennie had told him Donaldson frequently entertained at least one young rent-boy in the house for his sexual pleasure, Knox was suddenly grateful for his wife's fondness for silk scarves and opening the glove compartment, selected one from the three or four she always kept readily available in the car.

Selecting the darkest scarf he could find, a navy blue one, he shoved into his jacket pocket.

Getting out of the car, he pulled down the plaid bunnet, turned up the collar of his jacket and walking along the dimly lit road, passed by Donaldson's house.

Roughly thirty yards further on, he stopped, but other than the echo of a small dog barking from the nearby Kelvingrove Park, neither saw nor heard any sound of pedestrians or anyone he figured might be hanging around the area who might later describe him.

As satisfied as he could be that there was nobody about, he took a long breath to calm himself then retraced his steps to the house.

Climbing the seven stairs to the front door, he pulled Rosie's scarf from his pocket and wound it around his head his eyes narrowing as he briefly inhaled the scent of her perfume.

Knotting the scarf at the back of his head, it left just his eyes exposed under the plaid bunnet.

His right hand clutching the Beretta handgun in his jacket pocket, he rang the doorbell and stood back.

A half minute passed and he was about to ring the bell again when it was pulled open by a tubby, dark-haired youth about five feet four inches tall who Knox judged to be no more than sixteen or seventeen years of age.
The youth, he could see, was wearing a schoolboy uniform of white shirt, school tie and short, tight trousers, though his feet were bare.
What shocked Knox though, was the youth was wearing make-up of eye shadow rouge on his cheeks and a deep scarlet shade of lipstick and seemed to be tipsy or drugged.
Peering at Knox, he lazily asked, "Yes?"
Almost at the same time, the youth's eyes widened in shock as he realised the man at the door was masked, then his eyes dropped to the gun held in Knox's hand that was pointed at his stomach.
Still taken aback by the youth's appearance, Knox heard himself stutter, "Is Peter Donaldson at home?"
The youth, his hand still on the open door, his mouth now dropped open, could only nod.
Knox gulped and exhaling, suddenly stepped forward, then shoving the youth on the chest, slammed the door behind him.
Taken completely by surprise and suddenly fearful, the youth fell backwards, his hands flailing as he tried to break his fall.
Bending down to ram the barrel of the Beretta in the youth's cheek, Knox fervently hoped he had never met McGuire, when he hissed, "My name's Foxy, so shut the fuck up or I'll blow your head off!"
Terrified, his body noticeably trembling, the youth lay still and his face creased as he began to quietly sob.
Grabbing him by the front of his shirt, he pulled the youth to his feet, popping several buttons from the cheaply made garment as he did so and softly said, "Take me to Donaldson."
Turning the youth, Knox propelled him forward with his hand clutching the back of the youth's shoulder length hair.
Barefooted, the youth's feet made a slapping noise on the tiled floor and his hands raised, led Knox to a door at the rear of the hallway and beside the wide staircase.
The door was ajar and from inside the room, Knox could hear the sound of a man singing along to a song on the radio that was playing.
Pulling the youth backwards so that their heads were touching, Knox whispered, "How many people in the house?"

Quietly sobbing, the youth whispered back, "Just Peter and me. Please don't kill me! I'll do whatever you want! I'll be a good boy! Please!"

"Do as I say and you'll not be harmed," he snarled in the frightened youth's ear, then in the same low voice, pointed the Beretta at the partially open door and asked, "What's in that room?"

"It's the kitchen. Peter's making…"

But he didn't finish, for from the room they heard Donaldson call out, "Who was at the door, sweet cheeks?"

Knox stared at the youth and said, "Tell him it was a delivery for next door."

"It was a delivery for next door," the youth loudly simpered.

"Okay, this is nearly ready so…"

But as he was speaking, Knox pushed the cowering youth into the room and his arm extended, pointed the Beretta at Donaldson who was standing at the kitchen island, a ladle in his meaty hand and a pot in front of him.

Two deep plates lay beside the pot, waiting to be filled with the aromatic meal he had prepared while to one side the overlarge kitchen table had been formally set for dinner with white napkins, an open bottle of red wine bottle and a candelabra lit in the centre of the table.

To Knox's surprise, he saw the heavyset man was wearing a white cotton toga type garment and stared in astonishment at him.

Regaining his composure and almost with disdain, he addressed Knox, "I assume you haven't come for dinner or," he nodded with a wry smile towards the youth, "to share this delightful, plump boy's arse with me?"

Beneath the scarf his face twisted in disgust at the suggestion.

Waving the Beretta at the youth, he indicated he sit at one of the kitchen chairs.

Turning to Donaldson, he then said, "Find something to tie your toy boy to the chair."

"I don't really think…"

"Or would you rather I blow a hole in his kneecap," he interrupted as he moved around the island to stand a mere six feet from Donaldson, but with the Beretta pointed at the youth.

"That won't be necessary," Donaldson shook his head and was about to open a kitchen drawer when Knox cautiously called out, "Careful, now!"

With a wry smile, he slowly opened the drawer and withdrew a ball of thin white string, explaining, "I use this to tie the joints of meat." Knox watched as he first tied the youths wrists to the chair then at Knox's instruction, tied his ankles to the legs of the chair.

"Move away," he waved the gun at Donaldson, indicating he take a few steps backwards then satisfied himself that the weeping boy was now incapacitated.

"Why are you doing this?" Donaldson politely asked.

"Because I'm a man with a gun and I can."

"Ah, yes, but you must have a reason for coming to see me. Could this be something as simple as a robbery, for if it is, I assure you, you have no idea of the shit storm you are about to unleash upon yourself when my men find you."

In the warm kitchen and beneath the scarf, Knox's face was beginning to perspire and again waving the gun, told Donaldson, "Let's you and I move into another room."

He watched as the big man haughtily blew a kiss to the youth, telling him, "I won't be long, my dear boy, then we'll have some fun, eh?"

Listening to him, Knox had a sudden feeling of uncertainty and could not understand why Donaldson wasn't in fear of his life. Prodding the gun into his back, he forced Donaldson to step ahead of him into the roomy hallway then through to the front sitting room. Glancing about the room, Knox saw the drapes on the large sash windows were ajar and standing by the door, ordered Donaldson to pull them closed before he waved him into a chair.

Donaldson smiled, causing an anxious Knox to ask, "What the fuck's so funny?"

"Well, the mask you are wearing," his eyes narrowed. "A woman's scarf, I believe? I can even smell the perfume from here."

"What of it?"

"It means," he began to study the fingernails on his hand as he cockily continued, "that you don't want me to see your face. I can only deduce that being the case, that you fear me recognising you again and so I am of the opinion, my dear man, you have no intention of shooting me. So, my friend, what is it you *really* want? Money? Drugs? What?"

His eyes fluttered when Knox pulled down the scarf and smiled and as he did so.

Donaldson's face paled as he considered that perhaps he might have misjudged the situation. Staring at Knox, he asked, "Who the devil are you?"

He didn't immediately respond other than to reach into his jacket pocket from where carefully holding McGuire's gun that was still wrapped in the handkerchief, he lifted it into his left hand then placed the Beretta in the right-hand pocket.

Then, with the handkerchief draped over the handle of the gun, he transferred it to his right hand and levelled the Luger at Donaldson. Stepping towards him to narrow the distance to a few feet, Knox at last replied, "I'm the father of a lassie you turned to drugs and killed, the man you and McGuire tried to murder. Me and my five-year-old grandson, you evil bastard!" he snarled.

His lips quivering with horror, Donaldson realised now why he'd removed the scarf from his face and unable to help himself, his bowels suddenly loosened.

His voice weak and fearful, he stuttered, "George Knox."

But this wasn't a movie or a dramatic play where the man holding the gun explains and boasts to his victim about every little detail that brought them to this point, for Knox did not have time for any such theatrics.

Aiming the Lugar, he shot Donaldson in the face, the bullet ripping through his left cheek and exiting at his lower neck to wind up in the back of the cushioned chair.

When his body jerked with shock, the second bullet entered his throat then striking his spine, ricocheted upwards and through his tongue before exiting on the right side of his nose and careering vertically to embed in the ceiling above.

Still alive, but just barely, he continued to stare through tear filled eyes at Knox who fired again into his forehead.

The third bullet, the bullet that finally killed him, in a microsecond rattled around his skull then rooted itself in his brain.

Staring down at the dead man, Knox's nose wrinkled at the faecal smell seeping from between Donaldson's parted legs then nauseously retching, swallowed his disgust at what he had done.

Turning away, he hurriedly left the room.

At the front door, he stopped and glancing left and right, saw that the road appeared to be empty and that the three shots seemingly had not attracted any attention from the neighbours.

Making his way down the stairs to the pavement, he kept his head down, then stooping at a car parked a little further along the road, carefully placed the Luger on the roadway just beneath the front tyre on the driver's side where he believed the police would find it, before stuffing the handkerchief into his jacket pocket.

Taking a breath, he once more glanced around then seeing nobody about, rose to his feet and walking with his head down and his hands thrust into his jacket pockets, quickly made his way back to his car parked in Lynedoch Place.

CHAPTER TWENTY-SEVEN

Martin Benson woke early that Saturday morning with an aching head and listened to the drumming of the rain hitting the window spare of the bedroom.

He hadn't intended getting pissed, but as the DCI presenting both the farewell speech and the many gifts to one of his retiring DC's, he had participated in so many toasts that he'd lost count and when his wife came to collect him from the ex-serviceman's club, after they arrived home he'd been chaperoned into the spare bedroom.

The door opened to admit his wife, the bright light from the hallway steaming into the dark bedroom and hurting his eyes, but with a welcome mug of coffee in her hand and a not so welcome scowl on her face.

Five minutes and two paracetamol later, Benson was stood under a steaming hot shower and, aware he probably wasn't yet legally sober enough to drive, wondering how to broach with his irate wife the subject of a lift to the office.

Ten minutes later, showered, dressed and now seated at the kitchen table trying not to flinch at the sight of the fried breakfast, he heard her answer the telephone in the hallway.

When she returned to the kitchen, she curtly told him, "It's for you. Roddy Williams at Pollok."

Exhaling, he got up from the table and picking up the telephone, was greeted by Williams, who though Benson couldn't know it, grinned when he asked, "Morning, boss. You got your head on straight?"

"Barely," Benson sighed, then rubbing at the pain in his head, asked,

"What's up? You at the office already? I thought you and Willie were having a lie-in after your flight?"

"Aye, so did I," Williams sighed. "However, the Govan nightshift gave me a call ten minutes ago. They'd picked us up from the airport and on the way up the road, we'd told them the story about the dummy letter and the suspicion that Peter Donaldson and Foxy McGuire were suspect for our victim's murder. Anyway, as it happens, during their shift they were over in Partick Police Office interviewing a prisoner when all hell broke loose there. It's Donaldson. He's been found in his house, shot to death."

****

It had been a little after midnight when an exhausted Alex Hardie had got back to the hotel, for after Lennie Campbell had dropped him back at George Knox's house, he'd seen the parked Jaguar and called into the flat to ensure his friend was okay.

Though he'd spent no more than ten minutes there, he'd learned in a whispered conversation with Knox about the murder of Peter Donaldson, then held the kitchen chair as Knox returned the Beretta to the electrical box above the front door.

Having wearily nodding to the night porter as he made his way upstairs, he'd been surprised to find that a worried Avril, wearing one of his shirts as a nightie, had remained awake to await his return. Even more surprising, he found she'd ordered a tray with sandwiches and two bottles of beer to be sent up on the supposition that he'd be hungry when he arrived back.

Eating the sandwiches and washing them down with a beer, he'd told her of George Knox's rescue of his grandson, though omitted the details of the killing of Foxy McGuire by simply explaining that one of McGuire's men, who wanted no part in harming the wee boy, had instead assisted Knox as McGuire fled the scene.

Prudently, he made no mention of his part in disposing of the body nor of Knox's later visit to murder Peter Donaldson.

"And the wee boy?" her face had expressed her concern.

"He definitely got a fright," he'd explained, "but he's a resilient wee guy and being so young I expect he'll soon recover. If he remembers it at all, it will be like a bad nightmare that hopefully, he'll soon forget."

"I take it the police aren't involved," she'd stared at him.

"No," he'd smiled. "Let's just consider it to be a private matter."

"You must be very fond of this man Knox and his family."
"More than you would think," he'd agreed with a nod.
Wiping at his mouth with a white napkin from the tray, he'd smiled at her, seeing her long legs tucked under her and her hair in disarray. "You look gorgeous," he'd grinned.
She'd stared thoughtfully at him for several seconds, then slowly beginning to unbutton the shirt, she'd asked him, "Just how tired are you?"

****

George Knox slowly turned in the bed, conscious that his every movement might disturb both Rosie and their grandson, who was snuggled in between them.
When he'd returned home, he hadn't been surprised to find Clint fast asleep in their bed and though Rosie had suggested he used the spare bedroom, he'd shaken his head and said, "No, for one night and after everything that's happened, I'm happy that the three of us are welded together in the same bed."
She's laughed at that, being *welded* with her two favourite men and so, uncomfortable though it had been for them both, they'd nestled in beside Clint.
Now lying there fully awake, his thoughts turned to the previous evening and him shooting Donaldson.
Distasteful though it had been, he knew in his heart that it had to be done, that if he hadn't finished it last night, it would have left it open for the drug dealer at some point to send somebody after him and his family, whether they were abroad or not.
Yet though he knew that the men no longer presented a threat, the words uttered by McGuire continued to disturb him.
Is that what you think? That we killed her?
Why, he wondered if McGuire knew that he was going to kill me; *why* wouldn't he just admit they had murdered Kelly-Ann? Why not rub salt into an already open wound?
He almost stopped breathing when it came to him.
Because they hadn't killed her.
Hard as it was for him to face the truth, he'd been wrong.
It wasn't McGuire and Donaldson.
Some other bastard has killed her.

The sudden realisation that her killer might still be walking the street filled him with an uncontrollable rage and without thinking he swung his legs from the bed and sat up.

"George?" Rosie slowly sat up on the other side of the sleeping Clint. "Are you okay, love?"

"Yes," he sighed then in a low voice, added, "Sorry, I didn't mean to disturb you, hen. I need to make a phone call."

Standing upright, he padded to the door then quietly opening it, slid from the room.

****

Upon his arrival at Pollok Police station, Martin Benson met with Roddy Williams in the DI's office and questioned him about what he knew of Donaldson's murder.

"Not that much, other than what the nightshift told me before they signed off," Williams, looking a little worse the wear from lack of sleep, shook his head.

"When they were at Partick dealing with the ned they'd been looking for who'd committed a string of housebreakings on our side of the Clyde, one of the local DC's mentioned that about one o'clock this morning, a patrol car passing along the road had discovered the door to Donaldson's house lying wide open. Course he's well documented with B Division, so the cops did their nosey and when nobody came to the door, stepped in. Apparently they found Donaldson dead, shot so I'm told, and a rent boy tied up in the kitchen, greeting his eyes out."

He stared at Benson and asked, "What you thinking?"

After a few seconds pause, Benson slowly replied, "From what this man Ritchie told you, Alex Hardie, who's George Knox's man, had the real letter that indicated Ritchie suspected Donaldson and his sidekick McGuire of murdering Knox's lassie. Which means," his brow knitted, "that Knox will also know Ritchie suspected them too."

"You're thinking that maybe it was Knox who knocked him off?"

Benson didn't respond to Williams question, but instead asked, "Any idea who's the SIO for the murder, over there?"

"As you know it's Frankie Welch who's the DCI in B Division," Williams slowly shook his head, "but I know for a fact he's on the pat and mick with a hernia, so I'm not sure who's filling in for him."

Reaching for the phone, Benson nodded when he said, "I've a better idea."

Dialling the number, Williams heard him say, "Mr Meadows, Martin Benson, sir. Sorry to call you at home on a Saturday morning. I've heard about the murder of Peter Donaldson. I believe that I might have some relevant information that can assist the local guys, so can I have your permission to intrude in their investigation and be written in to whatever they find?"

He nodded then said, "DI Sheila Farquhar? Thanks and I'll let you know how I get on."

Replacing the handset, he stared keenly at Williams before he asked, "You look done in, Roddy. Would you prefer to maybe head home and get some kip?"

"At this stage of the game?" he grinned and shook his head. "No way."

Rising from his chair, he grabbed at his overcoat then said, "If you let Mhari know where we're going, boss, I'll grab us a set of car keys."

****

In the hotel room, Alex Hardie put down the phone and turning to Avril, said, "That was George Knox."

Without explaining how Knox had come by the information, he continued, "You remember George, my boss, he asked me to do something for him?"

He didn't think it worth mentioning that with all that went on the previous evening, he'd completely forgotten about tracking down the Indian cab driver.

"Yes, but you didn't tell me what it was you were doing?" she pouted.

"It's nothing too important," he shrugged and tried to play it down, "but he wants me to get onto it, today. That and he knows the polis are keen to speak with us, so he suggests we stay here at the hotel until you catch your flight. In the meantime, I'll stay on here and join you, maybe on Monday or Tuesday at the latest."

He didn't really know if he'd find Kelly Ann's killer by Monday, but thought that Avril might freak out if he suggested he could be a lot longer.

"That's *if* we get our new passports and the other documents," she reminded him.

"George mentioned that," he nodded. "He's going to phone Harry, the guy I mentioned before, and ask that Harry send them to us here at the hotel by courier, so we should get them by this lunchtime and it means we don't have to travel into the city centre and risk being spotted by the cops."

"God," she shook her head, "I'm beginning to think of myself as some sort of gangster."

"Gangster's moll," he corrected her with a grin. "It's me that's the gangster, remember?"

"Right," he suddenly sprung onto the bed and astride her, pinned her hands to the pillow.

With a cheesy smile, he said, "I'm going to have to go out soon, but before I go, how's about me and you have some more fun, just like last night."

She pretended to struggle, then with a suggestive smile, replied, "Is this how it's going to be, then? Me, the submissive woman?"

"I bloody hope so," he grinned then releasing her hands, bent forward towards her.

****

Unwilling to attend at Peter Donaldson's house and risk contaminating the crime scene, DCI Martin Benson learned that the SIO, DI Sheila Farquhar, had returned to the Partick Office and so had Roddy Williams drive them there.

"Do you know this woman, Roddy?"

"Sheila Farquhar? Aye," he nodded, "I've met her a couple of times on courses at Tulliallan. Big, fresh-faced, buxom lassie, like a farmer's wife," he smiled. "Never worked with her, but if I recall correctly, she hails from down Galloway somewhere. In fact," his eyebrows knitted, "I think she started down there with Dumfries and Galloway as a cop then transferred up to us."

"Oh," Benson smiled. "A D and G cop. A Doonhamer, is that what they're called from that part of the world?"

"Sheepshaggers, more likely," Williams dryly smiled, "but I think you'll find that a Doonhamer is somebody from Dumfries. Close enough though, I suppose."

Arriving at Partick Office, Williams parked in the rear yard then both men made their way upstairs to the incident room.

Striding into the room, they could see that the seven or eight detectives and civilian staff of the investigation team had already set up the incident room with a white board upon which were sellotaped headshot photographs of both the dead man and Foxy McGuire, as well as several photographs of the scene of the murder.

One photograph caught the eye of Benson who walking towards the white board, peered at the close-up photo of a handgun lying under a car.

It was then he heard his name called and turning, saw a sturdy, buxom woman with greying hair tightly bound in a bun walk and wearing a charcoal coloured jacket and dark coloured, pleated skirt, walk towards him, her hand extended and an open smile on her rosy cheeked face.

Recalling Williams description, he thought a farmer's wife indeed as he took her hand and said, "Sorry to intrude, DI Farquhar, eh, can I call you Sheila?"

"Aye, of course," she nodded.

"I assume you've had the phone call from Mr Meadows?"

"Aye," she nodded, "he called me about twenty minutes ago and told me to expect you."

She released her powerful grip on Benson's hand then taking Williams hand, beamed, "Long time no see, Roddy, and if I recall correctly, I haven't heard from you since that dinner and those bottles of red."

To Benson's inquiring glance, he blushed before turning to explain, "Long story boss."

"Right then, gentlemen," Farquhar beamed at them, "if you'd like to follow me, we can speak in the DCI's room."

Leading them to the door, she paused only to call out to a young woman sat at a desk to tell her, "Three coffees if you please, Lizzie. Thank you."

Once seated in the DCI's room, she asked, "What's your interest in Peter Donaldson, sir?"

Briefly, he reminded her of the murder of Kelly-Ann Knox and then related the letter that had allegedly been typed by a fugitive, Mark Ritchie, then handed to the investigation by Ritchie's secretary, Avril Collins.

"However, we've learned as recently as yesterday after Roddy here and Willie McBride, one of my DS's, tracked Ritchie down to Spain that the letter is a dummy and they learned the real letter had been handwritten. The contents apparently inferred Donaldson and his associate, Foxy McGuire, might have been responsible for the murder of our victim."

"Foxy McGuire, you say?" her thick eyebrows knitted.

"Aye, known to you, is he?"

She took a deep breath then leaning forward onto her forearms, stared at Benson and Williams in turn before relating the discovery by the attending officers of the young rent boy tied up in the kitchen. "The poor soul was in a hell of a state at first," she began, "and it took quite a while to calm him. Fifteen years of age, he is. A runaway from a children's home in Fife," her face paled and it was clear what her unspoken opinion was of her murder victim.

"Anyway, one of our younger, uniformed lassie's took the young lad under her wing and eventually got a statement out of him. It seems Donaldson had been plying the boy with cannabis, probably to make him more amenable for what Donaldson planned for him, so when the boy went to answer the door the killer was there with his face masked and a handgun pointed at the boy. It's likely the one you saw in the photo though I'm waiting on ballistics to confirm it."

Her brow creasing, she paused the continued, "The boy admits he was terrified and curiously, the masked man told the boy his name was Foxy."

"Foxy?" Benson repeated and turned to glance at Williams.

"That's what the lad said and he is scared enough to be credible. That and he tells us Donaldson had him brought to the house earlier that evening by some guy the lad had never met before and probably a pimp of some sorts. The ploy was he was going to get food and a bed for the night and paid for taking part in a play," she wiggled her forefingers in the air and almost growled at the lie.

She paused only to take out a small tin from her desk drawer from which, to Benson's surprise, she withdrew a Tom Thumb cigar that she lit.

"Anyway, the young lad," she continues.

"He tells us too that he'd never met either Donaldson or met or heard of Foxy McGuire. So, he's at the front door with this masked man who says he's Foxy, then frog-marched through to the kitchen where he made Donaldson tie the boy to a chair before both the men left the kitchen, presumably to go to the room where we found Donaldson's body."

"I take it Donaldson didn't call his killer by name nor did the killer remove his mask in the kitchen?" Benson asked.

"Not according to the boy, no," she shook her head.

"And the handgun that you discovered, Sheila," Williams leaned forward. "You suspect that to be the murder weapon?"

"Yes, and strangely, though the opposite side of the road leads down to Kelvingrove Park and it's a thickly covered in shrubs, we found the handgun as you saw in the photo, lying just under a parked car some twenty odd yards from the murder location."

"Dropped or put there for you to find?" asked Benson.

She shrugged before she replied, "Who knows. The Scene of Crime officer who took charge of it confirmed it to be a semi-automatic Luger, probably world war two vintage and that there was one round remaining in the breech, though the rest of the magazine was empty. And on that point," she nodded her head at Benson, "the SOCO were on the phone just before you arrived, sir. They're still at the locus and reported that they've discovered a bullet lodged in the wall in the kitchen."

"So, the killer fired a shot in the kitchen?"

"Not according to the young boy, no," she shook her head.

She paused as the young civilian, Lizzie, knocked the door and entered with a tray of mugs of coffee.

When Lizzie had left, Farquhar continued.

"If the lad's telling the truth and I have no reason to suspect otherwise, that bullet must have been fired at another time. Needless to say, the Ballistics people will compare it to the handgun that was found."

"How many times was Donaldson shot?" Williams asked.

"Three," she replied, then continued, "and that's what the lad says. He heard three loud bangs. Fortunately, I won't have to wait for the post mortem to recover the bullets. One was lodged in the ceiling after exiting his body and another discovered in the chair he had been sitting in when he was shot, so the Ballistics already have the bullets and the empty cases that were discharged from the Luger. At my request, they're treating the comparison examination as urgent."

"Fingerprints?" this from Benson.

"The SOCO are still working on it, but the Luger is already being fingerprinted, as we speak."

Benson turned to glance at Williams who said, "You're thinking the same as me, boss. It's a set-up, somebody is firing Foxy McGuire in as the killer."

However, it was Farquhar who replied when she said, "I'm also thinking the same. If McGuire did kill his business partner, why was there any need to wear a mask and yet tell the boy who he was? That and why did he need to be masked in front of his boss and again, why didn't Donaldson call him by his name in front of the boy?"

"We can ask him that when we find him, Sheila," Benson soberly replied then nodding, asked her, "Anything we can do to assist your investigation?"

"Nothing I can think of at the minute, sir, but needless to say whether I'm satisfied or not he is the killer, I'll need to be having a wee word with Mr McGuire, so I've posted a lookout for him. If you happen to come across him before my guys do…"

"Your phone will be ringing off the hook," he finished for her as both he and Williams rose from their chairs.

They were in the corridor outside the DI's room heading for the stairs when Benson heard his name called again and turning, saw Farquhar walking towards him.

"Just had a call from the Fingerprints Department at Pitt Street," she breathlessly began, tapping her cigar ash into the palm of her free hand. "They've checked the prints the Scene of Crime lifted off the Luger and they match Foxy McGuire."

Benson turned to stare at Williams before he responded with, "Well, I have to admit, I wasn't expecting that."

"Another nail in McGuire's coffin, boss?" Williams shrugged.

"Either that," his face creased, "or whoever's setting him up is making damn sure we don't go looking for the real killer."

It was when they returned to the CID car in the rear yard that Benson stared at Williams for a few seconds before, eyebrows raised, he asked, "Dinner and bottles of red?"

He took a breath before he replied, "Not my proudest moment, but suffice to say the last time I was on a course at Tulliallan with Sheila; well," he grimaced, "we'd had a few and one thing led to another, if you get my drift."

"Buxom girl," Benson worked at keeping his face straight.

"Indeed," Williams sighed heavily.

****

DS Mhari McGregor called together the six detectives she had tasked to trace Alex Hardie and Avril Collins, then warned them, "The boss is more than interested in hearing why they withheld information that was contained in the original letter, so get yourselves back to their addresses and I suggest you do not come back without them."

"What about us getting some breakfast first," asked a DC with the hung dog look of a man suffering from a hangover.

"Aye, you do that," she pleasantly smiled, "then when the boss radios to ask how you're getting on at Hardie's address, *you* can explain why you're not really there."

When he scowled, then replied, "That's a no, then?" she lowered her voice to tell him, "Don't be such a dunderhead. Grab something on the way or two of you stake out the address while one of you fetches something for the three of you. Christ, you're supposed to be *bloody* detectives. Work something out," she irritably waved them out of the incident room.

****

Just as the six detectives were leaving Pollok Police station, Alex Hardie was driving out of the Sherbrooke Hotel car park on his way to try and locate the Indian taxi driver, Janki Singh.

As he drove from Pollokshields towards the city centre, he thought again about Avril and realised he was becoming more fond of her than he'd meant to become.

Am I in love with her, he asked himself or is it some sort of infatuation?

Once more he considered the benefits of having a relationship with her and though more than a few women had passed through his life, he had become accustomed to living alone and so still had strong misgivings about sharing his life.

As he drove, he reflected once more on the only woman who had ever really touched him, Helen McCrory or Helen Philips, as she was now, married to and pregnant with his old pal Archie's baby. Every woman he'd been with, he suddenly realised, he'd compared to Helen, the woman he had for so long harboured his affections and once more, as he had done through the years, idly wondered what his life might have been like if he'd married her.

Certainly he'd not have taken up robbery, not with Helen as his wife, he unconsciously shook his head.

Turning from Clyde Place onto the King George V Bridge, his eyes fluttered when almost like some sort of self-admission, he knew what was wrong with him.

At the bridge's junction with the Broomielaw, the lights turned to red forcing him to stop.

Staring unseeingly forward, he realised he still yearned after Helen, but why, he asked himself, for that particular ship had sailed.

Helen was married, happily if she was to be believed when she spoke with him, and to a good man.

The van behind him beeped to indicate the lights had changed and he continued through the junction into Oswald Street, but in those few seconds of contemplation, he had made a decision.

No more would he pine for Helen.

She was gone and that was it.

Time, he gritted his teeth as he drove towards the Argyle Street junction, to get on with my life.

****

At his suggestion, Avril Collins took a long, leisurely bath then ordered breakfast to her room.

Just as Hardie had thought of her, she gave consideration to living with a man, something that other than her father she had never truly experienced.

Yes, admittedly, there had been more than a few boyfriends, but none with whom she had lived with for any longer than a few days and none she felt as safe with as she did Alex.

Staring at the bed, the sheets rumpled and the duvet cover lying on the floor, she blushingly smiled when she thought of their lovemaking, how forceful he could be, though without intimidating her or when she asked, how gentle he had been.

He's definitely had a lot of practise, she self-consciously grinned.

The phone by the bed rung and as she went to answer it, paused, for who would know she was here?

Taking a breath, she warily asked, "Hello?"

"Mrs Hardie," the receptionist greeted her. "A parcel has arrived addressed to Mr Hardie and it's to be signed for. Do you want the courier sent up or would you rather come to the reception?"

"Give me a minute, I'll be right down," she breathlessly replied.

Swiftly, she threw off the hotel dressing robe and pulled on pants, bra, navy-blue blouse and matching slacks then slipping on a pair of trainers, bundled her hair into a ponytail as she hurried from the room to the reception desk.

A bearded man in his late forties wearing biker leathers with a helmet tucked under his arm had her sign a clipboard before handing her a bulky, brown envelope.

Remembering to sign, 'Mrs A Hardie,' she smiled and passing the courier a five-pound note, brought a pleased smile to his face when she told him, "Thank you for waiting."

Hurrying back to the room, Avril tore open the envelope to find it contained passports, birth certificates, driving licences and two further envelopes that when opened, contained a tightly bound wad of Spanish pesetas while the second envelope contained two flight tickets.

Opening the passports, her hand involuntarily went to her mouth when staring at her photograph, saw she was now Grace Peters and that though her date and month of birth remained the same, she was now two years younger at thirty-one. Stunned, she glanced at the birth certificate and saw she had been born in Glasgow as Grace Wilson.

Alex's passport, she read, named him as Andrew James Peters with his real date and month of birth, but with two years added to his age to also make him thirty-one.

Both driving licences, she saw, mirrored the details on the passports. As she examined the documents, Avril marvelled that not only did they look genuine, but they also looked aged, particularly the birth certificates while the dates of issue for the passports, her eyes narrowed, was two years previously.

Studying the flight tickets, Avril's brow wrinkled when she saw that she was booked on an Iberian flight departing from Prestwick airport to Menorca the following day at eleven-thirty.

A slip of paper attached by a paper clip to the flight ticket indicated that upon landing in Mahon, a reservation in her new name had been made at the Hotel San Miguel, which was approximately a ten-minute taxi ride from the airport.

The same information was also attached to Alex's flight ticket, though when she examined the ticket, her face fell when saw there was no departure date, that it was an open ticket to be used on any date within two months of the date of issue.

Staring at the documents and the money spread out on the unmade bed, she knew she should be feeling at least a little excited.

So why, she wondered, am I feeling so deflated?

****

Returning to Pollok, Benson discovered that neither team sent to detain Alex Hardie and Avril Collins had any luck, that there was no trace of either at their homes.

Calling Roddy Williams and Mhari McGregor into the DI's room, where after bringing McGregor up to speed about their visit to Partick, he passed round a pack of cigarettes then said, "I'm open to suggestions where that pair might be."

It was McGregor who cautiously said, "At the risk of pissing you off, boss, is it really that important we bring them in? What I mean is, we already have the information that Mark Ritchie left for us, albeit retrospectively, so what more can Hardie and Collins tell us other than why they dummied up the typed letter? That and we're tying up six detectives looking for them," she shrugged.

"You think I'm out to get them because they messed us around, Mhari?"

She stared at him before slowly nodding then truthfully replied, "It did occur to me, yes, sir."

He slowly exhaled, then admitted, "You might be right. However, I still want to know what their reasons were for withholding the information from us in Ritchie's letter, so in the meantime, keep the troops at both the addresses for now in case they do return home and if they don't, we'll review the situation later this afternoon."

"Sir," she acknowledged and inwardly breathed a sigh of relief that the boss had accepted her argument.

"Now, the murder of Peter Donaldson. Though it's a B Division investigation, from what Ritchie told you, Roddy, he is of the opinion that Donaldson and McGuire might be implicated in our victim's murder. What's your take on Donaldson being killed? Do you think it was McGuire?"

"It would save us a lot of time and energy if that were true, boss, and we could pin our victim's murder of both, but the simple answer is, I don't know. If McGuire *did* kill Donaldson, he's on the run, but as you already know, why set himself up, leaving a witness alive to whom he's identified himself then getting rid of the murder weapon with his prints where, I might add, it was so easily found. No," he shook his head, "my gut tells me he's being set up."

"And does your gut tell you its George Knox who is setting him up?"

"Aye, boss, it does," he wearily rubbed at his forehead.

"I believe that you're both overthinking this," McGregor quietly said, staring from one to the other.

"How so?" Benson stared keenly at her.

"Well," she slowly drawled, "who has the most to gain from the murder of Peter Donaldson by his partner, McGuire? And let's not forget, both Donaldson and McGuire are major players in the drug scene in Glasgow and elsewhere, boss."

She sat forward, her mouth suddenly dry, but now into her assessment.

"Yes," she nodded, "it *might* have been a rival drugdealer who shot Donaldson, but the information contained in Mark Ritchie's letter was undoubtedly passed by Hardie to his associate, George Knox, so it's unlikely that Knox, given his criminal reputation as an armed bank robber, is going to ignore the fact that the two of them probably murdered his daughter."

"Go on," Benson thoughtfully nodded at her.

"If as we all three think, it *was* George Knox who shot Donaldson, sir, he's not only identified our victims' killers for us, but whether by design or accident, he's also dealt a major blow to the illicit drug industry in our police area. If we accept Mark Ritchie's statement to the DI here," she nodded towards Williams, "that our victim was being supplied with cocaine by Donaldson and McGuire and trying to force her to deal for them too, that indicates an association with our victim. If we further accept Ritchie's opinion that they might be implicated in her murder, that casts them as serious suspects. It's my own humble opinion that we or I should say, B Division, follow the evidence rather than our own doubts and suspicions. As we now know," she stared again at them in turn, "the evidence seems to indicate that Peter Donaldson was murdered by a man who is positively identified by a witness as calling himself Foxy, as well as McGuire's fingerprints discovered on the murder weapon."

Her assessment concluded, she sat back to await their reaction. However, before either man could respond, the telephone rang.

"DCI Benson," he replied then said, "Hold on, Sheila, I've Roddy here with me as well as my DS, Mhari McGregor, so I'll put you on to speaker."

"Hello, Roddy and Mhari, Sheila here," the voice boomed out over the speaker. "Just to let you all, know, I've had the Ballistics people on the phone. They did a hurry-up job and come up with a result. The three shell cases and two bullets recovered from the chair where the victim was sitting and the one lodged in the ceiling above him, all were proved to have been fired by the Luger. Interestingly, Mr Benson, you'll recall I mentioned a bullet recovered from the wall in the kitchen?"

"I do, yes," he agreed.

"Well, I'm told the bullet had apparently suffered some damage that the Ballistics thought was unusual because it was dug out of a plastered wall and so should not have been damaged. Anyway, the Ballistics people did their magic and traced the trajectory of the bullet when it had been fired and discovered it struck the metal frame of the cooker, scored the top of the marble worktop before coming to rest where it was discovered. Anyway, the long and short of it is that it too fits the Luger."

"And your assessment, Sheila, or should I say, the assessment of the Ballistics?" Benson asked.

"According to the experts, sir, when the bullet was fired it was either badly aimed or missed it's target. However, as you also might recall, our young witness is adamant there was no shot fired in the kitchen at the time of the murder and he heard just the three shots fired, the three that presumably killed Donaldson."

"So, we can't account for the fourth shot in the kitchen?"

"No, sir, regretfully not. However, though I have no evidence to substantiate this, it's just possible that the bullet discovered in the kitchen *might* have previously been aimed at Donaldson. What do you think?"

"A possibility, I suppose. Thank you, Sheila. Any update in your hunt for McGuire?"

"Nothing so far and when my guys put his door in, there was no trace of him at his home nor any indication he might have packed a suitcase and fled. However, Scene of Crime went over his flat in Dalmarnock and discovered a tin with an oily cloth inside that might have contained the Luger, or so I'm told. The cloth will be

Forensically examined to determine if it was used to wrap the Luger and if it was, that's another piece of indisputable evidence."

"Good, Sheila, and thank you for getting back to us," Benson finished the call.

Staring at McGregor, he slowly nodded.

"As you said, Mhari, I think you more or less voiced what the three of us are thinking and we might just have to follow the evidence, but I'll need to speak Mr Meadows before we come to any decision."

He sighed heavily, before he added, "Then we'll also need to have a word with George Knox and put it to him, did he murder Peter Donaldson?"

CHAPTER TWENTY-EIGHT

Putting down the phone, George Knox breathed a sigh of relief. He'd wondered how he would collect the passports and other documents from Harry Cavanagh and didn't like the thought of risking Rosie visiting the town centre, therefore Harry's idea of couriering the documents to the three of them was a far better idea. However, though he could not possibly know the Scottish Crime Squad had temporarily suspended their operation against him, he believed the police posed a viable threat and still worried that the surveillance might be watching the house.

His mind contemplating what the surveillance might see, he assumed the cops might intercept the courier after he'd made the delivery to find out both what was in the package and where it had come from. So, in agreement with Cavanagh who like Knox did not like the idea of the police tracing the package back to his office, he'd added his own subtle touch to the arrangement.

It was agreed with Harry that Rosie and their grandson would visit the shop along the road from their close. Then at precisely midday, the courier would make the delivery inside the shop, for Knox believed it was unlikely the polis would follow her into the premises just to watch her buy groceries.

All they would see, he reckoned, was a motorcyclist dismounting outside the shop, entering then shortly after, leaving, and the cops would be unaware of the handover.

Nothing to attract their attention, he fervently hoped.
When the phone in the hallway rang, he heard Rosie answer it then call his name.
"It's Jimmy," she handed him the phone, then shooed Clint into the front room to watch the television.
"Harry phone you?"
"Aye," Knox confirmed, the added, "We need to speak, face to face. I had a busy night last night."
"Oh?"
"You out in one of your burger vans at the football today?"
"No, I'm giving it a miss. I've told the lassies I've got working for me just to go ahead without me. That said, what about my favourite roll and sausage place?"
Knox smiled, aware that Dunlop was referring to the café adjacent to Lynch's Bar on the London Road, not far from the Trongate. Though neither man was a supporter of either Glasgow's Old Firm, Celtic or Rangers, they were both aware that the café, next door to the pub frequented by Irish republican supporters, was also a haunt of the pub's patrons and strange faces would be immediately identified and suspected of being the police.
However, both Knox and Dunlop were regular visitors to the café where they could discuss matters without the fear of being overheard.
"Say, one o'clock? We can grab lunch at the café."
"See you there," Dunlop replied, then added, "and you're on the bell."
****

Aware that the taxi driver he was looking for had started his shift at five the previous evening, Alex Hardie suspected Janki Singh would likely be off duty. However, he did have one card to play.
Also aware that by now the police would likely have the description of his red coloured Capri, he parked the car in multi-storey Buchanan Street car park in the knowledge that he was abandoning it for it was far too distinctive to be seen driving, then with a regretful pat on the roof of the Capri, headed into the bus station to find a phone.
Fetching his diary from his inside jacket pocket, he searched for the name and number then dialled.

It had been some time since Hardie had spoken with the man he was calling and mentally kicked himself, for had he thought about calling him first, he might have saved himself time in tracing the cab driver. When his call was answered by a woman, he politely asked, "Hello, can I speak with Agi, please?"
Told to wait, he listened until a deep Weegie voice said, "Hello, who's this?"
"Agi, it's Alex Hardie. You got a minute to speak?"
Agambir 'Agi' Sohal smiled when he replied, "Hello, shagger, how's it hanging? Haven't heard from you in a while. You still at the stewarding game or are some of these rumours I keep hearing about you true?"
"Aye, Agi, I *am* still stewarding so don't believe everything you hear," Hardie replied with a smile, his eyes darting back and forth as he kept a weather eye open for any police officers passing by who might be taking an interest in him.
"I'm on for a favour, Agi."
"Anything big man. I owe you a few favours for the jobs you've sent my way. Did you know I'm working full time now? I'm doing permanent security at Glasgow Airport and a wee bit of interpreting on the side as well, for the Immigration guys."
"Good for you, pal," Hardie smiled.
"Right, what can I do you for?" Agi joked.
"I'm trying to trace a Sikh taxi driver, Agi. A guy called Janki Singh. He wouldn't happen to be in your Temple, would he?"
"Bloody Christian," Agi laughed. "You think all us Sikh's in Glasgow know each other?"
"Sorry, Agi. It was just on the off chance you might have crossed paths," a disappointed Hardie replied.
"Hey, big man," Agi continued to laugh. "I'm saying I don't *know* him, but I think I might have heard of him. He's definitely not in my Temple, but I think there's a taxi driver with that name. Does he drive a black Hackney cab by any chance?"
"Aye, that's correct," Hardie quickly replied, a faint hope rising in his chest.
"If it's the same guy, big man, he goes to the Gurdwara in South Portland Street. That's the main Temple. Do you know it?"
"I know South Portland Street, aye, over off the Pollokshaws Road I think?"

"That's right. Do you want me to try and confirm that's where he is?"

"No, I'll just head over there myself and speak to someone. Do you know anyone I can ask?"

"Oh, you'll be all right. Whoever is there should be able to help you, so if need be just don't forget to mention you're a pal of mine," Agi cheerfully told him.

"I owe you, Agi, thanks."

"No problem, big man and good luck."

Hardie asked at the information desk and was told what bus would take him to Pollokshaws Road.

Ten minutes later, the bus pulled out of the station and he was on his way to South Portland Street.

****

"I've a bit of a quandary, sir," DCI Martin Benson spoke into the telephone, then continued, "I know it's a Saturday and you're at home, but I'm really needing some advice on how to progress this investigation."

"Anything we can discuss on the phone," sighed Detective Chief Superintendent Keith Meadows.

"In light of my visit to Partick and new evidence that has arisen, I'm keen to speak with George Knox, sir, but I'd prefer a meeting with you before I make that visit."

There was an audible sigh before Meadows said, "Wait for a minute, Martin, will you?"

Before Benson could respond, he heard the phone being laid down then the distant sound of voices, one of which was raised and guessed his request hadn't gone down well with Meadows wife.

The phone was lifted then Meadows said, "My office at Pitt Street, forty minutes."

"Thank you, sir," Benson replied, but Meadows had already ended the call.

****

Rosie Knox returned with her grandson in tow, his attention in the comic his Granny had bought him.

Handing her husband the package from her shopping bag, she shrugged, "Couldn't see anyone who looked suspicious."

Following her into the kitchen, Knox tore open the package and while Rosie boiled the kettle, inspecting the contents, laid them out in an orderly fashion on the kitchen table.

"Bloody cheek," he remarked.

Fearing something had gone wrong with the documents, she turned to ask, "What?"

"They've made me two years older than I am," he pouted, then with a wide grin, handed her a passport and said, "Say hello to Alison Wayne."

She sighed as she stared at her photograph and smiling, said, "They've made me two years younger."

"So, I've got myself a young thing, then?"

"I've always been a young thing," she laughed.

"Oh, that's a bit of smart thinking," his brow furrowed when he read the official looking letter.

"Harry's included a letter to the Immigration authorising us, his grandparents, to take our orphaned grandson out of the country."

Her face paled when she asked, "Who has authorised it?"

He shrugged when he said, "It's been notarised with two dummy signatures from a lawyer and a Sheriff at the Court in Ingram Street."

He smirked when he said, "I don't suppose he'll ever know about it, but the Sheriff is a real guy and known for being a right hard arse when he does the sentencing."

"Oh," she forced a smile when she asked, "And who is our grandson now?"

"He's Craig Wayne, the son of Craig senior and Elizabeth Wayne."

His face clouded and he shook his head when he softly said, "Harry's got his man to include death certificates in those names. A vehicle accident according to this," he handed her one of the certificates. "My God, Rosie, how the hell does the wee guy manage to come up with all this stuff?"

They stood for several minutes staring at the documents in their hands before Rosie, attempting to lighten the moment, asked him, "And who are you?"

"Me? I'm your husband, Thomas, Mrs Wayne. But you can call me Tam."

She stared thoughtfully at him then said, "This is going to take some getting used to, George…I mean Tam. Especially for the wee boy."

"He'll need to get used to it, so we'll have to invent some sort of game for him to get into the habit of it."

"Leave it to me," she nodded, her forehead creasing in thought. "I have an idea about that."

"Right, hen," he glanced at his wristwatch. "I'm heading out to meet Jimmy. He needs to know what happened last night."

"Be careful," she placed her hand on his arm.

"I'm always careful," he cockily replied, then sweeping her giggling into his arms, planted a sloppy kiss on her lips.

"Away you go, ya madman," she shoved him off her and her heart beating wildly, watched as he left the flat.

George Knox, she thought as she stared at the closed front door. You and the wee man are my whole world. Her eyes brimming as she clenched her hands so tightly the nails dug into her palms, she swallowed deeply and thought, don't get yourself arrested and do *not* get yourself killed.

****

Jumping from the platform of the bus onto the pavement outside the Laurieston Bar, Alex Hardie stared up at the falling rain and inwardly cursed his stupidity for not lifting the golf umbrella from the boot of the Capri.

Turning up his collar, he hurriedly made his way along Oxford Street then cast a wry smile at the Strathclyde Police Training School that was located on the corner of South Portland Street. Making his way along the street, he finally found the tenement building at number seventy-nine and ducking into the close out of the rain, almost collided with an Indian woman he thought to be in her sixties, dressed in bright colours and who stared irately at him before she asked in a strong Glasgow accent, "What's the hurry, young yin? You coming in to join us Sikh's?"

Hardie smiled, then replied, "Sorry, missus, I was looking to see if Janki Singh was anywhere about or if you might know where he lives?"

"Our Jan? Aye, he's upstairs. Follow me," lifting the hem of her dress the woman raced away so quickly, Hardie almost laughed as he tried to keep up with her.

Reaching the door of the Temple, the woman raised a hand and said, "Some are at prayer at the minute, but I'll see if Jan's free."

He waited no more than two minutes when the door was opened by a tall, bearded man in his forties who wore a black coloured turban and like the woman, said in a strong Glasgow accent, "I'm Jan Singh. You looking for me, brother?"

"Janki Singh, the Hackney cab driver?"

"Aye," the man's face expressed his curiosity as well as his suspicion.

"Jan, my name's Alex Hardie. I was a friend of the lassie that was murdered last week. You might have read about it?"

"The lassie from the Barrowland?" his eyes narrowed. "You're not the polis, then?"

"No, were you expecting them?"

"I thought by now they'd have given me a visit. I did make a phone call to my local station at Garscadden to say I was on duty that night in the rank at the Barrowland if anybody needed to speak to me, but I never heard anything back."

Bloody cops, Hardie inwardly thought, but instead said, "Her name was Kelly-Ann Knox. You might have seen her photo in the papers. Did you recognise her by any chance?"

"No, but see at that time of the night, pal, half the women are pissed anyway and I'm not being funny," he slowly shook his head, "but their own mothers wouldn't recognise them, they're that wrecked. Anyway, how did you come to find me?"

"It was one of the stewards at the Barrowland, a guy called Micky Rourke. He said he put Kelly-Ann into a…"

Hardie hesitated, worrying about offending Singh, then shrugging, continued. "He said he put her into a Paki's taxi, but I made inquiry and found it might have been you. Not a Pakistani guy. Part of that inquiry was speaking to a pal of mine, Agi Sohal."

"Agi Sohal? No," he shook his head and pursed his broad lips, "can't say I know him, but don't be worrying about me getting called a Paki. I've been called worse than that, believe me," he sighed. "Micky Rourke, you said? A steward at the Barrowland? I don't really know the guys that work there, but funny you should mention that," his brow furrowed into a deep crease. "I took one of the stewards' home that night with a bird and let me tell you," he shook his head again, "she was really out of it."

Though he couldn't explain it, a cold shiver run down Hardie's spine when he slowly asked, "Can you describe the steward for me?"

"Oh, I remember him," Singh humourlessly smiled. "I thought it funny at the time because the dancing was still on. That and the miserable sod asked for change for his tenner and didn't tip. As for his bird, pissed or drugged, I don't know, but he had to half carry her out of my cab. At one stage I thought she was arguing with him, but he told me she was always like that when she'd a drink in her."

"The steward?" Hardie prompted him.

"Eh," Singh's eyes narrowed as he tried to recall, then said, "About your height, hair down to his shoulders. I'm forty-four and he was younger than me, but," he squinted at Hardie, "aye, I'd say he was a bit older than you. Say mid to late thirties, maybe? Wearing a black suit and a white shirt and dickie bow like all the stewards wear, you know?"

One thought and one name invaded Hardie's mind.

Rourke had lied about putting Kelly-Ann into a taxi.

He'd got into the taxi with her.

His throat tight as bandsman's drum, he asked, "Do you recall where you dropped him and the woman off?"

Singh stared suspiciously at him before he asked, "You thinking that the lassie might have been your friend and if she was, had you not be better telling the cops about this?"

Forcing a smile, he replied, "If there's anything in it, believe me, I'll go to the police myself and try not to involve you."

"Oh, I'm not worried about telling the cops," Singh shook his head, then staring meaningfully at Hardie, he took a deep breath before he added, "but if someone hurt one of my daughters. Stand on me, brother, there would be no need for the polis to be involved."

He knew he was taking a chance on this man's integrity when Hardie slowly replied, "Then we're on the same page when it comes to hurting women?"

As if making up his mind, Singh took several seconds before he replied "I dropped them off outside a flat near the Corkerhill railway station. No, wait," his eyes narrowed in thought and he raised a hand to correct himself.

"Do you know the Cart Bar on the Corkerhill Road?"

"No," Hardie shook his head.

"Well," Singh's face tightened as in his mind, he plotted the route. Then he continued, "If you're coming down from the Paisley Road West side and you find the Cart Bar, then turn left into Corkerhill Place and drive to the end where there's a block of flats there in a cul-de-sac. I dropped them in the cul-de-sac and the last I saw them was heading for the close next to the big park," then as if in explanation, added, "The Pollok Park."

Recognising the name as the location Kelly-Ann's body was discovered, Hardie's throat tightened and he could feel his face pale when he asked, "The Pollok Park?"

"Aye, the cul-de-sac is right next door to the park."

Seeing Hardie's face pale, he frowned then asked, "Does that mean something to you?"

Hardie tightly smiled then clapping Singh on his arm, stared into his eyes before he asked, "Can we keep this conversation between us, man to man?"

As though reading into the comment, Singh slowly nodded then placing his own hand on top of Hardie's, quietly replied, "Whatever you need to do, brother, don't get caught."

****

Downstairs in the close entrance, Hardie stood for several moments, his mind in a whirl as he watched the rain falling.

Glancing at his wristwatch, he saw it was pushing one in the afternoon and dismissing travelling by bus, realised he'd need wheels to get around.

But it was Saturday afternoon and not only was he out without a cheque book to purchase a runner from any of the second-hand car dealerships that flourished in the waste grounds down at the docksides, but he didn't carry his driving licence so a hire was also out of the question.

That and there was no way he would trust a taxi to take him to Micky Rourke's flat to carry out the task he intended; not if he wanted to stay out of jail.

Frustrated, he was on the point of stepping out into the rain to return and collect his abandoned Capri when a knowing smile broke on his face as an idea came to him.

With a spring in his step, he hurried through the rain to the nearby Bridge Street to hail a taxi to take him to Summerston, in the north side of the city.

****

Sitting facing Detective Chief Superintendent Keith Meadows in his Pitt Street office, DCI Martin Benson recounted his meeting with DI Sheila Farquhar at Partick Police Office, then added, "Mhari McGregor was right though, sir. Regardless of what I or any of my team personally think, I should really be following the evidence and it all points to James McGuire being the killer of his associate, Peter Donaldson. So much so that Sheila's intimated she is already craving a warrant for McGuire's arrest on a charge of murder."

"Even though you believe it might have been George Knox taking revenge for the murder of his daughter?" Meadows stared thoughtfully at him.

"Aye, because as I've no need to tell you, what I think and what Sheila Farquhar can prove are two different things."

He sighed when he added; "I'd be laughed out of Crown Office if I tried to make a case against Knox for murder when the evidence clearly indicates it was Foxy who shot Donaldson."

"Though it *is* evidence you believe was planted by George Knox to incriminate McGuire?"

"Yes, sir," Benson slowly shook his head.

"So, Martin, why am I here?" Meadows face puckered. "What exactly is it that you want from me?"

"Now that I'm sitting here and having explained it all to you, I suppose I need your reassurance that when I challenge Knox about the murder, I'm not making a fool of myself."

Meadows slowly smiled before he replied, "Look, Martin, between you and me and these four walls," he waved a hand around the room, "the reality is that a bad bastard has been killed and another vicious criminal is being hunted for it. You're a good man and I know it will bother your conscience to think that an innocent man is being set-up for murder, but think about it. Assuming your suspicions are correct and it *was* George Knox settling the debt for his daughter's murder, ask yourself this. Is Foxy McGuire truly an innocent man?" his hands clasped, he leaned forward onto his elbows.

"Consider the hurt and damage he has done during his career in the drug industry. How many young lives have been lost because of the product he and Donaldson supplied? How many people have been viciously assaulted by him personally when he's acted on Donaldson's instructions?"

"You're suggesting that I simply ignore my suspicions and what, go with the flow, as they say?" he harshly stared at him.

"I'm suggesting you do what you're trained to do, Detective Chief Inspector," Meadows abruptly responded. "Trust the evidence that seems to indicate McGuire murdered Donaldson and permit DI

Farquhar to submit her application for a warrant so that McGuire might face the charge in court and let a *jury* decide if he's innocent or guilty. You, meantime, will continue to concentrate on finding the killer of George Knox's daughter."

"And if the killers were Donaldson and McGuire?"

"Then prove it, though from what you've told me," He sighed, "you only have this man Ritchie's suspicions, but no real evidence."

Benson took a deep breath then slowly exhaling, pushed himself to his feet.

He stared down at Meadows before he said, "I feel I've wasted your Saturday, sir."

A little more solicitously, Meadows shook his head before he replied, "Not at all, Martin. As you yourself said, you simply needed some reassurance that you're not wasting your time. And for what it's worth," he frowned, "I agree the law isn't all black and white. However, once we start straying into the grey areas between the lines, we risk losing focus on who the good guys are and who are really the bad guys. And don't forget what we already know," a soft smile played upon his lips when he added, "Justice and the law are not always the same thing."

Nodding his farewell, Benson wordlessly left the room.

****

Jimmy Dunlop, seated at a table in the rear of the café, was waiting on George Knox and when he saw his pal enter, turned and raised a hand towards the middle-aged man behind the counter who nodded in acknowledgement.

When Knox sat down, Dunlop told him, "I've ordered for us." Hunching forward onto the table, he asked, "So what happened last night that's so important you need a face to face?"

Before Knox could reply, the café owner arrived with two plates of rolls and sausage and mugs of tea then laying the tray down onto the table, grinned and said, "Here we go, gents."

When he'd retired back to behind the counter, Knox, in a quiet voice, told the stunned Dunlop of Clint's abduction and the resulting killing of Foxy McGuire.

To pre-empt Dunlop's question of why he hadn't called him, Knox explained that he had been given just twenty-five minutes to get to Ibrox and there was no time to call for either Dunlop or Hardie's assistance.

"Jesus Christ! Where's the body?"
"The guy that helped me, him and Alex took care of it."
"And Peter Donaldson?" Dunlop seethed, his face an angry red. "What are we going to do about that fat prick?"
"It's taken care of. I did him last night," Knox whispered then added, "The cops will be looking for McGuire for killing him."
Dunlop didn't bother asking any further questions about the murder, only, "Is Rosie and wean okay?"
"Aye, the wee guy got a fright, but he'll be fine. Now, did you get the stuff from Harry?"
"It arrived this morning, so I was going to put Liz onto the flight tomorrow, but if Donaldson and McGuire are turning up their toes, is there any need for the women to go on ahead without us?"
"That's the problem," Knox sighed, his rolls still untouched and related his suspicions that perhaps neither of the murdered men had killed Kelly-Ann.
"So, I've told Alex to go ahead and continue looking for the guy."
"Right, so we'll stay behind and help?"
Knox stared at Dunlop then softly smiling, replied, "No, Jimmy. I'll stay behind."
"No, that's not right, George. We're a team," Dunlop vigorously shook his head.
"Listen to me, pal, please," Knox continued to smile at him.
"I want you to go on the flight with Liz. Besides, we both know with her arthritis, she'll need all the help she can get. When or even *if* Alex finds this guy, we're enough to deal with it, the two of us."
"You sure?"
"I'm sure. Now, what about the tools?" asked Knox, referring to Dunlop's array of weapons.
"I'll be sad to see them go," he sighed, "but if they're not needed anyway, I'm retiring them and they're going for a wee swim tonight in the Clyde."
"Okay. How about getting to the airport? What are you planning?"
"Harry's booked us on an Edinburgh flight, so early tomorrow morning, I'm driving the motor to Edinburgh city centre, dumping it somewhere and getting a taxi to the airport from there. I'm not leaving it in the airport car park and giving the cops a clue we're away abroad."

"Good idea," Knox nodded. "I'm leaving the Jag at the house and getting a taxi from there to Glasgow Airport, too. No point in making it easy for the polis when they discover we're away," he smiled.

"The rolls okay, gents?" the café owner had unseeingly hovered over them.

"Aye, they're fine," Knox nodded at him. "Sorry, we just got caught up in conversation," then took a large bite from one of his rolls.

"Right then," the man cheerfully replied before asking, "More tea?"

"That will be grand," Dunlop handed him his empty mug.

Once again alone, he asked, "Are you sure about this? You and Alex hanging on for a while?"

"Of course I am," Knox grinned.

"And if you don't find her killer?"

"Then I'll need to live with it. Now," he removed a pen and scrap of paper from his jacket pocket, "once you've arrived, whereabouts in Cyprus can I contact you?"

****

The taxi dropped Alex Hardie at the front entrance of the multi-story high rise building in Glenavon Road.

Gambling the police would no longer be mounting a cordon at the building where Kevin Stobbie had been murdered, Hardie began to walk round the small car park, then sighed with relief when he saw Stobbie's black coloured Mercedes 190 saloon and guessed with Stobbie now dead, the police had no further interest in the car.

The Mercedes, barely a year old, had been Stobbie's pride and joy and as far as Hardie and the others knew, his only real financial outlay, for the wee man had led an austere and Spartan life with his only other hobby being his video collection of John Wayne movies.

Strolling towards the car, Hardie glanced about him and as far as he could see, no one was paying him any particular attention.

Now at the car, his plan hinged on whether or not Stobbie's spare car key was in the small metal box that was magnetically stuck to the underside of the rear wheel arch on the driver's side of the vehicle. Bending down between the car and its neighbour, a rusting Transit van, he fumbled for the box then sighed when his fingers touched it. A swift tug and the box fell into his hand.

"Yes," he involuntarily muttered when opening the box, he saw the key.

Aware that someone might be watching from the building, he quickly got into the driver's seat and starting the engine, drove out of the car park.

Five minutes later, he turned into a side street off Maryhill Road and stopped the car.

Opening the glove compartment, he found a Glasgow A to Z book as well as several other foldout maps of the Strathclyde area.

Opening the A to Z, he searched for Corkerhill Place. Satisfying himself he knew where he was going, he glanced round the car, taking note of both its cleanliness and the smell of polished leather, then idly pulled at the sun visor above him.

To his surprise, tucked into the flap that hid the mirror was a photograph of a smiling Clint, squinting against the sun as he stared into the camera. It was taken when he was about four years of age. The lad was squatting in the sand as he played with a pail and spade on a beach somewhere.

Kevin, you plonker he thought as he shook his head.

Why the hell didn't you just put your hands up to it? George and Rosie would have eventually understood.

All those wasted years you could have spent with your son.

****

Sitting in his Ford Cortina parked in Clydeholm Street, Lennie Campbell watched the last of the Saturday shift workers leave the building site some one hundred and fifty yards away, then waited a further twenty minutes to ensure no one returned to the site.

Getting out of the car in the lonely road, the winter sun now fading to a dim light, he carefully walked over the rough ground through the hole in the fence to the area where he'd watched the cement truck being guided to the different tasks.

At the spot where he and Alex Hardie had buried McGuire's body, he stared down at the newly laid concrete.

Grunting, he cleared his throat then spat down onto the rapidly hardening concrete.

Turning away, he shoved his hands in his pockets and walked off to return to his car.

CHAPTER TWENTY-NINE

Though still late afternoon, the clouds combined with the time of the year had further darkened the skies and with the light fall of rain, made for miserable driving conditions.

Nevertheless, Alex Hardie paid no heed to the weather for his mind was now totally focused on his task of finding Micky Rourke and getting the truth from him.

First though, he had to ensure that his trip to Rourke's home address wasn't a waste of time and sighting a phone box beside the road, pulled in beside it.

Fetching a handful of coins from his pocket, he phoned directory inquiries for the listed number of Lewis's department store, then calling the number, asked to be put through to the security office.

It was several rings before his call was answered by a laconic sounding female who informed him that no, Mr Rourke was not on duty, but if he were to contact him, he might wish to inform Mr Rourke that the security supervisor would like to speak with him regarding his current employment status.

Picking up the hint, Hardie asked, "Are you saying he's getting sacked?"

As if fearing being overheard, the woman lowered her voice to reply, "Just tell the lazy bugger if he doesn't get his arse in here to explain why he's missed his shift again, aye, he's getting the bullet, okay?"

Thanking her, he said he'd try to pass on her message then thoughtfully ended the call.

Missed his shift again?

To Hardie that meant only one thing.

His visit to meet with Rourke had panicked him and he'd gone to ground and hopefully, Hardie thought, to his house.

Returning to the car and as he drove off, he considered what he knew of Kelly-Ann's murder.

Her body had been discovered in the Pollok Park, the park adjacent to where he now knew Rourke lived.

His eyes narrowed as he recalled seeing Rourke for the first time, chatting up the pretty young assistant at the perfume counter. If he were honest though and he didn't excuse himself either, he sighed, Rourke wouldn't be the first or the last guy in the stewarding business to chance his arm with the women.

But why, he thought, did Rourke lie about putting Kelly-Ann in a taxi when it was likely that he'd brought her back to his flat with him?

Was it Kelly-Ann with Rourke or have I added two and two and made five, he wondered?

Passing through a set of traffic lights on Corkerhill Road at its junction with Mosspark Drive, he knew he was close to his destination.

When seconds later he drove the Mercedes up over a railway bridge, he saw the square shaped, single storey Cart Bar pub a further hundred yards on his left.

Slowing the car, he turned into Corkerhill Place and made his way to the cul-de-sac that Janki Singh had described then turned left into the dead end.

Switching off the engine, he stared through the rain at the council built, three-storey flats directly in front and seeing just two closes.

His eyes turned towards the nineteen-sixties built tenement and the huge grassy area by the building. Singh, he recalled, had said the man and woman had headed for the close next to the big park, so that, he reasoned, must be the close on his right.

Turning up the collar of his jacket, he got out of the car and made his way round the path that was separated from the uncut, patchy grass in front of the flats by a rusting, metal fence.

Lights were on in some of the flats and he could hear what sounded like jazz music loudly coming from an open window on the first floor of the close he was striding towards.

Entering the close, he stopped and listened, but other than the echoing noise of the jazz music, he couldn't hear any movement.

The door on his right seemed to him to be a council issued replacement door. Wooden, it had never seen a paintbrush and had the name 'P. ROURKE' written on the centre of the door in black felt pen, the writing dulled with age.

Halfway up the door was a Yale lock above a brass handle, though the brass on both the lock and handle was dull and unpolished.

His ear to the door, he listened, but could not hear any sound from within.

Conscious it was late Saturday afternoon, almost early evening now, he wondered if Rourke was at home, but if not, he was prepared to wait for him, though not in the chilly close.

Gently trying the door handle, it was as he thought, locked.
Seeing that there was no eyehole in the door, he decided to knock, but after three tries, there was no response.
He stopped and listened intently, but other than the music from upstairs, there was nothing to indicate his knocking at the door had attracted any attention.
Making his way through the close back door into the rear garden area, he saw that it was littered with rubbish that had been strewn about by the wind.
With the rain and darkness masking his movements, he stepped towards the two rear windows of the flat that were, he presumed, bedrooms.
The curtains were tightly closed in one room, while the other bedroom seemed to have been used as storage for it was filled with what looked like cardboard boxes, both on the floor and lying on top of the single bed. However, glancing up, he saw that the hopper window in the metal-framed window was slightly ajar.
Glancing around him, Hardie saw a tubular chair, its canvas seat torn, lying abandoned by the bin area. Carrying the chair to the window, he first tested his weight on its frame then stood upon it. The added height permitted him to reach the hopper window where he grabbed the frame and hauled himself up to stand on the ledge. Seconds later, his arm reached inside the hopper to lift up the metal catch, then pulled open the window and almost noiselessly dropped inside the room.
He stood for a few seconds in the darkness, but still there was no sound.
Walking to the door on his heels, his nose wrinkled at the damp, musty smell in the room and through what light remained of the day, he saw the cardboard boxes seemed to be filled with clothing and bedding.
At the room door, he gently turned the handle and stepped out in the darkness of the hallway, now growing more certain the flat was deserted.
With increasing confidence, he made his way through the other rooms, opening the doors and poking his head in to confirm that as he'd thought, Rourke wasn't at home.

With a sigh of disappointment, he decided to risk it and returning to the front room, switched on the light, but only after pulling the curtains tightly closed.

Once more his nose wrinkled at the combined smell of body odour, booze and cigarette smoke and he could see that the room was not just untidy, but filthy.

Dirty glasses of all shapes and sizes, plates, some with food still adhering to them and cigarette butts stubbed out on them, empty cartons and beer cans littered the coffee table and the grubby carpet by the armchair that faced the television in the corner.

If nothing else, Hardie thought with a sigh, Rourke should get the jail for living like a pig.

In the kitchen, he again closed the curtains before switching on the light to find the sink was barely visible beneath the assortment of pots and pans that lay in the greasy water with even more crockery and cutlery lying there too.

Pulling open the small fridge, he involuntarily took a step backwards, his face wrinkling at the smell of rotten food and soured milk emanating from the fridge.

Hurriedly closing the fridge door, his glance fell upon the small gateleg table located in the recess of the kitchen between the two built in cupboards and saw it was awash with mail, some of it unopened.

Flicking his fingers through the mail, Hardie's eyes narrowed when one brightly coloured envelope caught his eye, for the unopened envelope that was addressed to Mr Patrick Rourke, bore the cartoon image of a caravan beside the clear window. Tearing the envelope open, he pulled out the letter to find it was a second and final warning letter, that if the unpaid storage for Mr Patrick Rourke's caravan was not paid within the next thirty days, the caravan would be removed from its berth and left in the roadway outside the premises.

Thereafter, the letter threatened, the council would be notified of the caravan being illegally parked on the roadway.

Glancing at the letter heading, he saw it to be from a storage company based in Ashton Road in Rutherglen and dated just one week previously.

Patrick Rourke, he assumed must either be Micky Rourke's father or brother, but that question was answered when another unopened letter also caught his eye, for this time it was addressed to Mr Michael Rourke.

Tearing it open, he saw it to be dated some weeks previously and read that the Cooperative Funeral Service were pleased to inform Mr Michael Rourke that his father Patrick's ashes were, at his convenience, now available for collection.

But it was the letter from the storage company that had set Hardie thinking.

Leaving the mail on the table, he decided to search the rest of the flat, beginning with the bedroom with the closed curtains.

Opening the door, he switched on the light and gasped when the smell of body odour, stale urine, dampness and something else, something he couldn't quite distinguish, almost took his breath away.

Cheap gaudy posters of women, naked or in various stages of undress were thumbtacked to the walls where dampness had caused the wallpaper to come loose at the edges.

He stared down at the bed with the brass headboard, the quilt cover lying discarded on the floor on the opposite side of the bed.

But it was the lower crumpled sheet that attracted his attention, for it was stained a dark brown colour and his blood froze.

Barely able to breathe his eyes rose to stare at the pair of cheaply made handcuffs attached to each corner of the brass headboard, one with a pink coloured fluffy material still attached to it.

On the wooden bedside table lay what seemed to Hardie to be a police style wooden baton with a leather thong attached.

For how long he stood there immobile, staring at the bed, the handcuffs and the baton, he couldn't later say, but then found his feet moving towards the baton that he now saw was also stained with the same, sticky, brown substance.

A substance that like the stain on the bed, he inwardly now realised, that was dried blood.

Kelly-Ann Knox's blood.

His body shaking, he could feel the pulse in his temple throbbing as he tensed his body, tears of rage falling to his cheeks and his head held in his hands.

He fell backwards against the wall and slumped to the floor with his knees drawn up against his chest.

Sobbing, he wept uncontrollably like a baby, his mind racing with thoughts of the pain and indignity she must have helplessly suffered at the hands of Micky Rourke.

It was then, his eyes narrowing, he saw the green colour that lay beneath the bed and reaching forward, pulled it out.

His shoulders slumped when he recognised what it was.

The green, hooded coat so beloved by Kelly-Ann.

Dragging the coat towards him, that's when he also saw a brassiere and a pair of woman's knickers also lying under the bed alongside a woman's black handbag.

He did not need to search the handbag with its distinctive pattern for he had seen it often enough to know it belonged to Kelly-Ann.

Lifting the coat, he stared at it as he held it to him then, though he couldn't explain why, searched the two patch pockets. His fingers felt paper and pulling it out, saw it to be a torn wrapper of Trebor Soft Fruit Rolls, the favourite sweeties of Kelly-Ann's son, Clint.

Returning the sweeties wrapper to the pocket, he shoved the coat back under the bed.

But then once again the rage kicked in and he knew what he had to do.

He sat for several minutes as an idea formed in his head.

Frowning, he knew he had to find Rourke and make him pay and the first place he intended searching for him was the caravan storage facility.

Rising to his feet, he stumbled back to the other bedroom and closing the large window then pulled the bar of the hopper window closed to tightly lock it.

Returning to the hallway, he turned the Yale lock and his heart beating, slowly opened the front door and listened, but other than the music from upstairs, could not hear anyone in the close.

Stepping out the door, he pulled it closed behind him and heard the Yale lock click and secure the door.

Now, the house being closed, he knew there was no reason for the police to think that anyone had been in the house.

But he hadn't forgot about the tubular chair and silently moving through to the rear court, fetched it from under the bedroom window then replaced it at the bin area before making his way back through the close to where he had parked the car.

All he had to do now was find Rourke, but before he went hunting him, he had to visit George Knox, for he knew he would need some leverage when he did catch up with the man who had murdered Kelly-Ann Knox.

****

Liz Dunlop sat on the edge of the bed as she watched her husband Jimmy pack their suitcases and asked, "Are we really doing the right thing here, Jimmy? I mean, look what we're leaving behind, all our friends, our neighbours and, well, everything. Are we not too old to be starting again?"

He stopped and turning, replied, "Look, hen, how many times have we been over this? Yes, of course we're doing the right thing," he sighed, then sitting down beside her, gently took one of her hands in his and continued. "Every day when you watch those polis Forensic programmes on the telly, you see how they're always coming up with ideas how to catch bad guys like me. We both know that it's just a matter of time before they'll come for me and the boys, so the longer I stay here the better the chance the cops will eventually come up with something that could put me away. But the main thing is," he gradually raised her hand to his mouth and kissed it, "think of the benefit for you living in the sun. No more aches and pains from the Scottish weather and let's face it, hen, living in the west coast of Scotland, your arthritis isn't going to get any better, is it? Besides, with the grandweans living with our lassie and her man in Canada, what's really to keep us here? We can always get a flight to Canada from Cyprus, you know, and we'll have the money to do it, too," he smiled.

She glanced at the room around her, then sighed, "I'll miss the house."

"Don't worry about it," he got to his feet and grinned. "The council will soon have somebody else in here once they've figured out we've done a moonlight flit."

"And George is okay about you coming with me tomorrow morning? He doesn't need you to stay like you thought?"

"No hen, that's all sorted," he cheerily continued packing, yet inwardly hoped that when Knox finally did catch up with Kelly-Ann's killer, he didn't get himself caught murdering the bastard.

****

In the Sherbrooke Hotel room, Avril Collins had enough of watching television or reading newspapers and toyed with the idea of heading downstairs to the dining room for dinner.

Yet Alex had been firm about that.

"The less people see you, the less likely the police hear about you staying here," he had told her.

With a sigh, she picked up the phone and once more dialled for room service.

****

After returning to Pollok Police station, DCI Martin Benson had ordered Mhari McGregor to stand down the detectives at both Alex Hardie and Avril Collins addresses, but not before leaving some calling cards, instructing them both upon their return to contact Mr Benson at Pollok.

Calling Roddy Williams to him, he related his conversation with Keith Meadows then said, "I'm going to phone Knox now and inform him I'm on my way for a visit and I'd like you to accompany me."

"Righto, boss," Williams nodded. "I'll let Mhari know where we're going."

Minutes later, with Williams driving, they were on their way.

****

His work completed and the clients in receipt of their new identities and though it was Saturday evening, Harry Cavanagh sat back in his comfortable desk chair in his Wellington Street office.

Enjoyably puffing on his large Cuban cigar, he stared at the cigar and, imagined when it was created or so the urban legend said, being rolled upon the soft thighs of a Cuban maiden.

Ah, to be in Cuba right now, he smiled as the smoke swirled above his head.

His thoughts turned to George Knox and his companions.

If there were no hiccups, the clients and their women and the wee boy too, bless him, would be safely gone from Scotland either tomorrow or hopefully, within the next few days.

He knew that George was grateful for all the attention and details that went into creating the new identities, the transferring of their money into their individual accounts, the flight and hotel arrangements he had made on their behalf.

But, the truth was, Cavanagh *loved* it.

He loved the intrigue, the minute attention to detail the opportunity to put one over the establishment.
And besides, he modestly accepted that he made a pretty good living out of it, too.
That the money he laundered for his many clients was in the most part, the proceeds of criminality?
Yes, he smiled as he inhaled the rich fragrance of the cigar, he could live with that.
His thoughts turned to other issues and once more he glanced at the applications on his desk.
He'd had enough of that wizened face old cow out in the front office and finally decided it was time to replace her.
Of the three women and the young man he'd interviewed, two of the women were certainly very likely candidates; however, it was the youngest of the three who had intrigued him.
Helen was her name and his eyes narrowed as he smiled at the memory of her with her pink coloured hair that erupted from her head like a burst pillow, the black cropped top and a skirt that was so short it could hardly be described as such; however, the skirt showed off the most marvellous pair of legs, he smiled.
Aye, she had a mouth on her right enough, but there was definitely something about her.
Glancing down at her application, he decided that maybe she'd be worth another interview before he made up his mind.
****
Alex Hardie had spent ten minutes dissuading George Knox from accompanying him to find Micky Rourke, telling him only that Rourke was likely the man who had murdered Kelly-Ann, but nothing about what he had discovered in Rourke's flat.
It was then they had argued and pushed and shoved at each other. Hardie refusing details to protect the man who meant so much to him and Knox, his eyes wet with unshed tears, cursing and swearing and threatening and trying to persuade his young friend to tell him more about the man who had killed his daughter.
Rosie, in between the two of them, weeping and calling upon her husband to, "…listen to Alex! For God's sake, George, listen to what he's telling you!"

The small boy stood in the doorway of the front room, ignored and quietly sobbing as the two men pushed and shoved at each other and not understanding why.

Then the phone in the hallway rang.

Like a referee's bell at a boxing match, they breathlessly separated while Rosie snatched up the phone to snap, "Yes!"

They watched her face pale as she glanced from one to the other, then said, "Okay, we'll be in. Thank you."

They saw her take a nervous breath before she said, "That was the CID. The detective, that man Benson. He's coming to see us in about half an hour."

Now there was no question of George Knox leaving the house for to do so, they knew, might create suspicion at a time when they were so close to getting away.

Though it pained Hardie to ignore Knox's demands and pleas, he had finally persuaded him that their revenge was best left to Hardie to mete out the justice to their daughter's killer, with the guarantee that, "Yes, I'll make sure the bastard suffers. I promise you, he'll not die well."

The last thing he had done before leaving the flat was remove the Beretta from the electrical box and tuck it into the front waistband of his trousers.

Now en route to Rutherglen, he stopped at a licensed grocer to purchase a bottle of cheap, blended whisky that he had the assistant place into a plastic bag and a box of Swan Vesta matches. A mile further on, he pulled into a garage forecourt and from the boot of the car, fetched out the jerrycan that he filled with petrol.

Arriving at Rutherglen's Ashton Road, Hardie once more inwardly thanked Kevin Stobbie's foresight in keeping an A to Z map book in the glove compartment for it had led him directly to the dark and deserted industrial estate.

In the darkness with poor light from the overhead street lamps, the rain now pouring heavily down, he slowly drove through the estate till he saw the large number of caravans, more than he could count or guess at, parked side by side behind a wire fence that in places was lying askew or simply missing and had not been replaced.

Stopping the car, he sat for several minutes contemplating what he was about to do.

Breathing deeply, his mind spun at the memory of the bloodstained sheets, the baton and the handcuffs attached to the metal spars on the bed's headboard and knew it was a memory that would remain with him for a very long time.

Turning his head to glance about him, he satisfied himself there was no one around then getting out of the car, lifted the plastic bag containing the whisky from the rear seat and collected the jerry can and Beretta from the boot.

His nerves as taut as piano wire, he made his way into the area where the caravans were parked, taking his time over the rough and uneven ground, his senses alert for any sounds, then stopped dead. Some distance away, roughly one hundred yards he thought, a man moved among the caravans using the faint beam of a torch to light his way.

Stepping behind a caravan, Hardie could feel his heart beating wildly in his chest and wondered, is it Rourke, but then grimaced when the jerrycan struck the side of the caravan a glancing blow.

To Hardie, the jarring noise sounded like thunder.

Peeking through the window of the caravan he hid behind, he could see the torch beam shining in turn at the caravans as the man passed them by and realised, this wasn't a man trying to keep a low profile, so it must be a watchman.

As the torch beam approached, Hardie moved back along the side of the caravan to hide at the rear as the man passed by and sneaking a glance at him, saw him to be elderly and reasoned, probably a pensioner earning himself a few bob on the QT doing his night watchman.

As he breathed a sigh of relief, to his surprise, he saw the elderly man stop at a caravan then heard him call out, "Mind what we agreed, Micky boy. Don't be telling anybody about me letting you stay here, okay?"

He stood stock-still, hardly daring to breathe and heard a muffled response, but couldn't make it out though inwardly relieved that he'd been correct; Rourke had fled to his dead father's caravan.

However, whatever Rourke had replied caused the old man to laugh for Hardie heard him respond, "Aye right enough. Good night, then, son."

Moving back along the length of the caravan, Hardie watched the old man disappear towards the gates of the compound and presumably into a hut for the torch beam disappeared and in the quiet of the night, he heard a door slam closed.

His nerves shredded, he took a moment to compose himself then keeping to the shadows, slowly made his way along the line of caravans till he saw an old, dark coloured, mark one Ford Escort parked beside a dilapidated looking caravan.

As he neared the caravan, he could see through the net curtain a faint light flickered from within and presuming that none of the caravans would be connected to an electrical supply, guessed it to be a burning candle.

He didn't know anything about caravans, but guessed from the size of it Rourke's caravan was no more than a two-berth van. One of the tyres on the door side, he could see, was flat and both ends of the van were propped up onto breezeblocks to give it some form of stability.

At the door of the caravan, he listened and could hear a transistor radio playing from within and someone, Rourke he hoped, singing noisily along to the music.

Laying down the plastic bag and the jerrycan, he took the Beretta from his coat pocket then softly rapped his knuckles on the caravan door.

CHAPTER THIRTY

Rosie Knox, her face scrubbed clean of tears, forced a smile when she opened the door and invited the two detectives inside.

"George is in the front room," she told them, "so just go straight through. Can I get you gentlemen tea or coffee?"

Pokerfaced, both men declined with a polite thank you and made their way into the room to find Knox sitting reading that evenings edition of the 'Glasgow News.'

The small boy, the victim's son, was in his room playing with his railway set.

"Please," Knox invited them to sit down on the couch as Rosie entered to occupy the other armchair, "are you here with some good news?"

"Sadly, no," his eyebrows knitting, DCI Benson shook his head.

"However, we would like an explanation, Mr Knox, as to why your associate, Alex Hardie, retained a handwritten letter from Mark Ritchie and gave us the police an edited copy?"

Knox stared at him for a few seconds then frowning, he replied, "You'll need to explain that one, Mr Benson, and who this man Mark Ritchie is. No, wait," his eyes narrowed. "Isn't he the guy you said had gone abroad?"

"Oh, come now, let's not play games. Your man Hardie. He told you about the letter addressed to him that suggested Peter Donaldson and Foxy McGuire might have been responsible for your lassie's murder. Then, either on your instruction or his own volition, Hardie and his friend Avril Collins typed up a letter that was handed to us omitting that particular piece of information, information I might add that could have assisted us in our investigation to catch your daughter's killer!"

"So, have you asked Alex about this?"

"As likely you know," an increasingly red-faced Benson replied, "Hardie and his friend Avril Collins have made themselves scarce and so far avoided us. But don't be worrying on that account, Mr Knox. We will find them. Of that I've no doubt."

"This man Donaldson and the other one," Rosie butted in. Have you interviewed *them* about Kelly-Ann's murder?"

Benson stared at her for several seconds, then turned his glance towards Knox before he flatly responded with, "Peter Donaldson was himself murdered last night. Do you know anything about *that*, Mr Knox?"

Pretending surprise, Knox angrily asked, "Are you suggesting I have some knowledge of him being killed, Mr Benson?"

Realising the situation was becoming increasingly volatile, Williams calmly interjected with, "The upshot, Mr Knox, is that we believe you were told by Alex Hardie of Mark Ritchie's suspicions that Donaldson and McGuire killed Kelly-Ann. I've a daughter too and God forbid, if anything happened to her and if I thought I could take my revenge on who hurt her, I can appreciate if that was going through your head."

"So, now you're suggesting it was me who killed Donaldson?"

"It did cross our minds," Williams smiled at him.

"Well, you're wrong. I know who Peter Donaldson is, was," he corrected himself, "but if you're looking for whoever killed him, it wasn't me."

"Alex Hardie, perhaps?" Benson softly suggested.

"Extremely unlikely," Knox shook his head.

"What about your other pal, the weapons man, Jimmy Dunlop?"

Knox stared at him, then taking a deep breath, slowly exhaled before he slowly replied, "Let's not beat about the bush, here. It'll be no secret to you and your Squad colleagues, Mr Benson, that I run my team, so I can categorically tell you that neither Jimmy nor young Alex would kill Donaldson without my express permission so stand on me, they did not kill him."

"Mr Benson," they all three turned to stare at Rosie, her face pale, who softly continued, "we were relying on you to find our daughter's killer. When you and Mr Williams here first visited George and me, you told us that no matter what differences my man has with the police it would not interfere with how you conducted your investigation and that you would do everything you could to find who killed our daughter. Well," her voice rose an octave as she suddenly rose to her feet, "it seems from your line of questioning, you suspect my husband of killing this man Donaldson. When he tells you that neither he nor Jimmy Dunlop nor Alex Hardie killed this man, he means it. I'm sorry," her hands tightly clenched, she shook her head and now close to tears, stared at him, "but I feel that you have betrayed our confidence in your ability to be impartial and I'd like you to leave my home. *Now*, please."

Stunned, both men awkwardly rose to their feet as Benson replied, "It was not my intention to cause you further distress, Mrs Knox, but you must understand, I'm paid to ask the difficult questions. And yes," he nodded, "I take on board your comments and we will continue to try and find who killed Kelly-Ann. Good evening."

When they'd left the room, followed by Knox, she slumped down into her chair, her hands shaking as she held them to her breast and felt her beating heart.

When Knox returned to the room, he knelt by her and taking her hand in his, asked, "You okay, hen?"

"Nothing a cup of tea wouldn't solve," she muttered through her tears and forced a smile.

****

In the car downstairs, neither man spoke till Williams had driven off, then Benson said, "That was some performance she put on. He's as guilty as sin."

"You think he did it?" Williams risked a glance at him.

"Don't you?"

"Can I be brutally honest?"

"Go ahead."

"I'm just pleased to see a horrible bastard like Peter Donaldson taken out of the drug game and yes, there will always be somebody to take his place. But him and McGuire when we catch him? They'll not be missed."

"Even if it was Knox that murdered him?"

"Knox or some other bad bastard," he shrugged. "Let's face it, boss, does it really matter? Who really cares as long as it's not an innocent bystander that gets caught in the crossfire. As far as I'm concerned and I'm probably speaking for the majority of the public, they can murder each other for as long as they like. The more of them that get taken off the street, the better for us all."

"You're starting to sound like a right Fascist, Roddy."

Williams sighed before he nodded then said, "Maybe I'm getting a bit too long in the tooth or I'm just fed-up dealing with the scummies, but as far as the bloody public is concerned, today's front page is tomorrow's forgotten history."

A minute's silence followed, broken when Benson slowly smiled, then asked, "I know you'll be keen to get home, it being Saturday night, Roddy, but tell me this. Do you still keep a bottle in your bottom drawer?"

Risking a glance at him, Williams grinned before he replied, "Oh aye, I do."

****

"If you're back for another can, Willie…" Micky Rourke threw open the door, but seeing Alex Hardie stood there holding a gun that pointed towards his face, his eyes widened and the rest of the rebuke died on his lips.

"You?" he stuttered, his face expressing his fear as he recognised Hardie.

Hardie took a step backwards then nodding down at the plastic bag and the jerrycan on the metal step, said, "Pick them up and back away into the caravan."

His eyes flickering as he stared at the two objects, Rourke bent down and did as he was told, then walking backwards, stumbled and fell to sit onto the bench seat just inside the door, the petrol can and the plastic bag still tightly gripped in his hands.

"Move back a bit," Hardie waved the gun towards the rear of the caravan.

Doing as he was told, Rourke stared at the Beretta, then asked, "Why are you here? What the *fuck* do you want?"

"Lay the jerrycan and the bag on the floor, gently now with the bag," Hardie cautioned him and watched as he did so.

The transistor radio sitting on the small compact kitchen was tuned to Clyde One with Billy Joel belting out his hit number, *Uptown Girl*.

A half dozen empty Tennents cans litter the floor with two full ones sitting on the small, detachable table at the back window. An ashtray overflowed with butts and the familiar smell of body odour permeated throughout the van.

The light, as Hardie had guessed, came from a single candle that surprisingly lit up the interior of the van.

"What do you want?" he asked again and it was then that Hardie realised Rourke's voice was slurred and though not quite drunk, he was certainly tipsy.

"First, who's Willie?"

"Willie? He's the watchie. He keeps an eye on the vans during the night."

"Will he be back?"

"Naw, he usually kips in the…" then, his eyes narrowing as if realising he had made a mistake admitting it, quickly added, "Maybe. Aye, sometimes," he nodded.

"So, what is it you want, pal?"

"I want to ask you about Kelly-Ann," Hardie replied, the Beretta held in his right hand and pointed at Rourke's stomach.

"Who?" he replied, but so theatrically it was obvious to Hardie he was lying.

"When you took her back to that hovel of a flat you live in, then handcuffed her to the bed, was she still conscious?"

"Conscious? Aye, she was!" he spat the words out, now obviously deciding that Hardie knew and leering, then reached for a can, but stopped when Hardie waved the gun at him.

"She loved it, liked the idea of being trussed up, she did. Begged me for more when I'd cuffed her."

"And the baton?"

"Oh, that," he giggled drunkenly. "That's just a plaything, you know? Gets the women worked up and ready for me."

A cold fury overcame Hardie and he had to fight from laying into Rourke with the butt of the gun, his fists, his feet and his teeth. He wanted nothing more than to tear the sadistic bastard to pieces and had to inwardly fight to remain calm, for what he had planned needed to be done properly.

"And when did you realise you'd killed her?"

"Eh? Oh, it wasn't my fault," he tried to shake his head and almost fell off the bench seat.

Grabbing him by the front of his plaid shirt, Hardie propped him back up, then said, "What happened to her, then?"

"Had a heart attack or something. I don't know," he shrugged.

"You didn't strangle her, then?"

Rourke moodily stared at him, but didn't respond.

His silence, Hardie realised, was as much a confession as if he'd admitted it.

"Couldn't have been easy, carrying her into the park like you did."

"Naw," he giggled, "For a wee bird, she was a lot heavier than I thought and in the snow, too. Fucking freezing it was," his eyes were now drooping as he seemingly accepted that he was caught and was to be arrested.

The bile in his throat almost choking him, Hardie nodded down at the plastic bag, then said, "I brought you a present, Micky. Man to man, you know?"

"A present?" he seemed confused. "For me?"

"Go on, open it."

Warily, Rourke stared at the bag then licking nervously at his lips, lifted it and found the bottle of whisky.

"For me?" he asked again and his eyes flitting uncertainly towards the bottle, grinned nervously at Hardie.

"For you," he nodded.

"Do you want a wee drink, pal?"

"No, Mickey," he shook his head, the gun still held tightly in his fist.

"It's all for you. Drink up, *pal*, straight from the bottle if you like."

Uncorking the bottle, Rourke tossed back his head and took a deep swallow, smacking at his lips then coughing as the fiery liquid poured down his throat.

"Go on, have another swig."

"Naw I'll give it a minute…"

"Take another swig now or I'll blow your fucking head off!" Hardie snarled as he pointed the gun at Rourke's face.

Fearfully, his eyes fluttering, Rourke again upended the bottle and spluttered as the whisky poured down his throat and spilled out across his face.

Gasping, he began to hyperventilate and his body shuddered when Hardie leaned across and with the back of his hand, slapped him hard across the face.

"Again!" he ordered.

"But I…"

"Again!" he hissed, followed by another slap.

Once more the bottle was upended and by now half the contents were drunk.

"I can't take anymore of…" he slurred.

"Again!" another slap and as hard as the first two.

Rourke began to softly weep and clutching the bottle in both hands, drunk yet more whisky, though spilling almost as much as he consumed.

Hardie could see that in those short, ten or fifteen minutes he'd been in the van, he wasn't certain how much time had passed, the rapid ingestion of the alcohol on top of what Rourke had already drunk was taking an effect. His eyes were glazed, his speech fully slurred and even sitting on the bench seat, his balance was gone.

His body swaying and crying tears of remorse, he stuttered, "I'm sorry, I'm fucking *sorry*, alright? I didn't mean it. It was just fun."

"Aye," hissed Hardie, "fun for you, ya *bastard*, but not for Kelly-Ann!"

His head bowed and about to fall asleep, Rourke tried to stand, but instead fell sideways onto the bench seat.

Hardie waited for a couple of minutes as he stared at him, then lifting his legs, pinched Rourke's nose hard between his thumb and forefinger and when there was no visible reaction, was satisfied he really was out for the count.

There remained in the bottle just less than a quarter of whisky. Wrapping the plastic bag around the bottle, he lifted it and poured the remaining whisky over the unconscious Rourke's head, face and clothing, then dropping the bottle onto the floor, shoved the plastic bag into his jacket pocket.

He glanced at the jerrycan and undoing the cap, sniffed at the immediate smell of the petrol and his brow knitted with a sudden thought.

He'd watched a film on television some years previously and recalled the villain had been caught because using petrol to set fire to a house, he hadn't realised the smell of the petrol would linger long after the fire was extinguished.

The last thing Hardie wanted was any Forensic examination to indicate Rourke had been murdered.

"Bugger it," he irately muttered and staring down at the sleeping Rourke, thought about using the petrol anyway.

Irritated that his plan was unfolding, he glanced around the caravan and in the weak light, his eyes lit upon a Propane gas canister lying on its side at the far end of the van.

"Dancer," he muttered then lifting the canister, heard the liquid Propane gas swirling around inside and guessed it was at least half full.

His gaze then fell upon the lit candle.

It took him several minutes to prise open the nozzle of the gas canister, then laying it down onto its side by the bench seat where Rourke loudly snored, he could hear and smell the gas seeping from it.

He knew he was taking a chance with his own safety, but inwardly prayed he'd have time to get away.

Carefully lifting the three-inch stub of candle that stood upright on the saucer from the table top, he laid it down a few feet from the escaping gas and grabbing the jerrycan, quickly left the caravan, making sure to tightly close the door behind him.

He run through the darkness as fast as he could, then a mere thirty yards away stopped and turned to stare at the caravan.

Almost two minutes passed while he stood behind the corner of a caravan and watched, but when nothing happened, thought sod it.

Indecision raced through him, then with a grunt and intent on returning to Rourke's caravan to find out what had gone wrong, he dropped the jerrycan and had taken just two steps when there was an almighty flash and an ear shattering bang as the gas in the caravan ignited.

Thrown onto his back by the shockwave, Hardie stared in fascination as in a heartbeat, the sides and the roof of the caravan buckled out and upwards, the windows and flimsy door flying through the air to land just a few yards away and a great tongue of flame shot aloft, lighting up the dark sky.

The caravans parked on either side of Rourke's also suffered for both were rocked then pummelled against their neighbouring caravans by the explosion, suffering extensive damage to the side walls.

His eyes widened incredulously as a figure, Rourke he saw, staggered through the flames, his hair and clothes alight and his hands held out in front of him.

Hardie could not know it, but the whisky he had poured onto Rourke had acted as an accelerant causing the skin on Rourke's face and his exposed hands to be blackened and scorched into useless claws, while his eyes had liquefied in the intense heat.

Unable to even cry out in pain for at the point of the explosion, when he'd taken a deep and panicked breath, the heat had seared Rourke's throat and travelled down to scorch his lungs and he was no longer capable of breathing.

No more than three or four seconds passed before the body that had been Micky Rourke tumbled facedown to the ground.

Stunned by the sight, Hardie scrambled to his feet and backed away, picking up the jerrycan as he ran for the gap in the fence where the Mercedes was parked.

Throwing the jerrycan into the boot of the car, his heart thumping in his chest, he saw his hands were shaking as he turned the key and started the engine.

****

Though the rain was once more now hammering down, Hardie stopped the Mercedes on the Victoria Bridge and got out of the car, waving an apology to the driver of a bus who scowled as he negotiated the double-decker around the car.

Lifting the bonnet of the car, he ducked his head underneath which gave him the opportunity to check that there were no pedestrians walking on the bridge, then almost in one, fluid movement, walked to the grey coloured stone parapet and threw the Beretta into the dark waters of the River Clyde below.

Slamming the bonnet down, he re-entered the car and with a nervous sigh, drove off.

The disposal of the handgun, he guessed had taken no more than ten or fifteen seconds.

He had already decided there was little point in keeping the Mercedes, that he would return it to the car park outside the flats in Glenavon Road. Not that he thought the police would be keeping an eye on the car, but he didn't want to attract suspicion to the vehicle, particularly if for any reason it had been seen near the caravan site or on the Victoria Bridge.

He and Avril would catch a taxi the following morning from the hotel to Prestwick Airport and, he smiled for the first time that evening, bugger the cost of the long journey.

If the cops didn't know about them staying at the Sherbrooke Hotel, he believed there would be no reason for them to discover they had left there for the airport.

However, the first thing he had to do was find a phone.

Driving back towards Summerston, he chose a route that took him along Maryhill Road where he knew he would find a telephone box. Stopping beside one at the junction of Bilsland Drive, he checked it was working then dialled the number for George Knox.

It was Rosie who answered and when he asked to speak with Knox, he simply said, "It's me, boss. It's done and it's as I promised."

Before Knox could respond with questions, he ended the call.

Ten minutes later, the Mercedes delivered back to sit alongside the rusting Transit van, a weary and shaken Hardie walked to the Maryhill Road where he hailed a taxi to return him to the Sherbrooke Hotel.

EPILOGUE

The flight from Edinburgh Airport to Cyprus's Paphos Airport took off on time, as did the flight from Glasgow Airport to Palma de Mallorca Airport.

On the Mallorca flight, the pretty young Spanish stewardess was as enchanted by the extremely excited and wide-eyed, small boy who flying for the first time, was as shyly captivated with the dark-eyed beauty.

Her passenger manifest listed the small boy to be travelling with his grandparents, Mr and Mrs Wayne; however, leading him through to the rear of the plane to treat him to a juice and some sweets and though her English was above average, she was a little confused when he solemnly told her, "I used to be called Clint, but now I'm called Craig."

****

However, a little over thirty-six miles away from Glasgow, the young couple that had passed through Prestwick Airport Passport Control as Mr and Mrs Peters and who were now seated in the departure lounge, might have seemed to anyone who noticed to be a little anxious when without explanation, their Iberia Airways flight was announced as delayed for at least thirty minutes.

Tightly holding Alex Hardie's hand, Avril quietly asked, "Do you think there's something wrong? Is it the police?" she panickily whispered.

Forcing a smile, he squeezed her hand in return, then replied, "Probably just something mechanical. Relax, Mrs Peters," he grinned comfortingly at her. "It'll soon be all over."

A tense thirty minutes turned into forty minutes, then fifty-three anxious and worrying minutes after their due departure time, to their relief they heard the tannoy call for all passengers travelling to Mahon to make their way to the departure gate.

****

At the caravan storage facility in Rutherglen's Ashton Road, the heavy night rain thankfully now gone, the Sub-Divisional Fire Officer stood with the uniformed Inspector as they watched the police Scene of Crime and Forensic personnel sift through the remains of the burnt-out shell of the caravan.

Some thirty yards away, two couples, one elderly and one middle-aged, stood with the shocked site owner discussing the damage to their respective caravans that were parked beside the burnt out shell and damaged when Rourke's van had exploded.

"Bad business this," the fire officer shook his head.

"According to the watchman," the Inspector turned to him, "the guy wasn't supposed to be using the caravan, particularly as there isn't any electrics or toilet provision on the site, but he told the watchie he'd been flooded out of his flat or something and had nowhere else to go. Anyway, the watchie claims he told him off and asked him to leave, but says the guy was pissed and a bit aggressive, so being the age he is, he didn't want to get into a fight and left it with the intention of phoning his boss in the morning to report it."

They watched as a white-suited Forensic officer approached, then removing her face mask and pushing back her hood to reveal an unruly mop of fair, lazily pointed back towards the debris and said, "From what me and my guys can assess at the minute, it seems that the nozzle of a Propane gas cylinder has been partially opened and released the gas inside, then ignited and caused the explosion."

Her eyes narrowed when she asked the fire officer, "I understand he was using a naked candle in the caravan?"

"That's what my guys were told by the watchman when they got here," he confirmed with a nod.

She continued, "There's evidence he'd been drinking by the number of Tennents cans lying around and there's a whisky bottle that surprisingly, didn't shatter, so the Scene of Crime people have that and they'll likely be able to obtain some fingerprints to identify him or do you know who the victim is?"

The Inspector glanced down at his notebook and read out loud, "Michael Rourke, the watchie says. The site owner told my guys that his father owned the caravan, but he was lettered to get it off the site because of unpaid dues. The watchie described the son as a bit of an arse."

He peered at the Forensic officer and said, "The CID were here earlier on doing their nosey, so I have to ask. Can either of you," he turned to glance at the fire officer and the woman, "confirm if there's anything suspicious about the death?"

The woman glanced at the fire officer as if seeking agreement, then shaking her head, replied, "It seems like a straight forward accident, or if you'd rather, the bloody idiot caused his own death by having a gas cylinder in a small confined space where the top was loose, permitting a build-up of gas to occur. That and he used a naked candle," she sighed.

"So, straight forward accident it is then?"

"Seems so," she nodded.

"Agreed," the fire officer, well past his off-duty time, glanced at his watch.

"Right then," the Inspector nodded, "I'll have one of my guys coordinate with you for details when he's writing up the Sudden Death Report. Likely the Health and Safety people will want a copy too," he sighed. "In the meantime, the watchie has an emergency contact list of the caravan owners in his hut in case of any problems, so I'll find out where this guy Rourke lived and I'll get on to the local Division to try and trace his father or any relatives at the home address."

****

It was by a curious coincidence that the two uniformed officers tasked with delivering the death message to the flat at Corkerhill Place were Constables Pat Hanlon and Trudy McNamara, the officers who had attended the discovery of the body of Kelly-Ann Knox.

Stopping the Transit van, Golf Mike Four, in the cul-de-sac, Hanlon told his probationer neighbour, "You've not delivered a death message yet, Trood, so this will be good experience for you. It's the address of the father," he glanced down at the scrap of paper with the details, "Patrick Rourke. It's his son who's died in an accident at the father's caravan."

"Oh, joy," she muttered and braced herself, trying to remember what the training sergeant at Tulliallan had taught the class.

Entering the close, they saw the first ground floor flat had the name 'P. ROURKE' written on the unpainted door.

While McNamara mentally prepared herself to deliver the worse of news to a parent, her neighbour knocked on the door then waited, but receiving no response from within the flat, turned to the door opposite and knocked there.

The door was opened almost immediately by an ill-kept balding, unshaven man in his late seventies, his clothes reeking of tobacco and body odour, who peered suspiciously at them.

However, his speed in answering the knock suggested to Hanlon that he had seen them enter the close and been standing behind the door, listening.

"Sorry to bother you, sir," he politely began, "but we're trying to trace the occupant next door, Mr Patrick Rourke. Do you know if he's out working or anything?"

"Working? No, son," the man shook his head and sneered.

Forcing a smile, Hanlon said, "It's important we contact Mr Rourke, sir. Patrick Rourke, is that the householder?"

"Paddy? No son," the man shook his head, "not any longer. Paddy passed away a couple of months ago now. Maybe about three months," his brow furrowed as he tried to recall. "It's his boy that lives there now. Michael."

"Oh. Does anybody else live in the house with Michael or do you know of any relatives nearby?"

"No," again the man shook his head then staring at Hanlon, asked, "What's this about anyway?"

Inwardly taking a breath, Hanlon replied, "There's been a death. We're trying to contact anyone in the Rourke family."

"Oh, a death you say? Right," he shook his head, then in a low voice, continued, "Paddy's wife, Jeannie, she passed years ago and as far as I'm aware, son, there was only Paddy and his boy, Michael. He's not a nice guy," he pursed his lips and again shook his head in an expression of his disapproval of Michael Rourke.

"No other family then?"

"None that I know of and they never had visitors of that I'm certain."

Probably you're certain because you're a nosey old bugger, thought Hanlon, but instead said, "Well, thanks anyway," and turned away to indicate the interview was over.

When the old man's door was closed, McNamara quietly asked, "What do we do now?"

Taking a breath, then slowly exhaling, he replied, "Now, Trood, we ask permission to put the door in."

"Why?" her brow furrowed.

"Well," he slowly drawled, "we need to deliver the death message to somebody and there might be something in the flat to indicate the name and address of a next of kin."

He took a step back then pointing down at her shiny, bulled Doc Marten boots, grinned at her and asked, "Have you put a door in yet, hen?"

****

DCI Martin Benson had decided that he'd take Sunday off with the proviso that should anything of interest turn up, he be advised at home.

However, he didn't expect the phone call that sent him in his gardening clothes speeding from his home in Clarkston to the cul-de-sac in Corkerhill Place, where he saw a police Transit van, marked police panda car, two CID cars and a Scene of Crime Transit van already parked there.

Ignoring the curious glances of the building's tenants and from the houses nearby who nosily stared from their windows, he ducked under the blue and white chequered 'Police' tape, then nodding towards the pale-faced young female cop and her neighbour, Pat Hanlon, who manned the cordon, he strode purposefully towards the close.

DI Roddy Williams, wearing a one piece white Forensic suit with the hood down and a disposable mask hanging by its elasticated strap from one ear, met him at the close entrance and handing him a plastic bag containing a similar suit, nodded to the open door of the flat and said, "It seems to be the locus for our victim's murder."

While Benson struggled into the suit, Williams called Hanlon forward and said, "Tell the boss what you know, Pat."

Hanlon patiently recounted receiving the death message to deliver, then learning Patrick Rourke was deceased and receiving no reply at the door, he had his neighbour force it open only to discover the awfulness in the bedroom.

"And this man who's died, Michael Rourke, he's resident in the flat?"

"According to the next-door neighbour, sir, he lives there alone since his father died some time ago. I haven't spoken to anyone else in the building; thought I'd better let the CID do that."

Benson stared keenly at Hanlon then nodding, replied, "Good man." He was about to turn away, but then thoughtfully asked, "The young lassie outside. She okay?"

"Trood? It's been a tough lesson for her, sir, but aye," he nodded.

"She'll be okay. She's got the makings of a good cop."

"Right then thanks, Pat."

Dismissing Hanlon with a nod, he turned back to the DI and asked, "Do we know anything else about this guy Rourke?"

Williams replied, "I've got Mhari McGregor back at the office doing a background check, boss. She will let us know when she gets something. And there's one other thing."

"That is?"

"You recall mention of the green hooded coat our victim wore when she was last seen?"

"I do."

"It was discovered stuffed under the bed in the room. The SOCO guys have it bagged along with a woman's underwear and a black vinyl handbag that was also under the bed."

"Anything in the handbag that positively identifies her?"

"There's a set of house keys that I'm confident will fit her door lock, her purse with some pound notes and loose change and," he shook his head before he sighed, "a photograph of a wee boy in a school uniform who I recognised as George Knox's grandson."

Slowly nodding in acknowledgement, Benson first drew on a pair of Nitrile gloves then slipped the attached, elasticated hood over his head.

Sighing, he nodded towards the open door, then before slipping the disposable mask over his mouth, said, "Let's have a look then, Roddy."

****

It was two days later that the Fingerprint Department were able to categorically state that the fingerprints discovered on the whisky bottle recovered from the debris of the exploded caravan matched those of Michael Rourke, a convicted sex offender whose fingerprints were already on file. Other prints found on the bottle were not identified and as Rourke's prints were the predominant prints on the bottle and overlapped the others, it was presumed they belonged to staff from whatever shop Rourke had purchased the cheap and commonly sold whisky.

Those present during the post mortem conducted on the body of Michael Rourke included uniformed officers from F Division's Inquiry Department, who were tasked with reporting the Sudden Death to the Procurator Fiscal, DCI Benson and DI Roddy Williams from G Division whose interest lay in the fact that Rourke was now their primary suspect for the murder of Kelly-Ann Knox.

Benson and William's evidence of Rourke's culpability in her murder was already confirmed and documented for the victim's blood type was discovered on the bed in the room and on the truncheon that had been used to brutally violate her.

Blood and layers of torn skin were also discovered on the handcuffs attached to the bed where she had so obviously writhed in agony and torn the skin of her wrists in a frantic attempt to escape.

Hair follicles on the green hooded coat that matched the victim as well as her fingerprints on the metal headboard where she had seemingly held onto the rungs while being forcibly handcuffed.

Concluding his lengthy examination of the horror that was the charred corpse, the pathologist removed his safety glasses, then turned to the uniformed sergeant and politely said, "There seems little doubt that he was alive when the explosion occurred. His lungs are seared through, indicating he tried to take a deep breath and so was conscious. Regretfully, his organs are, well," he grimaced, "charred is the only word that comes to mind and so I'm unable to confirm just how inebriated he actually was. What I *can* confirm is that my examination of the external body indicates it is extremely damaged by fire; however, there is no indication or any suggestion that he might have suffered any injury prior to the explosion."

Shaking his head, he softly added, "This man died a death so painfully excruciating that even had immediate medical aid been available, he could not have been saved."

Turning to Benson and Williams and aware of their interest, he raised an eyebrow and said, "Gentlemen?"

A few seconds silence was broken when Benson softly replied, "In my service within the police, sir, I never believed I would utter these words, but having seen the agonising death this man put a young woman through, my only thoughts are, may he forever rot in hell."

****

Detective Inspector Sheila Farquhar's application for a warrant to arrest James 'Foxy' McGuire on suspicion of the murder of Peter Donaldson, was approved by the Procurator Fiscal and details logged on the Police National Computer.

Throughout the coming weeks then months, there were more than a few alleged sightings of McGuire, though to date the police believe he remains at large.

The warrant remains active.

****

DCI Michael Thorburn, the SIO in charge of investigating the murder of Kevin Stobbie, after several months of fruitless leads, was obliged to wind down the inquiry and though there is much speculation and mostly without any substance, about who might have been responsible for killing Stobbie, to date his murder remains unsolved.

****

Upon receipt of the complaint from Detective Chief Superintendent Keith Meadows, the Commander of the Scottish Crime Squad instructed that the three detective officers involved in falsifying the operational log on the date of Kevin Stobbie's murder, were returned to their parent Forces.

DI Alice Meechan, having embarrassed Tayside Constabulary by her actions that were brought the attention of the Deputy Chief Constable, found herself standing before the Chief Superintendent of the Personnel Department who had been instructed to find a uniformed post for the disgraced DI, where she could do no further harm.

Six weeks into her new assignment as the Force's uniformed Housing Officer with just a staff of two middle-aged female assistants who soon learned to ignore her and with no hope of any return to the CID let alone future promotion, Meechan made application for an Inspector post with the British Transport Police. Furnished with a glowing reference from Tayside Constabulary, she was the successful applicant and transferred to her new post in London.

For their part in the falsified log scandal and after they were returned to their parent Forces, neither Detective Sergeant Barney Fellowes or Shona Burns were treated too harshly.

Unknown to Burns, DCI Mike Thorburn, when relating the circumstances of the interview with the DI and the two DS's to Detective Chief Superintendent Keith Meadows, he had contended that the real culprit was the disgraced DI, Alice Meechan. Though aware that Meadows would have the final decision on Burns fate when she was returned to Strathclyde Police, Thorburn argued that the experienced Burns had been a loyal colleague to Fellowes, who had in turn been ordered against his wishes to participate in the falsification.

Upon her return to Strathclyde Police and at Thorburn's request, Burns was transferred directly to Maryhill CID at her current rank of DS and the reason for her dismissal from the Scottish Crime Squad omitted from her personnel file.

As he had correctly predicted, Fellowes was returned to uniform sergeant duties and likewise unaware that Meadows had fought Fellowes corner with his contemporary in the Lothian & Borders Force.

As a gesture of goodwill between the two Detective Chief Superintendents, Fellowes was immediately placed in charge of a shoplifting squad compromising of eight officers in plain clothes, who operated in Edinburgh city centre and would remain there for the next two years till the completion of his service.

****

However, the police were not yet done with George Knox and his team.

It was eight days after the discovery of the body of Kelly-Ann Knox that on a wet and chilly Monday, the thirtieth of January, and following their attendance at the post mortem of Michael Rourke, DCI Martin Benson and DI Roddy Williams called at the flat in Quarrywood Road.

Their purpose for the visit was to inform and confirm to George and Rosie Knox that the killer of their daughter had been identified and was himself now dead.

However, unaware that all three men and their partners had fled the country, the detectives received no response to their knocking and so Benson left a calling card requesting George Knox contact him at Pollok Police station.

Leaving the close, both men paused on the pavement outside and as Benson turned to stare up at the veranda, Williams remarked and nodded, "They can't be far. That's Knox's Jag parked there."

Neither man took any notice of the rusting Transit van parked a little further down the road outside the post office cum grocers and were unaware that they were being photographed.

Inside the dark interior of the van, a surveillance officer quietly spoke into his microphone to relate, "The two subjects have just exited the close and I might be mistaken, but they look to me like CID."

****

In a curious twist of fate, Lennie Campbell, who had turned against Foxy McGuire to assist George Knox, was the successful applicant for the vacant position of security officer that had been advertised by Lewis's when the incumbent security officer, Micky Rourke, had consistently failed to arrive for work nor responded to the letter of dismissal.

Campbell, a likeable big man, was welcomed into his first full-time employment for many years and was to become a great favourite with the staff.

****

Almost a full week passed before it became apparent to the Scottish Crime Squad surveillance team that their targets were not just in hiding, but had completely disappeared off the radar.

The Police National Computer logged not just George Knox, James Dunlop and Alexander Hardie as missing persons of interest, but also both spouses and Avril Collins too.

The Strathclyde Education Department were informed by the head teacher of Balornock Primary School that numerous phone calls and a letter to the grandparents of her pupil, Clint Knox, had failed to elicit a response as to why Clint was no longer attending school. An absence report was created by the Department who in turn sent a representative to the home address; however, just like the police, the woman was unable to gain any response to her visit.

As the days passed and with the agreement of the Commander of the Scottish Crime Squad, the circumstances were reported by Keith Meadows to the Procurator Fiscal in Glasgow, who satisfied that the disappearances were of such an unusual nature that inquiry must be made.

In due course, the PF authorised warrants to search the three homes of the missing criminals and also the Redpath Drive home of Avril Collins to try and ascertain their whereabouts.

Doors were forced and the homes searched, but nothing to indicate where the missing individuals were or anything in the homes that might imply they were the subjects of abduction or violence.

To date, the lookout request for the six adults and one child remains on the police PNC.

****

At the unofficial request of DI Roddy Williams, Detective Alejandro

Perez of the Policía Municipal de Madrid maintained a discreet, but covert watching brief on Mark Ritchie.

However, three months after Williams, McBride and Perez visited Ritchie, Perez had to regretfully inform Williams that Ritchie had disappeared from his Calle de Cuchilleros address. Unfortunately, Perez also reported that Ritchie's account with the Banco de Santander had also been closed and his money transferred to a Caribbean bank.

In due course. Strathclyde Police Fraud Squad successfully applied for an arrest warrant for Ritchie, though his current whereabouts remain unknown.

****

With Kelly-Ann Knox's killer positively identified, the PF decided that retaining her body served no purpose and so, as no relatives were immediately contactable or any others had come forward, in a longstanding agreement with Glasgow City Council, her body was released to the Council for internment in a pauper plot.

However, and unknown to the PF, a Glasgow based law firm contacted the Council and discreetly requested that instead the body be removed to local undertaker who would arrange a cremation, the cost of which would be borne by a benefactor who refused to be named.

Having no legal requirement to inform the PF of this proposal, the Council were only too happy to have the arrangements and costs taken off their hands and willingly agreed.

On a wet and windy day in March, the cremation was carried out at Daldowie Crematorium, the only mourner being a heavyset man who following the short ceremony and with a large Cuban cigar between his fingers, instructed the undertakers to inform him when the ashes were ready for collection.

Just over three weeks later, two unremarkable and elderly ladies cheerfully boarded a flight to Palma in Menorca for their free, weeklong holiday; the only condition being that secreted in their luggage they carry, a small, heavy-duty black plastic bag that contained a grey powder they were assured was not drugs.

Upon their arrival in Palma and as instructed, the two women met with a charming man to whom they delivered the black plastic bag. Two days later, the man formerly known as George Knox and his wife clutching the hand of their grandson, stood within the extensive rear garden of their stunning four-bedroom house in Palma's suburb Clinica Picasso where in a quiet corner under the branches of a spreading palm tree, laid the plastic bag into a small, prepared concrete lined hole that the man then covered with a marble slab.

****

Shaded from the October sun by the large, overhead green and white striped awning that reached out over four metres from the wall of his bar, Andy Peters stared out at the blue sea and took a long, leisurely breath.

Sitting on the comfortable, cushioned bamboo chair, wearing just an open neck, garishly brightly coloured shirt and khaki shorts, his long, tanned legs spread out with leather sandals on his feet, he glanced down at the wrought iron table as his forefinger traced a rivulet of icy water down the length of the bottle of San Miguel.

The bar was quiet, this slow afternoon with just the dozen or so customers, mostly tourists from Ireland, Holland and France and a couple of ex-pat regulars, all engaged in their own conversations and for the most part, ignoring him.

He half-turned in his chair when he heard her voice, her Spanish now almost fluent.

While he could speak and understand most of his neighbours, he didn't have the quick ear that she had. But, he inwardly smiled, as the days passed and the more he practised, even he realised he was definitely becoming more articulate.

Her blonde hair was tied up into a loose bundle on top of her head, her skin tanned and, he saw, the bright yellow coloured loosely fitted dress she wore suited her.

Like him, she was barelegged with just leather sandals on her feet and he thought she'd never looked more beautiful than she did right now.

He watched her as she set down the plates of tapas then cheerfully took the order from the elderly Dutch couple for more beer, seeing her unconsciously reach behind to rub at her aching back while laying her other hand protectively upon her swollen belly.

She turned and seeing him watching her, she smiled.

Walking to the door of the bar, she called out the customer's order to the waitress Isabella then strolled towards him.

He wasn't unaware that her healthy, radiant beauty turned more than a few eyes and took pride in the knowledge she belonged to him.

He drew up his legs as she settled upon his lap then wrapping her arms around his neck, softly smiled down at him.

"You just sit here, Mr Peters, and enjoy yourself and let me, a woman six months pregnant, run around after the customers."

He couldn't help himself and grinning, then said "Isabella and Felipe can handle the bar for now. Why don't we go for a walk?"

"Where to," she stared curiously at him.

He had considered it for some months now and realised it was what he wanted as much as he suspected she did too.

Taking a long breath, then slowly releasing it, he replied, "To find a priest."

****

Hi folks,

Once more, thank you for your support with the books.

Though it continues to be a really tough time for us all this year, like my family and I you'll likely be hoping that with the easing of the 'rules,' we might be on the turn from the wicked pandemic.

I hope in some way this story takes your mind off what going on outdoors.

As always, all the characters who appear in the story are *totally* fictitious and products of my overactive imagination.

Again, any resemblance to any person, living or dead or sounding like someone you might know is, I assure you, purely coincidental.

Most if not all of you will recognise the setting of the iconic Barrowland Ballroom that is a Glasgow institution and a rite of passage for most Weegie teenagers, as well as those of more advanced in years.

Of course, it's a well-run establishment and continues to be a real attraction – once we're back to a sense of normality, that is.

And talking about the Barrowland; did any of you know there are *two* Gibson Streets in Glasgow?

I didn't till I began this book.

Again, if you have read any of my previous books you will be aware I self-edit as well as self-publish on Amazon.
Not the best idea, I admit, but I can then claim that warts and all, the book is all mine.
Therefore, punctuation, spelling or grammatical errors are mine and mine alone and for those, I apologise and hope they did not interfere with the storyline.
As always, I keep the Kindle books @ two quid, but I have no control over Amazon's pricing of the printed books that range between £7 to £9. If you do buy the books, can I suggest you consider Kindle or similar e-devices?
So please, if you take the time to review this or any of my books, I will try to improve and the reviews that I do receive will hopefully be honest and help me develop.
I can also be contacted via my e-mail address at:
george.donald.books,@hotmail.co.uk

Regards to you all and importantly, stay safe.

George Donald